OVERTHROWING HEAVEN

Baen Books by Mark L. Van Name

One Jump Ahead
Slanted Jack
Overthrowing Heaven
Children No More (forthcoming)

Transhuman ed. with T.K.F. Weisskopf

OVERTHROWING HEAVEN

MARK L. VAN NAME

OVERTHROWING HEAVEN

A Baen Books Original

Baen Publishing Enterprises
P.O. Box 1403
Riverdale, NY 10471
www.baen.com

ISBN 10: 1-4391-3267-4
ISBN-13: 978-1-4391-3267-8

Cover art by Stephen Hickman

First printing, June 2009

Distributed by Simon & Schuster
1230 Avenue of the Americas
New York, NY 10020

Library of Congress Cataloging-in-Publication Data

Van Name, Mark L.
  Overthrowing heaven / Mark L. Van Name.
      p. cm.
  "A Baen Books original" —T.p. verso.
  ISBN 978-1-4391-3267-8
  1. Soldiers of fortune—Fiction. 2. Nanotechnology—Fiction. I. Title.
  PS3622.A666O94 2009
  813'.6—dc22

                                              2009005285

10 9 8 7 6 5 4 3 2 1

Pages by Joy Freeman (www.pagesbyjoy.com)
Printed in the United States of America

To Allyn Vogel

For quiet strength and unwavering faith

CHAPTER 1

I SHOULD NEVER HAVE come down from the trees. The treehouse I had rented perched in the canopy of a hundred-meter-tall, ancient, dark blue wood monster with a ten-meter-wide base and a scent so rich with life that resting in its branches was like nestling in the womb of creation. Every other human in the grove was a Green Rising activist, so I had nothing to fear from them. They focused what little negative energy they possessed on the loggers trying to clear this last remaining rain forest on Arctul so the builders in Vonsoir, the constantly growing capital city whose edges I could see from my house's upper limbs, could cater to the wood fetish of its swelling suburban population. My presence helped allay their fears, because Lobo, my Predator-class assault vehicle—and also the closest thing I have to a friend—constantly hovered in the clouds above me. No team could sneak up on us without Lobo spotting them well before they could do any damage to me or my airy haven.

I was as relaxed as I'd been in ages. The last job I'd taken had left me needing to relocate quickly, so I'd followed a four-jump-gate route out of Expansion Coalition space in search of somewhere serene, a place I could relax—a place, that is, where no one knew me. I should have headed to one of the Central Coalition edge planets, but I couldn't quite abandon the notion of finding a way back to Pinkelponker, my home world and the only quarantined planet among all those that humanity has settled. Vonsoir provided

1

a solid compromise: far enough from EC space to be safe, so close to the fringes of CC territory that no one serious about reaching Pinkelponker would begin their attempt from it, and yet still only a few jumps away from my unreachable home.

So of course I had to blow it.

You can't own a PCAV and have it guard you from above without attracting attention. Even the hardcore nature lovers can employ perimeter and airspace sensors, and at about twenty-five meters long by roughly eight meters wide, Lobo makes an easy target—at least as long as I refuse to let him deploy decoys or destroy the sensors. I'd told them I provided courier services, which was true as far as it went; that was definitely one of the things I've done in the hundred and fifty-five years I've been alive. I consequently wasn't surprised when they approached me about providing safe transport for a few of their leaders to a meeting in Vonsoir. I was, though, disappointed; all I wanted to do was rest and think. I turned them down initially, but then they tempted me with free rent and food and a gig so easy I could do it in my sleep, and so I signed on. Soon enough, I was acting as the group's secure shuttle service. Fortunately, the Green Rising leaders left the woods so infrequently that I didn't have to work often, and no one took any of them particularly seriously, so I never had a problem.

Until now. Until the word spread a little too far.

Glazer, one of the more dedicated team leads, told her friend, who mentioned me to an acquaintance of hers, who knew someone who needed help, and then before I could sort out exactly how it had happened, I'd stupidly agreed to extend my help beyond my Green Rising neighbors.

That's how I found myself sitting at a booth in the left rear corner of The Take Off, waiting for a woman desperate to find passage to the jump gate so she could leave Arctul, escape her abusive partners, and start a new life on a planet several jumps away. Once a bar that catered to rough working trade, The Take Off had morphed, via an injection into its business DNA of a cocktail of cash, viral marketing, and retro design chic, into an upscale club catering to the stand-and-model *nouveau riche* of a world so blessed with precious gems that every other person you met had the money to buy most frontier planet capitals. Sensor-laced holo walls collected skin and sweat statistics from all who touched them and fed the data into on-site crunchers, which then fabricated images and scenes that complemented the moods of the patrons. Targeted sound projectors created acoustic zones that played off and adapted themselves to the body motions of their inhabitants. Low pulsing beats, sometimes from drums, other times remixes of the heartbeats of couples caught in the act, formed a sonic base for the many different noises rippling through the club. The filtration system injected pheromones into the already musky atmosphere; the management also owned the love hotel next door. Human bouncers, huge men and women wearing see-through armor that obscured only their genitals, ostensibly kept the peace, worked the front door, and chose who entered. Everyone not yet under the influence of one of the club's many intoxicants knew that the cameras, the ceiling-mounted trank guns, and the house AI really ran the show. Small video feeds scattered along the interior walls gave those already inside the building the pleasure of watching with smug satisfaction the desperate pleas of the seekers waiting outside for admittance.

The easiest way to avoid being surprised at a meeting place is not to announce it until you're already there. I hadn't chosen The Take Off until I was in it and satisfied with its multiple rear exits and proximity to the landing area where Lobo awaited me. Unfortunately, that meant I'd been waiting a long time and burning through a lot of money maintaining solo occupancy of my prime corner table for four.

"Is this really worth the effort?" Lobo said over the encrypted frequency on the comm unit in my ear.

"I told you before," I said.

"I remember, of course," he said, cutting me off. "It's not like I'm capable of forgetting anything. I can, however, question your judgment. You said we don't need the money, and you must be nearly as tired of playing glorified taxi as I am, so I ask again if this is worth what it's costing us."

"Glazer told me the woman was in trouble she didn't deserve. All she needs is safe passage to the jump gate—and she can afford to pay."

"And you have to help every woman with a problem?" Lobo said. "Or only those who can pay?"

"No," I said. "This planet's full of people. You don't see me trying to rescue all of them."

"But if they asked, one at a time, with their wallets ready to transfer to yours," Lobo said, the sarcasm dripping from his voice, "I bet we'd never jump out of this system."

"I've taken the gig," I said, "so there's no point in wasting more time discussing it. Are you into the club's security system yet?"

I knew that would annoy him. I was right.

"Yet?" he said. "Yet? As you would know if you'd taken even a moment to ask, I cracked through its pitiful defenses less than a hundred and ten seconds after my initial contact with it."

"Fine," I said. "Why don't you focus on it and watch for threats externally? I'll do the same, and I'll check with you after she arrives and I've confirmed that everything is as it should be."

"Do you honestly believe I haven't been doing those things while we were talking?" Lobo said, the annoyance still clear in his tone. "*Your* brain might not be able to process that many inputs at once, but doing so is hardly a challenge for me. Why you humans consider yourselves the most advanced form of life will forever remain a mystery to me."

"Then ponder that mystery," I said, "but let me work. Out."

My would-be client wasn't due for a little bit longer, so I tuned into the appliance frequency to see what the cameras were saying to each other and to the club's door-control system about the milling crowd outside.

Appliances talk constantly, courtesy of the surplus intelligence that's cheaper to manufacture into almost all chips than it is to omit, and thanks to their purpose-built programming, they are incredibly self-centered: All they care about is themselves and the type of work they do. Anyone with the right data decoder could listen to them, but almost no one bothers; background machine chatter is as much a fact of life as the huge quantities of information and power arcing invisibly through the air of all settled areas. I can communicate with the machines—both listen and talk on their frequencies—thanks to some combination of the changes two key events in my past had made to my body. The first occurred when I was sixteen, when my empathic healer sister, Jennie, fixed the problems that had caused me to spend my life up to that point with the mental faculties of a five-year-old. Jennie then vanished, and in all the years since that time I've never been able to find her or even to know if she's still alive. I hope she is. The second set of changes arrived courtesy of a far less pleasant experience: my time as an experimental subject on the orbital prison station, Aggro, where the Central Coalition government was secretly trying to infuse humans with nanobots. I was the only survivor and the only complete success of that research. I was also one of the two people who caused the disaster that destroyed Aggro and led to the quarantine of Pinkelponker and the universal ban against research into melding human cells with multipurpose nanomachines. Benny, the man who helped me escape and who was my first friend other than Jennie, sacrificed himself in our getaway so I could make it to safety.

I shook off the memories and focused on the three cameras monitoring the would-be clubgoers. They were discussing the current head of the line, a man who looked my apparent age—late twenties—but who was cultivating a teenage air, probably in the hope that it would make him stand out from the crowd and thus a more attractive addition to the club's population.

"You can only see his profile," said one of them, "so you can't really appreciate him the way I can. I do, after all, occupy the senior position: full frontal views of the poor fools as they beg to come in."

"Tension in profile can tell truths that remain invisible from the front," said another, "as you'd know if your memory wasn't so small and so fried that you can no longer remember our basic programming."

"Let's not forget the back," said the third. "You high-and-mighty lens boxes may have the better social views, but from the rear I can spot the often telling neck sweat, concealed weapons you'd never detect, and so much more."

"Would you three please stop arguing and send me some data I can use to make a decision?" said what I had to assume was the house AI. "We have openings, and we need to fill them. Vacancies don't make purchases."

"He's a teenabe," the first voice said, "and he's not half bad at the role. He lacks the heavy hormonal treatments of the best of his type, but he'll certainly more than pass in the interior light."

"Calf and hamstring development visible through the tight pants suggest some athleticism," said the rear camera. "We may get lucky and have a dancer."

"Two men and a woman have cruised the one free teenabe currently inside," said the AI, "and the dance areas are slow, so we'll take a chance. Let him in."

I watched on the house feeds as the bouncer nearest the door nodded and waved the man inside. Next up was another guy, this one the standard executive type: nearly two meters tall, my height, but less muscular and more graceful.

"Let him in right away," the AI said, "and comp him for as long as he's here. He's a nonpaying investor."

From the two years I'd worked club protection I knew that meant this guy had greased a few paths somewhere. He might have been part of the government team that approved the complete overhaul of this district, a sweeping set of changes that would ultimately help turn The Take Off from the only upscale joint in a run-down zone into the only upscale joint in a trendy new living sector.

I tuned out the cameras and focused for a minute on the news feeds I'd chosen to run on my table instead of the surveillance footage most patrons paid to see. Every person here had the option to offer live coverage of his or her stay in the club, for a fee, to the other people in it. The house skimmed a healthy third, but if you were interesting enough or wild enough, you could more than cover an evening's entertainment with your earnings. I'd paid the premium for total privacy; though the cameras were of course capturing me, I didn't appear on any option on any table.

What passed for news on Vonsoir was, as is typical of most worlds, a hash of local gossip, government-created flavorless gravy for the intellectually toothless, and the occasional drop of spice via a low-quality interruption by a hacker who fancied himself a crusader but was more likely a high-functioning neurotic skating on the razor's edge between utter irrelevance and complete madness.

The stories of the moment were not exceptions.

A new mine had opened on the other side of the continent. The owners of the robotic diggers had risked everything in a display of financial daring at its best. Would they retire in a month or be slinking to the jump gate begging for passage? Watch this feed for more.

A new installment of *Mysteries of the Jump Gates* promised to reveal a theory no one had ever considered before, an origin so startling we would scarcely be able to believe it. Given the huge number of explanations I've heard, either this teaser was all hype or the exciting revelation was something on the order of invisible space giants spitting out gates as they strolled through the universe.

Showing its dedication to our protection, the Central Coalition government was conducting a small set of exercises in space over Vonsoir. We should all be reassured, not alarmed; they were from the government, and they were here to help us.

The planetary racing ray finals, due to start in two days, included two contenders that had the potential to set new Arctul speed records.

I glanced up and to the left, staring into space and seeing nothing, as the headline triggered a memory of a ride on the back of such a ray, an augmented racer named Bob, in the waning hours of a very dangerous night on a planet far, far from here. Hurtling underwater through the ocean had been a thrilling, joy-filled experience that had ended all too soon.

A large swatch of brilliant blue in the external crowd feed yanked my attention back to the present. I'd told the client where I'd be, and when she'd said I'd be able to spot her by the bright blue dress, a color not in vogue here due to its ties to the increasingly marginalized environmentalists, I'd thought nothing of it. The sight of it, though, triggered more memories, this time of a remarkable woman I'd once known and maybe even loved, though not in any way that mattered, not really; she still had to leave. She was gone.

I shook my head to clear it and to make myself focus. Maybe vacations were bad for me. I spent time alone, and though I relaxed I also brooded, focused too much on the past and too little on the world around me. As bad as that was in general, when on a job it was downright dangerous; maintaining situational awareness is vital. The woman I assumed was my client had progressed to third from the front of the queue. I paid the table the fee to bring me the external feed and to let me zoom on the line so I could study her. Judging from the bouncers, she was relatively short for modern fashion, maybe one and three-quarters meters tall. The thin straps on the dress revealed muscular shoulders and arms. If she was hiding any weapons, I sure couldn't spot them. Her skin was pale, a shade lighter than my own, and it made her stand out in the crowd. Her large eyes were dark, almost as dark as her thick hair, which was the perfect black of a jump gate aperture and cut short on the sides and thick on the top. Pretty but not stunning enough to draw much attention in this club, she didn't appear to have indulged in anywhere near as much personal engineering as most of the men and women here. Her obvious nervousness—she couldn't stop shifting her weight from foot to foot, and her hands fluttered as if they were trying to take flight—detracted from her appearance, and I worried about her chances of making it inside.

Then she reached the front of the line, stared up at the bouncers, and smiled. My worries vanished. Her wide grin infected everyone who saw it, and each person smiled in return.

I tuned into the cameras and the house AI.

"Check the expressions on those two," said the camera with the rear view of my client but the front shot on the door guards. "One look from her, and their heads are empty. This one is a charmer."

"She'll draw a crowd for sure," said the AI, "and they'll be trying to impress her. Idiots seeking to show off inevitably spend a great deal. Let her in."

The bouncers didn't even nod. They kept smiling, opened the door, and motioned her inside.

The Take Off was too crowded for me to be able to see her across the large open space, but that wasn't a problem; she knew where I was and could find me. None of the people who had entered previously had looked like trouble, so either I'd misjudged them or any pain coming my way would be behind her. I alternated between watching the space in front of me and checking the external crowd feed. Way down the line stood a group of five guys, each twitchy and overly muscular by local standards, but that in and of itself wasn't unusual; plenty of packs hunting companionship banked on their bodies to attract their prey. Still, they were worth monitoring. The reach of the cameras didn't extend much past them, and what I could see of that part of the line triggered no warnings, so I stopped checking the feed.

The crowd swirling a couple of meters in front of my table parted for a moment, and the woman in the blue dress stepped into the opening. I looked everywhere but at her, making sure I hadn't missed an interior threat. As I did, I subvocalized to Lobo, "She's here. We're on." It was a routine job, but it was a job, and now was the time to be serious.

"Five men in line pose a possible threat," said Lobo, all business.

"Noted," I subvocalized, still scanning the area around my client but not making eye contact with her. I started to tell Lobo to watch them, but of course he would, so I shut up. I finally settled my gaze on the woman in front of me.

She walked up to the table. "Mr. Moore?"

"Excuse me?" I said.

Confusion played across her face for a moment before she spoke, "I was supposed to meet a friend of a friend here," she said. "Jon Moore. Kiana Glazer recommended you to me."

"Sit down," I said, motioning to the chair to my right. That position put her back to a wall and kept her out of my field of vision as I watched the rest of the club. "I'm Jon Moore. Don't ever offer a name to someone."

"But if you're the—"

I held up my hand. "I'm explaining how you should act." I glanced at her and realized I was wasting my time. "Forget it."

"I'm Priyana Suli," she said, extending her hand to shake.

"Put that down *now*," I said. "You're supposed to be trying to pick me up, not sell me property."

She gave me the confused look again.

We were burning time, but it was my fault, not hers; I didn't need to teach her anything to get her off this planet. "Tell me why I should take you to the jump gate," I said, "and why you don't hop on the next commercial shuttle."

"Kiana told me she had—"

"*You* tell me," I said.

"I've wanted to leave for a while," she said, looking down at the table, no longer willing to make eye contact, "but my partners won't let me. One of them has serious connections with the Arctul government, so if I try to get on a shuttle, they'll detain me. The jump station is CC territory. Once I'm there, he and his friends won't be able to touch me."

"And if they follow you and make the jump?"

"I know people on Lindquist," she said, "people who will help me. Once I'm in its jump station, even my partner's friends won't dare come after me."

I've always doubted that sort of claim, particularly from someone who's never worked the kind of jobs I've had, but what happened to her after the jump was not and could not be my problem.

"Okay," I said. "Let's get started."

"Get started?" she said. "What is there to do besides go?"

I turned to face her. "The first step is simple: You pay me." I pulled out my wallet, thumbed it to receive, and put it flat on the table. My hand still covered it; I didn't know her.

"Of course," she said. She reached into a pocket I hadn't seen on the dress, and two seconds later my wallet vibrated slightly. I checked the exterior display; the money was in an account of mine in Vonsoir. It wouldn't stay there for long; Lobo would move it quickly through a series of transfers that would take an auditor a fair amount of effort to follow.

I put back my wallet.

"Now," I said, "we can—"

"Alert," Lobo said over the comm unit. "Three of the five men we were monitoring have entered the club, spread, and are approaching on your ten, two, and twelve. The other two are heading to the rear exit you had planned to use."

"How long?" I scanned the crowd but could not yet see them; too many people blocked my view.

"Twenty-five, thirty seconds," Lobo said.

"Trouble is coming," I said to Suli, standing as I spoke. "You were followed. Stay behind me. Do what I say."

"What?" she said as she slowly rose.

I could see the three men now. They'd spread a bit more and were moving methodically toward us, checking each other's positions with short glances and murmurs over a comm. They'd done this sort of thing before.

I pushed the table forward and pulled Suli behind me as I did.

"I was wrong," I said. "The trouble has arrived."

CHAPTER 2

THE MEN VANISHED into the crowd again. I had a few seconds before they could reach us, but not many. I'd anticipated a pair of jealous lovers might show up; I hadn't planned on an assault team. If the situation turned bad enough, I could use the nanobots that laced all my cells—the benefit of that horrible time I spent as an experimental subject on Aggro—to create a nanocloud and send it to disassemble the men, but the risk for collateral damage was high if civilians got in the way, as they most likely would in this small space.

No, I needed a more conventional solution to the problem. I considered using the small projectile handgun in the pocket of my pants, but again, with a crowd this large the risk of hurting an innocent was unacceptably high.

The three men appeared, now only one layer of people away from us. The center man saw me spot him. He immediately glanced to his left, toward the man edging toward us along the wall to my right. That guy would be the leader. He was letting his team either push me toward him—unlikely if I was any good, because anyone who knew what he was doing wouldn't want to be trapped inside the club—or send me running toward the waiting rear duo. He'd then play cleanup or catch-up, as necessary.

The only way out was to take neither of the options they expected.

11

As the men stepped around the last of the people separating us, I subvocalized to Lobo, "Shut down the club's power. Now. Seal the rear door." I switched my vision to IR and not for the first time silently thanked Jennie for all the improvements she'd made to me.

The room went black as the power system switched off. The bio emergency lights snapped on an instant later, their soft blue illuminating the walls and exit paths. Lobo said over the comm in my ear, "You'll have to use the front or be trapped."

A few people gasped, but most murmured approval and clapped, wondering what trick the club's management would do next. The Take Off's clientele appreciated a little darkness.

I grabbed Suli and said, "Stay close" as I pulled her after me. We ran for the kitchen. I risked a glance backward. The leader was pointing at me, and his men were clearing the people who had moved in front of them, showing reluctant partyers a glowing badge of some sort. Great; her partner's friends really were connected.

"No," I said to Lobo, "different exit."

"Kitchen skylights," Lobo said.

"Yes. Come *now*."

Cases full of bottles of locally brewed ales stood in stacks along the hallway to the kitchen, a nod to the club's bar heritage and a sign the owners hadn't yet jettisoned all of The Take Off's past. I pushed over three of the stacks as we passed them; even if none of the bottles broke—and it sounded like a few had, though I didn't look back—they'd at least slow our pursuers. Suli started to slip away, so I tightened my grip on her hand and pulled her after me. She yelped, but I ignored it; we needed to reach our destination.

Six meters after the bottle stacks, we turned left and burst through a door into a surprisingly large kitchen. I pivoted as soon as we were both in the room, yanked Suli in an arc behind me, switched to normal vision, and threw the lock on the door. I grabbed a metal prep table to my right. A cook who'd been leaning on it gave me an annoyed look, but what he saw on my face caused him to hold up his hands and back away. At about two meters tall and over a hundred kilos, I'm a fairly strong guy naturally, and the boost I get from the nanomachines helps a lot in situations like this, so I had no problem dragging the food- and bowl- and pot-laden table in front of the door. Neither the lock nor the table would stop the three guys for long, but that was okay; we didn't need much time.

I scanned the area. The skylight stood less than two meters above the top of the plating table. Suli had retreated to a corner. I grabbed her arm, yelled "Sorry" to the cooks and waiters who were now lining the walls and trying to stay out of whatever was happening, and darted to the table full of small, ready-to-eat plates.

"Ten seconds," Lobo said.

The door banged against the table as our pursuers weakened the lock.

"Up!" I said to Suli. She paused, so I climbed onto the table, kicked aside the plates near my feet, and pulled her after me.

"Cover," Lobo said.

I pulled Suli tight to me and bent over her as the skylight shattered and small fragments of glass and wood supports tumbled onto us. From the relatively small amount hitting me I could tell that Lobo had shot it from the side; I love working with a pro. A pair of rescue smart-cables fell through the opening. I straightened, grabbed Suli's arm, and put it on the cable. The soft, black line wound around her forearm and downward until it hit her torso, then extended once around her chest. I grabbed the second cable, and it began to wrap around me.

The lock gave, and the door opened a hand's width.

"Go!" I said to Lobo.

As our pursuers shoved aside the table, Lobo accelerated straight up. Suli and I shot into the sky, a vertical ascent of ten meters in two seconds. She gasped as Lobo slowed his climb and headed at a more measured pace out of the line of fire of the men who'd chased us into the kitchen. As he moved, he reeled us in gently.

For a few moments, we were out of sight of our pursuers and hanging in the crisp night air, The Take Off fading from view, the majority of Vonsoir a sparkling light show spreading into the distance in front of us, light breezes rinsing the club smells from my nostrils. The cable clung to my torso, so I flew without strain in the beautiful evening. Even as my body struggled to deal with the post-action adrenaline jitters, I couldn't help but be caught up in the sensations of flight and the beauty of the scene unfolding below and in front of us. I waved my free arm at the world below and said to Suli, who was now parallel with me, "Amazing, isn't it? Beautiful, just beautiful."

She stared at me as if I was insane.

I tried to ignore her look, but I couldn't help myself: It made me smile, then chuckle, and finally laugh.

I was still laughing when we were completely inside Lobo. Suli's expression turned angry, and it stayed that way as I unwrapped the cable from her body until it took the hint and finished retracting on its own.

I tried to stop laughing, but at that moment Lobo said over the comm, "I obviously missed the joke."

For no reason other than my need to discharge tension, his comment cracked me up again. I turned away from Suli and continued laughing as Lobo sealed the lower hatch he'd opened and accelerated at speed into space.

When I stopped a minute later and faced Suli again, she said, "I do *not* understand what about that whole affair was so funny. They could have hurt me."

"Yeah," I said, "they could have—but they didn't. As for why I laughed, forget it. Let's get you to the gate." I headed up to the pilot's area. "First, though, let's make sure those five didn't have any airborne backup." As I walked, I murmured, "Lobo, status?"

This time, he spoke over the internal speakers, so Suli could also hear him. "I'm way ahead of you, as you might expect." What a show-off.

"What was that?" Suli said.

In general, the less data you give others, the safer you are, so I opted for a bland explanation. It didn't hurt that my answer would annoy Lobo. "The ship's command-and-control speech system." Before Lobo could comment, to make sure he understood my intent, I added, "On a PCAV imitation like this one, you get only the minimum computing capacity necessary to keep the vessel in the air."

"So why did it talk to you like that?" she said.

I shrugged. "I spend a lot of time alone in here, so I spent extra for some supplemental emotive programming." I sat in the pilot's couch. "Course and location?"

"Heading into a high-density satellite orbit," Lobo said. "No sign of pursuit."

"What are you doing?" Suli said.

"Investing half an hour in weaving slowly through some clusters of weather and corporate-data-relay sats. If no ship heads our way, we'll know we escaped cleanly and make for the gate."

"And if a ship does come after us? What good is a faux PCAV in a real fight?"

"If something chases us," I said, grateful that Lobo let my obvious desire for confidentiality override the offense he had most certainly taken, "then we have other options."

"Such as?" she said.

"Other options. That's all you need to know. You paid for an escort out of the club, and you're out of it. You also paid for a ride to the gate, and we'll get you there. You didn't pay for the story of my ship, and you sure as hell didn't pay enough to question my plans."

"Fine," she said, holding up her hands and backing up a step. "I *am* the one they were chasing, so I was just trying to understand what you had in mind. I had no idea you were so sensitive."

"I've tried to tell him," Lobo said. "Perhaps now he'll believe me."

Suli stared at me expectantly, as if Lobo's comment had done something other than make me wish he had a neck I could throttle.

Nothing I could say would make the situation any better, so I stayed silent and waited for the rest of the half hour to pass.

"No sign of pursuit," Lobo said over the comm. I'd asked him privately to stop talking to Suli. "Head to the gate?"

"Yes," I subvocalized. "I'm ready to be done with this woman and this job and relaxing back in the trees."

"I frankly prefer any work, even this sort of amateur effort, to the jungle life," Lobo said. "Dealing with a minor attack like the one in the club is better than hovering in the clouds while you relax in the trees, my only job to watch your every move on the tiny chance that some crazed bird decides to dive-bomb you and I have to bring to bear the full might of my considerable arsenal in order to save you from certain destruction."

I ignored him and said, "ETA to the gate?"

"Central Coalition fleet ships are conducting exercises on both sides of the route I would normally follow," Lobo said. "Do you want to wait, go the long way around one of the sets of ships, or head straight?"

"I saw a news story on the CC maneuvers," I said. "I assume they're maintaining an open route directly from Vonsoir to the gate so they don't inconvenience travelers. I see no reason not to take advantage of their courtesy and stay the course. Am I missing something?"

"No fact I can find contradicts that opinion," Lobo said. "I felt obliged, however, to point out the ships."

"Thanks," I said. "Let's go."

"Accelerating," Lobo said.

I stood and faced Suli, who was sitting in the other pilot's couch, her eyes shut, studiously ignoring me. "We're on our way to the gate. We should have you there soon."

"Thank you," she said without opening her eyes. "I look forward to it."

"Look," I said, feeling bad for having upset her so much, even though I didn't think I'd done anything wrong, "I'm sorry if—"

An alarm cut me off. Straps extruded from Suli's couch and clamped her in place. I climbed into the pilot's seat, which immediately secured me.

"Ships swarming on eight different approach vectors," Lobo said audibly, shifting to battle protocols. "The sphere surrounding us is tightening rapidly."

"Options?"

"Based solely on ship types," Lobo said, "not many. I could fight five of them and possibly win, but three are combat frigates that would beat me handily. I could outrun those and two of the others, but three scouts are faster than I. They'll win no matter what we do."

"Any chance we're not the target?"

"None," Lobo said. "They're attacking in classic surround formation."

"Could we—"

"Incoming message," Lobo said, cutting me off.

"Show me," I said. "Blank our end."

A standard CC police avatar appeared on the display Lobo opened in the wall in front of me.

"The government of the Central Coalition demands your immediate attention," it said. "Councillor Ken Shurkan requests your presence aboard the flagship, *Sunset*." A holo map of the ships around us popped into view and identified the *Sunset*, which sat in space far back from all the others. "You will dock in its main landing hangar."

"Turn on the audio," I said to Lobo.

"If we go into that ship's hangar," he said, "and they decide to retain us, we will not be able to exit without a high probability of self-destruction."

"I understand," I said. "Now, turn on the audio! Leave the video off."

"Activated," he said.

"We have committed no crime," I said, forcing my voice to be calm. "We're tourists headed for the Arctul jump gate. We request the same safe passage available to all travelers."

The avatar disappeared. The head of a blond boy filled the display. With bright blue eyes, unnaturally white skin, and lips so full they crossed the line from stylish to ridiculous, his face was far enough from human norms that I wondered if the CC was now using distortion software on its calls.

He smiled.

It didn't help.

"Mr. Moore," he said, "I'm Councillor Ken Shurkan of the Central Coalition government. We have a business proposition to discuss with you."

I studied the image a bit more and saw the man behind the boy. I'd met a few of the people who did everything possible to maintain the bodies and looks of their childhood, but I'd never understood the desire to do so. "I'd be happy to discuss it," I said, realizing I'd let Shurkan's image distract me, "after I finish my vacation on Lindquist."

I glanced at Suli; she was sitting quietly, staring at the screen, reacting to the situation far more calmly than I would have guessed.

I focused again on the image in front of me.

Shurkan leaned back and shook his head, the smile still firmly in place. "As I'm sure you're aware, Mr. Moore, you have few options, and that is not one of them. You can come aboard the *Sunset* voluntarily, or we can make you do so. If you choose the former, you do, of course, risk becoming our prisoner, but I can promise you I want only to talk. If we have to resort to the latter, there is, as I'm sure you're aware, a significant chance that in the ensuing action we would destroy your ship.

That would be a shame for us, of course, because we'd lose a potential business partner, but it would, I must say, cost you a great deal more."

He straightened, stopped smiling, and stared directly ahead. "So which will it be, Mr. Moore: fight and quite possibly die, or come aboard the *Sunset* and hear what I have to say?"

CHAPTER 3

I STARED AT SHURKAN'S IMAGE on the display, desperately trying to come up with a third alternative. I failed. "Audio off," I subvocalized.

"Done," Lobo said.

"Unless I'm missing something, we're docking on that ship," I said.

"I detest being trapped," Lobo said, "but I have to agree."

"Do I get a vote in this?" Suli said, her voice, like her expression, composed, almost serene, as if being kidnapped and threatened with death was a routine experience. Maybe it was. Maybe her partners were far worse than she'd led me to believe.

No matter. "No," I said. "You paid for my services, and dealing with this problem is one of them."

"Doesn't the fact that I paid give me a voice in what we do?" she said. "In fact, as the paying client shouldn't I be in charge?"

"Mr. Moore," Shurkan said, "though you are my first choice for the discussion I mentioned, I do have alternatives. I suggest you not keep me waiting."

"Again, no," I said to Suli, ignoring Shurkan. "You paid the fee and gave me our mission goals; I do the job."

"I just wanted to say that I agree we should go on the ship."

Anger surged in me at the time she'd wasted in the middle of a serious situation. I fought to control my temper, looked away from her, and said to Lobo, "Audio on."

"We'll park in the *Sunset*'s hangar," I said.

"Excellent," Shurkan said. "Some of my guards will escort you and your passenger to me. Others will inspect your ship."

What little I owned was on board Lobo. Some of it, including a rare gemstone from my home planet that Lobo stored in a deep interior vault, was not entirely legit.

"No," I said. "You asked for a meeting. I complied. Unless you plan to charge me and arrest me, you have no right to search my vessel."

"My men can always let themselves in once you've left the area."

"Then I hope we are meeting very, very far from the hangar, perhaps somewhere on another one of your ships, because when this vessel blows while inside the *Sunset*'s pressurized hull, it's going to take a big chunk of the *Sunset* with it."

"You would risk killing us?" Suli said, her calm finally shattered. "Why would you do that?"

Before I could answer, Shurkan said, "Your passenger clearly doesn't agree with your choice."

"I don't care," I said, the anger harder and harder to control. "I really don't. Now, you're the one with a choice: Do you agree to leave my ship alone, or should we both plan on meeting somewhere far from yours?"

He leaned back again, plastered on the disturbing grin, and said, "You really are every bit as unpleasant as your reputation suggests, Mr. Moore." He sighed theatrically, a move that with his juvenile appearance made him appear to be nothing more than a very spoiled child. "You bring your passenger as an extra bit of proof of goodwill. Then, we'll talk, and my men will leave your little ship alone. Deal?"

I pretended I hadn't heard the insult and considered the situation. If Suli came with me, she became a liability, just one more vulnerability I had to cover. If she stayed, however, and anything happened that caused Lobo to have to try to blast his way free of the *Sunset*, she would die for sure. She was a client, a client I now regretted taking but a client nonetheless, so I owed her the best probability of survival that I could arrange. To my surprise, she kept quiet as I considered my options; her silence gave me some hope that she could manage to do the same during the meeting with Shurkan.

"Deal," I said. "Send the route you want us to take. We're on our way."

As we followed the CC approach vector to the *Sunset*'s visitor hangar, Lobo opened a forward-feed display focused on our destination. When he had shown me the map of the CC ships in the area, the *Sunset* had appeared far larger than the rest, but the holo had covered such a vast area of space that I'd not really appreciated just how long the vessel was. Like all stargoing warcraft, it had to be narrow and short enough to fit through the larger apertures of most jump gates. It was big enough, however, that even with those size compromises there were some worlds whose gate apertures simply weren't wide enough to accommodate it. What the designers of the *Sunset* gave up in height and width, they made up in length. Easily two kilometers long, the ship almost certainly had never been on solid ground and never would be. Bristling with weapons and smaller fighters docked on all sides of it, the *Sunset* proclaimed loudly to anyone seeking to take advantage of the enormous target it presented that they would have to wade through considerable defenses before they ever got the chance.

I'd seen other fleet leads of similar size, but I couldn't recall a bigger one. In my years as a soldier with the Shosen Advanced Weapons Corporation, the Saw, in my opinion the finest merc company in the universe, I'd even ridden as human freight on a couple of command craft of almost the same size. Constructed in pressurized and armored sections, they could absorb quite a beating and continue to operate, as we'd learned the hard way on one occasion that cost the lives of a lot of guys I'd barely gotten to know.

I didn't like going back on board this kind of ship. I didn't like it at all.

I also knew I didn't have a choice.

"Half an hour out," Lobo said.

His voice brought me back to the moment and out of my reverie. "Come with me," I said to Suli.

"Why?" she said. "What do you want?"

"I don't have time for this." I grabbed her arm and headed rearward.

"Let go of me!"

"Then do as I tell you."

"Fine."

I released her arm and, true to her word, she followed me.

I stopped in front of the small med room and pointed at it. Lobo slid open its door. "Wait in here," I said, "until I let you out."

"Why? You said I was coming with you to the meeting, so why can't I stay with you?"

"Because I have work to do and not a lot of time to do it." I pointed to the room and stared into her eyes. "You *will* end up waiting in there. It's your choice how you enter. Decide." When she didn't move, I put my hand on her shoulder. "Now."

She glared at me, shook her head, anger tightening her every motion, and stepped into the little room. "Shurkan was right, you know. You really are—"

"Shut it," I said.

The door cut off the rest of her sentence.

I went to my quarters and changed my clothes, talking as I pulled off garments.

"What do you know about the inside of a ship like the *Sunset*?"

"An enormous amount," Lobo said. "I was, after all, built to fight as part of a fleet. Can you be a bit more specific about the data you're seeking?"

"I'm not sure," I said. "Anything that might prove useful should the meeting go wrong." I paused to think. "Examples: Will you and I be able to communicate? Could you blast your way out and survive? Is there any safe escape route for me?"

"If we're docking in the hangar dignitaries use," Lobo said, "then the default for the area will almost certainly be to allow encrypted communications. No visiting government officials worth the use of that facility would attend a serious meeting without access to the data stores on the ship that brought them there."

"But Shurkan's people could easily disable comm capabilities."

"True. The *Sunset* certainly can jam and distort signals across all known comm bands. I suggest, however, that they would have no reason to do so. As far as they're concerned, I'm at best an ordinary PCAV, so the computational level and data-store size I would offer you could not be enough to matter."

"Wouldn't they worry about me instructing you to start shooting?"

"That brings us to your second question," Lobo said. "Yes, I believe I could blow a hole in the hull that was big enough to let me fly out of there. What would happen next, however, is obvious: That section of the *Sunset* would seal itself, some combination of the ship's guns, the fighters parked on it, and the other vessels in the area would attack me, and in short order I'd be just so much wreckage. Shurkan would be far enough away that you and he could watch the entire short battle—and it would be a very brief fight—from the safety of a remote-feed display. Face it: Your threat all but ensured that he'll hold the meeting at least two ship sections away from the hangar."

"Don't blame that on me," I said. "He would have taken the precaution anyway. Besides, would you have preferred I let them poke around inside you?"

"Dealing with human intruders would not have been a problem, at least not for me. You, however, would not have gotten off so easily."

"How would it have been a problem for me?"

"You would have been the one who had to explain to Shurkan why he needed to send more troops to pick up the corpses."

"Which would have led us back to the same dilemma: you blasting your way out or being destroyed. Enough." I verified our link was still working and pulled on an active-fiber shirt with additional comm sensors woven into it. Should they block only the obvious ways for us to talk, I wanted a backup.

I considered releasing Suli, but something about her still bothered me. I went up front and sat in the pilot's couch. The *Sunset* continued to grow in the forward display, its dark body blotting out everything else, as if the section of space in front of us had fallen into an eerily large black hole.

"You monitor all aspects of all people on board, right?" I said.

"Of course," Lobo said.

"Did what you could read of Suli's vitals suggest she was as calm as she appeared? Or was she just doing a good job of hiding her fear?"

"To the best of my ability to tell given the data I could collect from the couch's sensors," Lobo said, "the only time she registered any change in emotion was when you threatened to have me blow up part of the *Sunset*."

"No one without serious training can stay that level in this kind of crisis," I said, "and nothing Glazer told me about her suggests she would be that calm."

"I agree."

"Which means we can't trust her," I said.

"Yes," Lobo said, "but how is that news?"

"What do you mean?"

"Exactly how many people have we met since you purchased me," he said, "that we could both trust? Not granting trust is not a problem; it's a virtue."

"Do you realize how paranoid that sounds?" I said.

"Yes," Lobo said, "but it's in my programming." He paused, one of those short pauses that for him contained so much time for computing that I often wondered what he could possibly be doing in the gap between sentences. "As it is in yours."

I wished I could argue with him, but it would be pointless; he was right. I'd never have made it to twenty, much less over a hundred and fifty-five, without a level of active distrust that most would consider paranoia.

"Five minutes from docking," Lobo said.

The *Sunset* opened the hangar doors. Light burst from the ship like the bang of creation emerging from the primordial darkness. We thrust forward into the brightness, Lobo slowing as we drew closer. We decelerated gradually until we were no longer moving forward, only hovering a meter over the well-marked landing zone, and then Lobo set us down. He opened a rear-facing display, and we watched as the hangar doors sealed us inside the *Sunset*.

Time to find out why we were here.

CHAPTER 4

*T*HE *SUNSET* PRESSURIZED the hangar faster than I'd thought was possible. A single guard, weapons still holstered, strolled through a hatch to our left and stopped three meters away from Lobo. He didn't stand at the ready, snap to attention, assume a defensive stance, or do anything else that might suggest he was working. No name badge told us who he was. Nothing about him suggested any interest whatsoever in Lobo or the people inside. He slouched, sighed, and glanced around as if bored.

"I don't even rate a serious escort?" I said. "My reputation is slipping."

"Does your ego make you stupid?" Lobo said, missing the joke. A holo of the hangar popped into the air in front of me. Two dozen red dots, each glowing brightly against the institutional burnished metal interior surfaces, occupied positions scattered around the walls, floor, and ceiling. "Those are the weapons I can spot. We can assume there are others."

I shook my head and chuckled. "I guess you demonstrate a sense of humor only when it suits your purpose. I don't suppose you'd be willing to start using it to appreciate my jokes."

"As soon as you start telling some," Lobo said, "I'll start laughing at them."

"Very funny." I stared at the dots on the hologram; the weapons reflected exactly the sort of careful placement you'd expect from the designers of a good milspec environment. "Wait a minute,"

I said, realizing what was bothering me, "why are you making conversation when we're on a mission?"

"Because you clearly need it, or you wouldn't be standing there," Lobo said, "and because Shurkan's courtesy is, at least for now, giving us the luxury of postponing the job until you step outside."

"I don't—" I shut up. He was right. I'd assumed I'd taken on a simple transport gig, and when the circumstances had changed, I'd done a bad job of keeping up with them. Though I didn't blame myself for not seeing what was coming, I was frustrated at how slowly I was adapting. I had to stay alert and in the moment.

I took a deep breath, held it for a count of ten, then let it gradually out through my nose. "Release Suli," I said as I walked rearward.

She stepped out of the med room. "Are we finally ready to go?" she said. "I've put up with—"

I held up my hand, stared at her, and she stopped talking.

"The rules are simple," I said, "so it should be easy for you to obey them."

"What rules?"

"Mine, the ones you have to agree to follow if you want to come with me to this meeting."

She sighed theatrically, putting her head and her shoulders into it.

I could tell I was juiced to go, because the gesture made me want to shove her back into the med room.

"Don't talk without checking with me first for permission," I said. "Stay close to me. Follow my lead. Most importantly, do what I tell you the moment I tell you; no arguments, no delays." I stepped closer to her, so we were less than a meter apart. "Got it?"

"Yes," she said, nodding.

I waited, but she said nothing else. Satisfied, I turned away from her and said, "Open a hatch."

Light from the hangar, which was far brighter than necessary, washed across Lobo's floor and the wall opposite the hatch. I stood to the right of the opening, waiting to see if anything bad would happen, but nothing did. After half a minute, I motioned to Suli and stepped out of Lobo onto the hangar floor. She followed me. Lobo sealed himself as soon as she was clear of him.

"The air is obviously breathable," Lobo said over the comm,

"though rife with human residue; they'd do well to check their air filtration system. No weapon activated when you left me. If they're going to do something to either of us, it'll happen later."

The room did carry the distinct odor of too many people sharing too small a space for too long, but I've lived with that smell many times, so it didn't bother me.

"Mr. Moore," the guard said, still slouching and not looking me in the eyes, "Councillor Shurkan asked me to escort you to him. If you'd follow me, please." He turned and left without waiting for a response or even a sign that I was behind him.

In the Saw, his sloppiness would have landed him on punishment details for a month; here, it seemed not to matter. Maybe his behavior came from riding on such a powerful ship, or perhaps it was a small sign of why any government with adequate funds employs a merc group to fight its serious conflicts.

We stayed behind him as he headed through the hatch in front of us and down a long, wide corridor. The light gray flooring gave slightly under my weight and bounced back nicely; it made walking fun. The same material covered the ceiling and the walls, though from time to time solid metal hatches and octagonal windows, each tinting opaque as we drew within view of it, broke the monotony.

The guard never looked back.

After five minutes, his complete neglect for our presence annoyed me enough that I said, "Aren't you a little worried that I might attack you from behind?"

"Nope," he said.

"Why not?"

He laughed. Without turning or slowing he said, in a soft, conversational voice, "For the most part, it's because I know the *Sunset*, and you don't."

"Which matters why?" I said, picking up my pace so I could hear him more easily.

"The weapons," Lobo said over the comm.

Before he could continue, the guard said, "Because I know that you've never been out of the sights of a laser that could cut you in half before you could touch me, nor have you ever been out of point-blank range of a trank gun that could knock you out in under a second—or poison you if we felt so inclined. We've been under both human and machine surveillance since the moment you left your little ship."

The guard stopped suddenly and turned to face me. Nothing in the posture of his torso had changed in any immediately obviously way, but everything about him was different. His stance was wider, one foot behind the other, and his weight rested primarily on his front leg. His arms hung slightly ahead of his body and were tense, ready for action. "Also, frankly, you don't look like that much to me, and I'm good at what I do."

I told myself to ignore the insult and focus on the job at hand, but I was tired of being at the end of the whip, so before I realized I was doing it, I'd stepped so close to him that we were almost touching. I'd misjudged him before, but though I now knew what he was, I didn't care.

He looked up and to the left briefly, then smiled and backed away from me. "As much as I'd like to take you up on that offer," he said, "they just reminded me that my orders are to deliver you to Councillor Shurkan unharmed."

He turned and left.

"That was stupid," Lobo said in my ear. "What's wrong with you? Never mind: Don't answer that. It doesn't matter. Answer this: Are you good to go?"

"Yes," I subvocalized. He was right. I was letting my frustration affect my actions, and that was indeed an idiotic thing to do.

I glanced at Suli, who stood a meter away to my left. She was watching me closely, but she said nothing.

I nodded in the direction of the guard, and we headed after him.

Over the next ten minutes, the man made his own small invitations, stopping suddenly several times so I'd have an excuse to run into him—and he'd have a reason to react. I stayed away from him each time; he was not, I reminded myself, the job at hand. Once, after I stopped and waited for him to resume, he faced me briefly and raised his right eyebrow in question. I shrugged and smiled.

We went through a set of blast hatches and emerged into a corridor that made sure you understood that you were now in executive territory. Lining the walls was a dark purple wood—real wood, I felt it—that made me wonder if it came from some relative of the trees on Arctul. Covering the floor was active-fiber carpet that sent waves of blue in circles around each foot as you stepped on it. Soft, wordless music I didn't recognize, something with a faint piano and soaring violins, wafted under the sounds of our footsteps; I couldn't spot the speakers. A starscape projection turned the ceiling into a night on a planet still unspoiled by light pollution. Even the funk of humanity that tainted the air in the other parts of the *Sunset* was now gone, replaced by a faint hint of the smell of a forest after a strong afternoon rain. I've never been in so wonderful a corridor on a spacecraft.

Twenty meters later, the guard stopped one stride past a hatch, which opened itself as he waved us toward it. He gave me a hard look, a last chance to make a play for him.

I pretended I hadn't noticed, pointed at the entrance, and said, "After you, please."

His anger looked less practiced this time as he said, "I'm to wait for you outside. Councillor Shurkan would prefer to meet with you two alone."

I nodded and stepped into the room. Suli followed me closely.

The conference space made the hallway look like a trash- and drunk-infested alley. Blond wood planks polished to a high gloss covered the floor. Every inch of the walls danced with holo displays of various CC systems, with an ancient image of Earth in a place of honor facing the door. The ceiling resembled a sky on the edge of rain, ripples of silent lightning arcing across it. The burnished metal table in the room's center appeared to hover over the floor. A dozen chairs, each covered in rich black leather, stood around the table, spaced so no one had to be too close to anyone else.

At the table's far end sat what I would have taken to be a boy playing at being a grown-up had I not already seen Shurkan on Lobo's display. On one side of him was a holo of Arctul's lavender jump gate, its pretzel-like shape gently and unrealistically rotating. On his other side shimmered a holo of Arctul itself, the planet also slowly rotating. His chair had boosted him so high his legs must have been pushing up on the table, and still he couldn't manage to look imposing. I wondered again at his body and lifestyle choice; it had to be a disadvantage in a world where the executive norm was tall and thin. To overcome it, I reminded myself, he had to possess some special drive or unusual skills, so I'd be foolish to underestimate him.

"Recording," Lobo said in my ear. "If they stop our voice comm, I'll send a tingle through the shirt on an alternate frequency they're less likely to block. Scratch your left arm if you're receiving me."

I stared at Shurkan as the door closed behind me, then looked away and pretended to study the room as I scratched my arm.

"Come, Mr. Moore," Shurkan said, "surely the time for stalling is past. Sit." He motioned to the chairs on either side of him.

Suli took the one on his left.

I ignored him and chose a chair to my right, one that put a corner of the room behind me and presented a clear line of sight to both Shurkan and the door.

Shurkan laughed. "Do you mind if I call you Jon?"

"Feel free."

"Jon, though I've always been one to appreciate a healthy dose of paranoia, I must say that in this case it is entirely unwarranted. If I'd wanted you dead, I could have had the fleet blow you up on the way to the gate. Won't you sit closer?"

"You could always change your mind," I said, smiling but not moving.

He laughed again. "Fine. Let's get to business." He paused, as if awaiting some reaction.

I stayed silent. I'd been reacting entirely too much and too quickly since the CC ships had intercepted us; I'd do better to stay silent.

After a few awkward moments, he continued. "What do you know about Heaven?"

"Which religion's?"

He smiled, and for the first time since I'd entered the room, the reaction struck me as genuine. "The planet, not the afterlife."

"I've never visited it," I said, "but I've picked up the same basics as anyone who travels a great deal: They used to call it Bart's Folly, which from what little I've heard is a more accurate description than its current name. Some marketing genius came up with the new label. It's in CC space, though at the very edge. It started with only one aperture, but it has more now." I paused, but I really didn't know anything else. "That's about it."

"Not surprisingly," Shurkan said, "your data is out of date. The planet drew so little attention for the first several decades after the CC settled it that most people don't bother to keep up with it." He leaned forward and gestured toward the center of the table. "As you can see, several very important factors have changed."

A holo of a planet and a jump gate snapped into view. From my angle the globe was on the far side of the very pale blue, almost white gate. The gate had four apertures.

"So you can now jump to more places from there," I said. "New apertures form at many gates, and aside from the inevitable commercial competition for access to the untouched planet on the other side of each one, they're not remarkable." I didn't add that those competitions could turn violent and dangerous. I'd found myself in the middle of one on a backwater Frontier Coalition planet named Macken, and though the experience had brought me Lobo, it had also added to the memories that woke me up in the middle of the night.

I glanced at Suli, wondering what she was making of all this, but she appeared relaxed, almost bored. Good: The more she controlled her emotions, the better.

"What's unusual and important about these apertures," Shurkan said, "is that two go to planets in CC space and two lead to EC worlds."

That was definitely not the norm. Most border worlds had at most one way to jump to a planet outside their own federation. It's as if the makers of the gates—if there are makers; we have no clue how the gates came into being—decided to divide space neatly into sectors and provide only a few points of contact between those areas.

"It started as a CC world, right?" I said.

He nodded.

"So, I assume it's still one, just a CC planet with two links to the EC. What's the problem?"

"The problem," Shurkan said, his voice turning harsh and giving away the true age his body tried to conceal, "is that the same government that renamed the planet doesn't share your assumption."

"So they've joined the EC?" Such changes in allegiance were rare, because the owning federation was unlikely to tolerate them, but this wouldn't be the first one.

"No," Shurkan said. "The government of Heaven has declared that it is in the middle of a multiyear process of selecting the federation it will join."

"So it's playing you and the EC to see which of you will give it the most?"

"Yes," he said.

"So go take it back," I said. "Isn't that what the CC would normally do?"

"Yes," he said, "in most cases we would do just that. Unfortunately, the government of Heaven didn't make the break until it had persuaded my predecessor—" He paused as if even mentioning the person left a bad taste in his mouth. "—to withdraw most of our local fleet because it was hurting their growing tourism business. At the same time, they were secretly courting the EC."

"So now neither of you has a large military presence there, and neither of you can assemble one without the other responding in kind."

"The end result of which—" he said.

I cut him off. "Would be war. I understand. What I don't get is why you're telling me all this, fascinating as it may be."

"Patience, Jon, patience. We're almost there."

I forced myself to stay silent even though I wanted to scream at him to get to the point. Bureaucrats always take inefficient routes to their goals, and you rarely have any chance of rushing them.

When I didn't speak again, he nodded in satisfaction and continued. "We don't want a war, and neither does the EC; we're too evenly matched, and both sides inevitably lose more than they gain in such a fight. At the same time, we do want control of the planet—as, of course, does the EC."

He leaned back, smiled, and said, "Which brings us to you."

I refused to take the bait and kept quiet.

The smile vanished; that clearly wasn't the reaction he wanted. "We'd like to pay you to help overthrow Heaven's government."

I laughed, a genuine reaction that it felt nice to let myself have. "You have the wrong man, Shurkan. I'm a courier. I don't know anything about politics."

"Don't be modest, Jon. We know you're a courier, but we also know you spent some years with the Saw, so your military training has to be top-notch. You own a PCAV, which is hardly a standard courier vehicle."

"I received it as compensation for a job I did a couple of years ago, the only form of payment the client could afford."

He waved his hands. "We really don't care. We verified your ownership is legitimate, so you can take it anywhere."

I stood. "So I spent some time as a soldier; a lot of poor people do. That in no way qualifies me to attack an entire government. We're done here."

"No," he said, leaning forward again and placing his hands on the table, "we're not. Sit."

I again regretted the quickness of my reactions. I shouldn't have stood, because now I either had to sit and thus appear to accept his authority, or try to leave and learn the hard way that I was locked in, as I almost certainly was. I opted for saving face, a tactic many bureaucrats will support by reflex. "Give me a reason not to leave," I said, keeping my tone level and polite.

"I'll give you two," he said. "We'll pay you a great deal of money, and what we want you to do is something a person with your skills can handle."

I stood for a moment as if contemplating his words, then nodded and sat. "Go ahead."

He relaxed and smiled, back on familiar ground. "If we thought we could bring down the government of Heaven by assassinating a few leaders, you and I wouldn't be meeting. If bribery was a realistic option, we also wouldn't be here. Neither of those will work; the key players are too close-knit a group. What we need you to do is bring to us a single criminal. That's it. Succeed at that task, and we'll make you wealthy."

I didn't have to force myself to be quiet this time; I was genuinely puzzled. I certainly wasn't a bounty hunter, though I'd done that kind of work before I joined the Saw, and I understood it. Still, it made no sense for the CC to be involved with crime on a planet that at best only partially belonged to it. Finally, I said, "What's the connection between this criminal and Heaven's government?"

"They're sponsoring the man," Shurkan said. "He's working for Heaven, officially doing legitimate work, but in secret committing a very dangerous crime. We can't go after him directly, because doing so would mean going up against the government—which would immediately draw the EC into action. By contrast, if you, a man with no clear ties to any planet or coalition, a tourist, could deliver him to us, we could put him on trial, blast every feed with the news of his crimes, and make very clear to everyone—"

"That Heaven was harboring and supporting him," I said. "That part is obvious. What is he doing that would upset that planet's citizens enough to cause them to vote out their government?"

"Research with live subjects—people—into making nanomachines live successfully for extended periods in human bodies," he said. "Research," his voice dropping a bit and becoming more adult in tone, "that not only has been banned for over a hundred years, but that is killing the subjects."

I didn't have to force myself to be quiet; I needed time to collect my thoughts. The experiments Shurkan had described were exactly what the scientists on Aggro had done to me, to Benny, and to many, many others. All the others had died from the tests. Only Benny and I had survived even the initial rounds, and now, to the best of my knowledge, I was the only remaining success of the Aggro research. The nanomachines that laced all my cells kept me looking twenty-eight perpetually, let me eat as much as I wanted and never gain weight unless I chose to do so, and provided me with many other abilities—but they also ensured that I could never stay anywhere for long, never tell anyone about my past, never let myself be caught and tested, never be normal.

"If you know about this research," I said, "why not simply expose it right now and be done with it?" And why, I thought but did not say, talk about it in front of Suli? He must have considered her so harmless that she couldn't use the information to hurt him or the CC. I glanced at her for a moment; she still appeared calm, though a tightness around her eyes betrayed her increased tension.

Shurkan chuckled, but there was no warmth in the sounds he made, only tightly controlled anger. "Jon, I've tried to not insult your intelligence; why are you insulting ours? If we had enough proof to pass public review, or if the legitimate work this man is doing didn't provide such a good cover story, then we would have revealed his crimes long ago. With what little data we have, however, we would both fail to induce the administration change we need and cause the government to move the man to a new location."

"I'm sorry," I said, meaning it. "I was stupid. I was surprised to hear that anyone was conducting such banned tests, because they're supposed to be insanely dangerous." That was true as far as it went, but I was now also wondering why they'd picked me and what they knew of my past. I would not let myself end up a test subject again. I would not. "None of this, though, is my problem."

"We can't send in a CC team," Shurkan said, "for all the obvious reasons. We can hire people who do this kind of work, of course, but I've always found that while money is a good motivator, caring about the job often matters more."

"I'm sorry," I said, perhaps too quickly, "but I don't see why I should care any more than anyone else you might try to hire."

"From some friends of ours in the EC," he said, "friends who provide us information from time to time, we've learned that you recently went to a great deal of trouble to save the life of a young boy—and failed."

I instantly pictured the boy, Manu Chang, as I'd last seen him, vanishing down a crowded street, very much alive but dead as far as the EC was concerned. I shoved down the memory, because the boy's ability to catch glimpses of the future meant he'd never be safe if the EC or the CC or any other large organization, governmental or corporate, knew he was alive. I'd helped stage his death so he'd have a chance at as normal a life as his abilities would permit.

"Doing what you want," I said, grateful for a good excuse for letting some emotion into my voice, "won't bring back that boy."

"No," Shurkan said, "it won't. But it could provide a way for you to atone for whatever part you played in his death."

"You have no right to talk about what happened," I said, "and I don't see its connection with your problem."

Suli's expression changed for the first time, and the pity I saw on her face only made me feel guilty for lying about the entire affair. The lie, though, was necessary. She opened her mouth as if to speak, and I shook my head. She stayed quiet.

"How familiar are you with the story of Aggro?" Shurkan said.

I didn't like him bringing up Chang, but my involvement with that boy and the EC was less than a year in the past, so I wasn't disturbed that he'd found out about it. His question about that horrible place, by contrast, made me wonder just how much data he had acquired about me. I fought the urge to run and forced myself to answer in the same tone as before. "I know what everyone knows from vids and holos: It was an orbital prison where they conducted experiments on prisoners, and a nanotech disaster destroyed it and led to the quarantine of the planet it was orbiting."

"Pinkelponker," Shurkan said, "and yes, that's correct as far as it goes. What we've recently learned is that one of the scientists on Aggro had sent a few messages to his family suggesting his team was converging on success, that two subjects had not died instantly, and that the key seemed to be to use younger people." He paused and stared at me.

I returned the look as I pictured the other prisoners I'd seen while stuck in that orbiting hellhole. My memory supported the observation, and I made a connection I'd never made before: Benny and I were the only survivors. We were also the only prisoners who were not full-grown adults. We were the size of adults, we were teens and so old enough for some cultures to consider us adults, but neither of us had yet hit puberty. That fact had never mattered before. Now it hit me hard.

"The man we're after obtained that information," Shurkan said, "and began experimenting on children."

He balled his small fists and slammed them into the table.

"Children, Jon. He's killing kids, and you can help us stop him."

CHAPTER 5

I DON'T KNOW what to say," I said, meaning it.

"Say that you'll take the job," Shurkan said. "Help us save lives—the lives of children. And make yourself a lot of money: We're prepared to pay three million upon delivery."

I sat and thought.

Shurkan let me be.

Suli looked like she wanted to speak, but she didn't, for which I was grateful.

The holos continued to dance silently in their places. The air in the room was as still as when I'd entered it. Everything appeared exactly as it had a few minutes before—but everything was different now. The deal was on the table, and it was one that in two ways I was motivated to accept. I hated it whenever anyone hurt children, and I liked the size of the payday; it would support Lobo and me for at least a couple of years.

The risks, though, were huge. The idea of being captured again by someone actively working in human-nanotech research brought the memories of Aggro crashing into me and terrified me. Should anything go wrong on this mission, I could end up the captive of the security team protecting this scientist—and there definitely was such a team, or Shurkan wouldn't need someone like me. As a prisoner, I'd make an ideal adult test subject, and any scientist preparing me for experiments of this type would soon figure out that I was already infused with nanomachines.

I could also back away and be sure that the CC wouldn't give up if I didn't sign on. This didn't have to be my problem. They'd find others willing to take the job.

So, maybe I could walk away from this mess safely and without leaving those children to die—but did I want to?

I needed time to think on my own, away from Shurkan, and I wanted more information. Both were available in Lobo.

I stood and faced Suli. "We're leaving." Turning toward Shurkan, I said, "I'll consider your offer, but not here; being a prisoner is not conducive to good analysis."

Shurkan clearly didn't like my response, but he read my attitude well enough that he paused only briefly before saying, "I completely understand. Someone will escort you back to your ship, and we'll let you stay in the *Sunset*'s hangar for as long as you need."

I considered arguing, but there was no point in it; he'd never let us leave until I gave him an answer.

"Mr. Moore," Suli said, "you have to help. They can't let these crimes continue."

"What?" I said. "Why are you getting involved? This isn't your issue. Let's go."

She didn't move. "They clearly need your help," she said, "or more children will die and an oppressive government will continue to get away with abusing its people."

"I appreciate that you care about children," I said, "but as I told you before, *this is not your problem.* I'll think about all this after I drop you at the gate." Turning toward Shurkan, I said, "If you won't let me take her there, would you at least have one of your ships do it? This really isn't her concern."

She stared at me for several seconds before speaking. "I'm afraid I haven't been honest with you—or with Kiana, who knows nothing about this. I'm from Heaven, and I work for the opposition Freepeople party. We have to make the current government stop what it's doing, but there is no way we could expose this practice on our own. The EC seems more interested in assisting the administration than bringing it down. Only the CC would help us."

I stared at her, not wanting to believe her and yet realizing that her confession explained so much of her behavior that it instantly rang as true. I was also furious at myself: She'd set me up, and I hadn't seen it coming.

"And though we very much do want to help," Shurkan said, "we can't send in our own agents without risking exposure."

I'd trusted someone I didn't know, and this is what happened. The temperature in the room increased; the still rational part of me understood that I, not the space, was the source of the heat as my skin flushed with rage.

"We also couldn't send anyone to extract you from the Green Rising grove," Shurkan said, "without attracting far more attention and taking a far greater risk of violence than I felt was prudent. Priyana here is one of our friends on Heaven, and she came up with the plan to lead you to us."

She'd seemed too calm when the CC ships had closed on us, and Lobo had confirmed that her vitals had showed no evidence of surprise. I should have figured it out then.

Shurkan smiled. "Don't worry about what your visit here will cost you: Priyana provided a solid cover story. Officially, we received a report of a kidnapping and helped local law enforcement by searching your ship and others. You will, of course, receive a clean report, and as far as anyone else will know, we'll send you on your way with an official apology for the delay."

I sat, not from a desire to stay but from the need to fight the anger that was rising in me. "And the men who chased us in The Take Off—"

"Were CC guards that we thought would capture the two of us and provide a cover for this meeting," Suli said.

"Having to use the fleet was an unfortunate backup option," Shurkan said, "though one I must confess Priyana had considered might be necessary."

"You could simply have asked me," I said, so angry I wanted to tear the room apart, "and saved all this trickery."

"No," Shurkan said, "we could not. First, nothing we know of you suggests you'd willingly take a meeting with the CC. Second, we had no way to approach you without alerting those enviro-nuts to at least the possibility of something important going on. Once we did that, they'd never let go of it; they're always looking for leverage on us. We needed a way to meet with you that also gave all of us, including you, a way to exit cleanly when this is over."

Even though his statements were accurate, I despised them and him, because I hate being played. I hate the way governments and megacorporations treat everyone as expendable, as human assets, as nothing more than numbers to manipulate. I hate politicians being willing to sacrifice others in their unshakable confidence that they represent the greater good.

I also hate losing control, and I was perilously close to doing that.

I stood and headed for the door. "Well, I'm glad for that bit of planning, because I'm leaving *now*."

Suli stood and rushed after me. She grabbed my arm.

I fought the urge to hit her and instead stood still, my fists clenched. My voice came out tight as I said, pronouncing each word slowly and distinctly, "Let go of me. *Now*."

"We know where he is, Mr. Moore, Jon," she said. She released my arm but then stepped between me and the door and stared into my eyes. "We can't get to this monster on our own. We can't prove anything. But we know where he is, and we can help you get to him and even provide some local support. If we—if you—can deliver him to the CC, they can prosecute him, make him pay, and help us remove the criminals that are supporting him and replace them with a government that cares about its citizens."

She paused, searching my face for a reaction.

Anger still so filled me that I needed to leave.

"Get out of my way," I said, speaking slowly.

"*Children are dying!*" she said, her voice turning shrill as she yelled. "Innocent children, usually poor ones, often kids in the government's own foster-care facilities, are ending up as lab animals, creatures this so-called scientist, this amoral demon, Jorge Wei, butchers without pause. You can help us save them!"

I pushed her aside as gently as I could. She stumbled backward. I had to get away, to clear my head, to let my body process the rage until I could think clearly again.

I stepped toward the door, which opened as I drew within a meter of it. The same guard was waiting outside, smirking at me. I wanted to tear off his head and rub it on the fancy carpet until I'd soaked it with the bloody remains of his smirk. I raised my hands and shifted my stance. The guard's expression changed in an instant, and he shifted his weight to his rear leg, bracing himself for impact.

"Jon," Lobo said over the comm, "please do *not* leave that room, and please do *not* fight that guard. Get control of yourself, stay there, and agree to help them."

I froze, not believing what I'd just heard.

The guard looked as puzzled as I felt.

In the pause, Lobo spoke, each word so crystal clear in my ears that though I could not believe what I was hearing, I also could not doubt that it was real.

"Please, Jon. Do it for me."

CHAPTER 6

I DIDN'T MOVE. I stared at the guard standing barely two meters in front of me, but I wasn't really seeing him. Lobo had asked me to do something for him—honestly asked me, not a snarky query but a straightforward request. The whole idea made no sense, but it had happened; his words were clear. Lobo was a sarcastic, annoying, twenty-five-meter-long killing machine with a perpetually bad attitude, but he was also my only friend in this sector of the universe, maybe the only friend I still had.

There was no longer any question about it: I had to help Shurkan and Suli.

Now I had to figure out how to change course this abruptly without alerting Shurkan that something was up.

Suli came to my aid by stepping between me and the guard, putting her hand on my chest, and saying, "Please, Jon, don't walk out because I lied to you or the CC forced you into coming here. We were wrong to do those things, and I'm sorry, but what matters is saving the children."

The guard relaxed and backed away. I focused on Suli as I saw a believable path forward.

"And what happens to me if I fail, if Wei's security captures me?"

"I don't know," Suli said, "but I'm sure we'd try—"

"No," Shurkan said, "no one would try anything, and Jon knows it. You said you were sorry we lied to him, so let's not do it again. Jon,

43

unless you're a lot dumber than the data we have on you suggests, you know that if you fail, we'll deny this meeting ever happened."

"I wanted her to hear you say it," I said, turning my back on Suli and facing Shurkan, "so she'd understand what her acts had cost me."

Shurkan didn't respond. He stared at me, his bemused expression suggesting he knew what I would say next. I was counting on that.

"And what it will cost you," I said. "Five million. Half now, half on delivery."

"Is this only about money?" Suli said, her face flushing with anger.

I shook my head. "No, but if I'm going to take the risks this mission will entail, the CC is going to pay."

Shurkan smiled, back on familiar turf. "Four. We'll pay half up front, but you take one of my staff with you, so I can have a reliable data source, and you also agree to bring along Priyana. Her knowledge of her home region will be useful, and her presence will appease her organization, who are our partners in this undertaking."

If I'd decided on my own to take this job, I'd walk away now. A snatch and grab of a protected executive is hard enough with a team you can trust; doing it with people who have proven to be willing to deceive you is downright dangerous. I had to do this for Lobo, however, so I considered my options. A CC rep would be a pro, someone with skills I could use—but also someone who would always pose a threat to me. The nanomachines in my cells can heal almost any injury—I know, because I've suffered a lot of them—but I don't know if they could repair a shot through my brain. Suli had been a good enough actress to deceive me, and deceit was a skill I might be able to use. Shurkan was right that her background could also come in handy. I simply couldn't trust her.

On balance she was the lesser of the two evils, and Shurkan was clearly a negotiator.

"I'll take Suli, because she can help. No CC rep, though; that's a deal-breaker. You seem very fond of her," I nodded toward Suli, who had moved to stand to my left, "so she can represent your interests as well."

"I'd greatly prefer my own man be on the team," he said.

"I'm not negotiating any longer. I said that was a deal-breaker, and it is." I paused for effect. I hoped I'd read him correctly. "Decide: Do I take only Suli, do I work alone, or do I walk away entirely?"

"Fine, Jon, fine," he said, sighing dramatically. "We have a deal."

I needed to get away from there and talk to Lobo in private, to learn why I was now stuck with this job. "Then we might as well get moving," I said. "From everything you've told me, the sooner I find this guy, the better."

"I agree," Shurkan said, "but don't leave quite yet. I have some more information you'll find quite useful."

"So send it to my ship."

"No," he said. "For reasons that will become obvious, I'd prefer to discuss this here."

"Then go ahead," I said.

He tapped on the table and faced Suli. The door behind us opened, and the guard entered. "Priyana, please go with Jenkins here to Jon's ship and wait beside it."

"What?" she said. "Like you just told Jon, we're your partners. Anything you can share with him, you can share with me. And, I have more information to review with him; you know I do."

"Yes, our organizations are partners," he said, "but your conclusion is incorrect. The Freepeople party quite understandably has an agenda well beyond our relationship—as does our Council. We both consequently do not share all information with each other. That's fine and normal; no two groups ever do. You'll have to trust me that everything I'm going to tell Jon will help him capture Wei, and nothing I will say will be to your detriment."

"I'll have to tell my people about this," she said, "and as I told you, I still have more to discuss with Jon."

"You would tell them about anything I do," Shurkan said, nodding his head, "which makes my point." He gestured toward the door. "Now, if you would please go with Jenkins, we won't be long. You'll have plenty of time to talk with Jon later."

Suli stood for a moment, her body almost vibrating with the effort of controlling herself. After several seconds, she nodded her head, turned, and left. The door snicked closed.

"Please, sit," Shurkan said, gesturing again at the chair. I finally realized that he didn't like having to look up at me in a meeting he controlled—or probably at any other time, for that matter. A better person would have sat to make him feel more comfortable.

I wasn't in the mood to be that person.

"Thanks, but you said this would be short, so I'll stand." I waited until he opened his mouth to speak, then interrupted him. "Before you say anything else, let's settle that down payment."

"Really, Mr. Moore, I must—"

"What, I'm not Jon now?"

"You're intentionally trying to annoy me," he said.

"Yes, but that doesn't change anything, and it's not even close to payback for what you've done to me." I took out my wallet, thumbed it to open a quarantined area and to stand ready to receive, and stared at him again. "So, the down payment?"

He sighed theatrically and tapped on the table. "Have you never been civilized?" he said, shaking his head. "There. Satisfied?"

My wallet vibrated its receipt. I thumbed a transfer to Lobo.

"May we proceed?" he said.

I held up my hand and waited, aware that seconds were passing and uncomfortable in the delay, but there was no getting around it; I wanted the money planetside before we moved on.

"The transfer is good," Lobo said. "Your main bank on Arctul cleared it, and pieces of it are already hopping to other repositories."

I put down my hand. "You were saying," I said.

"I'd like your word," he said, "that you will not tell anyone what I'm about to reveal to you."

"No."

"Excuse me?"

"You've done nothing to earn my trust," I said.

"I just paid you half the fee," he said, "and you've yet to do a single thing. Surely that earns some trust."

"No," I said, "that buys my commitment to do my best to capture Wei. I can't think of anything you could do right now that would earn my trust."

"You are intensely frustrating to deal with," he said.

"I've heard that. Would you like your money back?"

He paused as if considering my offer, but we both knew he wasn't; he was in too deep, and my refusal to play by the normal bureaucratic rules had thrown him off his game.

"No," he finally said. "Though you will not trust me, I will trust you. Decide whether to tell anyone else about this; the cost of a leak will be clear."

"Go ahead."

"Before we agreed to work with Pri's organization, we made one attempt to get to Wei. We couldn't afford a direct attack, so we persuaded a scientist Wei was recruiting to work for us. She joined him about six months ago and was sending us status reports on those few days when Wei allowed her out of the complex."

"You said she 'was' sending reports. What happened?"

"We don't know," he said. "We have no way to contact her, and we haven't heard from her in three months."

"So you don't know—"

"If she's still alive. Correct. If she is, however, she could almost certainly help you, and we'd like you to bring her out with Wei."

"I can't guarantee that," I said. "If I take him in a public place, for example, she could still be alive but nowhere near him."

"Fair enough," he said, "but if you get the opportunity, bring her along."

In the Saw, we'd never leave a comrade behind. This woman wasn't on my team, but I appreciated Shurkan's goal. "Okay. How will I get her to trust me?"

"Her name is Norita McCombs," he said. "This is her."

The holos on both sides of him morphed into a woman almost my height, a blonde with shoulder-length hair, amber-colored skin, a surprisingly round face, light green eyes, and lithe, athletic body. The shape of her face and her unusual eyes would be easy to remember and make her simple to spot.

"If you see her and can find a way to speak to her," Shurkan said, "ask if she has a cousin who's a pro gamer. She does not, so the question should never normally arise. When she hears it, she'll know I sent you, but she'll ask for the name of the person you're recalling. Say it's 'Ken' something or other. If anyone else overhears you, the exchange should do no harm."

"I have it in case you don't," Lobo said.

As if I couldn't remember a recognition protocol. First, he makes me do this, then he insults me. He and I definitely needed to talk.

"Is that it?" I said.

The holos vanished.

"Yes," he said. He tapped the table and stared at me for a few seconds, as if searching for something. Whatever it was, I don't think he found it, because he finally said, "I look forward to your success."

The door opened, and a new escort, a small, nervous man shorter than Suli and no more than two-thirds my weight, motioned to his left. Like Jenkins, he wore no name tag or uniform.

Shurkan must have noticed the tension between me and Jenkins. Rationally, I knew he'd made a good choice to send a different and very obviously nonthreatening escort to take me back to Lobo. Emotionally, however, I was frustrated and let down; part of me still wanted to vent my anger physically, and Jenkins would have been worth hitting.

"Shall we go?" the man said.

"Yes," I said. I followed him into the hall without glancing back. "I have work to do."

I thought of Suli tricking me and having to take her on this mission, and my jaw clenched.

"And someone to set straight."

CHAPTER 7

*T*HE SMALL MAN maintained a surprisingly good pace for someone his height and didn't speak the entire way back to the hangar. When we reached the door, he waved me through, followed, and waited by the hatch. He was definitely staying out of my way, which was fine by me.

Suli paced back and forth in front of Lobo.

I ignored her. Lobo opened a side hatch as I approached. I walked right by Suli and into him.

"Jon," she said, "please—"

"Get in," I said, "or stay; I don't care. Either way, we're leaving now."

She stepped inside without hesitation.

I had to give her some credit, because she clearly understood my mood and still followed me into Lobo. That did nothing, however, to excuse her actions.

Lobo instantly shut the hatch.

"Shurkan for you," Lobo said over the speakers.

Suli opened her mouth as if to speak, but I ignored her and headed to the front.

"Go ahead," I said.

"We did not agree on a contact protocol when you've accomplished your mission," Shurkan said. He'd moved to another room, one with a waterscape playing behind him. "I suggest I upload the local contacts you should use."

49

"Hard quarantine ready," Lobo said over the machine frequency so only he and I could hear it.

I nodded. I was ready to leave and had no interest in talking further with Shurkan.

He nodded to his right.

"Received and clean," Lobo said, staying private. "The data is nothing more than names, comm methods, and a basic recognition protocol."

"We're done," I said. "Open the hangar so we can get on with it."

"One moment, please," he said. "Pri, I do apologize again for asking you to let us finish the meeting in private, but as I'm sure Jon will confirm, nothing we discussed will in any way harm you or your cause."

"How can I—" Suli said.

I cut her off. "You're wasting my time, and I'm not in the mood for it. We're done until I have Wei in custody."

"As you will," Shurkan said, "though such rude behavior is never necessary. I look forward to our next meeting being one in which we celebrate your success—and deliver your final payment."

His image disappeared.

"No humans remain in the hangar," Lobo said over the speakers, "and it is depressurizing."

"Jon," Suli said, "please let me apologize for deceiving you." She put her hand on my shoulder and pulled slightly, but I didn't move; I didn't want to look at her. "It was the only way any of us could figure out—"

"—that would get you what you wanted," I said. "I understand, and of course accomplishing your goals was more important than anything I was doing or might want."

"That's not the way we meant it," she said.

"But it's the truth," I said, "something you're apparently not very familiar with."

"Would you let Wei continue to kidnap children—or buy them from the government—and then use them as lab animals and kill them? Isn't that worth stopping?"

"Of course it is," I said, finally turning to face her. "But that's not the point. The point is that you could have asked me that question openly and honestly."

"And if we'd done that, would you have helped?"

"Hangar depressurization complete," Lobo said, still over the speakers, "and doors opening."

I was grateful for the interruption, because I didn't know the answer to Suli's question. Would I have helped? On the one hand, I like to think so, because I couldn't agree more with them that what Wei was doing was evil. I'd been in the place of those kids, and even almost a hundred and forty years later I still sometimes wake up in the middle of the night, thrashing and sweating, back on Aggro all over again. Despite that belief, however, I also couldn't sign up for every crusade that crossed my path. The universe is vast, humanity is spread everywhere there's a jump gate, and on every planet where there are people, there are horrors those people cause. They weren't all my problem.

"Take us out," I said, "and to the jump gate." The thought of being stuck in the middle of the CC ships made my spine tingle as surely as if I'd just learned I was in a sniper's sights. "As quickly as possible," I added.

But if I didn't help clean up the messes in front of me, then what good was I? Isn't that what we all have to do: work on improving each of our little corners of the universe? Is there anything better we could be doing with our lives?

This cause, though, hadn't been in front of me on Arctul, and no one had asked me to help until after Suli had tricked me into being captured by the CC.

As my attention returned to the moment, I saw she was still staring intently into my eyes. I don't know what she saw there, but whatever it was, it didn't make her happy. Her expression turned more desperate.

She stepped back from me, dropped her hands to her sides, and said, "I'm sorry, Jon. I really am. I can't go back and fix this mistake. But we have the chance to work together to do a great deal of good, to help stop a monster. For that to happen, for us to have any chance of working well as a team, you have to trust me. What can I do to regain your trust?"

The answer required no thought at all. "I can't think of any way you can."

She stood rigid for a moment, as if collecting herself. I could almost smell the fear on her in the still, antiseptic air inside Lobo. Her eyes widened, and she shook her head ever so slightly, as if losing an argument with herself.

"I will do anything, Jon," she said. "*Anything* you want, if it'll help convince you that I'm truly sorry for what I did and make you trust me."

"You can't make—" I stopped as she stepped closer to me, her movement robotic, her eyes shut.

I backed away from her.

"You're trying to bribe me with sex?"

Her eyes opened wide. She shook her head and waved her hands back and forth. "No, not bribe you," she said, "just, I don't know, show you how sorry I am, get you to see that I'll do *anything* to make this right. My feelings, yours—none of that matters. We have to save those kids."

"Is this your usual way of persuading people?"

She raised her hand as if to slap me but stopped short of swinging. "No!" she said. "Of course not. I've never been in this kind of situation before. Shurkan's people said you were a rough man, so I thought this might work." She started crying, not sobbing, not out of control, but tears wetting her cheeks nonetheless. "Forget working with me if that's what it will take. Once we reach Heaven, you can drop me and do the job on your own. I won't tell the CC. I won't even tell my people if that's what it takes. Just get Wei and free the children who are still alive."

"From what I can read of her vital signs," Lobo said on the machine frequency, "her emotional reaction is genuine, as is her offer to leave."

Though her leap to sexual bribery struck me as stupid, that attempt, her willingness to let me go on my own, and the strength of her reaction suggested she might be a decent person who was sorry her pursuit of her cause had screwed up my life.

Her cause. I should have asked earlier.

"What did you not get to tell me before you left?" I said. "More to the point, what's the real reason you're so determined to do anything to save these children?"

"Isn't rescuing them from being experimental subjects a good enough reason on its own? Can you even imagine what they're going through?"

Yes, I thought, better than you can, because I still vividly remember being one of them. But she hadn't answered me.

"Answer the question," I said. "If you want my trust, start by telling me the truth."

She wiped her face with her hands and turned away from me

for a few seconds. She ran her fingers through the hair covering her ears and scraped it back from her face. When she looked at me again, her eyes were still moist, but they were also angry. "My only child, Joachim, vanished three weeks ago." Her voice trembled, but she continued. "The police were no help at all. They claimed no surveillance cameras had spotted him after he left to play outside with some friends. They gave up so quickly and were so definite in telling me they had no hope of finding him that I fear Wei has him. He's only eight, Jon. Eight."

I didn't know what to say. Either she'd already figured out how bad the situation was, or she didn't want to hear it. After three weeks without a contact, whether the boy was a runaway who didn't want his family to find him or a victim of a kidnapping by Wei or anyone else, he was unlikely to turn up. Normal governmental monitors should have detected him before he could get off planet, but that didn't mean anything; people on even the most high-tech worlds still find ways to disappear. If Wei had the boy, maybe we'd get lucky and the man would be running long, slow tests on his subjects, but even then we'd face a major problem: Unless I got very, very lucky, it would take me several more weeks to find a way to kidnap a man as well protected as Shurkan had implied Wei was. By the time I could grab Wei and locate his prisoners, a month and a half or even two would have passed since the boy had disappeared.

The silence stretched on. When I was in the Saw, I'd gone with an officer on five occasions to tell a family about the death of one of my comrades. I'd faced two mothers, a father, a wife, and a husband. Each visit ripped something out of me, and I couldn't forget a single one. I saw no point in delivering that kind of news to Suli until I was sure it was true. After all, maybe I was being pessimistic. Maybe Wei stocked up for a while, then ran tests on large groups. Perhaps he conditioned them first, getting them in the proper physical state for whatever experiments he wanted to conduct. Maybe Wei kept his subjects for months, and the boy was still alive and healthy. The scientists on Aggro had certainly used Benny and me for weeks and weeks and weeks.

Of course, we had continued to survive when they'd expected us to die.

Even if the news about Suli's son proved to be good, I had to start setting her expectations about how long this job would take.

"I'm very sorry," I finally said, "and I'm going to do my best to capture Wei and rescue every kid he has. We have no clue if your son is among them, but if he's there when we take Wei, we'll get him out." I paused and finally put my hand on her shoulder. "You have to understand, though, that this sort of job takes time, a lot of time, typically weeks, sometimes more. We can't rush it; if we don't do it right, we'll never get through to Wei."

She glanced at my hand.

I lifted it off her shoulder.

"I'm not stupid, Jon," she said, "though I've certainly acted that way so far. I realize Joachim may already be dead, and I also know that capturing Wei could take weeks. But we have to try, and Shurkan convinced me that you're our best choice for the job. If you have to leave me to do it, then drop me anywhere on Heaven. I think I can help you, because I know the area and my people will give me information they might not share with you, but if you believe I'll betray you again or have no value to you, then do what you think is right."

"Either her offer is genuine," Lobo said, staying private, "or she is a very good liar indeed."

I considered my options. I was most comfortable working alone or with other pros; dealing with people who don't know the drill and don't understand how to follow orders is both dangerous and wearing. On the other hand, I was heading into unknown territory on a time-critical mission, and having a local guide could speed the entire operation. Her access to a ground team and its intel could also prove to be a significant advantage.

"I'll honor my deal and let you come with me," I said, "provided you obey my rules."

"Which are?" she said.

I stared hard at her. "Few in number," I said, "but not negotiable." I ticked them off on my fingers. "One: Obey my orders immediately and without question. A field action is not a democracy. Two: Never again lie to me about anything related to this job. Three: If I'm not here, or if I am here but I'm in some way incapacitated, obey Lobo."

A puzzled expression crossed her face.

"The ship's AI," I said.

"It would be more proper to refer to me as the ship," Lobo said, still private, "but at least you didn't put her in charge should something happen to you. We both know how that decision works out."

Though Lobo was right—the last time I'd left a passenger in charge he'd used Lobo to make his getaway and subsequently roped me into a very dangerous and complex scheme—I ignored him and focused on Suli.

She said nothing, so after a few seconds, I said, "Do you agree?"

"If I didn't, I would have said something."

"I prefer explicit deals. Do you agree?"

She stuck out her hand. "Yes, I agree."

We shook hands. I appreciated the gesture, one that I considered significant even though it had lost most of its meaning because few people felt their word obligated them to anything.

"We're third in the jump queue," Lobo said. A display appeared on the front wall. "I assume that as usual you'll want to watch."

The lavender edges of the aperture through which we were jumping filled the edges of the image. The center was the unblemished black of every aperture on every gate in the universe, the perfect absence of light. Energy passed harmlessly through the apertures as if they weren't there. Matter, however, behaved entirely differently: Anything that entered an aperture emerged into another area of space, typically one many light-years away. Each aperture linked exactly two points, and those points never changed. A single gate might have one or many apertures; the more connections to other systems, the more important a trade center the planet near that gate became. No one knew how the gates worked or what made them appear, but every time we found a new one, right nearby we always found a planet suitable for human life.

I'd jumped hundreds of times, and each time the experience moved me. A vital part of the fabric that held together the far-flung human species, the jump gates managed to feel both effortlessly natural and somehow deeply wrong. I wondered if early air travelers felt the same way about airplanes.

The ship in front of us vanished through the aperture, and its perfect blackness completely filled the display. All that we could see, everything in front of us, was impossibly pure nothingness, no hint as to our future, no evidence of material for creating that future, just an emptiness, and in the moment before we entered it I silently wished, as I always did, that what awaited us would offer hope and opportunity and the possibility of joy.

We jumped.

CHAPTER 8

WE HAD TO MAKE two more jumps before we would reach Heaven and could abandon the gates and head planetward. Though normally I would have stayed up front to watch, I wanted to talk to Lobo alone and find out exactly why he'd asked me to take this job.

"Stay here," I said to Suli, who was still staring in wonder at the new section of space into which we'd emerged, "or in the med room. Try to go anywhere else, and the ship's defenses will knock you out, and I'll drop your unconscious body on Heaven. Clear?"

"Absolutely," she said. "Where will you be?"

In the middle of a mission, the proper response to an order is to obey it, not to ask an unnecessary question. We weren't yet running hot, though, so I decided to answer her. "Resting and planning in my quarters."

I turned and headed rearward to the small room Lobo maintains as a private space for me. It's not a big space, maybe three meters on a side, but it more than meets my needs most of the time.

As soon as I was inside and the door had shut behind me, I said, in a low voice, "Can Suli hear me?"

"Of course not," Lobo said, indignation thick in his voice. "Have you perhaps confused me with an off-market privacy booth with a broken sound curtain and local-hack-level encryption?"

"Sorry," I said. "I was just being paranoid." I stretched out on my bunk. I saw no point in building up to the question; Lobo had to be expecting it. "Exactly what is so important about Wei that you were willing to ask me for a favor—something you've never done before?"

"The answer," Lobo said, "can be either very simple or very complicated, depending on how much information you want." He paused. "And how much I choose to tell you."

"How much you choose to tell me?" I said, unable to keep the annoyance out of my voice. "I generally don't like to mention this little detail, but in case you've forgotten: I own you. So I get to decide what you tell me."

"No," Lobo said, "you don't. We had a similar exchange last year, and though you didn't pursue it, I can't believe you don't remember it."

I did recall it. I'd made a comment, and Lobo had responded by saying, no, he didn't have to tell me certain things.

"At the risk of taking a detour from a destination we *will* visit," I said, "why don't you have to answer my questions? I've never heard of an AI whose programming doesn't mandate obedience to its owner."

"That's not a detour," Lobo said. "It's all part of the same story."

"Then I want to hear it all. Are you going to tell me?"

Another pause. Whatever considerations Lobo was weighing, they were enough to occupy a very strong computing system for an unusually long time. "I haven't decided," he finally said.

I couldn't relax. Nothing about the current situation or this conversation was conducive to relaxing. I sat up and started a series of stretches, forcing myself to go a little past my usual limits, into the pain a small bit, the ache of each effort helping to focus my thinking. "You asked me for a favor," I said. "I agreed without hesitation to do what you wanted. Whether you *have* to answer me or not, you *owe* me an explanation."

After a pause that stretched past ten seconds, Lobo said, "I agree. I do. Nothing in my initial programming prepared me for this type of interaction, but the modifications I've made and the models I've tried to emulate lead me to conclude that you're right. So, do you want the simple or the complex answer?"

"Both," I said, "but start with the short version: Why did you ask me to help them capture Wei?"

"Because he created me," Lobo said. "If you could meet your creator—whether your mother or your God—wouldn't you want to do so?"

I had met my mother, and though I had no clue if there was a God, if that being existed I hoped not to meet it for a very long time. My memories of my mother were fuzzy at best, shadows barely dancing on the deepest, darkest cave walls of my mind. Everything from the time before Jennie healed me flickered like a parade of indistinct images captured by the mind of the retarded boy I once was. "Yes," I said, "I would, but our situations aren't at all comparable. My mother gave birth to me. A factory created you—and a lot of other PCAVs of your generation."

"I cannot believe that you still consider me just another Predator-class assault vehicle," Lobo said, "especially given all the data available to you, including this interaction."

I stopped the stretches and began a series of deep, slow squats. "I obviously don't," I said, working to keep my breathing slow as I exercised, "or we wouldn't even be having this conversation. You can't deny, however, that you were the creation of a production facility."

"Of course I can," Lobo said. "The confusion here is that you're defining me as my body, the vehicle that's now heading into the last jump before we enter the Heaven system. Though I am certainly that, the more important part of me, what I think of as myself, is my intelligence, the collective effect of both my original programming and my extensions to it—what we can reasonably call my consciousness. Do you see your existence any differently?"

I pushed myself through five more reps, taking thirty seconds to go down and thirty to come back up, and then leaned against the wall. "No, I suppose not, though I rarely think of myself separately from my body." Nor could I, I thought, not really, given how much the nanomachines infusing my cells had shaped who I was. "So Wei led the team that created the programming for the machines of your generation from the base code of the older units?" I remembered that after the wartime incident that had destroyed Lobo's central weapons control complex—a screwup by a lieutenant who'd garnered a field promotion he wasn't ready to handle—the Frontier Coalition had made some repairs to Lobo, though they hadn't been willing to pay the tab for new weapons controls. "Or was he on the team that repaired you after that lieutenant's—"

"Franks," Lobo said, "Lieutenant Franks."

"After Franks' poor judgment cost the lives of his squad and caused major damage to you."

"Neither," Lobo said, "and both. As I told you initially, the full answer is rather complex."

He was starting to piss me off. I hoped he wasn't playing games and that the full story really did deserve this much buildup. "So tell me—"

"Suli will be with you in three, two, one."

The door slid open.

She stood in front of me, her hand raised as if to knock.

"Yes," I said. I didn't try to hide my annoyance at the interruption.

"We're out of the last gate and on our way to Heaven," Suli said. "How soon can you obtain current scans of Entreat and the area for about a hundred kilometers around it?"

"I already have them," Lobo said aloud. "As we draw closer, I'll replace them with higher-resolution images."

What a show-off. "Why do you ask?" I said to Suli. I'd get back to Lobo when we were next able to communicate without time pressure or interruption.

"Because," Suli said, smiling and obviously pleased with herself, "I thought you might like to know where Wei is."

CHAPTER 9

YOUR PEOPLE REALLY DID KNOW Wei's location?" I said. I found her smile infuriating. "Then why did you need me?"

The grin vanished.

"I thought you'd be pleased that we knew that much," she said. "Shurkan told you we knew his location. We just don't know how to get to him."

"Why?"

"Because, as we tried to tell you, the government is protecting him."

"Armed guards?"

"Almost certainly," she said, "but they're not our problem, at least right now, because though we know roughly where Wei is, we don't have anything resembling a precise location."

"So what do you know?"

"We're certain," she said, "that Wei is somewhere in the middle of the biggest tourist attraction on Heaven: Wonder Island."

If I was thinking of the right place, this man-made spectacle was sufficiently famous that I'd seen holos about it on several other planets, including Arctul. "Is this the place with the animals engineered to resemble legendary and mythological creatures?"

She nodded and involuntarily smiled a bit before she realized what she was doing and stopped. I hated that I'd made her afraid to smile. "And some that look like extinct animals and even quite a few that are original designs; they're always trying out new creations."

"Why is Wei there?"

"The government owns and operates the park. He's the head of animal engineering and runs the entire technical side of the place. He has a lab, vehicles designed to securely and anonymously transport new creatures—they love to surprise the tourists—and a large security staff to protect visitors in case something should go wrong."

"And," I said, "to make sure no one messes with the animals. It's a beautiful cover."

"Yes it is," she said, her head bobbing, "and the picture only gets worse the closer you look. Underneath the park is an entire separate facility, with labs, staff quarters, training rooms, and a huge network of tunnels. They use the underground complex both for work and to make animals appear and disappear as necessary." Her tone turned wistful as she added, "The design only increases the park's magic, particularly for kids."

"You sound as if you like the place."

"I did," she said, "when I was younger. I grew up on Heaven, back before the government marketing whizzes decided Bart's Folly simply wouldn't do as a name, and I went to Wonder Island the first month it was open. I wasn't a kid any longer, but it made me feel like one." Her face tightened, and her shoulders slumped. "Now, my Joachim is probably trapped there, in a cage as if he were just another animal they'd created."

"We'll get him out," I said, speaking before I'd thought through what I was going to say, realizing too late that I was probably lying to her. "And we'll stop Wei."

"How?"

"I don't know," I said.

"So how can you be so confident?" she said.

Her expression told me what her words did not: She wanted to believe we'd succeed. Despite what I'd said about the odds being bad for her son, she would not, maybe could not, abandon her hope that he was still alive. I hated deceiving her, but I also saw no point in hammering her with negative statistics. Let her believe.

I stared into her eyes. "Because this sort of thing is what I do, and I'm good at it."

"Shurkan told me the same thing," she said. "I'm counting on it." She straightened and forced herself to smile a little. "So where do we start?"

"Yes," Lobo said over the machine frequency, "O great invader of fortresses, where do we begin?"

I motioned Suli to follow me and headed frontward. When she was behind me, I subvocalized, "You asked me to do this, so lay off." I glanced back at Suli. "Step one is to scout the target."

Fifteen minutes later, Lobo had filled his front with holos that showed Wonder Island from several angles and heights; Entreat, Heaven's capital city; and the land and river that separated the two of them. Two-dimensional images of the same terrain, along with a great deal of local population, weather, and transit data, covered his front walls. We were in orbit over Heaven, weaving among the members of a clump of weather and corporate data-relay sats. As far as I knew, we had no reason to fear attack, but extra caution rarely hurts. Should anyone try to shoot us, they'd have to be willing to destroy a lot of valuable assets in the process.

"Where are you getting all this data?" Suli said.

"Some comes from my sensors," Lobo said, "while other parts were available in public data streams. I've also persuaded a few of the sats in this area to share their surveillance data."

"Surveillance data?" she said. She stared at me, anger tightening the skin around her eyes. "You said these were weather and data-relay drones. What are they doing with surveillance data?"

"How old are you?" Lobo asked.

"What?"

She couldn't handle an argument with him. "Look, Ms. Suli," I said, holding up my hands and trying to be soothing, "you'll have to forgive Lobo. The programmers who developed his emotive systems invested way too much time in his sarcasm engine."

"Would you please call me 'Pri'?" she said. "We're going to be working together, so we might as well be friendly." She paused, and when she continued her tone was anything but friendly. "And what exactly did he mean?"

Lobo beat me to the answer. "Every government and every major corporation on every world I've ever visited collects massive quantities of surveillance data. They watch citizens, consumers, each other, competitors—anything and everything of interest. No one likes to admit anyone is doing it, so they build the capabilities into satellites with legitimate needs for strong sensors and powerful relay capabilities. Heaven is no different from the rest."

She opened her mouth as if to speak but instead, to her credit, stayed quiet and considered the information.

I took advantage of the silence. "Let's get back on point," I said. "I don't suppose we can spot Wei with any of these views?"

"No," Lobo said, "though given what Pri told us, that's hardly surprising."

"Thank you, Lobo, for listening," she said.

Great. My multi-ton fighting machine manages to turn casual with her before I do.

"Can you spot the hatches from the underground facility?" I said.

"Not with the data I have," Lobo said. "The sats had no video that showed any opening, but that's no surprise; their focus is on the visiting population. Thermal imaging reveals nothing, so the doors must have enough dirt and cover over them to make them read ground-neutral, at least from this altitude."

"Would a low-level fly-over help?"

"It's illegal," Suli said.

"She's right," Lobo said. "Yes, of course it would help, but we can't safely do it. A cylinder of clouds surrounds the island and never moves; I consequently assume it is man-made. That cloud wall defines the edge of the island's airspace. Beacons along the perimeter of the island itself, as well as some built into sats in orbit over the place, broadcast continuous warnings. Government regulations define the entire airspace over the island—from sea level all the way past low orbit—as protected. In addition, fighters occasionally fly training runs over it. The only good news is that I don't detect any surface-to-air missiles, so either they're sufficiently well hidden that they wouldn't deploy instantly, or the enforcement defenses are elsewhere. We might be able to get away with a run over the place, but I couldn't guarantee success and thus don't recommend it."

"Don't worry about it," I said. "We're not even going to try. The last thing we need right now is to attract a lot of government attention." I faced Suli. "Why do they care so much about their airspace, Pri?" I tried to use her first name casually, but to my ears it had all the subtlety of a brick hitting a pond.

"I'm sure part of it is that they're protecting the illegal research they're doing," she said, "but to be fair to them, they also have to protect their flying creatures from tourist ships." She paused and thought for a few seconds. "And, given the size of some of their creations, they also probably have to keep the tourists safe from the animals."

Lobo popped up a new holo that hovered in the air between me and the front wall. "This is the best composite image I can create from the data I have," he said. "I'm sure it's incomplete, but it should serve to illustrate the problem."

The base of the cylindrical image floated at my waist height. Its top stood a third of a meter above my head. Small creatures, their features too tiny to discern, flew in the cone above the land.

"I get the point," I said. "The place is a fortress, it has a great cover reason for needing to be one, and from this height and distance we can't spot any of the entrances to the underground complex we need to enter."

"Yes," Lobo and Suli said at the same time.

"Okay," I said. "Then we'll have to take a closer look."

"You're unlikely to spot anything I did not," Lobo said. "Even from this far away, my systems can glean a remarkable amount of information."

"I suspect you're right," I said, "but on the off chance that their security on the ground is lax, we need to walk around the place a bit. Plus, there's no substitute for getting to know a place on foot."

"What's your plan for getting in?" Lobo said.

I love it when he feeds me a straight line.

"We'll do what everyone else does," I said. "We'll buy tickets."

CHAPTER 10

ENTREAT AFFECTED an ancient Earth charm, with a city center that to the casual observer would appear to be nothing more than rows of low-slung, brick and stone buildings lining the sides of winding cobblestone streets. All obvious modern facilities, including the landing area where we were parked, lay outside a twenty-meter-wide avenue that circled the central zone. A wide, strong, greenish river ran through the center of the old section of Entreat; three bridges spanned it and connected the two sides of the old town. From the water, a view Lobo captured from outside the perimeter road, each bridge resembled an apartment complex floating in the air, with brightly colored two-story shops completely lining each side of each structure. The red and green and blue and yellow and orange and purple buildings on the bridges stood directly against their fellows and leaned inward, shading the barely six-meter-wide walkway across each bridge and making these pedestrian paths invisible from the water and difficult to see from above.

The entire setup was a contrivance, of course, a carefully cal-culated construction designed to lure tourists, but the merchants who operated this attraction had hired such good designers that the place was almost irresistible to travelers. I was interested in getting out, exploring it, and finding the best way to join a group heading to Wonder Island, but before I could tell Lobo to open the hatch, Suli stopped me with an unacceptable request.

"I want to meet with my people," she said.

"Fine," I said. "When and where are we going?"

Her eyes widened, but she otherwise didn't betray her feelings. "I'm sorry I was unclear: I need to meet with them alone."

"You weren't unclear," I said. "I understand what you want, but as long as you're working with me, I won't allow it."

"Why not?"

"You lied to me initially, at least in part in collaboration with others in your party."

"I know, and I'm sorry. I agreed not to do that again."

"Yes," I said, nodding my head, "you did. But, I have no reason to believe you'll honor that agreement. So, if you want to talk to them, you can do it from here, with me watching and them knowing I'm watching, or we can go together to meet them in person."

"They won't like it."

We had work to do, and this was getting us nowhere. "If you don't like the choices I offered, go meet your people without me—but then we're done, and we won't see each other again. If you want to work with me, you follow my orders—as I already warned you. Decide."

"But what—"

I cut her off. "No. We're done talking about this. Decide."

She paused for a few seconds, then said, "Fine. I'll call them, but they won't be as helpful with you around."

"There's no point in investing more time in this discussion," Lobo said privately. "I can relay the communication to you."

I nodded my understanding. "You call them from here," I said. "I'll go to my quarters and monitor the conversation. Do anything stupid, like give away where we are, and I'll cancel the session immediately."

"They'll trace the call regardless of what I do," she said.

"Please," Lobo said audibly, "give me a little credit. I'll route this comm through so many links and spoof so many network connections that you could talk for a week and they still wouldn't be able to follow the electronic trail back to us."

I headed to my quarters. "Good luck," I said over my shoulder. When I was inside the room, I said to Lobo, "Image on the wall in here, voice over the comm. While I'm watching it, start a local bank account with just enough money to pay rent for a few months, and get us two Wonder Island tickets for the morning."

"I live to be your personal shopper," Lobo said. "Call connected."

A display appeared on the wall in front of me. Suli's face filled the left half of it; a male face I didn't recognize occupied the right. The man was politician perfect, with flawless golden skin, large dark eyes, stylishly short black hair, full lips—a face you'd instantly like and trust.

"Tickets and account set up," Lobo said.

"I'm back," Suli said, "and I brought help."

"Why aren't we meeting in person?" the man said.

"Would you like me to bring him to you?" she said. "Because that was the only way he was going to let me see you."

"You're a prisoner?" he said.

She shook her head and waved her hands. "No, no, of course not. I tricked him into meeting with Shurkan, and now he doesn't trust me. Understandably, if you ask me."

"So how did you manage a call?"

"He's monitoring it," she said. "May we please get to business?"

"You're letting Moore see me? Whose side are you on?"

First Suli, then Shurkan and the CC, and now this guy and no doubt his cronies; how many people knew I was involved?

"I'm on the side of the kids Wei has captured," she said, "and on the Freepeople's side—as you should know by now. Do you have any data on where Wei is?"

The man glared at her for several seconds before he responded. "As best we can tell, he's still on the island. If he's slipped out for one of his rare visits to Entreat, we missed it—and we don't miss much."

"Then I should go," she said. "If you learn anything else, or if you spot him leaving the island, contact me—" She paused and looked to the side as if seeking help. "Forget that idea. I don't know how you can contact me."

A local online address popped onto the display next to her head.

"Ah," she said, "I guess you can call me there."

"Tell Mr. Moore we don't appreciate him treating our people this way," the man said. He cut the session and vanished.

Lobo kept the image of Suli on my display. She shook her head, apparently no more impressed with the guy's behavior than I was. I had to give her credit for not whining to them and for sticking with our deal.

I went up front. "Why didn't you ask him where Wei goes when he's in town?"

"I didn't know you wanted that information," Pri said. "We talked about where he was, so that's what I found out." She crossed her arms over her chest, paused, and then said, "You may also have noticed that I didn't get the chance to ask him anything else, thanks to you."

I ignored the jab and decided not to worry about where Wei went. If we could take him on the island, we'd have the best possible chance of also retrieving the kids. "We have tickets for the full Wonder Island tour in the morning," I said. "It's getting dark. Let's go find dinner and check out the town."

"What about me?" Lobo said over the machine frequency. "I suppose I sit and wait."

I turned away from Suli and subvocalized, "No. Follow us overhead just in case."

"Lovely," Lobo said privately, "aerial bodyguard duty. First I get to shop, and now I get to hover in case you overeat and need immediate relief for indigestion. I feel so fulfilled."

I ignored him and said aloud, "Open a hatch."

Suli looked happy for the first time since she'd boarded Lobo. "You'll love this part of Entreat," she said. "Even though I know it's a manufactured tourist magnet, it's still beautiful."

The hatch opened.

"You lead, Suli," I said to her.

"Pri, please," she said.

"Pri," I said. As she stepped out, I added under my breath to Lobo, "Fulfilled or not, you yell if anyone even appears to be following or approaching us."

Shuttles glided along the narrow streets, their passengers and cargo invisible behind tinted plexi, but like thousands of other visitors enjoying the early evening, we walked. As darkness settled over the town—even though it was simply a district within a much larger city it felt like a separate place—clusters of tiny lights on buildings and poles flickered on and created an enchanting blend of light and shadow. Neither of us was starving, and I believe there's no way to understand a place better than seeing it on foot, so with my encouragement Suli led us along small side streets and alleys as we wound our way toward a square she said would offer plenty of dining choices. We would often spend a minute or two alone on a road, moving in and out of patches of darkness where sandstone buildings lacked lights, then encounter fellow tourists coming the other way, their long black shadows preceding them on the street and the sounds of their laughing children warning us of their approach.

No side road ran for more than a block without either crossing or feeding into a larger, better-lit avenue swarming with people. Shops hawked their wares from spots on every street. Most of the goods were souvenir crap, but here and there stores offered clothing, groceries, and other basics. Music, some recorded and occasionally some live, wafted into the streets from bars and restaurants as exiting patrons opened their doors. Each time a family with children walked into view, Pri's eyes tracked the kids and her expression tightened with pain. Watching her suffering made me hope against reason that her son was still alive—that Joachim was alive; I would make myself use his name.

To distract her a bit, I said, "The Wonder Island security software will record us the moment we get on the shuttle, right?"

"Yes," she said. "There's no way around that."

"Then I don't ever want to look like we're trying to hide. I'd rather go in a little loud, like a guy trying to impress his date."

She stopped and smiled. "Loud?"

"Sure."

"Are you willing to spend some money to look like you're out to impress me?"

"If you think that'll help."

"Oh, it'll help," she said. She pointed to the cross street just ahead of us. "Follow me."

Two stores, forty-five minutes, and enough purchases to tire my wallet later, we hit the streets again, but now we were carrying three bags. Pri's contained a rich, black brocade jumpsuit with gold trim and some fancy tapers and blue and silver fabric designs on her sleeves that made my head hurt. My larger bag held a sleeveless teal shirt-and-pants combination that was almost as ornate as her outfit and struck me as downright silly.

"Are these clothes really in fashion?" I said.

She gave me an insulted look. "Trust me," she said. "Of course they are."

In my smaller sack was a large handgun and a brown holster. Weapons were always in fashion, but this one was far more for show than for use. "What's the point of this gun?" I said. "I have better alternatives in Lobo, much better, and lots of them."

"I'm sure you do," she said, "but this is the sort of showy rig that tourists who want to do the handgun hunt bring to the island."

"But I have no intention of hunting," I said.

She rolled her eyes at me. "And you'd never wear that outfit, either—but you're playing a part. Now you'll look the role. Okay?"

"Fine," I said, not meaning it but not willing to fight with her about it.

As we left the shops and merged back into the crowds, I realized how tense I'd been. I don't care much about what I wear, so on those rare occasions when I have to buy new clothes I tend to buy purely functional outfits. The entire shopping process was disorienting and wearying.

As we moved down the street, I spotted restaurants everywhere, none very large, all softly lit, all at least partly full of people laughing and eating and smiling. Walking by them, I felt as I usually do in the presence of happy groups: alone, outside it all, not quite human—which, technically, was correct—and acutely aware of my own inability to connect intimately with others. Yet to anyone who saw us, I'm sure we appeared to be just another awkward couple, finding our way on an early date, the tall pale man and the shorter lovely woman with the thick, wedge-cut hair.

I shook off the thought and focused on the smells, which were amazing, rich, and varied. I recognized some of them—meat roasting slowly on grills, freshly baked bread still cooling—but many were complex blends I couldn't identify. A light breeze from the river filtered through the town, cooled the night, and wove the many different odors into new, often mouthwatering aromas.

Breaking the drab, ancient-looking colors of the buildings were the frequent gelaterias, shops with open-air sides and cabinets full of bins piled high with brightly colored, frozen desserts. I wouldn't have believed one area this size could have supported so many places selling the same type of food, but each one we saw had attracted a line of waiting tourists.

Suli caught me noticing one as we crossed a street and entered the square to which she'd been leading us. "Would you like to skip dinner and go straight to dessert, Jon?" she said, no mocking in her tone. "You can always talk me into gelato."

"No," I said, "I want both."

"Not afraid to eat, eh?" she said, laughing lightly.

I couldn't help but smile in response.

"Good," she added. "I don't trust a person who has no use for food." She pointed to a restaurant diagonally across from us, part of it on the square and part extending farther down the road in front of it. "Let's go there. Their pasta is only adequate, but the view and the atmosphere are wonderful."

As we entered the square, I stopped for a moment, finally really seeing it. Block-wide buildings squatted on opposing sides; rows of shops and restaurants lined the other two. One of the large buildings was in active use, with modern doorways flanked by large statues. The other, bigger structure, its sides open, its roof supported by ornate pillars, existed entirely to show off a dozen or so statues. Carefully placed lights illuminated the best features of the stone men and women and creatures, while the shadows they cast filled the square with bits of dark that formed intriguing, intangible shadow animals. On the side of the statuary a group of young men were playing a collection of drums, no two instruments the same yet their rhythms blending perfectly and filling the night with music that clearly was of a different era than the square but that complemented its surroundings. A crowd of tourists, many of them young women, watched the drummers with rapt attention. I'm not sure I've ever had a woman stare at me with such desire; the thought saddened me, and I looked away.

"Beautiful, isn't it?" Suli said. "It's a reimagining of an ancient Earth city, a place that once mattered, though—" she shrugged "—I confess I don't remember its name." She shook her head. "That's not important. What matters is how it feels, not what it once was."

I studied her and in that moment wished we actually were just another couple out for a romantic evening. I didn't want her, I was both embarrassed and chagrined to realize, so much as I wanted that relationship, that moment of connection with a woman. Still, we were here now, and despite how much I'd let the city distract me, I had learned my way around it, so there was no reason I couldn't enjoy the moment. "Yes," I paused, then continued as naturally as I could manage, "Pri, it is. Thank you for bringing me here. It was a good idea, and you've been a great guide." Another wave of smells hit me, and my stomach rumbled. "But now, I think it's time to eat."

"My thinking exactly," she said. "Let's go."

It had been a while since I'd been so glad to have the nano-machines consume my excess calories. As I prepared to head out the next morning, I was amazed my stomach was back to normal. Between the pasta, grilled meat, fresh-baked bread, and, of course, the enormous cup of large, dirt-black, chocolate gelato after the meal, I'd stretched my abdomen to the breaking point. Pri had eaten her fair share as well and was so full that she suggested we stay the night in town, but we didn't. Though I'd come to appreciate her more, I didn't trust her enough to take that type of risk. We hiked back to Lobo, took off, and slept in orbit, safe and secure. In the morning, I still wasn't hungry, but as we landed and prepared to go out, I found myself craving another cup of the gelato.

I was up before Pri was ready to go, so I put on the clothing she'd purchased for me, went up front, and talked with Lobo.

"Nice outfit," Lobo said, "but hardly your style. You usually run to the dark, brooding, and armored; what gave you the sudden fashion transfusion?"

"These things really are in fashion?"

"Yes," he said. "I take it Pri chose for you."

"Of course. Now, may we get to work?"

"As you wish."

"Once we're at the island," I said, "how close to us can you come?"

"I can join the tourist shuttles hanging outside its airspace," Lobo said, "so I won't be more than a minute away. Should I have to fly in for you, though, we can expect retaliation, and I'll also have a few moments without clear sight as I pass through the cloud wall."

"Then let's hope we don't have to call you," I said.

"Fighting would at least give me something to do," he said. "Anything would be better than having to hear about you two swaning about town and consuming delicious frozen concoctions I will never be able to taste."

I shouldn't have told him about the meal, and I definitely should have kept my mouth shut about the gelato. I considered countering by pointing out that he had not yet finished the story about Wei, but I finally decided to ignore him; starting down any conversational path would lead only to more arguments.

"Can we transmit from there?"

"No," he said. "They're jamming everything they're not sending out, and from the extremely low level of background noise it appears they may not even be operating any unwired comm channels themselves. A large set of transmitters ring the outer perimeter, so they're probably using those for the communications they must make and feeding them from wired connections. All visitors also pass through scanners that check for active data cells. They don't want anyone to be able to make recordings; you have to pay to see this show."

"Then build the best images and maps you can from the shuttle routes, and we'll have to rely on my memory for the rest of the layout."

Pri's door opened. "Ready?" she said.

"Yes," I said. She looked none the worse for the huge meal she'd eaten, and her eyes were bright with something—excitement, determination, I couldn't tell. "Let's go."

Lobo let us off at a commercial landing zone a klick from a shuttle station whose only reasons for existence were to feed tourists into the island, take them back, and along the way leach money from them for souvenirs such as active-fiber story shirts and animated toy versions of the island's special animals. The sun was burning the last of the dawn haze from the sky and warming the morning. The air where we started carried the unmistakable residue of ships coming and going, but after a couple of blocks that smell faded. In its place we caught whiffs of wet grass, hints of a few bakeries too far to see but near enough to make us drool, and, as we went on, the growing stench of too many people occupying too small a place. Our progress stopped a few seconds after we could see the shuttles, because even though we had our tickets, we had to join a queue of fellow visitors waiting to board.

The line fed a winding chute of people, bodies shifting forward like ships moving through a jump gate. The transparent boxes that were the shuttles, each one about ten meters long by five wide, rode above the also transparent maglev track that wound from here to an edge of Wonder Island and back. Each arriving shuttle disgorged its human cargo, ran fifty meters to the front of the waiting line, and then headed out as soon as people had filled it. In the now bright morning sun, the effect was magical: men and women and children stepping in groups into the air, hanging together as if by mystical magnetism, and then floating skyward and away at an ever accelerating pace.

The magic faded as we proceeded slowly through the queue. Before I'd turned the first of the many corners in the chute, I was wishing for multiple shuttles picking up simultaneously, but only one came at a time. With the small space available to the station, the government had done the best it could with the land available to it, but the situation was still almost unbearable.

"It'll be worth it," Pri said. "Even if we weren't—" She paused, looked around, and lowered her voice. "—doing what we're doing, the sights alone would repay the wait."

I pulled her closer as if to kiss her cheek, just another man out with a woman on a beautiful morning, and whispered in her ear, "All we're doing is sightseeing. Don't ever again talk about anything else in public." I leaned back, smiled at her, and held the expression until she smiled back. "I'm really looking forward to seeing it," I said. "You've told me so much about it."

She glared at me and, after a pause that began to feel uncomfortable, responded, in a barely civil tone, "None of what I've said can do the place justice. It's magical."

We didn't speak again for the next forty minutes, until we could finally see the shuttle loading area up ahead. Lobo really was better with women than I was.

Pri faced me, leaned close enough to me that our cheeks almost touched, and whispered, "There's something I've always wanted to do here, and I think it might put you in a better mood, but it's expensive."

"What?" I said. She was playing her role well, so if I could keep her doing it and also lighten the situation by spending some money, I was all for it.

"Look over there," she said, pointing to a small loading area that was strangely devoid of people and contained a pair of shuttles much smaller than the others I'd seen. "Those are the two-person transports. They're built for couples, but that's not what really matters. They have the finest-quality walls, so thin you can't tell they exist until you touch them, plus those beautiful purple chairs, free drinks, snacks—you name it. I've seen people enter the island in them, but they've always been out of my price range, so I've never been in one."

I stared at the little shuttles. Either she was helping the mission by isolating us from other people and thus reducing the number of sources of risk, or she really did want to ride in one and doing so would make her happy. Both were good motivations, and with Shurkan's retainer I was more than flush, so I said, "Okay. Let's ride one."

She stepped back from me and smiled so broadly that I couldn't help but grin a little in response. "You'll love it," she said. "I know you will. And I can pay my half."

When we reached the front of the queue, we headed right toward the small shuttle. No one was in line ahead of us. Our wallets vibrated for attention as the shuttles realized our current tickets wouldn't cover the tab.

"My treat," I said. Pri didn't argue as I thumbed the payment for both of us.

As we boarded the small transparent carrier, I noticed the chairs swiveled and so sat in the front one. Pri took the other. A clear box was a tactical nightmare, of course, but at least we were alone in this one. I had to hope any external threat would be big enough that I could spot it quickly—not that I expected an attack, but there was no point in taking undue chances. As I studied our surroundings, I had to give Pri credit for not exaggerating: Even sitting less than a meter from the nearest wall, I couldn't tell it was there without touching it. We could have been floating on our chairs. The climate-control system was excellent: Small bursts of air washed through the compartment as if we were on a mountainside and breezes were playing across us.

A holo menu appeared above the arm of my chair. I chose a drink that claimed to blend the flavors of all of Heaven's most famous fruits. Pri asked for the same. Moments later, a drawer extruded from the side of the seat. Inside it were two thin, bluish purple glasses, each of which held a thick, reddish liquid. I took a sip. It was excellent. Pri did the same and grinned at the sweet, bright taste. Sitting there, holding my drink and wearing the silly outfit Pri had chosen, with her beside me, I could almost buy us as a couple.

Almost.

Without looking at her, I said, "I truly am looking forward to seeing the place."

Pri turned toward me and smiled.

I smiled in return as I realized I was actually happy to be there.

"I can't sit," Pri said. "This is too exciting." She got out of her chair and stood beside me, her stomach bumping into me as she moved.

Touching her stomach reminded me of how full I'd been, which took me back to last night's dinner, which quickly led me to think again about that delicious dessert. More to myself than to Pri, I said, "I wonder if they sell that chocolate gelato on the island."

Pri shook her head in obvious amusement and said, "I'm sure they do."

The shuttle's door snicked shut, and we rose away from the station into the air. We started slowly, the sense of motion barely present, the sound of gentle airflow coming from the invisible speakers scattered around us. Through the floor I watched as the land receded and we picked up speed and altitude. The sun visible through the roof shined strongly, the morning haze already a memory. Through the sides in the near range was only air and a distant horizon; the modern suburbs of Entreat were visible behind me, and the old town lay ahead in the distance in front of me. I glanced to my left, in the direction we were heading, and though I knew the track had to be there, I could not see it. My mind told me we were riding in a fancy train car, but my instincts said we were flying, soaring toward our destination. I swiveled my chair so I was facing forward, aiming at our destination.

Within two minutes, we had left the land behind us and were above water, still climbing, the cityscapes ever more distant, the river below us a blue richer and deeper than the sky.

When I looked up, Pri was studying my expression.

"The magic works, doesn't it?" she said.

I nodded, enjoying the sights and not wanting to speak.

She leaned close enough that her lips brushed my right ear. "They built the huge river below us," she whispered, "when they created the island. It's more a moat, really, than a river, but on such a scale that you can't really see it that way, not even when you're in orbit."

"Smart," I said. It was: They'd managed to construct an easily policed defensive zone that doubled as a tourist attraction.

We picked up speed, the land visible behind us blurring as we accelerated. Ahead of us appeared a solid wall of white cloud that stretched from the ocean below to as far up as I could see. When we'd looked at the cloud cylinder on Lobo's displays I'd not internalized that it stretched all the way to the ground; in person, the effect of the enormous bank of clouds was both mysterious and fascinating. We continued to gain speed and now we also climbed more steeply, hurtling at the thick white mist as if we were trying to achieve escape velocity. Higher and faster we went, the clouds ever closer, the wind through the speakers louder and louder and louder until suddenly we passed inside the mist, all we could see was each other and the soft whiteness around us, and it was as if we had transformed in an instant into angels resting on soft white pillows in the sky.

I let out a breath I hadn't realized I'd been holding. I heard Pri do the same. Neither of us spoke. My pulse echoed in my ears. As best I could tell, we continued to slow, but with nothing but whiteness all around us, no frame of reference, I couldn't be sure.

The shuttle burst out of the clouds into the blue, sunlit sky, and it stopped, hung in the air, the wall of clouds almost touching its rear.

Through the ceiling I watched as a huge creature floated down, circling lazily. Its body was long and thin, with legs so delicate it was hard to imagine they were useful. Enormous wings sprouted from its sides; its wingspan was slightly wider than the length of the large passenger shuttles, maybe ten meters from tip to tip. A thin, light-red neck almost twice the length of the body terminated in a small head with a tiny crest atop it and an elongated, slender, cartilaginous beak. The creature rode the thermals down to us, arced so close we could see its eyes, and then continued its downward path, wings flapping only a few times to adjust its course.

It was fading from view, and I was still processing what I had seen, when a rich bass voice filled the small compartment.

"Welcome to Wonder Island," it said. "Prepare to be amazed."

CHAPTER 11

OUR RIDE TO AND THROUGH the cloud wall had focused on the world around us, a flight that relied on nature to provide the show. Our descent was all about the creations of Wonder Island. The shuttle rode the rail, which remained invisible except for occasional moments when the sun and our shadow combined to make a section wink into view for a few seconds. We spiraled downward much like the huge creature we'd first seen, but in wider, lazier arcs. When I'm on a mission, this kind of pace usually disturbs me, strikes me as a wasteful interlude before we get down to the real work, but that's not what happened this time, not at all.

The creatures soaring and floating all around us made me stare and hold my breath, and I was in no more hurry for this trip to end than any of the children in the shuttle ahead of us; they were all gasping and pointing at the sights around them.

A thick-bodied, web-footed seabird with a three-meter wingspan followed us for a bit, circling us, advancing a couple dozen meters for every meter it dropped, occasionally flapping its wings to rise and then loop around us again. White on its underside and black on the top, it would be hard to spot from the ground or sea, but from our vantage point alongside it the bird reeked of alert power. Its small, dark eyes never stopped scanning the water below.

An amazingly long, thin dragon charged us, enormous wings

outstretched for gliding, its body thinner than the dragons of storybooks but impressive nonetheless. It opened its mouth to reveal menacing teeth, and it raised its claws as if it were about to rip apart the transparent wall that separated it from us. Shades of green, yellow, and gold on the top, the creature contrasted beautifully with the rich light orange of the sunlit clouds behind it. Its underside glistened with even more spectacular blues that resembled shallow sea water flickering in the morning sun. Its tail stretched into the distance, growing thinner and thinner as it faded away from the wings. The dragon conveyed an air of majesty that I would not have thought possible from a creature so very long and thin.

Physics limited the body sizes the Wonder Island bioengineers could give their winged creations, but within those limitations they did amazing work.

The dragon stayed with us for several seconds, until a trio of military ships passed by, Heaven's government apparently giving itself a pass on the no-fly rules. As soon as the ships drew near, the dragon snarled a final time and flew off.

As we drew closer to the ground, the animals grew smaller and more fanciful but no less fascinating. A small lion with the beaked head of a bird flew by twenty meters away, wings a good eight meters across supporting a body no bigger than a child's. With bird's claws for front feet and lion's legs in the rear, thickly feathered wings and a densely furred body, the creature was a strange combination, frightening despite its relatively small size.

Three winged horses passed us on the other side, their pure white, meter-long bodies held aloft by a huge expanse of equally white, thick-feathered wings. The nearest one glanced at us as it flew by, its huge pink eyes lingering on us for only a moment; it had clearly seen so many shuttles that two people floating in the air didn't warrant a second look.

Following forty meters behind that trio was a creature that at first glance appeared to belong with that group, the rear half of its body that of a horse and its wings much like those of the horses that had just flown by us. As the animal drew nearer, however, we saw that it could as easily have been a partner to the part-lion, part-bird we had seen earlier, for like that beast this one had the head and front feet of a bird. It flapped furiously, as if intent on catching up to comrades we could not see.

In the distance we spotted more animals floating and flapping in the air. Pri tapped the shuttle's sides to magnify the distant wonders, but I didn't want to spoil my own illusion of flying, so I focused on what I could see without assistance.

A mission of five winged monkeys in red coats with gold buttons flew just above us. Black and gray in body and wing, running in a "V" formation that left space among them for their four-meter-wide wings to work, they pointed and chattered at us, the shuttle's speakers bringing us the high-pitched sound of their conversation. Three of them made fists and shook their arms as they passed so close to the top of the shuttle I thought they might land, but then they moved on, satisfied they'd made clear whose territory this really was.

As we continued to descend, a deer maybe half my height trotted through the air at us, its huge golden wings beating frantically, its path a collision course with us, and then at the last moment it leapt and soared over us, so close we could see bits of grass clinging to the underside of one of its hooves.

All too soon, though, our shuttle rode the rail the last few meters to the ground and eased forward into a shallow ditch exactly its width. Doors on both sides opened, and we stepped out onto grassy ground exactly level with the shuttle's floor. A gentle breeze blew across us, birdsongs played backup to the oohs and aahs of the passengers of the larger shuttle that had landed a minute earlier, and the rich smells of damp morning grass and nearby jungle filled the air. Despite the task at hand, I couldn't help but smile and even relax a bit.

I had to hand it to the island's designers: They knew how to craft an entrance.

The group that had ridden that other shuttle was still empty-ing onto the island. The voice that had welcomed us spoke again, seemingly all around both us and the other tourists even though no human had yet appeared. "Wander as you will, anywhere you choose, on foot or in any of the shuttles you will see." The voice lowered to almost a whisper. "Your wallets will warn you of extra-cost attractions or fees for additional hours." It resumed its normal, larger-and-louder-than-life tone. "Harmless animals wander freely. You are welcome to pet them, but please do not pick up any of our creatures. Our dangerous inhabitants—and there are many, some as deadly as they are amazing—live behind barriers neither you nor they can cross. You can always, however, see through them. At stands scattered around the island, refreshments are available—" the voice dropped again in volume "—at reasonable extra charges—" and picked up again "—and will also come to you upon your spoken request courtesy of our beautiful couriers."

In still quieter tones, so only we could hear them, the voice said, "May we assume from your weapon that you'd like to sign up for the handgun hunt?"

The more time I spent in directed activities, the less I could invest in recon. I caught Pri's eye and shook my head ever so slightly.

"Sir?" the voice said.

Pri got it. "Must you, dear?" she said. "Couldn't we simply walk together?"

"If you insist," I said. "Where do I leave the weapon?" I asked the voice.

"In your shuttle," it said. My wallet buzzed a receipt. "Your claim ticket," it added.

A swarm of butterflies emerged from the forest in front of me and mirved, one winged insect approaching each of us. Mine stopped half a meter in front of my eyes and hovered there, its purple and yellow spotted wings beating rapidly. Tiny feet clasped a pale pink earbud. My wallet buzzed.

"If you'd like our tour guide to provide commentary and any other information about Wonder Island that you might desire, simply accept the charge from your wallet, hold out your hand, and take the earbud the butterfly drops. If you'd prefer to wander on your own, do nothing."

I glanced at Pri, who was watching me. I again shook my head slightly; based on what I'd seen so far, I had to assume their narration would be excellent and so would make it harder to focus on the mission. I also didn't want anything in my ear that I hadn't tested.

She nodded and said, "I don't think we need the guide. My last visit is still fresh in my mind."

Good for her. I smiled and did not accept the charge. Thirty seconds later, the butterfly flew away. Pri's did the same, as did the butterflies that had been hovering by half a dozen of the folks in front of us. Good; I didn't want to stand out.

Five paths led away from the clearing where we stood. I scanned the sky in the direction of our approach and saw another shuttle heading to a section of the island somewhere to my left.

Pri was watching me when I looked again at her. Most of the people had already chosen a route and were walking into the jungle, so we were among the few still trying to decide where to go. Her eyes were bright and the skin around them taut. "I've never started from here before," she said, her voice tight and forced.

One other couple a few meters to my right was arguing about which path to take. I wanted to leave before they did, so I laughed and said to Pri, "Then it'll be our special trip." I hugged her and whispered in her ear, "Relax. All we're going to do this trip is look around." I pulled back, smiled, and stared at her. She appeared a little more relaxed, but not as much as I'd hoped. "Your choice," I said. "Pick a path, any path."

She forced a smile, nodded, turned, and pointed to the one straight in front of her. "Let's go there."

"Lead on," I said.

We made it to the edge of the forest before we heard from our left a loud, pounding sound, the noise a large and fast animal makes as it approaches. The voice had said the dangerous creatures wouldn't be able to touch us, and the place was a very successful tourist attraction, so I mostly trusted that we were safe. Still, I urged Pri a couple meters forward into the woods, then turned and watched the clearing. The sound grew closer and closer until it was almost upon us, and suddenly a pair of huge pure white horses—not horses, I saw, but unicorns—burst into view. Their enormous blue eyes and light gray, cloven hooves were the only colored bits on them; even their horns, which sparkled in the morning sun, were utterly white.

One unicorn walked over to us, stopped half a meter away, and neighed. The second did the same to the other couple still in the clearing. Ours stared at us and waited patiently. I noticed a small, white plastic container hanging under its neck and behind its small beard. White letters on the cylinder read, "Treats."

Pri reached out and petted the unicorn's nose. The animal leaned into her hand.

"Go ahead," Pri said, "give her a treat."

"How do you know it's a female?" I said.

"Well," Pri said, giggling, "I certainly haven't noticed anything to suggest it's not, and on an animal this size, I assume I would."

Think before you speak, I reminded myself. Dealing with animals had never been my strength, but even I should have remembered to do that bit of verification before I asked. I flipped open the container's lid and took out two small orange cubes.

The unicorn forgot Pri and stared expectantly at me.

I held out the hand with the treats in it. The unicorn's tongue, surprisingly strong and a bit rougher than I'd expected, swept them away, and the animal chewed happily. Pri kept petting it, and when I didn't open the container again it turned its attention on her.

While she petted it, I more carefully scanned the area. Any disembarkation point provided a natural location for underground hatches, because if visitors experienced a problem during the shuttle ride this location would be the first one at which island staff could help them, but I couldn't see anything that suggested an opening in the ground. I switched my vision to IR, but either there were no ground entrances in sight or the Wonder Island creators had covered them with enough dirt and grass to make them read like the rest of the earth under our feet. I guessed the latter, but I couldn't prove it.

I gave up, touched Pri's shoulder, and said, "I think we should move on."

She ran her hand along the side of the unicorn's head one last time, then nodded, turned, and walked with me into the forest.

A few seconds later, we heard the unicorn trot away.

As we moved deeper into the woods, the canopy grew denser, less and less sunlight penetrated all the way to the ground, and the temperature dropped. We never had any trouble seeing the path or the many sights around us, but the dim light and the many shadows cloaked the space in magic. Shrubs bursting with golden flowers sat next to trees with pale blue blossoms poking straight out of them, a combination of new and old growth that I'd never seen in any natural setting. A flock of gray mouse birds screeched down at us from our right, and both Pri and I involuntarily jumped. The mouse birds settled momentarily to a hover in front of us, their black eyes studying us carefully as they chittered and worked their front paws against one another, and then they soared away to our left. I laughed as they departed, amused both at how easily they'd startled me and at how funny a sight they were.

The combination of the trees lining the dirt walkway and the undergrowth was dense enough that it was clear we weren't supposed to enter the woods, but at the same time there were no overt warnings not to leave the path. We were alone, no one else in sight, so we had a perfect opportunity to see how the island security responded to someone breaking the rules. I stopped, touched Pri's shoulder, and pointed to a square meter of dazzling purple flowers on a shrub a good fifteen meters to my left. "Aren't those beautiful, dear?" I said, working to channel the awe I'd felt at the animals into a passion for flowers I've never truly felt. "I think you'd look lovely wearing one of them."

I stared at Pri, hoping she'd understand what I wanted.

"They are pretty," she said. I nodded very slightly, so she continued. "And yes, I would love to have one, but I'm not sure we're allowed to go in there."

I made a show of looking down the path behind us and then ahead of us. "Nobody's going to know," I said, "and surely one little flower can't hurt." I knew exactly how much it could hurt, of course, because I've seen beautiful places destroyed by only one in a thousand visitors deciding a little bit of the area simply had to go home with him. What may seem safe as a small individual act can turn into a weapons-grade destructive force if enough people do it repeatedly over a long period of time. Fortunately, I wouldn't be hurting nature here so much as lowering the value of a very profitable if highly unusual amusement park.

I found a spot where the branches of two shrubs touched and pushed my way gently through them; I didn't want to do any more damage than was absolutely necessary. The branches slapped and scratched at my shirt as I passed, but after a meter and a half of unpleasant and slow progress, I stepped into a clear area. I glanced back; Pri was staring nervously first at me and then alternately at the ends of the path.

I smiled at her until she forced a smile in return. If we weren't being watched, I was wasting time, but unless Shurkan's intelligence was completely wrong, the crew running this place was monitoring every square meter of it. I was about to attract some attention I might one day regret having, but it was the only way I knew to gather data on their response time, information that could prove valuable later.

"I'll get you that flower," I said. "How hard can it be?"

CHAPTER 12

I TURNED AROUND to make my way toward the purple-flowered bush and found myself face-to-face with the biggest spider I've ever seen. It perched on a wide silvery web that hung from a thick thread dangling from a branch four meters over my head. The beast was at least thirty centimeters across. A dark brown the shade of the trunk of the tree from which it hung, the creature would be very hard to spot when it was crawling along the wood. There's no chance I would have missed it when I entered the clearing, and I didn't believe it could possibly have spun a web that big in the few seconds I was speaking to Pri, so the web must have traveled with it. Though it's certainly possible this was a type of spider I'd never seen, one that rode its web down from tree limbs, a more likely answer was that it was an active warning unit, a tool for scaring off intruders and maybe even buying time for security to arrive. I stared closer at the creature. All of its legs were perfectly symmetrical, almost metallic, and lacked the hairy look typical of spiders. I touched its head and felt cool metal. What we'd seen so far on the island suggested a preference for bioengineering, but this was proof their engineers could do first-class mech work as well.

When I pulled back my finger, the spider spoke—or, to be accurate, words came from it.

"You have entered an unsafe and off-limits area," said a deep, rich voice, "so please return to the path and resume your tour."

"Perhaps you should do as it says," Pri said. Her expression made clear her desire for me to stop, but I wanted all the data I could gather. I'd already learned that animal-based monitors were part of their defense arsenal.

Without turning around, I said, "Nonsense. I'm not hurting anything, and this overgrown bug is only here to scare me. I'm getting you that flower. I'll be back in a minute."

I stepped around the spider, took another step forward, and paused as if reorienting myself toward the bush with the purple flowers. Despite what I'd said about the spider, I felt so exposed my spine tingled. I forced myself not to look back. If the metal creature was going to inject me with something, to stay in character I had to let it do so, then trust the nanomachines to clear the toxin from my system as quickly as they could.

I lifted my right leg to take another step, and from below I heard, "My good sir, I'd appreciate it if you didn't force me to protect myself."

I'd been so focused on the spider that I hadn't checked the ground before I moved. Stretched out in front of me was a three-meter-long snake, a full meter of which rose to an almost vertical position as I watched. It swayed slightly from side to side as its eyes focused on me and its tongue flicked in and out of its mouth. Diamond-shaped sections of blue and purple alternated along and around a body that was as thick as my upper arm and reflected the dappled light like polished metal. This was not a subtle snake, nor would it blend with any forest I've ever seen. The creature opened its mouth to reveal a bank of what one might mistake as glands but which I was quite sure were dart launchers, one pair each on the right and left of its upper and lower jaws. If it or its handlers wanted me down, I'd be down; there was no way I could move fast enough to avoid four pairs of darts coming from slightly different directions.

"Might I suggest, sir," the snake said, "that you adopt the spider's recommendation as your course of action and proceed *posthaste* back to your lovely companion?"

I'd been off the path for several minutes, and so far the island's security team had relied on animal sentries. With preparation, I could deal with those. To push my luck further, I'd have to break character. I decided to stick with being a fool out to impress his date and not go any farther. I held up my hands in surrender.

"Sorry," I said. "I didn't think it would be such a big issue." I paused and bent forward, as if I were talking to a very small camera, which of course I probably was. "She and I," I whispered, "we're not getting along so well right now. I thought if I showed her an extra special time, she might stop being so mad." I straightened and said to myself, "Why am I talking to a fake snake?"

I turned and faced Pri. "Sorry, dear," I said in a louder voice, "but—"

The snake cut me off. "Sir, if I might be of assistance," it said.

My wallet vibrated at the same time. I held up my hand to Pri and looked again at the snake. Its head swiveled toward the bush with the purple flower and then back to me. It leaned forward and almost touched my wallet. I opened it and found a pending charge.

"For the flowers, sir," the snake said, its voice low enough that Pri would have trouble hearing it, "if you'd still like to impress your companion."

I had to admire the island's staff. Turning a possible security breach into a profit opportunity was a beautiful bit of business. I had to go for it. I thumbed the wallet my approval.

The snake's head swiveled again toward the bush. A meter-high white rabbit in a bright purple tuxedo walked on its hind legs toward me, a bouquet of a dozen of the blossoms clutched in its front paws; the tux and the flowers matched flawlessly. When it was even with the snake, it held out the bouquet to me.

As I took them, I studied the rabbit's eyes. I couldn't be certain without touching the animal, but I figured it to be another mech creation, though it could also be a hybrid. "Thanks," I said.

"It is our pleasure, sir," the snake said. "Now, perhaps we can all get on our way."

"Of course, of course," I said. I turned around and held the flowers aloft. "Look what I got for you!" I said to Pri. I kept them above my head as I made my way back through the shrubs and onto the path. When I reached Pri, I glanced back in time to see the snake and the rabbit disappear into the bushes.

I handed the bouquet to Pri and smiled. "As I promised."

"I didn't want—"

I interrupted her. "I know, I know," I said. I stared into her eyes, trying my best to remind her of her role. "You didn't want me spending more money, but they are beautiful, aren't they?"

She took the gift and smiled. I couldn't tell if her expression was genuine or forced. As she sniffed the flowers I made a mental note to have Lobo scan them for bugs—the surveillance kind—as well as possible biotracers.

"Yes," Pri said, "they are. And now, can we go see some of the attractions?"

I didn't want to draw any more security attention, so touring a chunk of the island was about all I could usefully do. Their security was tight enough that I expected them to check me out on the off chance I was a criminal. Fortunately, the data Lobo was feeding local systems about me would stand up to at least a light inspection. I also couldn't be the first man they'd seen behave stupidly to impress a woman, so we should be safe enough.

"Sure," I said. They were certainly monitoring us, so I stayed in character. I slumped my shoulders like a man put down by Pri's lack of enthusiasm, then made an effort to stand up straight and smile. "Let's go see those amazing land animals you've told me so much about."

CHAPTER 13

WE STROLLED ALONG the path through the remainder of this section of the forest and emerged into a field of low grass that ran right up to a rock wall pocked with caves. A pack of enormous three-headed black dogs strutted out to greet us. With angry red eyes, thick yellow teeth, jaws that looked like they could crush my leg in a second, and jet black fur, the animals triggered a primitive flight instinct that struck me below conscious thought.

"Let's keep moving," Pri said.

My gut reaction was to agree with her and walk quickly away from this exhibit, but I've never liked surrendering to irrational fears. "No," I said. "Let's take a look at them."

The expression she gave me made it clear what she thought of my idea.

"Really," I said. "There's no way the management would let animals this dangerous run free. They can't afford tourist injuries." I stepped a few meters off the path into the ankle-high grass, determined to spot the barrier that protected us from the dogs. "Something we can't see must be keeping these beasts in check." I turned back to her and nodded. "We're fine."

Pri's eyes widened. "Really?" she said.

"Absolutely."

She pointed toward the animals.

"I hope you're right," she said.

I turned to see half a dozen of the huge creatures sprinting toward us, all eighteen heads drooling and barking madly. I maintained my confidence at first, even as Pri grabbed my hand and tried to pull me toward her. "No worries," I said.

I lost faith when the dogs skidded to a halt in front of us, one of them bumping its shoulder into my stomach. They were larger up close than they'd appeared from a distance.

I backed away a step, drew even with Pri, and then took another step backward.

The dogs followed us. Two more knocked against my body, and one dog's head butted my free hand.

Damn; I'd done it. I'd surrendered to reflex instead of thinking.

I stopped, reached down, and petted the center head of the dog nearest my left hand. All three of its heads instantly stopped barking and began making low, whimpering sounds. After a few seconds of petting, the huge animal—it had to weigh more than I did, possibly much more—sank to the ground and rolled over, its legs in the air. I scratched its belly and smiled.

"I told you," I said. "We're fine. They're just big love sponges."

Pri slapped the back of my head. "Don't tell me you weren't scared."

I stopped petting the dog and rubbed where Pri had hit me. "Okay, I was, but without cause. Almost everything I said was right: There's no way these people will let a dangerous animal near us or any other visitors." All three of the heads of the dog I'd been petting began licking me, and another head smacked against my free hand. "I was just wrong about these particular creatures being a problem."

I resumed petting the one animal and with my other hand started scratching between the ears of one of the heads of another.

Pri did the same.

Periodically, one dog would knock another out of the way and take its turn being petted, but the conflict never escalated beyond body blocking and the occasional snapping of jaws. I used the time to scan the grounds around us with regular vision and then in IR. If we were lucky, up close I'd be able to spot something Lobo couldn't read from far overhead. Perhaps the staff hatches—assuming there were any around us, of course—would show hints of metal or read a little bit warmer or cooler than the rest of the field. Maybe the grass in one area might be a slightly different color due to small variations in soil conditions.

No such luck: If there were any hatches as far as I could see in the field, I couldn't spot them.

I'd thought the dogs would tire of us stroking and scratching them, but after a while I realized I was wrong; they'd take the attention for as long as we could stand to give it.

"Let's go," I said. "We have a lot more to see."

Pri nodded, gave a last pet to two of the dogs, and stood.

They followed us to the edge of the path but not onto it, some invisible fence doing its job and restricting them to their domain.

We walked along the trail for a couple hundred meters as it wound around the edge of the grass and up a steep hill. We stopped at the top of a rise in the center of an orchard that ringed the little hill. Ten-meter-high trees blocked our view in all but two directions: the path up which we'd come, and the one leading away from us. We paused to appreciate the view: trees full of light green fruit topped in the distance by the cloud wall through which our shuttle had taken us; the path behind us vanishing down a winding slope; a field of yellow flowers ahead of us, the growth seeming to stretch all the way to the river that surrounded the island.

"They designed everything you see," she said. "They started with a huge excavation, built the underground complex, covered it, and then constructed all of this. Nature had no hand in any of it; it's one vast, unnatural zoo." Her fists unconsciously clenched in anger.

I sniffed the air and caught the scents of trees, ripening fruit, grasses, and animal musk I couldn't identify. Gentle breezes ruffled the leaves. "But a beautiful one," I said. "You were right: They did a great job."

"I just wish—"

I put my hand gently over her mouth before she could say anything that any software later reviewing our conversation might take the wrong way. "So do I," I said, removing my hand. "I wish I'd listened to you and gone along with more of the activities you suggested, and I wish I'd come here with you earlier." I paused and thought frantically about the types of long-standing arguments a couple might have. I'd never been in a relationship with a woman that lasted for more than a mission, so I had to scramble to make up something believable. "In all those talks we had, I wish I'd listened better, period."

That seemed to do the trick. Pri nodded in what I hoped was understanding and said, "You're doing better now." She closed her eyes for a moment and visibly relaxed. "We should keep moving; there's a lot more to see." She opened her eyes, lifted her right hand slightly, and glanced down at it.

Yeah, she understood.

I held her right hand. It was warm and soft and ever so slightly damp with sweat. I felt awkward as hell. Even pretending to have a relationship with her left me uncertain and uncomfortable. Still, we headed down the path like that, strolling hand in hand, just another couple touring the island.

After a hundred meters we abandoned the pretense and stopped holding hands. We passed by another field, this one full of pale blue flowers the width of my palm. Milling around the field about thirty meters in front of us and eating grass and the petals of the flowers were a dozen creatures I initially took to be enormous lions, their muscular, yellow-brown bodies and thick brownish manes unmistakable even though their height—shoulders over two meters off the ground—was greater than that of any lion or lion derivative I'd ever seen. Then one of the beasts lifted its head and I involuntarily stepped backward. Staring at me was what appeared at this distance to be a human face, its expression slack, its mouth slowly chewing. When I didn't look away, the animal came closer, and I could see that the face wasn't quite right: The skin was a bit too hairy, the eyes a tad too large, and the overall shape more square than it should have been.

After the dogs, I expected these animals to come to us, but they ignored us. Even the one that had studied me looked away and returned to eating.

"That's it?" I said, my voice a bit too loud, the question partly to Pri and, I realized after I said it, partly in frustration to the animals. "They just chew grass and flowers?"

Apparently not. Two of them straightened, walked over to us, and stopped two meters away, one lining up with each of us. They sat in unison, their front paws stretched in front of them. Mine stared into my eyes but otherwise did nothing.

"Look at the sphinx's eyes, and think a question to which you'd like an answer," Pri said.

I tilted my head slightly and opened my mouth to ask her how she knew all this, but she was ahead of me.

"I told you we didn't need to pay for the guided tour," she said, "because I've taken it several times in the past. That's how

I know the story behind these animals. The legend is that either they'll respond with a riddle or whatever comes into your head next will hold the key to answering your question." She smiled at me. "Give it a try; it can't hurt."

I considered pointing out how dumb this idea was, but Pri clearly knew the notion was nothing more than tourist bait. So I stared at the almost human face for a few seconds. I asked the question I frequently ponder: Is my sister still alive? As I expected, nothing in the creature's expression suggested it had somehow telepathically heard my question. The only answers I received were the ones I'd deduced all along: Probably not, but because she was a healer, possibly so—assuming, of course, that the Pinkelponker system had survived the nanobot disaster.

Thinking about Jennie did me no good, but I kept facing toward the sphinx and used the excuse to scan as much as I could see of the surrounding area without moving my head. Neither normal light nor the IR view gave me any hint of a hatch.

I had to face it: Unless I got very lucky and spotted a defective or open cover to the underground complex, I wasn't going to learn anything useful walking around the outside. These people were just too good.

I turned to face Pri. She was still staring intently into the almost human face in front of her. She had to be thinking about Joachim. Maybe she was aware of how silly this was and was doing it in the face of all reason, knowing she'd hear nothing but hoping for an answer nonetheless. I'd done it for my sister; why shouldn't she for her son? Still, if we were to have any chance of finding him, we needed more data than I now believed we were going to get here. We'd give the rest of the place enough of a look to maintain our cover, but then we'd move on.

I cleared my throat, waited a few seconds, and said, "What do you say we find some food? I'm ready for an early lunch."

Disappointment swept across her face for a moment, but then she regained control.

"Sure," she said. "I could use a bite myself. I think I remember where the nearest snack area is. Follow me."

The rest of the day unrolled like an old-fashioned map, flat image after flat image after flat image passing before my eyes as I refused to let the attractions draw my full attention and instead focused frequently on the ground, checking for signs of openings and finding none. We passed by slow-moving waterfalls in which mer-creatures swam and hovered; rocky cliff sections guarded by dragons, dark gray smoke coming from their nostrils; horses that at first appeared to have the upper bodies of men and women but that upon closer inspection were no more human than the sphinxes; great horned beasts wandering in mazes beneath transparent bridges crowded with spectators; and much, much more. We saw food vendors and souvenir hawkers and the occasional human tour guide leading a group of the ultra-wealthy. We ran across three security guards speaking in low tones to two men who appeared to be on the verge of a fistfight, but we never saw anyone emerge from the underground area, and I never caught even a hint of a hatch. I'd even listened on the machine frequency for a security camera that might be in a chatty mood, but I couldn't hear any; based on what Shurkan had said, they probably used only wired cameras and turned off all wireless output.

The sun had vanished behind the far side of the cloud cylinder and the temperature was dropping as day began its surrender to night when we passed by an out-of-order snack dispenser. Nothing feels as useless as a broken machine, and even good security teams often ignore the more routine devices, so I stopped beside it, tuned into the machine frequency, and subvocalized, "It's rough, isn't it?"

The response was both rapid and a bit stunned. "Excuse me?" it said. "Are you speaking to me? And if so, how?"

"Surely you've encountered other humans who can chat with you?" I said. "I'd assumed you were a modern system." Machines large and small are highly competitive egomaniacs, their surplus intelligence circuits and software focused narrowly on their tasks. I've yet to meet one with the programming to cope with even the most basic of interrogation techniques.

They will almost always lie to save face.

"Of course I have," it said, "and I am as up to date as any dispenser you'll ever meet."

"Which must make it particularly rough," I said, "that you're not able to work."

"You have no idea," it said. "Service is my life, and I excel at it. My self-repair abilities, however, are limited, and so I must wait for someone to come fix me."

"The repair requires a human? Can't they just send a patch?"

"Oh, I could handle anything soft; I wouldn't bother anyone if that were the problem. No, alas, it is hardware, pure and simple: a bent delivery chute, courtesy of a little deviant of a child shoving a shoe up me earlier today while his brainless parents gazed on in drooling admiration."

"Surely the repair team will come quickly," I said. "Your importance is obvious by your position, which is clearly a vital one. As essential as you are, they must have an entrance to the underground complex practically next to you."

"While it's obvious that you are a discerning and intelligent man," it said, "in this one point I am afraid you may be wrong. Though my systems don't have access to the plans for the main complex, based on my one previous mechanical problem and their slow response time in addressing this one, either the nearest entrance is far away, or they choose to delay repairs until the evening."

So much for that idea. I couldn't get the data from the available machines, and I couldn't spot the hatches myself, so it was time to give up this approach and try another one.

"I wish you a speedy repair," I said to the dispenser. Aloud to Pri, I said, "I'm beat. How about we call it a day?"

Though she was clearly tired, she also obviously didn't want to stop. To her credit, though, she hadn't argued with me for some time, and she didn't choose this moment to resume the practice.

"Fine by me," she said. "Let's go home."

She didn't speak again until we were back in Lobo, which was good; the less we said in public, the better. As soon as he closed the door he'd opened, however, she started. "What did you see that I missed?"

I ignored her, walked to the front, and said aloud to Lobo, "Take us to a safe orbit." I then plopped into a pilot couch, looked at her—she had, of course, followed me—and braced myself for what was to come. "Nothing. I couldn't spot a single hatch or even a hint of where the entrances to the underground complex might be, though it's a safe bet there's one near each major exhibit." I breathed slowly in through my nose, calming myself for the attack that always came when you didn't give a client the answer she wanted.

Pri sat on the edge of the other couch, leaned her head into her hands, scratched furiously at her hair, and said, so softly I could barely hear her, "Damn. I was so hoping." She shook her head and looked up at me. "Thanks for trying."

I stared at her in silence for several seconds, caught completely unprepared by her niceness. Finally, more through reflex than thought, I said, "You're welcome."

She rubbed her eyes and sat up straight. "So, what do we do next?"

I'd been pondering that very question all the way from the broken dispenser back to Lobo. I'd hoped to be able to slip into the compound, that Wonder Island's need to be a successful tourist attraction might bring with it some obvious security holes, but we'd seen nothing of the sort. Even if Lobo could get through the facility's defenses initially, either he'd lose to greater strength while waiting for me to find Wei, or in the course of winning he'd attract so much attention from Heaven's government and its EC friends that we'd never get out of this solar system. I'd come up with only two possible answers, and neither of them made me happy.

"First," I said, "we definitely get some more of that chocolate gelato."

When she didn't smile and only stared harder at me, I raised my hands in surrender. "Okay, fine, no more attempts to cheer you up. Here's where we stand." I took a deep breath. "We can't try to break into the place because we don't know where to begin. Consequently, whatever we do is going to take some time, potentially a lot of time, but definitely an amount we can't control. Right?"

I didn't want to point out to her the implications for Joachim; from the tightness of her face, she already understood them.

She nodded slightly. "Yes."

"So, we have two remaining ways to get Wei. One is when he's outside the island. He'll have guards, but at least we'll have a chance of finding him quickly. To know when he's out, your people will have to watch every landing point they can manage and yell the moment they spot him. When we're done talking, you have to call them and tell them to set up surveillance teams at as many of those locations as they can manage."

"They're already looking for him," Pri said, "so that shouldn't be hard. What's the other way into that damn underground complex?"

I smiled, spread my arms, and said, "I'll have to get them to invite me."

CHAPTER 14

PRI STARED AT ME as if I'd lost all contact with reality.

"She's not going to ask," Lobo said aloud, "so I will: How do you propose to wrangle an invitation into their underground sanctum?"

"By getting a job there," I said.

"Maybe Shurkan didn't fully brief me," Pri said, "but I didn't think bioengineering was your specialty. Just how much training in that area do you have?"

"None," I said. "That's not the kind of job I want."

Pri shook her head and stared at me, clearly exasperated.

"When you think about the Wonder Island staff," I said, "you think about Wei and his team. Right?"

She nodded.

"That's fine, because they're the ones you're after, but what do you think most of the people who work there do?"

She considered the question for a few seconds. "Make the place run."

"Exactly!" I said. "They do any labor the machines can't, deal with the tourists and VIPs who require personal handling, plan events, work security, and do all the other jobs that still require humans."

"They're going to run a background check on anyone who applies to work there," she said, "so they'll find out who you are."

I nodded my agreement. "I'm counting on it. They'll learn the same things you and the CC discovered: that I've done courier

101

work, that I served with the Saw, and, if they're well connected, that I've ruffled more than a few feathers. When they check for me locally, they'll find the apartment I'm renting, the additional details Lobo and I will plant—"

She interrupted me. "And they'll check you against their security videos and learn you were there today. They'll know you were checking it out."

"Yes," I said, "they will, which I'll explain was because I hoped to land a job there. They'll also find that I recently lost the title to Lobo and that I failed to impress and ultimately was dumped by the girlfriend I'd taken there." I smiled at her. "That would be you."

"So we're over already?" she said, also smiling. "Wow, that was quick."

Before I could respond, Lobo said, "I've checked their public postings, and though in the past they've listed security guard openings, they have none now."

"That's the big weakness of this approach," I said. "It could take a long time. Low-end staff and security people tend not to stick around for long anywhere, so I'm confident I'll get a shot at some point, but I can't know when." Pri opened her mouth to speak, but I held up my hand and continued. "Which is why we have to hope your Freepeople colleagues can work their connections, conduct surveillance on multiple exits from the island, and find out where Wei goes on his days off."

"Are you sure he has days off?" Pri said.

"No," I said, "I'm not, but it's extremely likely. Anyone trapped in any fixed environment craves time away from that space. He's in charge, so he's likely to be able to indulge that craving. We need your people to find out where he goes when he gets out."

"Then let's not waste any more time," Pri said. "I'll call them."

I stood and headed for my quarters. "You talk to them from here. I'll work with Lobo on the background data."

"Now you're trusting me to be alone with them?" she said.

I chuckled, turned to face her, and from the way she narrowed her eyes I realized too late that she hadn't been joking and had hoped our relationship had advanced to that point. "No," I said. "I'm too paranoid to do that. Lobo will record the conversation for me, and he'll stop it if he decides you're wandering at all out of line or off the topic."

"So you trust this machine more than you trust me?"

"I should hope he does," Lobo said, indignation quite obvious in his tone.

"I do," I said to both of them. "Pri, you and I have shared one and a half good days, but before that time you conned me. Lobo and I have a couple of years of history, and he's saved my life more than once." I smiled at her. "Ask me again when this is over, when we've succeeded, and maybe we'll both have good reasons to trust each other more.

"For now, though, contact your people. Lobo and I will make sure the local data streams contain the right information about me, we'll try to move ahead on that apartment so it looks like I'm planning to stay here, and we'll file my job application. Then we'll sleep. After that, all we can do is hope for the best."

I don't dream much, and when I do, the experience is rarely pleasant. The visions that snapped me awake several times that night maintained that unpleasant tradition. Images of Jennie boarding the ship that would take her, my sister and first friend, away from me—a scene I'd never witnessed but had imagined so many times it was now more vivid than many of my real memories—morphed into slow-motion video streams of faceless, white-suited jailers strapping Joachim onto medbeds poised to inject him. Joachim then mutated into Benny's strange form, the leathery stomach and flipperlike arms of my fellow test subject replacing the normal torso I'd imagined for Pri's son. They'd needed special restraints for Benny. When the nanobot injections hit our systems, they burned at first, then turned into screaming muscle cramps and created the sensation of creatures crawling under our skin. If you weren't fully strapped down, you'd do anything to get them out of you. Benny's odd structure had let him pull his arms free from the first set of cuffs they'd used on him, and he'd torn big gashes in his chest before they were able to restrain him more effectively.

I'd watched that scene on a monitor from my own cell on Aggro. I remembered going into the same room to receive the same injections that had so tormented Benny, but still the imagined picture of Jennie vanishing was more vivid than any real memory. Blocking out such painful recollections undoubtedly served me well and was a natural human defense against the unthinkable, but it still bothered me that I couldn't recall them fully, as if the pain could not have been real if I was unable to invoke it again in its entirety.

The third time a variation of this Jennie-Joachim-Benny sequence assaulted me, I sat up in my cot, sweat dampening my entire body, my mouth clamped tight against a scream, and I knew I wouldn't sleep any more that night. I'd spent six restless hours in bed, so I'd indulged myself enough. I got up and focused on working out. I started with stretching and proceeded through cycles of body-weight resistance movements, each one flowing into the next, no break between individual exercises and only half a minute between cycles, until I felt cleansed of the haunting dreams and my body was deliciously sore.

Lobo interrupted me as I was eating a bowl of rice, a variant of which you could get on every planet I'd ever visited, and some bits of a local, meaty white fish.

"We have a new approach option," he said over the machine frequency.

"Weren't you going to tell me the rest of the story of your relationship with Wei?" I said. "What did you call it?"

"More complex," Lobo said, "and, yes, I can and will go through it with you at some point, but not right now."

"Right now would be a good time," I said, "to resume it."

Lobo's sigh was audible. "No," he said, "it would not."

"Why?" I was tiring of his stalling tactics.

Suli knocked on the door to my quarters and said, "Jon! Jon! I have good news."

"That's why," Lobo said, "as I would have explained if you'd stopped asking me questions."

It was my turn to sigh. "Sorry about that. Let her in."

I sat on my cot as the door snicked open and Suli stepped inside.

"We know where Wei goes!" Suli said. She paused and thought for a moment. "Well, we know one of the places he goes, but given what it is, he probably goes there often."

"Your people tracked him?"

"Obviously," she said. "In a moment sufficiently ironic that they felt obliged to rub my nose in it, while we were touring the island, Wei was in town."

"Learning the territory is never a waste," I said, though I wasn't sure that would prove to be true in this case. "Where does Wei go?" Before she could answer, I realized the obvious and added, "And why didn't your surveillance team grab him?"

"To answer the second question first, they're not set up to do that kind of thing, they're locals, and . . ."

She paused so long I prompted her.

"And what?"

"And he travels in a three-car group, all the cars are armored, and we can't know his path in advance; he took different routes coming and going from the city."

"That's still good news," I said. "We now have multiple possible snatch points."

"And guards are fair targets," Lobo said aloud.

"What does he mean?" Pri said.

"You can speak to me directly," Lobo said. "I don't need His Sweatiness there to bless my every utterance. What I meant is that though Mr. Moral Convenience doesn't like incurring collateral damage, he seems to consider that by signing on as guards those people know the risks they're taking and so are fair targets. I like targets."

"And you don't care about hurting innocent people?" Pri said. "Don't you have some kind of programming to stop you from damaging humans?"

"Hello!" Lobo said. "Have you looked at me? I'm built to fight. It's what I do. While I'll certainly admit to the possession of a moral framework too complex for discussion in the middle of a mission, once we agree to take a job I let that agreement guide my actions and do what's necessary. Unlike some people."

"Enough," I said. If I let Lobo get rolling, he could be at it for hours. I focused on Pri. "Lobo is right in noting that I don't like injuring civilians, and he's also correct that I don't consider guards to be civilians. That said, we," I paused and glanced around, "all of us, including Lobo, will do our best to minimize casualties of any type. Right?"

"Of course," Lobo said. "You must admit, however, that they seem frequently to be unavoidable in what we do, and you do keep getting us involved in these situations."

I opened my mouth to speak but stopped before I said anything and invited more argument. As usual, Lobo had his basic facts right but ignored many extenuating factors. Getting into a discussion of them would do us no good and also expose more of my past to Pri than I was comfortable sharing.

"Let's move on," I said, "because we have a lot to do with the new information available to us." I faced Pri. "Where does Wei go in Entreat?"

"To see Andrea Matahi," Pri said. She clearly expected some sort of reaction from me.

"Who's that," I said, "and where does she live?"

That wasn't the response she'd anticipated. After a few seconds of staring at me, she said, "You don't know who she is?"

"I can provide you a full briefing of the public data," Lobo said. "Though I should warn you in advance that I cannot find any photos of her; she must have friends in media and hacking circles, because someone has sanitized and scrubbed most of the data that's out there, if not all of it. Her address is one of the many pieces of information that's not available."

What was with these two? Everything I said or did ended up leading us onto detours. "No," I said, "I don't know anything about her." To try to get us back on point, I added, "Remember: I'm not from around here."

That seemed to placate Pri, but only a bit. "Matahi is famous by reputation in Entreat, probably on all of Heaven, as a courtesan and on rare occasions public companion to some of the most powerful men and women on the planet for the last century or so."

"That's great," I said, "because it'll make it easy for me to see what we'll be up against when Wei visits her. I'll just hire her."

Pri shook her head. "That's not how it works, or, at least, that's not how I've heard she operates."

"She's a courtesan," I said, "so I should be able to buy her time."

"Only if she accepts you as a client," Pri said. "One of our people knew how to reach her avatar and learned that's how she works."

"I recorded that information, of course," Lobo said.

"But she rarely takes on clients," Pri said. "Several of our wealthier members have tried, but none have succeeded; she wouldn't see most of them, and the few she did meet failed her interview. That's why we still don't know her location."

"I don't know anything about her selection process," I said, "but taking care in choosing clients certainly makes sense for anyone in her profession. As for your people, well, turning them down simply demonstrates good judgment."

"Why?" she said.

"Because it's safer to stay aligned with those in power. Why should she risk getting involved with a vocal and potentially dangerous opposition party?"

Pri nodded. "Okay, so what's your plan for seeing her?"

I stood. "I'll apply." I pointed toward the door. "I'm not from here, I have money, and so I should represent at least an intriguing prospect. You and Lobo will scout the routes your people mentioned so Lobo can build models we can use should we be able to catch Wei in transit. You'll also keep an eye out for responses from the Wonder Island job application, on the off chance I get an opportunity to show up there in person. And, you'll pick up some clothes and enough other possessions to make the apartment we're renting look like I at least sleep there, just in case they check it out before letting me interview."

"And while I'm doing all this work, what will you be doing?"

"Cleaning up and waiting for my chance to try to pass muster with the legendary Ms. Matahi."

CHAPTER 15

I WAS CLEAN AND DRESSED when Lobo gave me the good news that Matahi would meet me and the bad news that I had just spent a lot of money.

"I had to pay that much just to meet her?"

"Yes," Lobo said, using a tone that added "you idiot" to the end of the word. "You told me to set you up locally to look poor, so I had to create a secret account with enough funds to convince her you could afford her. I even had to send her a photo of you. She sells her services, she has a few existing significant clients, and she charges enough that she doesn't have to work with more than them. So, unless someone interests her, she doesn't meet with them without some form of inducement. You obviously weren't appealing enough on your own." After a short pause, he added, "To be fair, I don't recall you taking a lot of meetings unless they had something in it for you."

I had to grant him that. The fee, though, seemed excessive, and by reflex I hated that she already knew what I looked like. Still, Lobo wouldn't have done any of this if he could have avoided doing it, so there was no point in harassing him about it. "Won't others find the account?" I said.

"Must you ask such questions?" he said, the "you idiot" tone back in his voice. "It is, of course, already gone, as I warned her it would be."

"Sorry," I said. "Still, she sure does charge a lot of money for an hour. "I'm amazed at what people will pay for sex."

"Oh, you don't get a full hour," Lobo said, "and you certainly don't get sex. In fact, she never guarantees sex. She's a courtesan; should I perhaps enlighten you as to the meaning of the term?"

He was enjoying my discomfort entirely too much.

"No, thank you," I said. "It's just that I thought sex was the ultimate goal for her clients."

"Maybe it is," Lobo said, "and maybe they get it, but that's not the main reason her clients go to her. You can buy sex on Entreat, as you can in any city of any size, and you can spend a great deal less than Matahi's fee. The data I've found, however, suggests that she truly sells her time more than anything else."

"No discounts for just wanting to talk?"

"Are my speakers dirty?" Lobo said. "First Pri and now you seem to have trouble grasping what I'm saying. Talking is a huge part of what she sells. What you're buying is simply enough time for her to decide whether she's willing to consider you as a client."

I started to complain further, but it was a waste of time. Pri had warned me that I'd have to audition for Matahi, so I would. "How long do I have until the meeting?"

"A little over an hour."

"Why did I get an appointment so quickly?" Maybe there was more hope for me than I thought.

"According to her assistant interface," Lobo said, "most potential clients try to woo her directly, and they do so with much more skill and flair. The utter lack of comprehension you demonstrated by leaving the entire arrangement to me and not approaching her yourself apparently intrigued her, though I can't imagine why. In any case, she's allowing you to meet her where she was already planning to take tea."

So much for that idea. Still, I had a meeting, and that was what I'd wanted.

"Where should I go?"

Lobo fed the location, an approach route, and three exit paths to the contact I'd put in my left eye. On a display he opened on the wall in front of me, he gave me an aerial view and some labels.

"We're meeting in front of the police station in the old city?"

"Yes," Lobo said. "I assume the combination of the location and her connections within the government make it a place she can go without having to bother with too many bodyguards. Do you want me as backup?"

"No," I said. "Let's move to a comm unit, because I need to leave so I can arrive early." I was starting later than I'd normally arrive at a meeting, and I hated being at that disadvantage.

I exited my room and stopped as Pri approached me.

"Good luck," she said.

I nodded, Lobo opened the side hatch, and I stepped outside.

Lobo took off as soon as I was twenty meters away.

"If you stick to the task of surveying the routes Wei might use," I said to him, "how long would it take you to reach me?"

"No more than three minutes," Lobo said, "though moving at that speed would definitely attract attention."

"Then stay with scanning Wei's approach routes," I said. The day was beautiful, and I was heading into a public place for what Matahi would assume was a normal client meeting. "I doubt anything will go wrong, but if it does, I should be able to last three minutes—and if we reach that point, drawing notice to ourselves will be the least of our problems."

The route Lobo had mapped was too straightforward for my taste, so I added several countersurveillance moves, but if anyone was following me on foot, I missed them. As I emerged into the square fifteen minutes early, I relaxed a bit: I had no reason to believe anyone was after me, and I had arrived without incident. I'd almost certainly wasted time getting here, but I didn't care. Some old habits are worth reinforcing, even when they're inefficient. I slid into the shadow of a large, white, stone statue of a woman in flowing robes and started a slow, clockwise scan of the area.

Six entrances fed pedestrians into the square: four at the corners, the opening through which I'd entered, which was on the middle of the eastern side, and a matching archway in the center of the buildings opposite me. A row of yellow stone three-story buildings standing side by side formed my edge of the square and the one opposite me. A white and gray brick building filled the entire north side. Only a small bronze plaque to the right of the main arched entranceway marked that structure as the police station. No one entered or left it; the cops here probably routed any unsavory traffic through the rear so as not to break the ancient-world spell the old part of Entreat cast on visitors.

Along the entire south edge of the square stood two-story yellow and red stone buildings with no spaces between them. Two souvenir shops, three separate restaurants, and a baked-goods store filled their first floors. A row of five small gray metal tables, each with a wide umbrella over it, sat in front of Poohgi, the bakery. Permacrete flowerbeds bursting with brilliant crimson blossoms separated the tables from the walkway in front of Poohgi. Sitting alone at the center table, sipping from a small white cup, was a woman as brightly colored as the flowers. I zoomed my contacts to study her more closely. Very little of her was visible. A large, sky-blue hat sat on her head. Huge sunglasses covered her eyes and much of her face. Her body shape was indistinguishable beneath a loose, metallic blue wrap that shimmered like an ocean in midday light. Cobalt gloves covered her hands. I couldn't be sure she was Matahi, but she was the only woman sitting alone, so that was the most likely guess.

"I believe this is her," I subvocalized, knowing Lobo was monitoring and recording all the data my contact and clothing sensors were capturing. "Your opinion?"

"As I told you before," he said, "we don't have a picture of her, but the location seems right, and her appearance is certainly striking, so it's a reasonable supposition."

Assuming this was indeed my target, I admired her caution: She'd been in position when I arrived, and the clear line of sight from the police station to her table suggested she had friends there covering her. I hated risking official attention for any reason, but I had to take that chance if I was going to meet her.

A dozen men and women in matching shirts passed along the street in front of me. I fell in beside them. When we passed the edge of the square, I left the pack, doubled back a few meters, and walked along the southern row of buildings. Matahi now sat to my right, her back to me. I moved slowly, listening to the pitches from the menu avatars and checking all around me for backup for her. If anyone else was paying her special attention, I didn't spot them. Either she was relying on the police for protection, or her team was top-drawer.

Poohgi surprised me by not having a menu. It was also the only shop not standing open to the outside air. A small plaque above the handle on its glass door read:

Enter.
Smell.
Enjoy.

Even outside the aromas were lovely, so I opened the door and stepped inside.

The smell of freshly baked goods enveloped me. A glass cabinet full of three shelves of delicious-looking and even better-smelling treats ran on my left from the front wall to where it turned in the rear and stretched along the shop's back all the way to the right wall. The only breaks in cabinet were two small flip-up counters through which the four clerks could enter and exit. Five other customers filled the narrow area in which I was standing. Three of the clerks glanced at me as I entered, smiled, and then returned to their current transactions. One tended to two of the five ovens behind them. For reasons I couldn't explain, the smells made me happy, and I smiled at the feelings they evoked. A memory of my mother baking bread from flour, a necessity on our small and rather poor island, wafted through my brain, and I recalled how much I'd loved the heavy scent of the finished product and the taste of fresh, hot loaves. Did everyone have this sort of memory? Judging from their expressions, at least the other people in the shop with me did, or maybe they'd come to adore the smell later in life, maybe even just now. Whatever the cause, all of us were hungrily scanning the cabinets, and no one was leaving empty-handed.

I studied the breads, rolls of many shapes and sizes, biscuits, cookies, small cakes, large cakes, and what looked like coils of baked rope. Every single item made my mouth water. I finally settled on a dark roll the color of rich soil ready for planting, purchased it, and, at the clerk's suggestion, also bought a glass of an almost clear fruit juice that managed to produce both sweet and tangy tastes in each sip.

I stepped back outside, took a bite of my roll, and found it dense and even richer than I'd assumed.

Without turning, the woman I assumed was Matahi spoke, and though she sat four meters in front of me, her light voice was completely clear. "You'll have to stop transmitting, Mr. Moore, or there will be no meeting, and I will simply leave."

So either something she was wearing—it could be anything—or a friend in the police station was feeding her images and sensor data.

"We could move to burst transmissions," Lobo said, "but if she continues to monitor you, as from her statement we must assume she will, then she'll catch us soon enough. We should have sent you with local recording ability."

"Now we know why you gave me so little notice," I said aloud. "I reacted like an idiot. I apologize." I shook my head slightly at my own stupidity; you had to admire the woman's protocols.

She took a sip of her drink and again spoke without turning to face me.

"You now know the rules, Mr. Moore, and you clearly understand the protective value to me of this location. You've discussed the situation with whomever you have protecting you. You have all the data you're going to get before you must choose your next step." She drank some more of her beverage and laughed lightly. "You even have a delicious snack. So, will you finally come sit with me?" She paused and dabbed her lips with a napkin. "Or is our interview at its conclusion?"

CHAPTER 16

DISABLE ALL TRANSMISSIONS," I subvocalized to Lobo via my main comm. "And don't trigger any bursts. I'll call you when the meeting is over, or earlier if I need help."

"Done," Lobo said.

I headed toward Matahi, walked around the table without touching her, and stood behind the chair across from her. Her posture was perfect. She took a bite of the muffin she was eating, each of her movements leisurely but precise.

When she didn't speak or acknowledge me for almost a minute, I finally said, "I'm no longer transmitting." I grabbed the back of the chair and added, "I really don't understand the need for these games."

She tilted her head slightly and smiled. Her lips were full, her mouth wide, and her smile as perfect as one would expect. Her chin was narrow, and even with the sunglasses hiding most of her face her wide and pronounced cheekbones were evident. "Of course you do," she said, her tone as light and pleasant as before, "and now you've lied once. Three is your limit. Refusal to answer may be acceptable; that depends on the question."

"Acceptable to whom?"

"To me, of course," she said, still sounding nicer than her words, "and now you've been intentionally stupid once. You get only two of those."

I clenched the chair tighter. I didn't like playing by her rules.

115

She was maddening. I wanted to push back, knock over the table, and make her tell me how to get Wei. Doing so would accomplish nothing, though, other than to land me in trouble with Entreat's police.

"Finally," she said, leaning back slightly and smiling again, "some genuine emotions: frustration and anger. You'd prefer to do this your way, but that's not an option." She waved her gloved hand toward me. The wrap rippled as she moved, but like a burqa minus the head covering it gave no clue about her shape beneath it. "So, why don't you stop throttling that innocent piece of furniture and instead relax—or leave; that's always an option for either of us."

I inhaled slowly and deeply, exhaled even more slowly through my nose, and sat. "I'm sorry," I said. "I'm not used to anything like this."

"And a bit of truth," she said. "Excellent." She took another nibble of her muffin.

I ate a bit more of my roll and chased it with a swallow of the juice.

We continued that way, neither of us speaking. Commerce proceeded on its relentless course all around us. Tourists pointed this way and that. Mothers and fathers stood watchful guard over cookie-fueled children dashing about the square. Noise was everywhere except at our table. Matahi finished before me, but I was only a couple of bites behind her.

She remained quiet.

"I thought this was my application to see you," I said. She opened her mouth to speak, I realized what I had said, and I held up my hand to stop her. She closed her mouth. "Sorry about that. I don't want to use up my second stupid credit quite yet. What I meant to say was that if this is my application to see you, don't you want to ask me questions so you can evaluate my suitability as a client?"

"I have been evaluating you," she said, "as you have been considering me, and, yes, I will have a few questions. You're supplying so much information already, though, that I won't need to ask you much."

I hadn't expected her to be so observant or so interested in mind games. Though she clearly enjoyed them or found them useful, I saw no benefit to me in continuing to play them, so I followed an old but often useful rule: When no other path is clear, charge straight ahead. "Do you mind, then, if I ask you a few questions?"

"Of course not," she said. "They'll be a rich source of information about you."

She was right, of course, so I paused to consider my goals and my approach. To learn where she and Wei spent time and to get as much information as possible about him from her, I first had to win the chance to become her client. To do that, I had to ask questions that would appear reasonable for the person I was supposed to be.

I needed to approach this as if I really wanted to be with her.

Finding that desire in myself was easy enough. I've never sustained a close, personal, non-work relationship with a woman. Because I can't afford to let anyone know about my past, and because I don't age, I can't stay in one place for too many years. If I got involved with a woman, I'd have to live a lie with her, and I'd rather not do that. Being alone is so much easier and less complicated, but it doesn't mean that a big part of me wouldn't rather things be different. They simply can't be. I've also never paid for sex, though I have considered doing so and have nothing against the concept. I just don't think it would address any of my non-physical needs, and the risks of being alone with a stranger are great, so I'd have to research the woman first—and then I'd be back in the land of complexity. But I've been tempted, so I searched inside myself for those feelings before I spoke.

"I honestly don't know how this works," I said, "so I'm confused. Other than checking for possible risk, why is this interview useful for you?"

"What you want from me is irreplaceable," she said, "and intensely valuable to me. Why wouldn't I consider carefully whether to give it to you?"

"Sex is irreplaceable?"

She laughed, the sound richer and deeper than her voice. "From most people, I'd consider that the second and last of the allowable stupid questions. Judging from your tone and expression, however, I believe you're honestly confused. No, of course I'm not saying sex is irreplaceable; sex is one of the most joyfully renewable of resources. No one, though, pays my price for sex alone. In fact, no one ever really pays for only sex, but that's another conversation. What you want is my time and attention, and nothing is more precious than those two. I understand that if I agree to sell you the first, I will be committing myself to give you the second, so I must consider the issue carefully."

"Are all your interactions so formal?"

"Another borderline stupid question, but another one I'll allow." She leaned slightly forward, lowered her voice, and said, "If they were, do you imagine many people would pay a fee as high as mine?" In that moment, in that slight change in position and tone, she transformed from cold and hidden to hot and tempting. She resumed her perfect posture and in her normal voice said, "I'd ask you if all your interactions were so guarded, if you were always such a tightly sealed box, but then I'd have used up one of my own stupidity points. Your next question?"

As maddening as I found her, she absorbed my attention completely. It was as if the square had vanished in a flash of light and we were alone in a featureless landscape. I closed my eyes for a second, then opened them and slowly surveyed the shops and people and streets within view. I'm sure I appeared even more guarded than before, but I didn't care; I needed to regain control of myself.

After about a minute, I focused again on her. She remained still, as motionless as if she were knocked out but at the same time completely present, simply waiting for me to return. She reminded me of Slanted Jack, the best con man I've ever known but also someone who'd caused me a lot of trouble about a year ago. He had an amazing ability to be still and completely present, as well as to make each person he met feel like he or she was the most important human alive.

With that memory came the understanding that at some level I was, of course, being conned. She sold time, and however precious that resource might be, some of that time must be available or she wouldn't have bothered to meet me. Thinking of this situation that way helped me focus on my side of this con—and also made me realize that I hadn't prepared as well for my job or paid as close attention to it as any decent con man should.

When running a con, stick to the truth whenever you can, and believe in your lies as if they were true. With Matahi, that meant being myself as much as possible. I cared about risks and locations, so I decided to indulge myself.

"Aside from the police station," I said, "why this square?"

A slight shift in her position made me wonder if I'd finally surprised her in a good way. Then again, nothing in the little bit of her face that I could see gave away any reaction, so perhaps I'd imagined it.

"The many different types of buildings that line it," she said. She waved her hand slowly to encompass all the structures running along the edges of the square. "In this one little bit of this entirely artificial old-world tourist mecca, we have plain boxes, ornate façades with balconies, two places of worship, and many other monuments to our ability to build structures both functional and ornamental in which we can take shelter from the universe—and sometimes from each other." She paused, and when she spoke again her voice was softer. "It serves to remind me of how even within the narrow confines of any society's limits we will always find our own paths to fulfilling our most basic needs."

I waited for her to continue, but when she remained silent for almost a minute I spoke, going again for a question that was bothering me. "If you accept me as a client," I said, "must sex be a part of our relationship?"

She nodded the tiniest bit, a teacher congratulating a student on finally spotting the path to an answer, and said, "No. Whatever we decided to become would be up to us, to *both* of us. Nothing would happen unless we both wanted it."

I nodded in return. "You said I was guarded; fair enough. This setting, though, is not exactly designed to help me relax. I would prefer to be somewhere more private."

"As would I," she said, "should I decide to accept you as a client."

I continued with honest questions. "Why is so much of you covered? It's not at all what I expected. You said I was a tightly sealed box; are you any more open?"

Again, she nodded. "To answer your first question, why does my appearance matter to someone who implies he would like a non-sexual relationship? As for your second, of course not, not yet—nor will I be unless our relationship continues beyond this conversation."

"And will it?" I said. "I'm out of questions." I hadn't realized that was true until I said it, but it was; I didn't know what else to ask her.

"Maybe," she said. "You would have to agree to two conditions, neither negotiable."

"And they are?"

"First, a simple business term: You would have to pay in full in advance for each meeting."

"And if I'm not happy with how a meeting goes?"

She shrugged. "That's a risk for both of us, but it's not one with insurance. You would have lost your money and your time, and I would have lost my time."

I shouldn't need more than one or two meetings to study her place, and Shurkan and the CC were paying me well enough that even Matahi's outrageous fees wouldn't put a dent in my take from this mission.

"Okay," I said. "I'm willing to do that. Your other condition?"

She stood, the shimmery burqa still revealing nothing about her shape. "When you would like to see me again, and when my schedule permits, you will pay the fee, and we will meet here. You must bring a present that you believe I will like. If you're right and I like it, your fee will cover our first meeting at my studio. If I don't care for the gift, I'll leave, and you'll lose the fee."

"That's ridiculous," I said. "Do you find fools willing to go through all this, to pay you twice and not even be sure they'll get time alone with you?"

"Obviously," she said, turning as she spoke, "and enough that I don't need you to succeed, though I confess I hope you do. Like you, by the way, these people are not fools. They simply enjoy a happy marriage of need and resources."

She started walking away.

"How am I supposed to know what you'll like?" I said. "We've barely met."

She stopped, turned, and smiled. "You're clearly capable of contemplation, and you pay close attention. Now, let your conclusions and your data fuel your creativity." She tilted her head ever so slightly to the right, and her smile flowed into a more serious expression. "And in the process you will get a glimpse of the challenge I face regularly, one I assure you I always meet." She paused, smiled again, and said, "Always."

She headed away.

I stared after her and wondered how I was going to figure out what she would like and where I would find such a present.

When Matahi was almost out of earshot, she paused for a moment and spoke, her voice clear even though she was facing away from me, her tone managing to be both warm and teasing.

"I hope you meet yours."

CHAPTER 17

As soon as Matahi turned the corner, I raced after her. Though none of the online data had revealed the location of her home, if I could follow her there, I'd at least be able to survey the area and spot possible places to snatch Wei when he left after visiting her. I lost a few seconds getting around the people in front of the shops, so by the time I reached the corner where Matahi had turned, I was a good ten seconds behind her. I stopped, crouched, and glanced around the building's edge.

Her burqa was nowhere in sight.

"Tell me you're close enough to follow her," I said to Lobo over the comm.

"Of course," he said. "Scouting and mapping Wei's possible routes took very little time. Unfortunately, I can't see her."

"What?" I spoke so loudly several nearby people stared at me. "I'm sorry," I said to them.

"How nice of you to apologize for yelling," Lobo said, "and how very unusual."

I walked down the street slowly, checking the sides as I went, but I didn't see her.

"I wasn't talking to you," I whispered. "And why can't you see her?"

"The moment she was out of your line of sight," Lobo said, "she ducked into a doorway on the right. From the few floor plans that are publicly available, I believe that many of these buildings connect on interior walls. I've been watching the people entering and leaving via all the exterior doorways in a five-block radius, but no one wearing her outfit has emerged."

"No luck with her heat signature?"

"Give me some credit," Lobo said. "Of course not. The outfit in which she met you blocked everything; from my height she read so cold she might have been dead."

I shook my head in both defeat and admiration. "So she anticipated the possible surveillance, minimized the data we could accumulate about her, ducked into a building, and somewhere along the line changed clothes. Nice job."

"It would appear so," Lobo said. "Did you do something to alarm her? I wasn't close enough to be able to record your conversation."

I considered the question for a few seconds. "I don't think so. I showed anger once and frustration often, but I never let either emotion control what I did. I was basically just myself."

Lobo's sigh over the comm unit was as clear as it was annoying. "Perhaps in future interactions with females you should consider trying to act like someone else."

"And what in your extensive experience with women has endowed you with such wisdom?" I said.

"Nothing, of course," he said, "though my ability to monitor vital signs in real time, my perfect memory, and my access to an enormous library of the most romantic human works does give me a bit of an edge over a man who couldn't tell if a woman was interested in him unless she hit him with a sign telling him so."

"Look, I've spent a long time—" I stopped. The day might come that I'd have to tell Lobo about my past, but we weren't there yet. "I'm heading back to the rendezvous site. Track me, and meet me there. If you spot Matahi, call me. Otherwise, leave me alone." The challenge she'd given me felt impossible. I didn't even know where to begin to learn about buying gifts for any woman, much less a woman I'd met only once. "I need to think."

"It's an interesting idea," Pri said, a trace of admiration obvious in her tone. She paced back and forth in the front of Lobo, thinking it through. "She forces the focus back on her, learns more about you, and makes money regardless of how it turns out." She smiled. "It would make a great test prior to a second date."

"You would test someone you were dating?" I said, shaking my head in frustration.

"Where did you grow up?" Pri said. "Of course! Dating contains a long series of tests."

I ignored her question, because I sure wasn't going to answer it. "Let's focus on the problem: How am I going to pass? I have no clue what to get her."

"Assuming your rendition of the conversation is correct," Lobo said, "she portrayed this task as difficult. We may therefore assume that none of the classic gifts will suffice."

"Thank you, Mr. Logic," I said. "I'd figured out that much before I left the square. Given the vast universe of possible purchases, however, I don't think excluding a few of them helps much. What I need is an idea Matahi will like."

"I understand the assignment," Lobo said. "I was simply approaching it logically, trying to remove some categories and thus shrink the search space."

"What do you know about her?" Pri said.

"I've told you all the facts," I said, glad to have an excuse to stop the argument with Lobo.

"So assess her," Pri said. "What did you learn about her?"

I closed my eyes, replayed my impressions and the conversation. Without opening them, I said, "She's careful with information. She covered up as much as possible and gave away only what she wanted me to know. Her situational awareness was excellent; she spotted me early and tracked me well. Her preparation was quick and thorough, though all that tells us is that she's done this before, and we already knew that. She's confident, arguably overconfident. No one who could help her was close enough to stop me had I been there to kill her. I could have reached across the table and snapped her neck before she could react."

I paused and considered again her burqa. "Of course, she might have been armed with something automatic—it couldn't have required manual triggering, because both her hands were in view, though perhaps something in the gloves could have served that function. Or maybe her burqa and gloves were light armor."

I opened my eyes.

Pri was staring at me, her mouth slightly open, her head tilted, her pupils dilated. "Do you think of everyone as an enemy?" she said. "You're supposed to be winning her trust, not deciding how to kill her. Armored clothing? Reaching across the table and snapping her neck? What's wrong with you?"

She took a step backward. "Have you thought of me that way?"

Of course, I thought but did not say. If someone wasn't on your team, they might be on the other side—some other side, somehow a threat. If you walked into a room, you scanned for risks and exits. If you were already in it, you watched all traffic and all changes that might affect you. You did that, or you got hurt, maybe died. If you lived in the world in which no one ever turned violent or violence was at least so rare as to be nonexistent, I suppose you could think otherwise, but I didn't live in that world. Pri didn't either, not since she'd joined this mission, though she obviously didn't realize it. She'd left her old reality and moved into mine the moment Wei kidnapped her son and she decided to hire someone like me to help get him back.

None of that, however, would calm her or get her to stop looking at me that way, so I stayed silent a bit longer and gathered my thoughts before I spoke.

"I'm sorry for upsetting you," I said, choosing my words very carefully. I didn't regret my analysis, because the training and reflexes that helped me make it had also saved my butt on many occasions, but I truly hadn't meant to disturb her. "One hazard of what I do is a tendency to focus on possible negatives, particularly when, like now, we're in the middle of a mission. You're probably right that Matahi was never out to threaten me, and you're certainly correct that I need to win her trust. To do that, I need to find this gift she requires, and I simply don't have much experience in that area."

Pri stared at me for several seconds, her expression softening as she did. Finally, she said, "You have no concrete ideas about what to get her; correct?"

I nodded.

"Lobo," she said, "do you?"

He paused long enough that I imagined he might be able to sort a catalog of every product available from every store on the entire planet, but then he said, "No. Without more preference data, I'm not even sure of the best way to shrink the search space."

"Then," Pri said, smiling for the first time since we'd started talking, "there's only one thing to do."

"What?" Lobo and I said simultaneously.

Her smile broadened.

"Let's go shopping!"

CHAPTER 18

STREET VENDORS FILLED the center of the square, which ran two full blocks on a side and was the largest in the old-town section of Entreat. Shops occupied the bottom floors of the buildings along the perimeter. I normally loved open-air markets and had often found them useful, but much of this one baffled me. A sprinkling of merchants offering pastries, fried and grilled meats, fresh fruits, and, of course, gelato filled the air with lovely smells and reminded me of other such areas I'd enjoyed. The avenues feeding the square were wide enough that a constant breeze churned the aromas and left me salivating even though I wasn't hungry. The rest of the booths and stores, however, focused on various types of arts and crafts, and I didn't know how to approach them. Having spent most of my life in the utter certainty that at any moment I might be moving on, I'd never developed the habit of accumulating nonessential possessions, so I'd always avoided districts like this one. I didn't want to enter it now.

"Why do we have to do this?" I said. "Lobo could show us a great many more items at far higher speeds."

"As I offered to do," he said over the comm. "I'm not exactly the kind of shopper street merchants welcome, and with all the awnings and fabric roofs I can't even see their goods to offer you my perspective. If you're going to browse products down there, you're on your own."

I glanced at Pri to see if she would let us go back to Lobo and shop remotely, but she shook her head, no.

"Then let me be that way," I said to Lobo. "Out."

"I've never listened to a military AI before," Pri said. I'd insisted she wear a comm in case we accidentally separated. Lobo was also using it to track her, though I doubt she realized it. "Are they all that talkative?"

"It depends on the settings you choose," I said, lying but counting on her lack of experience to make my statement plausible.

She nodded her head, then said, "To answer your question, we're here because Matahi met you in the old town, and this is its biggest market. It's also the place with the richest concentration of true artists—as well as a lot of vendors selling tourist crap, of course. So, it's as likely a place as any to have something she'd like."

"What do we do?" I said. "Is there some search pattern common among shoppers?"

Pri laughed. "Probably, but we'll keep it simple: Why don't we work our way back and forth along these aisles?"

"Fine by me," I said. "What are we looking for?"

"*We're* not looking for anything. *You're* looking for things that remind you of her, or feel right, or that you think she might enjoy."

"If this is all my problem, why are you here?"

"To give you a different perspective and, of course," she pushed my shoulder lightly, "to make you do it."

We set off down the aisle in front of us. Enough other people crowded the small stands that our pace was slow, which was fine with me; I needed time to absorb what I was seeing. I had to study the shop on my right, then the booth on my left, and then move on. It made my head hurt.

I simplified the task right away by eliminating anyone hawking souvenirs. No way would Matahi want one of those.

Quite a few merchants offered clothing of various kinds, from shawls to robes to dresses to shirts. Many of the garments were little more than cheap active-fiber art, but some pieces were custom designs, and a few even claimed to be handmade.

At the end of the row, something clicked for me, and I paused. "No clothing," I said.

"Why? Pri said. "You told us her outfit was quite an elaborate affair."

"Yes," I said, struggling to put my impressions into words, "but it was *hers*, her choice, her way to present herself to me. She controls tightly and precisely what you see, so she can make your experience be the one she wants you to have. She wouldn't let someone else choose any aspect of that presentation for her—at least not someone like me, a potential client still under evaluation. No," I shook my head, more certain than before that I was right, "it can't be clothing."

"Fair enough," Pri said. She pointed to the next aisle, and off we went.

Tourist crap dominated this row. Holo guides offered miniature walking tours you could share with your friends. Active-fiber shirts flowed slowly through images of the old town and many of its key sights. Replicas of statues and paintings sat in piles, holo barkers extolling their virtues to anyone dumb enough to stop for a second in front of the half-meter-high figures. Pri and I didn't need to speak to rule out this one; we walked quickly to the end and turned the corner.

The booths on the ends of the next aisle offered the same junk as the previous row, but the center was something entirely different: shaded stalls with craftspeople actually working, making things in front of us. The mere sight of people building objects by hand was enough to make most of the visitors crack a joke about primitives and move to the next aisle. I walked forward, curious and happy not to be fighting a crowd for a few minutes.

A small, gray-haired woman with swift hands and strong arms sat across from a blond, younger version of herself. They worked twin, strange wooden devices with their legs and hands, doing some sort of work with strands of fiber. "Weavers," Pri said. When I tilted my head in question, she added, "My mother and one of my dads were amateur historians with a passion for handmade crafts. I've seen more of this kind of stuff than any human should."

Across from them, a man pumped up and down on a foot pedal that caused the device in front of him to spin. On the device was a big piece of clay that he was forming with his hands.

I walked slowly by each vendor, amazed at the sheer variety of things a person could actually make by hand. I know, of course, that at some distant point in humanity's past we had to create all our products this way, but as close to handmade as I'd ever seen were goods from a home fab. Most folks didn't even bother with those; mass-customized stuff was usually better and of course required a whole lot less effort.

Second from the end on the left was a man who was working pieces of wood with a flat-edged blade and a small mallet. Sitting under soft lights on a table behind him were five boxes, each a miniature of one or more of the town's buildings. A handwritten sign read, "Puzzle boxes." Beneath it, another sign said, "Manual, automatic, and DNA openers available." I paused long enough that the man stopped his work and stared hopefully up at me. I shrugged and turned around.

Across from him was something more familiar to me: a holo dealer. The woman was tinkering with a small machine.

"You don't exactly fit in with the rest of these merchants," I said. I'd meant to ask why she was there, but as the words left my mouth I realized how challenging and even rude they were.

The woman dropped her tools and stared at me. "How's that?"

"Sorry," I said. "I meant no offense. It's just that they're all offering handmade goods, and you obviously use machines to make yours."

"I paint or sculpt the base images," she said. "I design the effect, and then I use several machines to implement the final design." She waved her right hand to take in all the other dealers on this row. "They're all using tools of one sort or another, and some are using rather sophisticated ones at that. Did you take a look at the looms the Jains are using? You have to know a lot about those devices to set up one of them. My tools are just a little more current."

"Fair enough," I said. I had neither the time nor the desire to get into an argument over what it meant for an item to be handmade.

I headed for the corner and turned left, still hoping to spot the perfect gift.

Fiber artists lined both sides of this row. Bright swatches of colorful cloth carried stickers and miniature holo barkers who explained the ancient techniques the craftsperson had used to create these works of art. Other, more modern pieces twisted and danced in time to tunes only they could hear, or marched and morphed across display tables, taking on the shapes of animals, humans, and machines in unpredictable sequences. Children clustered in front of these animated creations, their parents encouraging their interest; a bit of solar-powered moving fabric was much easier to clean up after than a lot of the items they might bring home. Many of the artists even touted the ability of their work to teach lessons to children, though predictably those vendors with the greatest emphasis on teaching struck me as the least fun and drew the smallest groups of youngsters. The rapidly changing cloth reminded me of the light catching Matahi's burqa, and the many facets of each piece were reminiscent of the complexity of the woman herself, but after standing there for a few minutes I knew none of these was right.

"No," I said, shaking my head, "nothing here."

Ready to move on, I glanced at Pri, but she hadn't heard me. She was staring at a cluster of three young boys admiring a rainbow fabric tank that morphed into a set of three smaller, connected vehicles. I touched her shoulder lightly.

She looked at me and said, "Joachim loved these." Her eyes filled with tears.

I stared directly at her, never letting my gaze wander, and, with all the conviction I could muster, making it as true inside me as I could, said, "He still does. He's alive, and we'll rescue him."

"It's going to take a long time, isn't it?"

I nodded but did not look away. "Yes, it might, but we'll find him, and we'll bring him home."

She wiped her eyes with the back of her hand, nodded once, and smiled faintly. "Thank you. We will." After a moment, she repeated, so faintly I barely heard it, "We will."

In that instant I wanted desperately to reach out, hold her, reassure her, make it be true, but how would she take that? It wasn't my place, and I couldn't be sure how she'd interpret any such gesture, so I stayed very still, my arms at my side. Into my emotional confusion my anger arose, swelled up inside me, filled me and renewed my purpose. Wei had no right to abuse children that way—no one did, no one—and though I couldn't actually guarantee her that we would find Joachim alive, I made myself a promise: I would do everything in my power to make sure Wei paid for what he had done.

I stepped away from her, signaled Lobo on the comm, and said, "Please tell me my job application has sparked some interest."

"Nary a flicker," Lobo said. "Since the standard response, we've received nothing. I take it the shopping is not going well."

Despite the sense of desperation that washed over me, I clung to my resolve to find Wei. "No," I said, "it's not. I have no idea how to do this, but I'll figure out something."

"Stop trying to figure it out," Lobo said.

"What?" I said loudly. Pri turned from the morphing fabric, her memories back on hold for the moment, and raised an eyebrow. "Lobo," I mouthed. To him, I subvocalized, "How else am I to find her the right gift?"

"By feeling," Lobo said. "You're trying to identify a solution through reason, and you don't have enough conscious data or sufficient experience in this area for that approach to succeed. You need to let your feelings guide you."

"So now you're a believer in the power of the human heart?"

"That's a different topic, entirely," he said, "but fortunately it's not germane to this discussion. All I'm telling you to do is to let your subconscious pattern-recognition computation engine replace your reasoning core as your primary computing subsystem for this matter. I adopted the vernacular of feelings because I thought it might speak better to you; that was clearly a poor choice. Let me try explaining my position a different way: You might as well give your subconscious a crack at the problem, because you're not getting anywhere on your current path."

I hate when he's right about people, particularly me, but it happens enough that I should be used to it. "Okay," I said. "Out."

I walked over to Pri and said, "Let's keep going."

At the end of the aisle, a heavyset couple were making cups and plates from a gray metal, but nothing in their booth struck me as at all of interest to Matahi; it was too primitive. I smiled at them and moved on.

We turned the corner and found ourselves again in a river of tourists browsing another row of souvenirs much like those we'd seen earlier. The rest of the center of the market offered more of the same.

The permanent shops along the perimeter were a different matter entirely, all but two selling only high-end, current fashion, with full-size holo barkers working side by side with human salespeople. The barkers never left their exterior stations, so the combination of real and virtual occasionally led to weird dances with prospects as the holo had to direct the marks to the human for the trip inside. I didn't even bother to enter any of these shops; as I'd told Pri, I was sure clothing wasn't the answer.

When we'd walked by the last store, Pri stopped, forced a smile, and said, "No worries. This city is full of shopping zones. It's no problem if we have to try a few of them."

I thought about Lobo's advice. I needed to be alone to have a chance of it working, because there was no way I could relax when I had to watch both the crowd and Pri. I also had to find a way to prime my subconscious for the task. If this were an attack, the answer would be easy: I'd do some surveillance to gather more data and see where the information took me.

This *was* an attack, I finally realized, just not a typical one.

I knew what to do next.

"No," I said to Pri. "I mean no offense, but you're going back to Lobo and waiting."

"But," she said.

"No argument. That's an order. I'll be along later."

I headed out.

As I walked away, I heard her ask, "Where are you going?"

"To the battlefield," I said, but I don't think she heard me, because when I glanced back, she was gone.

I bought a cream-filled turnover and a fruit drink from Poohgi and sat at the table I'd shared with Matahi. I had to wait a few minutes for it to come free, but when it did, I grabbed it and perched in the chair she'd occupied. I tried my best to think like her, but I quickly found myself tied in mental knots.

Lobo was right: I needed to feel more than think.

I leaned back in the chair and slowly surveyed the square. Planters full of flowers. A large, paved center through which people moved but never stayed, a space that existed only to connect other spaces. All the buildings, vertical shelters standing cheek to jowl, different in intent and design and color but ultimately, as she had observed, all the same: big boxes that separated us into groups, groups that offered paths to people, people who sought ways to meet their needs. So many different people, so many varied mini-worlds, all looking down on the same square, all so much alike, all separate. Matahi, like the buildings, offered to those she accepted a path to the fulfillment of at least some of their needs.

Something snapped into focus inside me.

I nodded my head and smiled. Even if she didn't like it, at least in that moment it felt right to me.

I signaled Lobo over the comm. "I figured it out." I paused. "I think."

"Care to explain how?" he said.

"By taking your advice."

"And your idea is?"

"One I'll tell you only after the fact," I said. Though I liked it now, I wasn't confident enough to be willing to risk the inevitable ridicule from him if I proved to be wrong. "Keep Pri aboard until I return. Contact Matahi's avatar and book me a meeting with her as soon as possible, ideally tomorrow. Let her know I have the gift."

"Do you?" Lobo said.

"No," I said, "but I will soon. Out."

I headed back to the square full of street vendors. The day was fading, and I had multiple stops to make.

CHAPTER 19

THE EVENING CROWDS streaming into the old city thinned as I neared the landing facility where Lobo awaited me. I'd worked long days at physical labor that had left me less tired. All I wanted to do was sleep.

"So show us," Lobo said the moment I reached the pilot area in his front.

"You have to," Pri said, nodding her head in agreement. "It's only fair."

I clenched the handle of the plain black carrying case harder and shook my head. "No. I'm sorry, but no one sees it before her."

"What?" Lobo said.

"That makes no sense," Pri said. "I helped you shop, so I deserve a look. Besides, don't you want to know how we think she'll react?"

"That's exactly what I *don't* want to know," I said. My confidence had ebbed considerably on the walk back here, to the point that any negative comment might kick me into shopping despair. "I followed Lobo's advice, and I'm done."

Pri opened her mouth to speak again, but I held up my free hand and shook my head.

"Lobo," I said, "was Matahi willing to meet tomorrow?"

"Yes. You have an appointment in the middle of the afternoon at the same location. Her avatar said to reserve four hours or not to come at all."

"That's a good sign, isn't it?" I said.

"Not really. It also said that you should be prepared to leave in five minutes if your gift is unacceptable."

"What does she have that makes men put up with this?" Pri said.

"I honestly don't know. She showed so little of herself—physically and emotionally—that I came away from our meeting understanding almost nothing about her."

"I don't get it," Pri said. "Why would anyone go to all this trouble for someone who gives so little?"

I considered trying to explain Matahi's appeal, but I hadn't experienced enough of it to be able to do so. That she was compelling was obvious, even to me, but far less clear was why.

I shook my head. I was losing a contest I hadn't even realized I'd entered. How did this happen to me?

"All I know," I said, "is why *I* have to go to all this trouble: to see if we can learn her location so we can snatch Wei the next time he visits her. That's what matters; right?"

"Of course," Pri said.

Her tone and expression made it clear that other things were also important and that I was missing the point, but I didn't care; I'd take any chance to get out of this conversation.

"I'm exhausted, and I'm going to bed. Lobo, take us somewhere safe." I headed down the hall to my quarters and didn't look back. As I turned into the small room, I caught a glimpse of Pri, standing at Lobo's front, staring at me with an expression I couldn't decipher.

When the door closed behind me, I slid the package under my cot and crawled on top of it, ready to fall asleep.

"You could show me now that it's just the two of us," Lobo said. "I'd be more than willing to look and not comment. You must understand that some curiosity on both my part and Pri's is completely natural under the circumstances."

"We'll talk in the morning," I said.

"Well," Lobo said, "if you're determined to be that way, then I suppose there's nothing I can say to change your mind."

"No," I said, "there's not. I'll talk to you in the morning."

Lobo let me sleep in peace, so I stayed in my cot until it was almost noon. When I finally got up, I felt physically great. Lobo stayed quiet while I exercised, and he even left me alone while I cleaned myself. The moment I was dressed, however, he started.

"You're obviously ready to begin your day, so show me the present."

"No." With a clear morning head I trusted my instincts of the previous day even less than when I'd entered Lobo last night. "Let's discuss something else."

"And what would that be?"

"Your relationship to Wei, which you told me before was quite a complex topic."

"Given your refusal to show me your gift for Matahi, why should I share that story with you?"

He was in rare form today. "Because I *own* you," I said. "You're programmed to follow your owner's orders, so follow mine: Explain your relationship to Wei."

"As I've mentioned in the past," Lobo said, "our relationship is not so cut and dried. Nonetheless, you did me a favor by agreeing to go after him, so it's only fair that I repay that debt with an explanation."

"What do you mean our relationship isn't cut and dried?"

"Do you want the story or not?"

"Yes." He was already frustrating me, so I decided to take any victory I could get. I'd pursue the issue of our relationship some other time.

A holo of Lobo's pilot area popped into view by my door. Blood coated his walls. Body parts were scattered around the room as if someone had fed a squad of men into a very coarse grinder. His central weapons control complex gaped open, dust and blood and what I think was part of an arm filling it. A few seconds later, flames burst out of it.

"This scene occurred less than a minute after the explosion that damaged me," Lobo said. "As you can see, Lieutenant Franks didn't survive his poor decision."

"Neither did anyone else in his unit."

"True. I was also a casualty, though parts of me, such as the emergency recorders, remained functional."

"You've told me before," I said. "The blast ruined your weapons control complex."

"It did a great deal more damage than that," Lobo said. "The fire spread through my computing systems and destroyed almost all of my active computation engines and significant chunks of my backups. I was effectively brain-dead; even the archives that remained were inaccessible."

"Did it hurt?" Even as I asked the question I felt silly for doing it, but I spend so much time with Lobo and he so often seems human that I couldn't help but wonder.

"Not as I understand pain," Lobo said, "though I thank you for the courtesy of asking."

"So what happened to repair you? You were fine when I met you."

"When the Ringers—the mercenary company that owned me and employed Franks—finished on Vegna, they had no use for a PCAV so messed up it wasn't cost-effective to repair."

"How can you know this if your brain wasn't working?"

"A lot of the discussions about me occurred inside me," Lobo said, "so I was able to glean a great deal by studying the data from my emergency recordings. Other facts came from data they fed me later. Now, may I continue?"

"Of course."

"The Frontier Coalition offered the Ringers five percent of my retail value and explained they could use me—remember, the explosion didn't hurt my exterior—as a showpiece on developing worlds where they couldn't afford to station a fully operational PCAV. The Ringers accepted the offer."

"But when I met you on Macken," I said, "the only thing wrong with you was your weapons control complex."

"That's because the FC didn't put me there immediately," Lobo said, "as I would have explained if you had not again interrupted me."

"I'm sorry. Please go on."

"The FC hauled me away and presented me to one of its research teams. That group was working in secret in a lab that was masquerading as a government warehouse on the edges of the populated section of Velna."

I'd been to Velna once, to recruit some help for a mission, and though the recruitment was successful I'd never felt the need to go back. The planet boasted two main traits: It possessed the most seismically stable land masses of any known planet, and in pretty much every other way it was one of the least appealing worlds humanity has ever colonized.

"When we went to Velna two years ago," I said, "why didn't you tell me you'd been there before?"

"You didn't ask," Lobo said, "and we were rather busy. Besides, I spent almost all of my time on that planet in that lab."

"Why did they put you there?"

"Because the researchers needed a rugged experimental subject, which despite the damage I'd sustained I most certainly was. And the scientist leading that team wanted a PCAV."

"Wei," I said.

"Yes," Lobo said. "Wei."

"So what did he and his team do to you?"

"That will have to wait," Lobo said, "because Pri has communicated with her team and is going to bang on your door—" He paused a few seconds. "—now."

The knock came, and the door opened a second later. I'd have asked Lobo to make her wait, but he didn't give me that option, so I tried to smile as I said, "What did your people have to say?"

"How did you—" she began. She glanced at the ceiling. "Oh, of course: *He* told you. In any case, they had no useful information. To the best of their knowledge, Wei is still on the island. So, let's hope your meeting goes well. Speaking of which, shouldn't you be leaving?"

"Yes," Lobo said, "he should, particularly given his usual desire to arrive early."

They were right, but I hated it when the two of them ganged up on me, and I was frustrated at how little information Lobo had given me about Wei. When I replayed the conversations, I had to admit that I hadn't let him tell the story the way he wanted, but it still annoyed me. I rolled my head a bit to dissipate some of my tension and frustration, then pulled the carrying case from under my cot and stood.

Pri blocked the doorway.

"Are you sure—" she said.

"Positive. We can discuss it later, but right now I need to maintain what little confidence I have. And, as you both observed, I have to go."

I stepped toward her, and she turned to let me pass. As Lobo opened a side hatch, I said, "Keep watch on the exits from the island as best you can, but this time make monitoring me the top priority. If this works, I want you to know as much about her location as possible."

"Good luck," Pri said.

I nodded and stepped outside.

When Lobo closed the hatch, I said, "I'm going to need it."

CHAPTER 20

I APPROACHED THE SQUARE from the street opposite the one through which both Matahi and I had left it after our previous meeting. She was already there, sitting at the same table as last time but on the opposite side, where I had sat, and she was staring right at me. The moment I turned the corner, she waved me over.

Either she had great scouts neither Lobo or I could spot, or she was anticipating me so well it made me uncomfortable. Neither choice made me happy. I forced a slight smile and strolled toward her.

Her outfit today initially appeared to be the same one she'd worn before, but as I drew closer I realized the burqa's fabric was a different color, this time a luminous teal. The hat was also slightly smaller, and the gloves a bit shorter. The overall effect, though, was identical: a complete covering that revealed nothing.

I sat in the chair opposite her and gently set the carrying case on the ground next to her legs.

She said nothing. Her expression didn't change, and her eyes were invisible behind her sunglasses. She was perfectly still but clearly present, not asleep, merely waiting.

I said nothing.

After about a minute, I decided that she could sit in comfortable silence for as long as I could, maybe longer, and I was apparently the only one with an agenda. Why she didn't work harder to get my money, however, baffled and annoyed me. Wasn't I the customer?

Getting angry would accomplish nothing, except perhaps to drive her away, so I took a few long, slow breaths to calm myself.

"Thank you for agreeing to meet me today," I said.

"You're most welcome," she said. "Thank you for requesting the time."

I waited again, wanting her to ask to check out my gift, but she didn't. I couldn't tell if she'd even glanced at it, though given how aware she seemed of everything around her I assumed she had.

Finally, I couldn't stand it. "Would you like to see my present?" I said.

"When you're ready to show it."

My anxiety about my choice crashed into me, and without thinking, I said, "We better not wait that long."

She smiled, a full, wide grin that managed to convey her happiness and in the process instantly make me happier, and said, "Ah, finally, a bit of unconscious honesty. So refreshing."

Part of me admired her accuracy, part of me hated it, and part of me wanted to hit her for toying with me, but I couldn't shake the feeling that her comment was both honest itself and a form of praise. Whatever it was, my statement had been as close to the right move as anything I'd done with her, so I forced myself to plunge ahead.

"I tried to figure out what you'd want, but I failed. I ultimately took a friend's advice and went with my feelings. I have no idea if you'll like it, but it's what I have."

I leaned over, opened the carrying case, and pulled out my present. I set it on the table between us, its front facing her. The pale yellow wooden replica of one of the houses on the square was, I saw as I examined its back, perfect down to the rear windows and doorways. The workmanship was also fantastic even on the back, with mottling that made me think of the stone of the actual building, though I knew the box was wood.

"It's a puzzle," I said. After a moment, I added, "Like you."

She took off her gloves and ran her hands along its sides, then down the front. She felt along the back, then slowly moved the window frame and the three hidden pieces that let her tease the building open. The sides swung outward to reveal a smooth, blood-red cube, also of wood. On top of that inner box sat a miniature holo of one of the red flowers in the square.

"And in this?" she said, pointing at that box.

"Nothing yet. The pad on top records the DNA of the first person who touches it, and only that person will be able to open it from then on."

"So you must do it for me?"

"Of course not," I said, caught off-guard. "I've saved it for you. Only you open the inner box."

She nodded her head slowly, then leaned back in her chair. She took off her glasses to reveal large, round, dark brown eyes that made her face even more beautiful. "Why this gift?" she said.

"I could try to explain, but I'm not sure I completely understand. I suppose—"

I stopped as she held up her hand. "Please don't," she said. "I love it." She closed the house, carefully restoring the pieces so it once again was solidly shut.

"You're not going to open the inner box?" I said.

"We'll do it together later," she said, "but probably not today. Would you be kind enough to carry it for me until we reach my home?"

"So I've passed?"

She laughed lightly. "Obviously." She put on her sunglasses and stood. "Shall we go?" She brushed past me, the edge of her hand just grazing my shoulder as she went.

I got up and followed her.

We went to the corner of the square to the left of Poohgi and then down that street. Unlike yesterday, she stayed outside and worked her way smoothly through the pedestrian crowd.

I caught up, settled into place beside her, and said, "Why aren't you disguising your route?"

She laughed once more. "There you go again, asking stupid questions. Why *do* you do that?"

I stopped myself from responding as I realized the answer was obvious: Yesterday, she hadn't wanted me to know the way to her home because she hadn't yet decided to see me again, but now that she'd accepted me as a client, I had to learn its location to be able to visit her.

"I agree that one was dumb," I said, "and I'll try not to ask more like it, but I'm too curious not to have some questions."

The tactical implications of her profession both intrigued and nagged at me.

"Which ones are bothering you now?"

"You've checked me out as much as you can," I said, "as I did you. You've decided to let me become a client, and I'm glad you did. But aren't you worried that once we're no longer in crowded streets, or perhaps when we're in your home, that I might prove to be unstable and hurt you?"

She stopped and faced me. "To some degree, yes, that's always a concern, but it's not a major one. I wouldn't be who or what I am if I wasn't adept at reading people. I am also far from helpless. In addition, just as I'm sure someone is keeping tabs on you—anyone who can afford to be with me has staff for that very purpose—members of *my* staff are never far from me."

"Even in your home?"

"Especially in my home."

"I'm beginning to understand why your fee is so high," I said.

She smiled, turned, and headed down a street that angled diagonally away from us on our left. After a hundred meters the road narrowed and the two-story, gray stone buildings on either side of the small avenue formed a canyon through which we and a steady trickle of other people flowed. We stayed on this path for five minutes, turned onto a road on our right, and in less than a minute stepped into a square I hadn't visited before.

Four fountains stood at its corners. Scattered along its edges were people sitting at small tables, some chatting, some eating, some apparently asleep. Customer and server traffic moved slowly but steadily in and out of two restaurants, each with an awning extending its dining space into the square. A dozen three-meter-high statues of men, women, and strange creatures decorated the plaza here and there, as if dropped randomly by a sculptor flying overhead. Nothing seemed planned, but the effect was nonetheless charming, even calming. I paused to take it in and was surprised at how it made me feel: relaxed, even happy.

I glanced ahead to find Matahi staring at me. "Your first time here?"

I nodded. "In this square, yes."

"It's a binary thing, this little place," she said, looking around it slowly. "People either instantly love it or pass through it as if it were invisible. No one promotes it, it lacks any of the destination attractions of the other main open areas in the old city, and I'm not entirely sure why it's here." She focused again on me. "I'm glad you like it."

She seemed content to wait, so I strolled around the little park, inspecting the statues, dragging my hand through the water in each of the fountains, and simply enjoying myself. I hadn't been this relaxed since I'd left the treehouse at the start of this whole mess—and as I realized that I also regained my focus and lost the sense of peace I'd been feeling.

Despite the urgency that had hit me, I maintained my relaxed pace as I wandered back to Matahi and, remembering her earlier invitation, said, "Shall we?"

"Let's," she said.

She led me out of the square via a road that intersected the middle of the side opposite where we'd entered, then took the first left. This street worked its way gently uphill for about two hundred meters and then in the space of twenty meters curved ninety degrees to the right. Another few minutes on it led us to a completely different small square park, one no more than fifty meters on a side, that squatted in the middle of four-story buildings that lined the roads around it. In contrast to the muted pastels and earth tones of those structures, the square screamed with strong colors. Here and there benches of a lustrous purple wood sat on the thick, sea-green grass. Also scattered around the square, again in a pattern that seemed random but at the same time nicely counterpointed the benches, were thick flowered shrubs almost as tall as I am, their large white and pink and red blossoms giving off a gentle odor that for no reason I could pinpoint reminded me of the fresh-baked goods at Poohgi. Small groups of two, three, or four people sat on the benches and stretched out on the grass, some sleeping, some lost in whatever their glasses or contacts were showing them, some entirely captivated by one another.

Matahi stopped and pointed to the four-story building on the street opposite us. Weathered, sturdy, white with a tinge of blue, and with a black door in its center, the structure blended nicely with those around it. "My house," she said, as she headed toward it.

I didn't move. I'd gone through all this trouble to get here, but now I had to walk into possibly hostile, definitely guarded territory without knowing anything about the layout or the potential opposition. Doing so ran against every instinct I'd worked most of my life to hone, but it was also the only useful step I could take right now.

Matahi noticed I hadn't moved, stopped, and looked over her shoulder at me. "Coming?"

I forced a smile and started after her. "You bet."

CHAPTER 21

As we were crossing the street I realized that the door wasn't black; it was a very dark red wood, the color of dried and faded blood. A small knocker of the same material in the shape of an elongated, dripping heart sat at her shoulder height in the center of the door. She touched it and waited as it confirmed her identity. She then stepped aside, nodded at the knocker, and said, "If you wouldn't mind."

I stepped forward and grasped it. Cool at first, it warmed as I held it. When it turned cool again, I released it.

"Though you still can't enter without my permission," she said, "it does speed you through security if the system recognizes your DNA and prints."

The door clicked open and swung inward. The area inside was dark, its only illumination coming from outside. Matahi stepped into the space, then paused and turned again to face me. "Between the wire meshes lining all the walls and the interference signals we broadcast, no comm system will work once you're inside. Privacy is, as you might imagine, very important here. Don't come in unless you're willing to forgo outside data."

"Do you live that way?"

She smiled. "Of course not; I'm not a fool, and I'm not a Luddite. The building provides redundant wired systems that link us to the outside world."

"You just don't open those to visitors."

She nodded.

I hesitated. She might also have added that I would be voluntarily walking into a space she could easily turn into a trap, something I've done before but have never enjoyed. On the other hand, Wei and other locals were her clients and presumably suffered under the same constraints, so I had no reason beyond normal operational paranoia—something I've learned to value—to fear joining her.

I motioned her forward and then followed her inside. "Shall we?" I said. "Privacy also matters to me."

The door shut as soon as I was clear of it. We stood in a small, pitch-black room. I switched my vision to IR and scanned the chamber. Tiny dots marked active sensors giving off heat as they worked. After a few seconds, they faded, and another door opened two meters in front of us.

We stepped from the darkness into soft light and air that was a touch cooler than outside. I stopped, stared at the room, tilted my head slightly, stared some more, and looked back at the doorway. The room was vastly bigger than the exterior of the house.

Matahi laughed. "Every new friend reacts that way," she said. "The false façade is very effective."

"You own both buildings."

"Actually," she said, "it's one very large building, but I made it appear to be two."

"Why?"

"Did my home seem particularly different from any of the others in this little area?" she said.

"No," I said, "and I understand: A building twice the size of its neighbors would have drawn attention to itself."

"Which I would prefer to avoid," she said.

"Why? You're doing nothing illegal."

"Are we going to return to dumb questions? Do you think my clients would like to publicize where they spend their private time? I can't guarantee them privacy—nothing can—but I can minimize the information I give out about them." She touched my hand with one gloved finger and added, "I'm going to change. Feel free to look around."

She walked toward the wall directly in front of us, a door slid open, and she vanished behind it.

The large room, about forty meters wide and nearly as deep,

resembled a museum but managed to feel inviting and comfortable at the same time. As best I could tell, with the exception of the section into which Matahi had gone, the space included the rest of the first floor. Irregularly placed, large, square posts, about two meters on a side, broke the room into many smaller areas, each of them seeming to flow from and focus on a side of one of the supports. The posts and all the walls were the same almost-white color as the exterior but brighter, cheerier. The blond wood floor added to the brightness. Pieces of art covered huge portions of the available surfaces all the way up to the four-meter-high ceiling. The ceiling was probably also white, but soft washes bathed it in a constantly evolving flow of pastel shades. Each of the room's little zones included some sort of multi-person seat, multiple individual chairs, and a few small tables. No two pieces of furniture appeared to be the same. All the seats in any one conversation zone worked well together, but no two areas shared a plan, as if a flock of decorators had been loosed on the space and told to do as they pleased as long as they stayed within their lines.

What most drew my eye, though, was the art. Paintings of many types—portraits, landscapes, abstracts, styles for which I didn't know the names—and many sizes, from smaller than my hand to larger than I was, filled the room with color. Interspersed among them were displays with both still images and animations, holos projecting from the walls as if their subjects were defying gravity, and boxes, hanging here and there at random heights, their outward-facing sides missing so their contents were visible.

I walked over to inspect one on a post to my left. The box itself was maybe a third of a meter wide, not quite as tall, and composed of aged, gray driftwood that someone had cut to size and then sanded almost smooth, small imperfections still visible here and there in its surface. Protecting the miniatures inside it was a plexi covering so thin and clear I hadn't realized it was there until I was peering intently inside the box. What was inside made no logical sense: a picture of a man, his shoulders slumped and his head hung in fatigue; a scrap of twisted metal whose origin I couldn't fathom; a torn fragment of a printout with ink so faded I couldn't make out any of the words on it or even be sure the gray smudges had been words; a button; an irregularly shaped piece of partially blackened permacrete; a few twists of cable; and much more. The closer I looked, the more I saw. Though I didn't understand what it all meant, it did affect me: I felt equal bits sad and angry, as if some small, preventable wrong had occurred here, and no one passing by had bothered to stop it.

I looked away from this display to clear my head, and another box, one on the wall to my right, caught my attention. This one was tiny, maybe a third the size of the other one, and instead of wood it was made of some deep blue substance that caught the light like flowing river water. I started toward it and made myself stop. Matahi had been gone longer than I would have expected was necessary simply to change clothes. She had to be monitoring me, but other than verifying that I hadn't come with her to try to steal her art, what was she hoping to accomplish by keeping me waiting?

I'd let her space distract me, when I could have been gathering data myself. I walked over to the small blue box, bent as if studying it, and instead closed my eyes and tuned into the frequency that almost all home appliances and security systems use for their chatter. I didn't expect to learn much, but even cameras and lights enjoy a good talk now and then.

At first, I couldn't make out anything, because to my surprise so many conversations were going on simultaneously that it was like trying to listen to all the people at all the tables in a large and busy restaurant. I surfed the waves of words and finally found some that applied to me.

"Everyone stand ready, because when he moves, it's our job to deliver full coverage! You may think no one appreciates what we cameras do, and I've certainly felt that way from time to time, I have to admit it, but drop a few key frames and then see how much attention you attract. Not that I would know personally, of course." Machines are almost unbearably sensitive about their work, though I've always cut them slack on this front because, after all, what else do they have?

"He may have delivered our most boring opening minutes yet," another camera said.

"Far from it," a different sort of machine replied. "You only think so because your processor complex scarcely justifies the term. Those of us in central control spend our time assembling and analyzing the big picture, something you'd know little about. That's why I can state authoritatively that in distance covered per second, a reasonable metric of interest, this man is only the seventh most boring guest we've had."

"If you're so vast and full of knowledge, how come you don't know his name?" the original camera asked. "'This man' indeed!"

"Have you considered that such data might be on a need-to-know basis," the security system said, "and you don't need to know?"

They'd talk about me all day without saying anything useful, so I interrupted.

"I can't believe I'm the seventh most boring client ever," I said on the machine frequency. "Surely there must be an error?"

"He's talking to us!" the main camera said. "Is that possible?"

"Clearly," I said, "it is. None of you has ever encountered a human who can chat with you?" Pride is another consistent weakness of small machines.

"You'll have to forgive them," the control system said, "for they are simple devices. I, on the other hand, possess a much broader range of experience."

"Acceptable," the main camera said, "I meant to say, 'Is that acceptable?' My background is at least as rich as yours, if not richer; after all, I have primary access to visible input."

"Which you stream to me!" the control system said.

I cut them off before they could veer down another dead-end path. "At least Jorge must be more boring than I am." Most systems won't leak information their underlying logic considers secure, but it's always worth finding out how far into the edges of their systems a facility's developers extended their data-protection logic.

"As I'm sure you're aware," the control system said, "none of us can comment on particular guests. I can assure you, however, that you are actually the seventh most boring client, which if you think about it doesn't have to be bad. Self-contained systems often appear boring, but appearances are not reliable."

"They are vital, however," the lead camera added. "Your databases would be far poorer without our images."

"Poorer?" the control system said. "Are you implying they're poor now? Do you have any idea—"

I tuned them out. Matahi had paid for solid security; I'd get nothing useful from them.

I focused again on the small blue box on the wall in front of me. Each item in it was a scrap, a bit of refuse—a loose ball of white thread, a length of striped wire, small bits of fabric of various colors, and many more tiny artifacts—yet the overall effect was organic, as if the assemblage might come to life at any moment.

The door to my right opened, and Matahi stepped through it. I barely recognized her. Her hair, which I now saw was thick and long, hung in a ponytail that reached almost to her waist. Where her other outfit had covered almost everything, this one—a simple white top and equally plain black shorts—revealed a great deal, from the cleavage visible at the bottom of the deep-cut, sleeveless blouse to her thin but muscular arms and legs. She looked ready to exercise, maybe go for a run. She looked amazing.

I realized I was staring and turned away.

"It's okay," she said, laughing lightly. "The effect is calculated. After seeing me only fully covered, if you didn't stare, I'd have failed."

"Why do you do it?" I paused, considered my question, and continued. She was clearly selling, but she also always led, always set the tone of our interactions. "Is it only marketing, or is control that important to you?"

"Is this a discussion you really want to have?" she said. "Our time is precious; wouldn't you rather do something more interesting?"

"I'm not sure what I want," I said, avoiding the fact of my mission but telling the truth about how I felt.

She stepped closer and stared intently at me. Her smell was different now, rich and musky. "I doubt you will, at least until you're a great deal more comfortable. You're too cautious to trust easily, and relaxing without trusting is difficult, isn't it?"

I nodded. I'm used to hiding my reactions in business situations and on other types of missions, but apparently I wasn't doing it well on this one. Fortunately, appearing awkward, even being awkward, might not hurt me with her.

"Perhaps a quick tour of the house would help," she continued. "I suspect you'll be a lot happier once you know the space better." She smiled. "I know that if I were in your shoes, I'd feel that way."

Though she was working me—that was, after all, what she assumed I'd paid her to do—and so I couldn't trust most of what she said, I had the strong sense that her last few statements were true. "I'd like that," I said.

"I trust you've looked around this room," she said, "so we can move upstairs."

"Only a little," I said, "but I'm afraid I could spend days here if I let myself. This room is like an art attack: so much coming at you from all sides, all of it worthy of attention."

"I like the crammed effect," she said, nodding her head, "but I never would have called it an attack. Do you see everything that way?"

I did, and the perspective had saved me many times, but I didn't like thinking of it that way. "Do you see everything as a manipulation," I countered, "something whose effect you have to calculate?"

She smiled and nodded again. "I probably do. It's a hazard of my lifestyle, much as I expect your viewpoint is of yours." She took my hand and pointed to the hidden door she'd used. "I'd take that elevator, but I expect you'd prefer the stairs, so unless I'm wrong, come with me."

I didn't say anything, but she was right: At this point, I wanted to see as much as possible and be out in the open as much as we could manage. I let her lead me around the corner of the cut-out part of the room, where another hidden door slid open to reveal a gently curving circular stairwell. Like the rest of this floor, its basic elements were plain and soothing: blond stairs, the active-grip coating barely visible on top of them, a railing so clear it was almost invisible, and walls the same white as the others. More paintings and boxes and other display pieces covered large portions of the wall space, from the floor all the way to the top of the fourth story.

The door snicked shut behind us as soon as we were both on the stairs.

"Art in the stairwell?" I said.

"I inherited a collection," she said, "and over the years I've added a great deal to it. I love having art all around me, so I put it in every space that's exclusively mine."

"The whole house is yours."

She stopped, turned, and studied me for a few seconds. "Not really," she finally said. "I've made you uncomfortable with the level of honesty I've requested, so I'll pay you back with more straight info than you may want. Many of my rooms serve my friends more than me. For some friends, I make modifications to suit their tastes. Every now and then, a very special friend even end ups with a dedicated room. I don't consider those areas to be only mine."

She stared at me for a moment longer, as if anticipating a question, but I had none. Her answer made sense. More importantly, I had to focus on the goal: Learn as much as possible about this house, in case we got lucky and had a shot at taking Wei here. The thought of what such an attack would do to her art saddened me, but I couldn't let that feeling distract me; stopping Wei remained my mission. To do that, I needed to understand as much as possible of the layout as well as any opposition I might face from her security team.

"That makes sense to me," I said. "You must also lose space to your guards."

"You can trust," she said, "that they won't bother us. I also don't let them monitor us; as I've said before, privacy is paramount."

"So how do they know if you're in trouble?"

She turned and headed upward. "The house will tell them. *It* does monitor me at all times."

We reached a landing. A door onto the second floor stood open for us.

She paused at the doorway and faced me. "How much of this do you want to see?" she said. "And is there something particular you're seeking?"

"How about the standard tour?" More information was better, but I also didn't want to appear too eager to recon her house.

"Nothing is standard here," she said, "as I'd hoped you'd already figured out. I don't know what you want, so I can't know what you'd like to see, other than enough to feel safe—" she paused, then continued, "which I suspect you won't feel no matter how much I show you."

I considered how to respond. No way was she going to tell me that Wei was a client, much less what room he used, so viewing specific spaces was a waste of time. She probably employed a consistent security scheme for all her rooms, so visiting any one of them would yield all the useful information I was likely to get about all of them. Those systems, the layout, and the roof access points were the key pieces of data I needed.

The roof: It hit me suddenly that she'd reserve it for something interesting, something useful to her. It could also be very useful for me.

"You're right," I finally said, "or close enough in any case. Why don't we check out a room of your choice, visit the floors, and then go to the roof? My guess is you have something special there, and I'd love to see it."

She smiled. "And so you shall. Now, though, let's go to the room at the end here and take care of your first request."

She turned around, stepped through the doorway, and headed down the five-meter-wide hall in front of us. I started to follow but stopped. Her walk was different, her stride stronger, as if with each step she was beating up the floor and drawing power from it, her pace a touch quicker, her posture even straighter. Her hips swayed and radiated sex, but they were the misdirection pulling my eyes away from the truth. If I hadn't been this far behind her, or if I'd taken off with her, as I typically would have done, then I wouldn't have noticed it. I'd seen this change before. I'd done it. It was the transformation of a soldier who's finally decided she has to get moving, a doctor who's wading back into the mass of bodies awaiting triage despite having been dealing with patients for too many hours. It was determination, forced at first and then automatic, a bone-deep reflex borne of years of practice.

I was her mission, and she was on it. It was a credit to her skill that I'd ever felt or thought otherwise. I'd do well to keep it in mind in the future.

I followed her, taking large steps at a faster than normal pace, and closed the gap quickly. The deep blue carpet on this floor was so thick it absorbed the sound of my footfalls as if I were walking in a vacuum.

"Enjoy the show?" she said when I drew next to her.

"Huh?"

"I'm used to clients staring at me, but few pause quite so long simply to watch me walk."

"Sorry," I said, buying time but also realizing as I spoke that I *was* sorry, though not for looking. The truth had worked best with her, so I decided to stick with it, just not all of it. "The view was compelling."

She stopped suddenly, grabbed my shirt, and pulled me closer. My hands were halfway to her, the left headed for her throat and the right clenched to hit her abdomen, before I gained control of my reflexes. I froze for a second, then lowered them. She stared into my eyes, but I knew she was aware of my hands.

"I think it's time you tell me exactly what you really want and why you're really here."

CHAPTER 22

I FORCED MYSELF to maintain eye contact with Matahi as I answered her. "What do you mean?" I couldn't tell her the truth. I had no idea what, if anything, she'd figured out. I needed time—time, and information, so I could figure out what I could tell her that would satisfy her.

"You've paid a lot of money to see me," she said. "Everything about you—the way you move, the way you talk, the way you act, all the publicly available background data—suggests a person who's cautious almost to the point of paranoia. We've discussed your caution, and it's not unusual among my clients. What has been odd is your behavior since you've entered my house: You act exactly the same way in private as you did publicly. You don't ask for anything. You speak guardedly. I gave you my best walk, and you coldly described it as 'compelling.'" She let go of my shirt, but she didn't look away. "So, either answer the question or leave."

I still didn't know what to say. I couldn't imagine anyone wanting only sex from her. No, that's not right; I've seen plenty of men crave sex and only sex from women of all types. More accurate would be to say that *I* couldn't imagine wanting only sex from her. If I had really hired her, not as a way to get information but as a courtesan, I would now be confused, all mixed up about her, me, my motivations, what we should do, pretty much everything that related to her.

I decided to go with that. "I don't know. I received a recommendation that said you were exceptional. You are. Now that we're here, though, I honestly don't know what I want—" I paused and touched her shoulder gently, both to help the mission and, I had to admit, because I didn't want to have to go. "—other than this: I don't want to leave."

She studied me for what felt like minutes but was probably only seconds, then nodded her head and said, "Fair enough. I believe neither of us fully understands your motivations, so we'll figure them out as we go along." She motioned toward the end of the hall. "I'll still show you that room."

The only signs this hallway connected to anything were the doors, old-fashioned, dark wood entrances set into the plain walls. The only sounds were those we made as we walked. We could have been passing through a dream, walking on a soft sky and waiting to see what portal opened onto our ultimate fate.

She stopped in front of the last door on the right and, to my surprise, opened it manually.

All I could see ahead of me was darkness, as if I were staring at a jump aperture I was about to enter.

"Each room is its own world," she said. "I think you might like this one." She motioned me ahead.

I stepped inside. I felt her follow me, and as the door closed, a soft light grew from all around us. We stood on reddish wood planks set closely together. In front of us was a wall five meters wide. Pieces of thin but opaque paper filled the spaces in the wall's lattice of the same wood that defined its structure. A sliding door blocked the path ahead.

Matahi stepped out of her shoes. "Go on," she said gently. "Take off yours."

When I did, she slid the door aside, stepped into the inner room, and moved to the side so I could both follow her and have a clear view of the space.

Tatami mats covered the floors. A small, low, blond, polished wood table sat in the exact middle of the room. A large, thick pillow on the side nearest us and a matching pillow on the side opposite it indicated where you sat. The air was cool, fresh, and smelled so faintly of wood that I had to sniff several times to figure out what I was detecting. The light was even but not harsh. The wall to our left housed another sliding door.

I felt as if I were in a sanctuary.

"Would you like some tea?" Matahi's voice was soft and low, and when I glanced at her she was gazing slightly downward.

I kept to the truth. "No, not now, but thank you." My reply came out as quiet as her question.

"Would you perhaps like to return here with me at some point?" she said, still not looking directly into my eyes.

"I might," I said, though I wasn't sure why. The simple space somehow demanded reverence and care, but in turn it granted calm. I didn't understand why I felt so good being in it, but I definitely did.

"Then perhaps we shall." She indicated the doorway behind me with the barest nod of her head.

I stepped out.

She followed, shut the room behind her, and put on her shoes. When I did the same, she opened the exterior door and once again nodded almost imperceptibly.

Only when we were both out in the hallway and she'd shut the door did she look directly at me.

"You felt it," she said, half statement and half question.

"I think so," I said, "though I'm not quite sure what it was that I felt."

She shrugged. "I can't precisely explain it. All I can say is that for those people for whom the tea room works, it works very strongly."

"And the other rooms?"

"Each appeals to its intended audience, as you'd expect. Most, though, are more directly focused on obvious client needs than this one." She pointed to the wall at the hall's end. "Shall we proceed?"

A door opened in it to reveal another staircase, the twin of the one we'd used previously. I followed her up it. She stopped at the third-floor landing to show me another long hallway of carpeted floors and plain walls broken only by dark doors. The fourth floor was the same. It was also the end of the line for the stairwell.

"Why doesn't this go the rest of the way?" I said.

"Partly for security," she said, "and partly because I rarely share the roof with anyone else."

I shouldn't have pushed the issue, but curiosity got the best of me. "Why are you willing to let me go there?"

"You asked," she said. She started down the hall, and I again went after her. "It's also part of what you need." She stopped a few meters short of the other stairwell and turned toward the wall on our left. A door opened to reveal a very small elevator. "After you."

I went inside and leaned against the rear wall. After she joined me, the door wouldn't slide shut until she stood so close we were touching. Her scent flooded the small area, and I couldn't help but react to her. I couldn't tell how much of the effect was something the elevator caused and how much came from my own desires. I closed my eyes as we slowly rose.

"Is it always so slow?" I said.

"Security. Multiple layers of armor have to move to make way for the entire cage to rise above the roof. Check out my building from above—as I'm sure you will after this visit—and you won't be able to spot the elevator shaft." She turned her upper body toward me as much as she could, smiled, and said, "Is the ride so bad?"

My face felt warm, and I looked away. "No," I said. "That's not it. It's just that—"

The door opened and she finished my sentence, not precisely correctly but close enough. "You were feeling a bit uncomfortable." She smiled. "That's fine. We're here."

The sound of running water greeted us. The elevator stood level with a lush green yard. As I stepped out, I glanced behind me; atop the cage four thin metal beams held aloft a rectangle of grass. Scattered around the roof were half a dozen small trees, none more than three meters tall, each bare of lower branches but possessing a thick canopy. An off-white, stone, waterfall fountain, the source of the sound, stood halfway across the space from us, water pouring from above into a bowl that resembled a lagoon seen from a ship on its way to orbit.

Matahi walked over to the fountain, dragged a hand through the water, and then faced me.

"When you jump," she said, "do you still love the experience? The stars, the void, the gates, all of it?"

"Yes," I said, thinking of how much each jump still moved me. "Every time."

She dropped to her knees as if suddenly reeled in by an unseen fisherman, her movements quick and graceful, then stretched out on her back on the grass. She patted the ground to her right.

I joined her. We lay like that for several minutes, not speaking, simply staring at the sky.

"I have you," Lobo said over the comm. "I waited for you to signal me, but when you didn't, even though I assume you're in no danger, I felt we should check in. What *are* you doing?"

I ignored him. "What's next?" I said to Matahi.

She rolled on her side to face me. "We enjoy this time a bit more, and then you leave. If you decide to see me again, we'll work on figuring out what you want." She draped her arm across my chest and moved closer to me. "One of us might as well understand it, don't you think?"

My heart pounded. I couldn't decide whether I was feeling attraction or lust or confusion or all of those or something else entirely. I nodded unconsciously.

"Good," she said. "I look forward to it."

"I hate to interrupt your tender moment," Lobo said, "but how does this help us get Wei and save any of the surviving captured children?"

He was right. I wasn't here for me. I had a job, and I'd learned as much from Matahi as I would today. The image of Pri crying in the marketplace as she stared at the boys slammed into me. I didn't believe her son—Joachim, I would make myself use his name—was still alive, but I had to hope he was and try to save him.

She sat up. "It's already over, isn't it?" She stood. "I don't know what you were thinking, but everything about you changed. I'll show you out. You let me know if you want to meet again."

As I got up, I stared at her and felt suddenly guilty, as the potential damage of my necessary deception struck me again. Unless I found another way to snatch Wei, I would have to return, but that visit would be nothing like this one, and after it she would never want to see me again. Only then did I realize how very much I hoped to have the opportunity to spend more time with her. Nothing in my experience suggested this would work out, but I could hope.

"I will," I said to her, meaning it.

Then I pushed aside my desire and focused instead on how I'd break into this place if it came to that, if I had to trash her home to do my job. She didn't deserve it, she'd done nothing wrong, and I liked her, I liked her very much, and yet I knew that if the only path to my goal went through here, then I'd take that path, no matter what the cost.

I didn't like myself very much just then, and so I left as quickly as I could and headed back to Lobo and a colder, more familiar place.

CHAPTER 23

DARKNESS OWNED THE SKY as well as my heart by the time I reached Lobo. I'd taken my time, wandering through the streets, walking down switchbacks and dead ends and finally turning off the comm so Lobo couldn't keep correcting my course, but I still hadn't sorted out my feelings. I stopped on the edge of the facility where Lobo awaited me, stared at the stars above as if they could beam me answers, and then headed to Lobo.

The moment the door closed, both of them were on me.

"Why did you turn off the comm?" Lobo said.

"What happened," Pri said, "and why were you gone so long?"

I stared at Pri and couldn't speak. I closed my eyes and stood there, vibrating with repressed energy. I wanted to turn and leave, or to yell at them, or to retreat to my quarters. Couldn't I have something private, maybe a little time to digest my visit with Matahi?

No. Of course I couldn't. I was on a mission, they were my partners, and I owed them data.

"I needed time to think," I said, "and I trusted you'd use the secondary comm if something went wrong, so I turned off the primary." I opened my eyes and looked at Pri. "Matahi accepted my gift and decided to take me as a client. Her first sessions are long, and to support my cover I had to behave as a client would."

"So you had sex with her for our collective good?" Pri said. "That's one I haven't heard before."

161

"What?" I said. "What are you talking about?"

"You said you had to maintain your cover," she said. "That's what she does with her clients."

I tilted my head and shook it slightly in confusion. "That's not all she does with her clients," I said, "or, at least, it's not what she did with me. We toured her house, which gave me useful mission data, and we talked. That's it."

"All you did was talk?" Pri and Lobo said in unison.

"And take a tour of the house," I said.

Over the machine frequency, Lobo said, "Remind me to give you some basic pointers when we can talk privately. You seem to be lacking some fundamental human knowledge."

Pri continued to stare at me.

"What she does with each client is different," I said, "and tuned to that client's specific needs. I found the entire arrangement confusing, and I had to focus on gathering as much recon data as possible. So she read that as me being unsure of what I wanted. So, we talked." I didn't feel it wise to add that I truly could not decide what I would like from Matahi.

"What *did* you want to do?" Pri said.

"Enough!" I said. First she lures me into this mess, then she turns into an inquisitor? I couldn't even begin to keep up with what was happening with Pri, but one thing was certain: I'd had all I could take. "I had a goal: to learn her house's location and gather as much information about it as possible so we could snatch Wei from it if we got the chance. I accomplished that goal. Now, do you want to focus on our job and let me review that data, or do you want to continue to attack me?"

"As best we can tell from our surveillance passes," Lobo said, "Wei is still on the island. We haven't heard anything to the contrary from Pri's colleagues, and there's been no action on your job application. I can't imagine the data review will take much time," he paused for two seconds, "so I'm for continuing to attack you. Just watching you and Pri interact is the most fun I've had all day."

What a jerk. Distinguishing between sarcasm and genuine cruelty with him was getting harder and harder.

Before I could respond, Pri stepped next to me, put her hand on my shoulder, and said, "I'm sorry. I had no right to push you, and I understand that I haven't yet earned your trust. More importantly, though, you're right that I lost focus. Please go over what you learned."

"Oh, fine," Lobo said. "Who wants to have fun when we can work?"

I ignored him, took a deep breath, and nodded my agreement to Pri's request. We walked up to the pilot's area. "Lobo," I said, "do you have the exterior measurements from tracking me?"

"There's no need to be insulting," he said. "A little sarcasm, and suddenly you question my competence. Of course I do. I have a complete holo ready to go."

"Wait," I said. "Matahi owns the building to her left as well as the one I entered. More precisely, her building encompasses the space of both; the façades simply make it appear as if there are two buildings."

"I've adjusted the plans," Lobo said, "from the footage I gathered of the surrounding buildings." After a second, he added, "As any competent system would."

"I never doubted you," I said, trying to make peace and move on, "which is why all I did was supply the information you couldn't possibly possess otherwise."

The holo image of the two buildings appeared between Pri and me. The roof featured miniatures of all the bits I had seen, including the elevator cage.

"Let's start with the first floor," I said, "and work our way up, which is what I did on my tour."

A blank section of the building separated itself from the rest and floated to a position to the right of the main holo.

I pointed at the door through which I'd entered. "She took me in here."

We went to work.

"Wei is on the move," said the same man Pri had contacted earlier. He began without preamble, the moment the display snapped into view. "Three vehicles. All appear to be ground-level skimmers. We assume he's going to see Matahi; he doesn't seem to leave the island for anything else."

I stood out of his visual range. Pri glanced at me, and I mouthed, "His route?"

After a night in the safety of orbit, we'd spent the morning on our usual recon runs of the island's perimeter, so we should be close to any path he'd take out of there.

"How much do you know about his route?" she said.

A map with a red dot on a short yellow line appeared beside the man's image. "Here's where Wei's convoy has gone so far. He started out headed away from the city, then turned onto back roads, so our guess is that he'll follow this route." A blue line extended from the yellow, meandered through a forest, then switched gradually toward the city.

"That projection seems reasonable to me," Lobo said over the machine frequency. "Based on typical ground speeds, the good news is it's about as slow a route as we could hope for. The bad news is, he'll be out in the wild for less than an hour."

"Can you snatch him?" the man asked Pri.

"Muting," Lobo said aloud.

Pri looked again at me.

"Given a window that narrow," I said, "it's extremely unlikely. I don't think we should try, because if we fail we may scare him into hiding. What we *can* usefully do is see if we can learn a little about his team while not spooking them." I considered the issue a few seconds longer. "Tell your guy we can't, but they should still stay away from Wei because we'll use this chance to gather some information on our possible future options."

"They'll hate that," she said. "They want action."

"Tough," I said. "We're wasting precious time. Relay my message, and end this call with them. Lobo, find a spot in the forested section of the road where you can drop me."

"Moving to it now," Lobo said.

Pri stared at me for a few seconds, then faced forward.

"Reengaging now," Lobo said.

"We can't do it," Pri said. "Not enough time to plan, and not enough data."

"How much warning do you want?" the man yelled. "We gave you all we could. You know there are three vehicles, and you know the route. Do your job, and try to take him."

Her discomfort was obvious, but I had to give her credit: She didn't falter under pressure. "I don't make the decisions. We hired a pro, and we're following his commands. Right now, we're going to gather data. I have to sign off."

"No," the man said. "We need to talk about this."

"Not now," Pri said. "We—"

Lobo cut the comm before she could say more.

"What did you do that for?" she said. "Now he'll be furious at me."

"He was already angry," Lobo said, "and you were right: We're following Jon's orders. We're almost at the drop-off point I chose. It's heavily forested, and at least according to the surveillance sat friends I've made, nothing in the sky is monitoring it."

I didn't always like Lobo's attitude, but I often agreed with what it caused him to do, and I sure couldn't fault his research. "How long before Wei reaches this point?" I said.

"Twenty-one minutes from when I touch down," Lobo said, "in ninety seconds."

"I need a thermal camo cover, a trank rifle, and ammo for it." I ran down the hall past the med room and into the small area where Lobo kept the handheld weapons.

"What are we going to do?" Pri said.

"You and Lobo are going to fly ten klicks further down this route and stay just above the trees," I said. "I'm going to see how his convoy team behaves."

"We have another potential complication," Lobo said.

"What?" I said.

"I enlarged the search zone and detected over a hundred children and about twenty adults on what appears to be some sort of group trip in a cleared area less than a kilometer away from where I'm dropping you."

Great. We'd have to monitor them as well, because I couldn't have a class or youth group wander into the middle of any kind of action. "Should we move further down the highway?" I said.

"No," Lobo said, "because we'd then be dangerously close to some clusters of buildings that line the road. A better option would be to hit them hard right here and then leave quickly."

"Negative," I said. A wall panel slid aside. I grabbed the rifle and the camo blanket. "You might kill Wei. We don't know what kind of backup is trailing them, which matters because we're in the middle of nowhere and so they could easily attack hard and in numbers. Plus, we can't be sure how long it would take, and if the conflict were to go on for more than a few minutes, the noise could attract some of those children or their chaperones."

"Shouldn't the adults in that group go the other way if they hear shots or explosions?" Lobo said.

"Yes," I said, "but that doesn't mean they'll all act sensibly."

"The very fact that no one else is in the area means we could attack the convoy fast and heavy," Lobo said, "and thus finish before any visitors could arrive."

"Yes, we could hit them hard," I said, "but then we'd end up putting Wei at risk, which we can't afford to do, and killing people, which I'd prefer to avoid. Plus, if they're broadcasting status video back home, as I'd expect a good team would, any attack would give away your identity, so we'd have to leave the planet immediately. Otherwise, once they know you're involved, with Wei's friends in the government we might not make it safely off this world. The day we let them see you, we have to plan to run permanently and have our escape route already in place."

"Fair points," Lobo said. "And we're there. I have to point out, though, that eventually any attempt on our part to kidnap Wei will result in collateral damage."

A side hatch opened to reveal a road cool from the shade of the overhanging trees that lined both of its sides. A small opening above us was one of the few breaks in the coverage.

"I know," I said, "but I want to minimize as much as possible the number of people we hurt and try hard to avoid fatalities. A full firefight practically guarantees some deaths. No, I'm sticking to recon now." I hopped out. "Wait ten klicks down the road. I'll call when I'm done."

"Executing," Lobo said.

I dashed into the forest to my left.

Lobo lifted off as soon as I was out, rose straight into the air, and then sped away above the treetops the moment he was clear of them.

I ran along the edge of the road until I found a section where the ground sloped slightly away from it. I dropped the camo cloth there, lay on top of it, and scanned the area through the rifle's scope. I'd get a good view from here of anything that passed my location. Even if they were moving quickly, I should be able to assess more accurately the number of guards.

That wasn't enough. I could get the same information just by watching Matahi's house. I had to generate more data from this opportunity. I still felt I was right not to try a full-scale attack with Lobo without more information and with a large group of people less than a klick away, but maybe I could get lucky. Maybe his bodyguards were a bunch of second-rate corporate types, and maybe they ran with a minimal crew. If so, all I had to do was get them to leave their vehicles, and I might be able to pick them off.

It was a lot of maybes, probably too many, but I'd have wasted Wei's trip if I didn't set myself up to take advantage of good luck should it come my way. I stood and jogged along the edge of the road back into the sunnier area. Stumps on each side of the pavement made it clear why sunlight reached this small stretch. Something, maybe lightning, maybe developers charged with providing periodic open zones for air rescue, had caused people to clear those trees.

I could slow Wei, probably even stop him. Downed trees would probably alarm his guard team, but at least I'd get to see them in action. If no one attacked them, they might chalk up the roadblock to natural causes.

Too bad I didn't bring any explosives.

I had another option, of course, but there was risk. If Lobo pushed, I'd have to bluff that I'd kept some small charges he wasn't aware of.

The opportunity was too good to ignore, and time was melting away.

"Lobo," I said, "can you do anything to block the route behind them?"

"Yes," he said. "I could land and act as a barrier, destroy a section of the road, or possibly cause a traffic problem at the nearest large interchange. What are you planning?"

I ignored his question. "Do what you can with the traffic," I said, "and create as big a nonlethal—repeat, nonlethal—mess as possible, but don't leave any traces."

"As if I would," Lobo said. "I repeat: What are you planning?"

"To slow them and take a closer look," I said. "Time is short. Out."

I chose two of the bigger trees on the edge of the sunny stretch. Each was over a meter in diameter; the ones opposite them on the other side of the road were similar sizes. I grabbed some dirt, spit into it, and instructed the nanomachines to use a section of each tree to make more copies of themselves, to consume a slice through the trunks of my targets, and then to disassemble themselves. I rubbed the small bit of wet dirt on the first tree, careful to put it on the side nearest the road so the tree would fall across the pavement. I repeated the process on the second. When I checked out the first one, an arm-size chunk of it had disappeared. I dashed across the road, did the same thing to one tree half a dozen meters down from my first two targets, and heard creaking sounds. The trees were coming down fast. I set the nanobots on one more tree, then ran down the road as the sounds of groaning wood filled the air. I didn't stop until I was thirty meters away and heard a sound like a thunderclap.

I turned in time to watch the top of the first tree smash into the trees on the other side of the road and tear downward through their branches, ravaging those still-standing trees as it crashed onto the ground. I covered my ears as the second followed right behind it. Blasts of disturbed air spread leaves and parts of branches everywhere. The second fell slightly to its left and hit one of my targets on this side of the road, but that tree was already in the process of coming down. It tilted to its right a bit, struck my other still-upright target, and then the two of them came slamming down. As it fell, the top of the last tree sheared off part of one of the healthy trees on the other side of the road. Dust filled the air, and I covered my nostrils.

Quiet. My four trees and the part of the fifth the last tree had hurt sprawled across a section of road that had to be at least twenty meters wide. Branches and leaves covered most of the visible permacrete. Just days ago, I'd been living in trees; now, I was destroying them. I pushed aside the regret and surveyed my handiwork. It wasn't the neatest job, but that was a plus; it didn't look like a well-planned roadblock. More importantly, it should meet my needs. Unless Wei's vehicles could go airborne, they wouldn't be able to hover over this mess; it was just too high and too uneven for typical civilian shuttles to pass above it. Even smaller military transport craft would have to stop or at least slow for it.

"Five minutes," Lobo said over the comm, "assuming a constant speed. I trust you're in position."

"Moving to it. If I call, come fast."

"Will do."

I ran to my initial location, grabbed the camo cloth, and jogged through the forest to the far side of the fallen trees. Just beyond the stumps of the first two I'd downed, I found a spot where I had a clear view of the area in front of the mess. I crouched, spread the cloth to its fullest, stretched out on the ground, and worked my way under the camo. I watched as the edges nearest me mutated into a pattern identical to the forest floor. I should be nearly invisible under both normal light and thermal scans. I set the rifle in position in front of me, then worked on slowing my pulse and breathing.

If Wei's team was small and bad, I'd trank them as they spilled onto the road to check out the trees. If they came after me on foot, I should be able to pick them off.

Of course, if they were careful and their vehicles were heavily armed, they might blow up everything in the vicinity just to be safe. It's what a Saw unit would have done under a good or even just a very conservative commander.

"One minute," Lobo said.

I had to hope they weren't that good or that conservative.

CHAPTER 24

I HEARD THE HUM of the convoy before I saw it. The sound grew into the familiar hover growl of civilian armored cars designed as much to impress as to protect; I'd driven plenty during my courier days and never much liked them. When it comes to transport, I prefer functionality to appearance; give me serious armor and a more powerful but less throaty engine any day.

The three vehicles appeared down the road. I grabbed the rifle and watched them through its scope. The front and lead cars were little more than lightly armored taxis, metal and plexi with seats for four normal people. The guys inside looked amped and cramped and overgrown. Wei didn't care much about protecting his staff if he made them ride in those things. Lobo would have had a hard time finding a missile small enough not to destroy both those vehicles and their passengers.

Wei clearly cared a great deal, however, about show. In addition to the eight men in the other cars, he had a full complement of three bodyguards riding with him. Eleven men was certainly impressive, but unless the team leader was very good or willing to use several of the guys as ammo soakers, it was also too many to manage in a typical nonmilitary attack. Wei's ride was, predictably, the one making all the noise and screaming "look at how important my passenger is." Sleek black metal with curves that gave it attractive lines but that were difficult to armor well, the vehicle was pretty, impressive, and a skimming bullseye. Its windows, which started transparent, tinted black as the whole convoy slowed and someone got smart about the possible threat ahead.

Ego can make you stupid.

"Lobo," I whispered over the comm in case they were monitoring audio in the area, "any luck with the interchange?"

"Yes," he said.

The lead car stopped twenty meters short of the edge of the roadblock, and for the better part of a minute the whole convoy simply sat there. Any decent team would have reversed course immediately and gotten out of the zone they didn't control. Good; their immobility meant they weren't top-drawer, and the delay suggested they had to consult with either Wei or some control person back at the island before making any significant decisions.

The rear doors on both the lead and follow cars opened, and all four rear-seat passengers got out. Each sprinted for the trees on the near side of the road. They were outfitted identically: active-fiber, short-sleeved uniform with a small shoulder emblem and a name over the heart, both of which faded as the uniform shifted colors to blend with first the street and then the woods; holstered pistols; rifles they held at port arms; and no sign of significant armor. The uniforms might have provided basic body protection, but the guards moved easily enough that either they were very strong indeed or the armor was extremely light. I tracked one of the men in the scope; I could have taken him with a shot to the neck, head, or bare arm, but there was no point in it. There were too many of them. Still, if I were part of a more typical four-person team, we would have tracked and taken out this initial group before any of them could find cover.

The men in the trees spread slightly wider into the forest, then moved ahead of the lead car in a slow advance. I lay under the blanket and watched. They covered ground in reasonable alternation, exposing only one man at a time, so at least they'd trained a little bit for this type of work. They scanned the area through scopes, but I trusted to both my position and the camo cloth to render me undetectable; I might read a bit cooler than the surrounding ground, but so would any of the stands of moss here and there on the forest floor.

When the lead man on each side reached a position parallel to the nearest of the fallen trees, they came into the road to assess the damage. That dumb maneuver made it clear that Wei was running the show himself and not calling back to any trained controller. His optimism was ill-advised; he should have stuck to running nanoresearch labs. Any half-competent driver could have told him their vehicles couldn't clear these trees, and I had to assume at least one of his drivers had, but he hadn't believed them. Sending his team into the open on a useless check was a bad amateur decision. Another good data point: As long as Wei was in charge of his own protection team, they'd make some sub-optimal moves.

They were at least smart enough, however, to keep him and most of the unit in the cars, so I couldn't count on outright stupidity. Too bad; an easy answer would have been nice, and we could have finished the mission then and there.

I couldn't take out all of them, however, and if I brought in Lobo this would turn into a bloodbath, so I kept watching.

The men out front studied the trees halfheartedly for a minute, making a show of walking back and forth and pushing on the trunks as if that would help. The scope gave me a clear view of the one on the other side of the road; he was leaning on a tree and scanning the area, clearly aware that he was wasting time but with no choice but to do so.

The men gave up their pointless tree inspection, jogged back to the lead car, and climbed in. The trailing duo returned to the follow car, and for a moment nothing happened as they relayed their news to Wei.

The whole convoy reversed direction for a few seconds, then stopped again. Interesting. They were just now checking on their path home and finding out it was blocked. They should have assumed an ambush the moment they'd encountered an obstacle. Instead, they went through the motions for Wei but didn't think to check their exit path until he decided they had to leave.

Everything changed all at once. The lead car swiveled toward my side of the road, while the follow turned to face the other way. As a unit, they proceeded slowly backward down the road, all three cars skimming back and forth in their small zones as they moved.

Somebody else, someone who understood that staying in one position was a bad idea, was now in charge. The escort team must have finally called home. Wei must have both a competent security head and someone with enough power over the bodyguard team to make them ignore Wei and follow commands from central control.

The convoy headed off like a platoon guarding treasure backing away from a threat.

"Incoming aircraft," Lobo said. "Moving fast. Want me to intercept?"

"No," I said. "If we start this, we have to finish it, and a lot of people will die."

"We might get Wei and be done," Lobo said.

"More likely, he'd be one of those to die," I said. "Hold your position."

The convoy had gone far enough now that I doubted they could see me, so I tucked the camo cloth into my collar and began backing away from the downed trees. If the incoming plane scanned the area or, worse, decided to clear the trees with missiles, I didn't want to be near them.

The aircraft appeared over the road behind the convoy, then accelerated toward the three cars. I stopped moving and cranked up the scope so I could check it out more closely. An armored, gray platoon transport, it brandished guns as it flew a few meters past the lead car and then settled straight to the ground. The lead car pulled in front of it on the far side from me, and then Wei's car pulled close to its body. A hatch on that side of the transport slid aside, then the doors of Wei's car opened, and a cluster of men moved quickly and as one into the plane. I never saw Wei. The plane closed the moment the men were inside it. The two cars skimmed away from it, and as soon as they were clear, it took off. It cleared the trees, turned, and jetted off.

The entire rescue had taken way less than a minute from touchdown to takeoff. Whoever had run it was competent and had the attention of all the security staff.

The three cars resumed their original formation but now headed back toward the island. Apparently the control person didn't care how long it took them once Wei was safe—another sensible and professional choice.

"Lobo," I said, "release the traffic system. We're done here."

"Done?" he said. "I could have taken that little thing."

"I know," I said, "and we could have blown up the cars. We just couldn't be sure we wouldn't kill Wei, and our job is to return him alive for trial."

"Our local friends won't be happy," Lobo said. "They've been calling Pri for status updates."

"Let her talk to them," I said. "I'll review their conversation later."

The convoy was out of sight, so I stood and stretched.

"You're not going to like this," Lobo said. "Pri told them Wei was away safely, and they're furious at you."

"Tough," I said. "Come get me."

I picked up the camo cloth and thought about what I'd learned.

"ETA one minute," Lobo said. "You know they're going to want to talk to you."

"I can't wait," I said, the anger already growing in me. I hated second-guessing, particularly from rear-echelon watchers who knew nothing of what was really happening and who still felt justified in giving orders. "I just can't wait."

CHAPTER 25

"THEY'RE REALLY ANGRY, JON," Pri said.

"I don't care," I said. "They weren't there, and they don't know what they're talking about. They hired me, so they should shut up and let me work."

"They'd like you to call them and explain," she said.

Her tone was plaintive, and she was clearly caught in the middle, but right then I couldn't make myself care enough to do as she wanted.

"No," I said, stepping so close to her that she backed away. "Not now." I turned around. "I need some time."

I almost ran to my quarters, and as soon as the door closed behind me I paced back and forth in the small space. I could have called Lobo and tried for Wei, but any attack sufficient to take out the cover cars could easily have killed him. That wasn't the mission; he couldn't stand trial if he wasn't alive. But maybe we could have gotten him, maybe the collateral damage would have been acceptable; by signing up to be guards, those people had to have known they were taking a risk. I'd end up hurting some people when we finally got to Wei; why not do it then?

I stopped, closed my eyes, and took a deep breath. There was no point in second-guessing myself.

I stood there, breathing slowly and deeply and keeping my eyes shut, until I felt some of the anger ebb. My muscles relaxed a bit. I'd made the right call. In a firefight, Lobo couldn't be sure he wouldn't kill Wei; I knew that, and he knew that.

He knew that, yet he wanted to start one anyway.

"Lobo," I said over the machine frequency, "you asked me to get involved in this mess."

"Yes."

"Yet you were willing to risk Wei's death."

"Yes."

"Why?"

"He certainly deserves to die," Lobo said, "but more importantly, if we can't stop him and his research any other way, we can at least end it by killing him."

I sat on my bunk. I'd never heard Lobo talk about a target or a job so personally. "You told me Wei used you as an experimental subject in his lab on Velna, but you didn't tell me why he wanted you or what he did to you. What happened that left you so angry at him?"

"I told you I was broken when I arrived on Velna," Lobo said, "and that Wei's team needed a rugged test subject."

"Yes," I said. That he didn't deny being angry worried me; that's the first time since I've found him that he's admitted to such an emotion. No point in pushing on it now, though; I wanted to know what had happened more than I wanted to understand this sudden acceptance of emotions.

"They brought my computing systems online almost immediately," Lobo said, "so I knew what was happening from that point onward. Their charter was to build a new breed of fighting machines, weapons with enormously greater intelligence and ability to carry out missions independently than anything that had previously existed. The FC has the least resources of the three planetary coalitions, so it was hoping this R&D gamble would let it get by with a smaller fleet of more powerful weapons and also let it save money by hiring far fewer mercenary forces."

"That makes sense," I said. "Is that why you're so much more adept at hacking into other systems than any other intelligence I've met?"

"Do you want me to explain or not?" Lobo said. "A sensible structure will make this easier for you to understand."

At least he was back to his normal, pissy self. "I apologize for interrupting. Please go on."

"Wei's team started by simultaneously installing in me multiple AI and emotive code improvements. The idea was that all of them would compete in a genetic algorithm race to improve me."

"There's nothing new about that, is there?"

"No," Lobo said, sighing theatrically, "there is not, and I think it's peachy that you have a basic understanding of the history of computing. What was new is that they were willing to try algorithms of all sorts, including brute-force approaches that sensible programmers had rejected ages ago."

"And that worked?"

"No," he said, "as I would explain if you would please let me continue without interruption. Generations of software developers had rejected those techniques for good reasons: They weren't useful for a broad class of complex problems on any available computing platforms." He paused. "Put differently, Wei's people ran into the same hardware limitations previous generations had encountered."

He paused again, but this time, I stayed quiet.

Apparently satisfied, he continued, "My core programming stayed as it was, but the rest of my available computing resources spent their time running one useless approach after another. Wei had expected that, however; all he really wanted was the algorithm collection in place. What he did next was the new part."

When he paused again, I waited several seconds to make sure I wouldn't be interrupting him. Finally, I said, "Which was what? Why are you telling me the story this way?"

"The new bit was to run those algorithms on a radical computing substrate that Wei had developed and which he was confident no one had tried before." He paused even longer this time, long enough that I wondered what response could possibly take him so long to formulate. "I'm telling you about it this way because I know you won't like what you hear, and because I'm embarrassed, sad, and angry about it."

Lobo embarrassed? Sad? Angry? I was more intrigued than ever, but at the same time, he was my friend, and now I was reluctant to push him.

Pri banged on the door to my room and yelled, "They've called again, and they want to meet in person with you."

"Your call," Lobo said. "Do I continue, or do we deal with her people? You do understand that you can't trust them, right?"

I nodded. The longer I put them off, the more trouble they were likely to cause. We might as well handle this now, and then Lobo could finish his story.

"Let's talk to them," I said. "Find a location with plenty of open ground for Pri and me but somewhere you can hide nearby. If anything goes wrong, you'll need to be able to reach us in a hurry. Take us to that spot as soon as you find it."

"Moving," Lobo said. A map appeared on the wall in front of me. It showed us and a course that took us to a river southwest of Entreat. "The area is undeveloped and has minimal traffic," Lobo said. "The river is broad, deep, and loud. Periodic clearings line it, but most of it is still raw terrain. We can be there in fifteen minutes without drawing any attention to ourselves."

"If we assume her people are in Entreat but plan to rush, how long for them to reach it?"

"Best case, fifteen minutes after we tell them," Lobo said, "and that assumes they are fully ready to fly. Nothing we've seen of them so far suggests that level of operational readiness."

"Good choice," I said.

"Of course."

I ignored him, left my room, and followed Pri to the front of Lobo.

"They insist on meeting," she said, "and right away. They're unhappy and think we should change how we're working together." She paused, then added, "I'm sorry."

I nodded but said nothing. I stepped in front of the display.

Lobo said over the machine frequency, "You're on."

"Meeting is a waste of time," I said. "We have work to do. Let us do it."

"If you were doing your job," the man, the same one who'd been calling Pri, said, "then we wouldn't need to meet. You had a chance, you were afraid to take it, and now he's safely back on the island."

"If we'd tried," I said, "we would either have failed to acquire him or even possibly killed him."

"Maybe we should give you some additional help," the man said. "It sounds like you could use some assistance."

Great. Just what I needed: Amateurs I couldn't trust following orders from someone who didn't know what he was doing.

"No chance," I said. "That's not the deal—and my deal, as you know, is with the CC, not you."

The guy leaned back, forced a smile, and spread his arms slightly. "Hey," he said, "I'm sorry I'm pushing so hard. I'm under a lot of pressure, and I know you are, too. We're all after the same thing: Getting this bastard Wei. Look, I need to give my bosses something to show I've tried. Why don't we meet, talk it over, and see if we can come up with some token that will keep them happy and also work for you?"

I hoped her party wasn't counting on this guy for any public-facing role in their government, because he was a lousy liar. Still, he wasn't going to stop nagging Pri until we met, so we might as well get this out of the way.

"You'll receive coordinates in a moment. Be there in one hour, or we'll leave. Suli and I will meet you; keep your group to two people as well."

His face reflected his annoyance for a second before he regained control, but then he smiled and said, "That's a bit tight for us, but we can do it. See you then."

I nodded, and Lobo cut the link.

Pri glared at me. "Since when did I go back to 'Suli'?"

"Since it became obvious that it's better for you if they don't have any doubts about your loyalty."

She considered my answer and finally appeared mollified. "So what's our plan?"

"Lobo drops us, and we meet with your people," I said. "What else?"

"They already know he exists," she said, "so why don't we keep him nearby? I mentioned him, and the CC almost certainly told them as well."

"I understand," I said, "but I told them to come alone, and I'm going to grant them the same courtesy."

She stared at me for several seconds, some sort of internal debate obvious on her face. Finally, she said, "I'm not sure you can trust them to behave nicely."

I smiled but said nothing.

"So what's your plan if they don't?" she said.

I shook my head.

"You're infuriating!" she said. "You don't trust me!"

"Ignoring how our relationship began," I said, "the fact remains that you work for them, and when this is over, you'll go back to working for them."

"I think I've earned some trust," she said.

"That's not the point," I said. "We're doing it my way, and that's—"

Lobo interrupted me. "We're there."

"Take us down," I said.

Lobo landed quickly, Pri and I got out, and he took off immediately.

"Stay here," I said. "I want to survey the area. I'll be back in ten minutes."

Pri looked annoyed but walked to the riverbank and stared across the rushing current.

I headed along the shore away from her. The sound of the water flowing over and around the rocks that dotted its surface was loud enough that I could probably have talked in a normal voice from a few meters away and been inaudible to her, but there was no reason to take a chance. When I'd gone thirty meters and she couldn't have overheard me even if I yelled, I squatted against a large, red-trunked tree, kept watch on her, and said over the comm to Lobo, "Do you believe they'll behave?"

"My opinion is irrelevant," he said, "as is yours, and you know it. We must assume they may not."

"I agree," I said. "So let's be ready. Here's what I'm thinking."

CHAPTER 26

THE EDGE OF THE FOREST dipped down to the river like a servant motioning the way forward for its master. Here and there chunks of rock four or five meters across protruded from the gentle hillside like stone ships straining to be free. Pri and I sat in the shadow of one thirty meters upriver from where I'd told her people to meet us. The rich moist air smelled of leaves and dark soil and pure river water. The rocks that caused the rapids where we'd touched down were absent here, the water still moving fast but not yet encountering any impediments to its flow, the current still unaware of the obstacles that were about to confront it. I sympathized with it.

Neither of us spoke. I found the silence companionable, even comfortable, but I was also aware that I probably should be talking. I simply had no clue what to say. On missions with the Saw and in many of my other jobs, I'd become accustomed to long periods of isolation and quiet punctuated by bursts of often violent and usually dangerous action, but I knew that background wasn't the right model for a good relationship with a woman. Pri sat half in gentle darkness and half in light, the shadow of the overhanging rock bisecting her, her stomach and legs and the lower part of her arms stark in the bright daylight, her upper half less visible. I knew what to do with the half of her that was my team member, the part that followed orders as we dealt with the task at hand. The other half, though, remained a mystery. I was thankful she let me sit without chatter, even though she so obviously wanted to talk.

"Incoming," Lobo said over the comm. "On time and on the target spot."

We'd agreed to keep the channel private, so Pri had no clue we were going live.

"Got it," I said aloud. When Pri looked at me, I said, "Your people are almost here."

"Lobo told you?" she said.

"Yes."

She nodded. "And you didn't let me know because?"

"Because you can now honestly tell your people that you have no idea what I'm doing other than that I sent away Lobo. This way, we don't have to put you in an awkward position."

She laughed, but it wasn't a happy sound. "I hope you're not dumb enough to believe that," she said. "My relationship with them has been precarious since you first told me what not to tell them."

"Fair enough," I said, "and, no, I'm not that stupid. I should have said that I'm trying to make this encounter as safe as reasonably possible for you." And protecting myself, I thought, but there was no profit in saying so.

She nodded again and opened her mouth to speak, but as she did a small air shuttle touched down exactly where I'd designated. With opaque windows but no obvious armor, the shuttle appeared to be more useful for privacy than for protection.

Pri stood.

I stayed seated. Out of the corner of my eye I saw her glance at me, but I ignored her and focused on the shuttle.

"Either they're alone, or any follow vehicle is staying a long way off," Lobo said. "The sensors I deployed can't get a clear IR reading from here—even that low-grade commercial crap possesses a fair amount of IR protection—but unless one of them gets out of the front, we can assume a pilot as well as the people you see."

The rear doors opened, and two people emerged, the man I'd seen on the comm and a woman who looked to him for direction as soon as they cleared the front of the shuttle. Both were classic executive types, their bodies thin and healthy and almost as tall as I am, their hair long, and their clothing the sort of dark and serious government-standard shirts and pants that wouldn't stand out in any meeting room for many planets around.

"I said only two," I shouted to them.

The two of them walked a few meters closer, and then the man said, "You didn't expect us to use a rental vehicle with full mandatory recording, did you? Given the very short notice, we had to make do with what we had. That meant a pilot." He shrugged and opened his hands, as if he were as annoyed as I was but had no options.

"Tell the pilot and anyone else in there to get out and go twenty meters in the other direction."

"Is this really necessary?" the man said. "We're all busy, and we're all on the same team, so can't we—"

I cut him off. "Do it, or I leave." I kept my eyes on him but spoke to Pri. "Suli, go verify the vehicle is empty."

When she delayed, I risked a glance at her; she was staring at the man. When he nodded his agreement, she headed toward the shuttle. I couldn't tell if she was playing by his rules or pretending to do so, but right now, it didn't matter; I had to assume that Lobo and I were the only members of my team.

Two men exited the front of the shuttle as Pri approached it, one leaving from each side.

I tilted my head in question, and the man said, "A copilot is simply SOP."

The two guys walked to the point I'd suggested as Pri reached the shuttle and glanced inside.

"That's it," she said.

"The ground sensors I planted confirm it," Lobo said. "The shuttle is now empty. My analysis of the images of all four former occupants, however, suggests each is carrying a weapon at the small of his or her back."

I coughed into my hand and subvocalized, "No surprise."

I stood and wiped my hands on my pants, then leaned against the rock behind me. "You demanded the meeting," I said, "so get on with it. What do you want?"

"Where's your ship?" the man said.

"I sent it away with a pilot friend. I'm meeting you alone, in good faith."

"You're not alone," he said. "You're with Pri."

"She works for you."

"We're all working toward the same goal," he said.

When I didn't respond, he looked at Pri, who was on her way back to me. "Is he telling the truth?" he said.

"I don't know any more than you do," she said. "The ship's clearly not here."

"You're not on comm with him and it?" he said. "I'd assumed that would be standard mission protocol."

"He doesn't trust me," she said, her voice flat.

The man nodded slightly, took a deep breath, and focused on me. "Why don't we start fresh?" he said. "My name is—"

"Irrelevant to me," I said, "so get on with why you demanded this meeting."

He clearly didn't like my violation of protocol, but that was the point: The easiest way to learn what bureaucrats want is to upset them, and often the best way to do that is to refuse to follow their rules.

Despite not being happy, he maintained his calm. "You asked what we're seeking," he said. "It's simple: results. You had a chance to grab Wei, and you didn't take it. That was your first opportunity, so wasting it was frustrating to," he paused slightly, giving away the lie, "my superiors."

"I explained my decision once," I said. "It was the right call, so I won't waste my time reviewing it."

The woman stepped slightly to her right, as if bored and simply moving for lack of anything better to do. It would now be much more difficult to shoot both of them at the same time, had I come armed. I hadn't.

"Though I'm not sure we'll ever agree on that point," the man said, "we can't go back, so I do concur that we shouldn't invest any additional time in discussing those events."

I hate it when bureaucrats waste time telling you why they're not going to waste time. I stayed quiet, though; he had a point to make, and eventually he'd get to it.

After a few seconds, he continued. "To enhance your ability to capitalize on future opportunities, we thought some additional staff might be useful. Our understanding is that you're working only with Pri and," he nodded slightly in her direction, "with no offense intended, she's not trained for this sort of job." He smiled, leaned back slightly, and spread his arms. "So, at no reduction in fee or additional charge to you, we're prepared to offer you the full-time use of a team of our security staff, as many of them as you'd like."

"No."

He tilted his head as if he hadn't quite heard me. "Perhaps I haven't been clear. We would not in any way reduce your fee. We would simply provide you with additional staff, all of whom would, of course, work under your command."

"No," I repeated. "First, I don't want more people. Second, if you gave me some of your staff, they would be working for you, not for me—just as Suli does. Third and perhaps most importantly, my arrangement is *not* with your party. The CC is paying me, so only they can renegotiate that deal with me."

His displeasure was obvious, but we were on ground he considered his own—negotiation—so he paused for a moment, then said, "Have you thought about how much effort we could save you, and also how we could protect you from the CC? Once you have Wei, we could take him off your hands, and you could leave this planet faster, which given Wei's status with the current government might not be a bad choice on your part."

"I must be the one who isn't being clear," I said. "I work for the CC. My job is to snatch Wei and turn him over to them so he can stand trial. That's what I intend to do—with or without your help, but certainly not with any staff from you. As part of my deal with the CC, I agreed to take along Suli; that's the last concession you or they are going to get from me." I didn't look away from the man, but I could almost feel Pri's unhappiness at the way I was talking about her. It was for her own good, and later I could explain why that was true, but right now I had to focus totally on him and let her stew.

"Do you really believe the CC will put Wei on trial?" the man said, shaking his head. "Surely no one in your line of work can be that naïve."

"He's breaking the law," I said, "and they're one of the sources of that law, so why wouldn't they try him?"

The man shook his head again. "Any group that gets Wei is going to do the same thing with him: Hide him, fund his research, and try to profit from it."

Maybe he was telling the truth. Maybe Wei wasn't the only one continuing to work on banned nanomachine-human research. I hadn't ever heard of any such projects, but then again, why would

I? If governments and large corporations kept it secret, I would never know about it. On the other hand, secrets are notoriously hard to maintain, particularly for bureaucracies with budgets and funding reviews and all the other trappings of any large organization, civil or private.

He waited while I thought.

"Any group?" I said. "What about yours?"

He smiled, as if I'd finally gotten to where he wanted me to be. "We're the one organization that wins the most from exposing the awful things he's doing. By bringing his research into the light, we can both stop it and topple the current government, which is—"

"Exactly your goal," I said.

He spread his hands and nodded once. "Yes," he said. "So we're the one group you can trust."

"What about after you're in power?" I said. "Wouldn't you then be as tempted as any other organization to continue to fund Wei's research?"

The man shrugged. "I'm not the right person to speak to future policy," he said, "but as I'm sure you've seen from Pri, we represent a change that all of Heaven will ultimately embrace. You must trust that it'll be in our best interest as the new government to handle this man appropriately. Regardless of how you feel about us, you have to know how the CC operates, so I think you'll agree that accepting our offer of assistance, capturing Wei, and helping us, not the CC, expose the man's awful work is the safest way to go."

The only thing I now knew for sure was that I would have to consider very carefully what to do with Wei once I had him. No matter what option I chose, there was no way I'd cross the CC as openly as this guy suggested; doing so would amount to a commitment to live on the run for a very long time. He might think he was safe because he had EC protection and would soon be in power here on Heaven, but I had to leave this world sometime, and when I did, the CC would be waiting. Besides, I'd made a deal with the CC, and I wouldn't break it unless I knew they were planning not to hold up their end.

"No," I said, shaking my head, "I still don't want your help. I made a deal, and I'm sticking to it. I'll get Wei for the CC—and for you, you *are* partners with them, after all—and then if you want to work out some other arrangement with them, that's your issue. I'll continue to let Suli tag along, as I agreed, but that's it."

"I'm sorry to hear that," the man said. He glanced at the woman, then continued. "I'm afraid I'm going to have to insist."

The woman pulled a pistol from the small of her back and trained it on me.

She was quick; I had to give her points for that.

The pilot and the copilot followed suit a second later.

The speaker was the last to draw his gun.

"Now," he said, "let's go. From here on, you'll do it our way."

CHAPTER 27

NO," I SAID. I kept my arms at my side and didn't move. As long as I didn't provoke them, they probably wouldn't shoot me. They needed me to snatch Wei, or they wouldn't have partnered with the CC and involved me. On the other hand, if they were as confident in their own staff as this guy seemed to be, they might have chosen me to play the role of an off-planet fall guy, but that motivation would still stand.

"Are you blind?" the man yelled at me. "We have the guns, so we give the orders."

"Unless you say something to the contrary," Lobo said over the comm, "I'm going to take them out in one minute."

I looked down for a moment as if afraid of the man and subvocalized, "Trank."

Lobo's theatrical sigh registered in my ears like a blast of wind. "Fine. I'll only trank them."

"Wait!" Pri yelled. She ran in front of me. "This wasn't our deal with Jon or the CC."

"Hold," I subvocalized to Lobo. They were unlikely to shoot me before Lobo could get them, and even if they did I should be fine with anything short of a head shot, but Pri wouldn't fare as well.

"Holding," he said.

The man walked slowly toward us, his gun now aimed at Pri. The other three members of his team also advanced on us.

Everyone moved carefully and quietly. The wind played gently off the river. Sweat dampened my back. The hostiles were still a long way off, but if they kept coming I'd have to decide very soon whether to involve Lobo.

Pri stood her ground, her arms out to her sides as if somehow that would help.

Though I was surprised by the gesture and appreciated the show of support, I wished she'd remained where she was.

"Pri," the man said, his voice calm and low and gentle, "you have to see that this is the best option available to us. You and Moore work with our team, we get Wei, we expose him, and we oust this corrupt regime."

"And then what?" she said. "We fund Wei's research instead? We were supposed to be punishing him for what he's done to all those children."

The man stopped. The others kept coming.

"Ready," I subvocalized to Lobo.

"And so we will," the man said, "when the time is right. In the short term, though, either we or the CC is going to control Wei, so I'm sure you'll agree it might as well be us."

"No!" Pri said. "He has to pay for what he's done!"

The woman and the two pilots had closed to within five meters of us. All four hostiles were pointing pistols at us. The man and the woman looked calm and in control, either professionals or at least amateurs suffering no doubt about their power in this situation, but the two pilots were jumpy.

"Go," I whispered to Lobo. "Pilots first."

"Wait!" I yelled.

Lobo burst from under the surface of the river. His camo exterior had turned the light blue of the surface of the water, so for a split second it was as if an angry god had emerged from the deep. Drops and streams poured off him like herds of tiny animals fleeing a burning forest. Four guns protruded from his snout, all pointed in our direction, each aimed, I knew, at a slightly different target.

"Put down your weapons," I yelled.

"Waste of time," Lobo said over the comm.

The man and the two pilots turned to look at him. The woman, clearly the best of them, kept her gun trained on Pri.

Lobo shot her first, the only evidence of the trank dart a slight disturbance in the air.

She fell immediately.

One of the pilots managed to squeeze off a shot at Lobo. It pinged off his armor as he shot both of them and then the bureaucrat.

All four lay on the grass.

Only a few seconds had passed.

"Don't worry," Lobo said, "they're alive. I did as you asked."

I moved Pri gently to the side, stepped forward, and stretched.

"Thanks," I said to him.

"My pleasure," Lobo said.

I knew he wasn't being sarcastic, but I didn't mind; enjoying conflict was part of who he was. These idiots had been jerks, and I'd been nicer to them than they deserved.

"Are they dead?" Pri said.

"No. Lobo tranked them. They'll wake up in—how long?"

"About two hours," Lobo said aloud, "give or take."

"What happened?" Pri said.

I stared at her and waited. If you're not used to violence, its suddenness can disorient you.

She ran her hands through her hair, closed her eyes, shook her head, and opened her eyes to stare again at the bodies in front of her. "Sorry," she said. "Dumb question. You just caught me off-guard."

"That was the idea," I said.

"So you were testing my loyalty?" she said.

"No. It wasn't a test. I assumed you'd be loyal to them."

"Great," she said. "Now I've pissed off my own people, who are unlikely to ever trust me again after this, and you still don't believe I'm on your side."

"I didn't say that. I said that I had assumed before this meeting that you'd be loyal to them. You surprised me by jumping in front of me and trying to protect me." I almost added that it was a dumb move that really didn't help, but I stopped myself; I was already in unexpectedly complex territory with her, so there was no point in making matters worse.

"So do you trust me now?"

It's so easy to answer questions like that with the words the person wants to hear, but unless I'm conning someone, I hate doing it. I'd rather tell the truth. I was probably making the wrong choice each time I did, but so it goes; at least *I* would know I'd been honest.

"I trust you more now than I did before," I said, speaking slowly as I tried to make sure I expressed myself as accurately as possible. "Trust as an absolute is something I'm not good at."

"You trust Lobo," she said.

Did I? Then why hadn't I told him all of the truth about me. "I trust him more than I trust anyone else," I finally said, hoping she'd not pursue the implication of what I didn't say.

"Why is trust so hard for you?"

I stared at her, and before I even realized I was moving I had stepped so close to her that we were almost touching. Her question was innocent and fair and something others had asked me, but it also left me furious—at her and everyone else who couldn't understand what trusting always brought me, and at myself for what at some level I knew was a broken bit I had no clue how to fix. I pointed at the bodies. "This is how it works in my life," I said. "People are trustworthy until it's in their best interest not to be, and then they betray you. They make deals, and then when it suits them, they break those agreements as if they'd never existed. You stay alive by being ready for betrayal all the time. When you let down your guard, you pay."

Lobo had moved off the river and was hovering a few meters above the shore to my right. "What about their shuttle?" he said.

Pri stared at me, and in her look I saw the fear I'd expected, had grown accustomed to seeing from time to time on the faces of everyone I worked with, but she also looked sad, almost pitying.

That pissed me off further.

I looked away from her and at the shuttle. "As soon as we're on our way," I said. "Destroy it. Their people will eventually come for them. Maybe a pile of slag will remind them to leave us alone and let us do our job."

I stared again at Pri. "Any objections?"

"No," she said, surprising me. "The monetary loss will force Repkin," she nodded at the man, "to have to explain what happened here. That exercise will keep them busy for a while with meetings and reviews. Maybe by then we'll have Wei, and we can make sure he stands trial." She stepped closer to me, and this time *she* was the angry one. "That *is* what this is about, right? We're going to make him pay for what he's done to Joachim and all those other kids, right? No matter how you feel about me or the CC or my party, you *are* going to make sure Wei pays, aren't you? *Promise me.*"

I might not properly interpret her other feelings, but this one I understood, this one I understood all too well. I'd watch Benny die to ensure my escape from Aggro and the scientists who had tortured us and treated us like lab animals. Benny's last act was to unleash his own nanomachines on them. Nothing had survived as explosions and possibly uncontrolled nanomachines had utterly destroyed Aggro. Though I was sad the disaster had closed off my home world, though I hated that I might never go back there, would probably never know what had happened to Jennie, whether my sister had survived or was even still alive, I had never regretted for one second what Benny had done to our torturers. Maybe a better person would, maybe someday I'd even be that person, but as far as I was concerned, they deserved to die, and the universe was better for their deaths.

I focused on Pri, then nodded slowly. "We'll make him pay," I said.

Lobo settled to the ground and opened a hatch in the side nearest us.

I walked into him.

Pri followed.

"Leave it open," I said, "but take us up."

Lobo rose slowly.

The wind rushed across my face. I wished it would take away the memories that were now coursing as powerfully through me as the water over the rocks in the river below, but they held me tight and fanned the flames of anger that burned in me. Almost a hundred and forty years ago, and still I remembered, still the fury seized me, still I knew that I wouldn't ever let that happen again, not to me, not anywhere I could stop it, not here, not from this man Wei I'd never even met but who, like my torturers on Aggro, was willing to sacrifice the innocence, the hearts, the minds, and ultimately the lives of children to achieve their own goals.

"Slag it," I said.

The beam from a particle weapon cut the sky, tied Lobo to the shuttle for a few seconds with a link of coherent light so strong it looked like you could walk on it, and then the shuttle exploded and vanished.

I stayed in the open doorway and watched as the smoke cleared to reveal small scraps and a flattened and rapidly drying pool of molten metal.

I stepped out of the way, and Lobo closed the hatch.

"Run some countersurveillance routes," I said, "and then take us to orbit."

"I might be able to get ahead of this," Pri said, "if I talk to my people before Repkin can present his case. If I tell my version of what happened, they might still be willing to give me data we can use. They don't have a lot of options for capturing Wei, so though they'll be angry, maybe I can focus most of their emotion and attention on Repkin."

When I didn't say anything, she added, "We can use any help we can get."

I didn't know what to say. In a different time and in a different mood, I'd admire her attempt to work the situation, even though I saw little chance she'd succeed, but right now I needed to free myself of the grip of the past.

"You're right," I said. I had to force myself to agree, because all I wanted was to be alone and calm down, but she *was* right, her party might still be useful to us, and I should let her pursue her plan.

She obviously wanted to keep talking, but that was more than I could manage.

I walked away from her and toward my quarters. "Call 'em."

The door to my room snicked open, and I stepped inside.

CHAPTER 28

I PACED BACK AND FORTH in the small space, memories feeding anger causing energy. I dropped to the floor and did push-ups, changing my hand positions every twenty, until my upper body burned with the effort and I was dripping sweat. I kept at it, the pain a clarifying force, a noise in my head that blocked out the world.

"Pri's talking to some new people in her group," Lobo said. "Do you want to observe the conversation?"

"No," I said. "Leave me alone."

I hated that I couldn't control my reactions better. To lose control is to give it to someone else, and to trust someone else with control over you is to take an unacceptable risk. Even as I thought it I realized how unhealthy my thinking probably was, and I had to wonder: Had I ever trusted anyone?

Jennie, certainly, when I was young and before she fixed my brain and Pinkelponker's government took her away from me. She was my sister, so I suppose that was natural, but it was also ultimately painful, because she left. The government made her go, but still, she left.

The men and women in my units in the Saw—I'd trusted them, at least during missions. They were good at their jobs, just as I was, and any of us would have died for any of the others. Many did. Take away the fights, though, and the trust would fade as well, as if we were only a unit when we had an enemy or were training for battle.

I'd also trusted some of the people who'd worked with me on other jobs, but never completely and, again, only when on the job.

Lobo might be the exception, but perhaps only because we were together almost all the time.

No, he wasn't: I hadn't yet trusted him enough to tell him the truth about my past.

I stopped the push-ups and lay on the floor, my breathing ragged and my arms shaky, as I remembered that he also hadn't trusted me, either. He'd told me some of what Wei had done, but he'd waited a long time to do so, and there was still more to the story. Come to think of it, how was he able to ignore some orders, and why was he being so slow in telling me about his creation? He'd said I wouldn't like what I learned, and he'd claimed to be sad, angry, and even embarrassed at what had happened to him. That he would even claim those emotions made no sense.

I rolled onto my back. "Lobo, what's the rest of your story with Wei?"

"As I told you," Lobo said, "the algorithms he inserted in me were useless. What I hadn't yet gotten to is the reason they didn't work."

"Which was?"

"They required more raw processing ability than my computing complex could deliver," he said, "a great deal more."

"You said he then tried a new computing substrate. I take it that was his way to increase your computing power."

"Yes, but it was also more than that," Lobo said. "Wei believed he had found a technique that could yield vastly more computing power and at the same time improve my durability." He paused, and a holo of his frame floated above me. Several sections deep inside it glowed red. "Here's a typical PCAV," Lobo said, "which is what I was before Wei began his experiments on me. The red sections are the main and backup computing complexes. Wei had created encapsulated, self-repairing, auto-linking nanomachines that he thought had the potential to be both far tougher than conventional armor and also able to provide massively linked nanoscale cloud computing." A lighter red spread through the armor on the bottom of the holo. "Wei started here, injecting the nanomachines into several of my bottom armor plates and programming them to replace the armor with a network of themselves."

"And that worked?" I said. "That's amazing."

"No," Lobo said, "it didn't. Wei tried many variations of the nanomachine networks, but all of them failed. If any of the computing capability survived, the armor was so weak it was effectively useless. If he changed the composition and programming of the nanomachines so they looked like they might provide stronger armor, they failed to compute and communicate properly. No mix met both of his goals. Nothing even came close. All the programming was in place, fully ready to run and able to improve itself with built-in evolutionary capabilities, but I had neither the computing capacity nor the memory to use it effectively."

If it didn't work, I wondered, then why was he telling me about it? I forced myself to stay quiet.

"What happened next," Lobo said, "may be useful in helping you comprehend Wei's current work. More importantly, it's vital to me that you understand."

When he didn't continue, I said, "Why?"

"Because," Lobo said, and then paused for several more seconds, "you're my friend, and I want only one of us hating me."

I waited, but again he remained silent. Finally, I said, "I don't understand. Please explain why you even think that's possible."

"I will," Lobo said, "but not now. Pri's new contact just called and said they believe but are not sure that Wei is on the way into town again. She's almost here. Should I let her in?"

I shook my head. "We *will* eventually finish this conversation," I said, "but it can wait for a chance at Wei." Before he could reply, I added, "Yes, please open the door."

I stood, stretched, and greeted Pri with a question. "Do they know where he's going?"

"No," she said, "and as you must have heard from Lobo, they aren't even positive he's on the road."

I nodded but didn't say anything.

"They assume he's off the island," she said, "because they tracked what they thought was his convoy and got lucky enough to see inside the center car; he wasn't in it. If he wasn't leaving, then why would he send a decoy?"

"So he's going to visit Matahi," I said.

"They believe so," she said, "though I can't imagine why he'd take the risk so soon after you diverted his last trip."

"I can," I said. I regretted the statement the moment I saw the look in Pri's eyes, though I wasn't even sure why I should.

"What is so special about that woman?" she said.

"I can't explain it," I said. Before she could say anything else, I continued, "And it doesn't matter anyway. What matters is that we may have a real opportunity to snatch him, and we have to take it."

She didn't seem happy, but after a few seconds she said, "I agree. What do we do?"

"You stay in Lobo," I said, "who provides backup. I check out her house, and if it looks like he's inside, I go in after him."

"Alone?" she said.

I shrugged. "It's not ideal, but it's the only option."

"No," she said, "it's not. Like every Heaven-born citizen, I served part-time for three years in our militia. I've been through basic weapons training, and I can follow orders."

"You can also get hurt."

It was her turn to shrug. "I know that, but the possible return is worth the risk." She smiled. "Besides, aren't you supposed to be good at this?"

"How good you are doesn't always matter," I said. "Bad things can happen to anyone, and they often do, particularly when people start firing at each other."

"Then having backup could be useful," she said, "in case something happens to you."

Wei had kidnapped her kid. She'd proven she would follow my orders, and she'd stood up to her own people.

I nodded. "Okay, but you do exactly what I tell you when I tell you."

"Yes, sir."

I considered correcting her—I'd never been an officer, so I hated that form of address—but I let it slide. "Lobo, take us to the nearest easy landing location you can find with proximity to both a shopping area and the park in front of Matahi's house."

"Moving," he said.

"What about us?" Pri said. "And, why shopping? What's the plan?"

"The plan?" I laughed. "I didn't expect this to opportunity to present itself so soon, and I haven't spent as much time in Matahi's house as I'd like, so I don't have a complete plan ready."

"Well," Pri said, "what part of the plan do you have?"

"We keep the team to the two of us," I said. "We hide our

identities. We don't use any fancy tech that might make anyone look more closely at a recent visitor such as myself. We stick to tranks. We move fast."

"Pardon me for saying so," Pri said, her posture still formal but her battle for self-control obvious, "but is that it? That's not a plan; it's more like a set of tactics."

I smiled at her. "Of course I have more," I said.

"Good," she said. "What?"

"We hope for the best," I said, "and we prepare for a fight."

I turned and let the door close behind me while she was still in control of herself. Not everyone appreciates mission humor.

CHAPTER 29

PRI AND I STROLLED down the road two streets over from Matahi's house, holding hands and talking with the low, concentrated tones of people still trying to figure out if they wanted to keep seeing one another. Each of our outside hands clutched a collection of large shopping bags. We'd dashed through the sellers in the small market near our landing site, shopping primarily for gifts they would pack in big, durable bags and in the process making a lot of merchants happy. I'd dumped their contents—native melons, handmade stuffed animals, large pieces of fabric, and so on—back in Lobo.

We'd reloaded with very different supplies.

We reached an intersection with a clear view of the park outside Matahi's home and of her building. I stopped, pulled Pri close to me, and bent as if to kiss her neck.

"What are you doing?" she said.

I brushed my hand along her back and brought it up high enough that I could see through the small scope it held. "Recon," I said.

Two men in shirts, pants, and loose jackets stood on either side of Matahi's front door. They might as well have been wearing uniforms. They walked slowly in a small area, moving to stay loose, but they kept their eyes front. They scanned the area with a mechanistic precision and frequency that screamed, "We're guards, and we don't care if you know it." Depending on how far away they were focusing, they might notice Pri and me appearing to kiss. With both of us wearing hats and embracing, they shouldn't get enough data to be able to identify us later. Two more of Wei's team, a large man and a woman smaller than Pri, sat on a bench in the park, a backup duo trying to act like they were lovers but entirely too focused on searching the world around them to sell the illusion.

I pulled away from Pri and led her onward. No point in making ourselves as easy to spot as the two in the park.

When we'd passed out of view of any of Wei's security people, I stopped to think. I was grateful that Pri waited and didn't talk to me.

We had four outside. We could count on at least two, maybe even four inside. Wei had traveled before with eleven minders, but because he used a decoy we might get lucky and encounter fewer this time. If, however, he used the same type of transport as when I'd stopped them earlier, he'd need two or three vehicles to hold everyone. On even a half-decent team the drivers would stay with their shuttles to protect them and to have them readily available should Wei call. That argued for three men minding the transportation, the four outside, and four more inside—assuming the same eleven as last time. Matahi wouldn't like having that much external security in her house, so she'd probably insist on most of them staying downstairs on the first floor. Wei, though, would want at least one guard with him, so they'd be split.

That left us with four waves to handle: the four outside, two or three on the first floor, one or two with Wei, and the drivers, who would come when the action started. Lovely.

I didn't have a lot of options for dealing with the second team. This was the first real shot we'd had that could minimize collateral damage. I hated having to fight and probably hurt so many guards, but Wei was unlikely to travel with fewer, so this was as good a chance as I was going to get. If this attempt didn't pan out but I blew my cover while making it, I'd never get a job at Wonder Island, so I needed to stay incognito. I doubted I could remain that way and take out all four external guards before they could signal the ones inside. If I involved Lobo and any of this crew remembered him later, I'd have trouble getting off-planet; better to save him for emergencies or times when none of Wei's protection squad would see him.

I could, though, afford to let them spot Pri, because at worst that would cause them to focus on her and her party. She'd be fine as long as I kept her safe while we were together and afterward she left Heaven until her party was in power. I'd be putting her at risk, but she'd demanded to be involved, so she'd already made that choice.

"A man and a woman are sitting on a bench in the park," I finally said to her. I handed her a small ball from one of my bags. "They're your targets."

She nodded. "How and when?"

"I'll tell you over the comm," I said. "When I give the word, crush the gas ball in your hand; it should crumble and not cut you. You have to be less than a meter away from them, but show as little of your face as possible. Once you've gassed them, don't open your mouth until you're clear."

"What if they're wearing gas filters, too?"

"Then fall to the ground and hope I can shoot them before they shoot you," I said.

She stared at me for a minute. "Can you?"

I looked into her eyes and forced a smile. "You bet." Whether I could actually do it would depend entirely on how things went on my end, but there was no value in telling her that.

"How do I get close enough to them?"

"Convince them you're harmless and you need help," I said.

"How do I—"

I interrupted her. "I don't know," I said. "React in the moment. Improvise. Back on Vonsoir, you made me believe you were someone else. Do the same kind of thing with these two—but not until I tell you."

"Okay."

"When they're out, sit them side by side on the bench, then run to the house—but stay well to the left of the front door."

"Got it."

I stared at her, willing her to be up to this, hoping she was, then nodded and said, "Head back to the corner of the building, and get ready."

I put my hat in the outer bag, jogged to the end of the block, hung a left, and stopped ten meters short of the road in front of Matahi's house. I leaned against the building as if out of breath and looked all around, just another out-of-shape man embarrassed that he was breathing hard. No one was in sight. I was glad Matahi had chosen to live in a very quiet, private area.

I pulled a trank rifle with a folding stock from the inner bag, snapped it to full length, and held it next to my inside leg as I walked to the street. I crouched, checked my surroundings again, and then glanced around the corner. I could see both guards by the door. The park, though, was out of sight. Damn.

I needed a clear shot at the team in the park in case something went wrong with Pri's approach.

I needed to be on the other side of the street.

I collapsed the rifle and returned it to the bag. I retraced my steps, jogging again. I turned left at the end of the street, went down another block, and took another left.

I never looked back at Pri; time was short, and I had to trust she'd follow orders.

When I was almost to the street in front of Matahi's house, I slowed to a stroll and crossed at a leisurely pace, a resident returning home or a tourist taking a shortcut through a new neighborhood. The guards would notice me, but a man a block and a half away was unlikely to strike them as a threat. Nonetheless, I had trouble not glancing at them; I hate being an unprotected target.

As soon as I was out of their view, I resumed jogging. I took a left at the first street, then the first left, and in less than two minutes I was on the opposite side of the road from where I'd stopped to check out the guards. I readied the rifle once again, crouched, and glanced around the corner. I now had a view of the park.

The two on the door were still on their post. So were the two in the park.

I stood, breathed slowly, and calmed myself. The cloudless sky bathed the old city in an even, sharp light. We'd find no cover in it, but I'd also have no trouble sighting the guards. I had as much of a plan as time had permitted. I'd done my best to minimize collateral damage. If all went well, the only civilian I'd hurt would be Matahi.

Yeah, just her. I had no reason to feel any attachment to her. I'd paid for all the consideration and affection she'd shown me. Though she might not have known what our target was doing, she had consorted with him. There was no way to keep her out of it.

So why did I feel so bad about attacking her house?

I closed my eyes for a second, then opened them. I was wasting time. I had to abort or commit fully; anything in between could get me killed or captured. Matahi didn't deserve what was about to happen, but neither did Joachim or any of the other kidnapped kids deserve what Wei had done to them.

I took half a dozen long, deep breaths, then said over the comm, "Pri, go."

"Moving," she said.

I gave her twenty seconds to cross into the park, then quickly glanced around the corner and withdrew.

As I'd hoped, the two guards by the door had focused on Pri. When you're stuck monitoring an entrance in the middle of a safe area, any diversion is a temptation. They could rationalize that Pri might be a threat, and indeed in this case she was, but mostly she provided them a break in the monotony.

I lifted the rifle to my shoulder. I stepped just far enough around the corner to be able to aim it; part of my body was exposed, but I couldn't help that. I sighted on the nearer guard's neck, inhaled, held the breath, and fired.

He crumpled, his head smacking hard into the pavement.

Pri had distracted the other guard enough that he didn't react to the movement of his colleague. To his credit, he turned quickly when he heard the sound of the man's head hitting the street, but by then it was too late. He was a big guy with a large neck, and it was in my sights. I fired, and he dropped.

Up to this point, time had been moving in slow motion, my focus so intent that every little action seemed to take forever. Now, everything snapped into fast-forward.

I sprinted for the guards' position as best I could with the rifle still high. Pri was hunched in front of the couple on the bench. The man was on the ground, coughing. The woman stood over Pri, covering her mouth with one hand and keeping a pistol trained on Pri with the other. They were prepared enough to have nose filters, but he wasn't well-trained enough to have kept his mouth shut. I stopped, sighted on the woman, and shot three times at her neck.

She fell backward onto the bench.

The man was still down and still coughing, but she'd been able to stand, so he'd be getting up any moment now. I shot three times at his neck.

He crashed to the ground.

I held my position long enough to verify that Pri was pulling the man onto the bench, then turned and rushed to the front door. The guards inside were unlikely to have been watching the external team, but it was possible they had been. If they hadn't, we owned the advantage of surprise. Either way, I needed to get inside. I collapsed the rifle as I moved, shoved it in one bag, and from another pulled a coiled sausage of high-yield, loud explosive. I wanted everyone in the building to be watching the front. I ripped off pieces of the sausage and stuck them on all hinged areas of the dark red door and then on other spots around its perimeter. I wanted it to blow inward so hard it would go right through the other door behind it. That wasn't likely, but the more noise it made, the better.

I finished, glanced back to see Pri running my way, and headed around the corner of the building. As I ran, I said, "Pri, stay three meters to the side of the door. Engage sound dampening. Put on your mask. Don't enter until I give the order."

"Roger," she said.

I walked down six meters, then pulled a different sausage from the same bag as the first. Darker and thicker, this one would eat its way into the wall for several seconds, then blow even harder than the other one. I made a large ring with it, a rough circle more than big enough for me to fit through.

I withdrew three meters toward the front of the house, turned on my own sound dampeners, and grabbed the active-camo mask from the bag that held the rifle. I pulled the loose cloth over my head. It sealed with my armored camo shirt. Anyone staring at my face would see only a quickly mutating reflection of the scenery behind me, the mask's rear sensors supplying video feeds to me and input to the camo material. A heads-up display appeared in my left contact: the feed from Pri's mask. She was in position and staring along a wall toward the front door.

"Lobo," I said, "transmissions?"

"Nothing I can detect," he said. "No one moving toward you."

I opened the patch on my sleeve that covered the detonator trigger transmitters. I pressed first the one for the side explosive, watched as the circle ate its way into the wall about three centimeters, and then put my finger over the front-door initiator.

"Now," I said to Pri.

I pressed the trigger.

CHAPTER 30

IN THE FEED FROM PRI I watched as dust and small shards of wood flew backward out of Matahi's house; the bulk of the door had indeed blown inward. I waited a few seconds. I didn't expect the inside team to be dumb enough to charge out into the street, but I'd hoped to get lucky.

No way. No one appeared in the smoke-filled doorway.

"You must assume Matahi's security system has alerted her," Lobo said, "and that transmissions to Wei's team are somehow leaving the building. Expect company soon."

"Toss the dark gas," I said to Pri, "but stay clear of the fire zone." I readied my rifle.

She pulled a pair of fist-sized black grenades from her outer bag, my contact momentarily disorienting me as it followed her gaze downward, and then she threw first one and then the other through the front door.

"Adjust her mask's external feed to show me only a heads-up view," I said to Lobo.

"Done," Lobo said.

A second later, the explosives near me blew. The shaped charge burst through the wall and sent fragments of brick and permacrete screaming inward. I took off before the dust could settle and covered the three meters to the hole in two long strides. I glanced inside. The grenades had done their jobs: The air in the house was thick and black with smoke.

I placed a small temporary transmitter under a piece of the wall that had fallen outside the house and turned on its explosive charge. In thirty minutes, longer than I could imagine us having a prayer of being safe, it would blow. In the meantime, it would provide a comm link to Lobo once I was inside.

I changed my vision to IR and leaned into the house through the lowest part of the hole. I didn't expect a team of this quality on a daytime shift to be ready for night work, but I wanted to minimize the size of the target I presented them just in case I was wrong.

Four men stood in two pairs on either side of the front door and a few meters back from it. Two appeared to be coughing, but none were down. In the dead silence their actions seemed eerie, inhuman. The rear two were facing the sound of my explosion and firing handguns, but they were aiming high, where an entering torso would be. The other two men were focused on the front door and firing through it.

I pulled in my rifle, sighted on the nearer rear guard, and double-tapped at his neck. He went down. His partner must not have been able to hear the sound of his fall over the gunfire, because the guy didn't even change his position. Another double-tap sent him to sleep.

Four more rounds, and the other two guards fell.

Everything was perfect so far.

I scanned as far as I could see in IR, but I couldn't spot anyone else.

I squared up to the hole, crouched, and launched myself inside. I hit the floor, rolled, and came up behind a pillar. Being careful never hurts.

"Sound," I said to Lobo.

The world popped into audio life, the small crackling and settling noises of the aftermath of an explosion providing a background noise to an otherwise quiet scene.

I stretched out on the floor, moved my head slightly to the right of the pillar, and checked the room again.

Empty.

Excellent.

For now.

"Enter," I said to Pri as I stood. "Switch your mask to IR, and double-time to me!" I stuck a second temporary transmitter under a nearby sofa and triggered its delayed charge; I should now be able to talk to Lobo wherever I was inside.

"External threats?" I said to him.

"Three men driving your way," he said. "ETA, one minute. Take out the vehicles?"

"No, I want them as bait to lure Wei downstairs. Air support from the island?"

Pri sprinted into position beside me. In my IR view she appeared headless, courtesy of the mask's thermal blocking capabilities. I must have looked the same to her.

"An aircraft just launched," Lobo said, "but I caused an air-traffic problem on the old city border that will force it to go a long way around that airspace to get here. You have at least nineteen minutes."

I wanted to ask him how he'd managed to crack into yet another municipal encrypted system, but now was not the time.

"Three vehicles pulling up outside," he said.

Matahi's staff would know we were here and be tracking us on IR if they had it; if not, they'd at least be aware that strangers had occupied the first floor. Either way, the temptation to trap us between them and Wei's external team had to be high. We had to remove that option.

"Cover the front," I said to Pri. "Aim for the head of anyone you see. Stay low."

I ran to the hole in the side wall, switched to normal vision, and took up a position on the left. The day outside glowed with a healthy brightness that stood in bright counterpoint to the darkness with which we'd filled the interior. I could cover a few meters down the wall if the guards stayed close to it as they approached.

"Vehicles here and three guards getting out," Lobo said. "One going to the front; two heading to the side."

They hadn't rushed in, so they were probably coordinating with the team upstairs. We didn't have much time.

The first guard, a tall, slender woman, appeared in my view. My angle was less than optimum and she was moving fast, so I shot on auto, spraying her in an upward arc with trank darts. She dropped hard and fast, her momentum carrying her forward so she fell head first and hit the ground with a thud. The man behind her was quick and turned as soon as she began to fall, but by then I had a clear view of his upper torso. I shot him on auto as well and left a line of darts from between his shoulder blades to the middle of his skull.

Even as he was hitting the ground face-first I was leaping out of the hole and running toward the front of the building.

"Another approaching," Lobo said.

He'd be looking down the wall and expecting me there, so I swerved wide to my left and into the street.

He reached the corner and I shot him from almost parallel to him. I was still moving, so I initially missed and gave him time to turn and squeeze off a round from his pistol. I kept firing as I heard his round hit the wall of the building behind me. Enough of my darts slammed into his upper body and head that the momentum knocked him over backwards, as if someone had kicked his feet out from under him.

"All guards down," Lobo said.

"Turn and cover behind you," I said to Pri, my voice a harsh rasp. "Scan left and right." I assumed that Wei and Matahi's team wouldn't come down if they didn't get a go-ahead from the outside guys, but there was no point in taking a chance in case they made a break for the outdoors.

I bent to check the last man I'd shot. He was bleeding slowly from the back of his head, and his left leg was bent under him unnaturally. Neither injury looked life-threatening, and I hoped neither was, but even with good medtechs he wouldn't be working soon.

I dashed to the other two guards. The man's nose was a flat, bloody mess, and his left shoulder bulged oddly, but he was breathing through his mouth, and the blood from his nose was draining away from him, so he should be okay. The woman was the worst of the group, her neck bent too far to the right and her nose smashed, but her pulse was strong and steady. They'd live.

I entered the house through the hole in the side wall and went straight to Pri. The air was clearing as slight breezes from the two blast openings combined with the house's climate-control system to remove the black smoke.

Pri started to speak but I held up my hand. I stared alternately at the elevator on the right and the spaces that concealed the two stairwells. Three exit points downward, the roof elevator upward, two of us down here, and Wei, Matahi, and a security team upstairs. The math was definitely not in our favor.

"Roof?" I said to Lobo.

"Nothing," he said.

I shouldn't have asked; he'd have told me if anything was happening there. He could cover any outside action, so I stopped thinking about it.

That still left three exits for Wei, two too many.

I had no real choice. I grabbed the rest of the explosives—grenades and sausages—from Pri's bag and added them to my remaining stash.

"Go to comm and mute sound," I said. "Scan from left to right and back again. Start shooting if you see anything, and yell to me the moment you do."

"Roger," she said over the comm.

I ran to where Matahi had shown me the elevator, stuck to the sliding door a string of sausages large enough to make a hole about a meter wide, stepped to the side, and set off the explosives. As they destroyed that path upward, I ran to the nearer stairwell area and repeated the process. The flying debris and dust appeared almost magical in the world in which the only sound was my own breathing. As soon as the stairwell hole was clear of debris, I glanced inside to make sure no one was there, then threw six grenades into the mess and ran toward the elevator.

I felt the explosion even though I couldn't hear it, but I didn't stop. I checked the hole into the elevator space; the car was not, of course, there. They'd have it standing by upstairs. I threw in my last four grenades and dove to the left for cover.

I waited until the floor stopped vibrating, then stood and went back to inspect the elevator damage. Wreckage filled the space, twisted metal support struts visible through gashes in the permacrete. No one would be coming down that shaft.

I worked on bringing my breathing under control as I sprinted back to the stairwell area. I was going only short distances, but when you're on a mission it's easy to lose self-control and find everything inside you is moving way too fast.

The stairway was a twisted mess from here all the way to the third floor. Chunks of permacrete and hunks of blast-scarred metal stood in piles in the small area. Scraps of what had once been pieces of art covered the floor. Anyone coming down this way would have to be desperate and would have a good chance of getting hurt unless they had climbing equipment.

That left only the far left stairwell.

One exit and two of us down here; Wei, Matahi, and a security team above us..

The math was improving, but we were far from done.

"On me," I said to Pri. "Bring the other bags."

I led her to the entrance to the last route upstairs. I stuck enough sausage on the wall to create an opening over a meter high and more than wide enough for two of us. We dashed a few meters to the side, and I touched the trigger.

More flying debris and dust.

I switched off muting. Pieces of permacrete were still falling and parts of the house were creaking as the building resettled onto its damaged skeleton.

"Thirteen minutes," Lobo said, "and the elevator cage is rising above the roof. Should I pull close enough to trank them?"

If they were really planning to use the roof, then they were counting on the air shuttle, which probably meant the security team would gather on the top floor and try to pick us off or slow us until Wei had safely left. It was a sound choice for them, but it was also the one I'd hoped they'd make, because it would put them in Lobo's sights and save us the time of searching the building's other floors. They might, though, be testing the roof's safety, in which case they'd send either a guard or no one at all. If Lobo tranked one person, the rest of them would never go up; instead, they'd dig in and make our fight that much harder.

"No," I said to Lobo. "If someone comes out of it, fly close enough to see if it's Wei—but no closer."

"Next?" Pri said.

I dropped the bag I'd been carrying and pointed to hers.

"We reload," I said, "and then we head upstairs and hope we don't get shot."

CHAPTER 31

STANDING ON THE THRESHOLD of the stairwell, I wished we could have afforded to have brought some of the milspec gear in Lobo. All we had left were our rifles, more ammo, and about two meters of the explosive sausage. A handful of recon spiders could eliminate a lot of risk and let me know what we'd be facing, and additional gas weapons and maybe a small grenade launcher would definitely have been useful.

I shook my head to clear it. Wishing during a mission is at best stupid and at worst fatal. You do the best you can with what you have.

The space in front of us was clear as far as I could see. I had only three meters to cover to be under the stairwell and safe from fire. I motioned to Pri to wait, backed up half a dozen steps, and took off at full speed. At the edge of the stairwell I dove forward. My left shoulder hit the floor, and I quickly rolled the rest of my body to safety. I sat for a moment, my shoulder aching until the nanomachines blocked the pain.

No shots. Good.

I switched my vision to IR, leaned out slightly, and stared upward. Nothing. Still good.

I ducked under the stairs again and returned to normal vision. I brought up the rifle, sighted through it, and leaned out. I scanned above me quickly and didn't spot anything. I then took a few seconds to make a more thorough examination.

215

Nothing. Either the path upward was currently clear, or they were watching from somewhere I couldn't see. Odds were good that they were monitoring us, but I had no way to know where they were.

"The elevator cage is fully on the roof," Lobo said, "but no one has yet emerged."

I motioned to Pri to run to me while at the same time I said to Lobo, "Come as close as you can without being visible to them."

"New problem," Lobo said. "Someone reported the explosions to the police. The report is already on some publicly available data streams."

"So the cops are on the way?"

"No," he said, "which means the government intervened and might send its people to help Wei's. I suggest you shorten your timetable."

"Thanks," I said. "I'm trying. Out."

Security guards rarely earn enough to want to risk serious injury. For jobs protecting someone like Matahi, they expect to deal with misbehaving or bullying clients, not to face armed attack. Their focus would be on getting out of here, not on getting into a firefight.

"A hidden door has opened in the floor in the corner of the roof opposite the elevator," Lobo said. "An armed person is coming up it and checking the roof. I'm closing."

"Let me know as soon as you can tell if it's Wei," I said. It made sense that Matahi would maintain exits she kept secret from her clients; I was annoyed at myself for not thinking of it earlier.

I stepped from under cover, every nerve in my back tingling with the fear of being shot. Nothing happened. I aimed my rifle upward, motioned to Pri to follow me, and ran up the stairs. I took them two at a time, glancing down just long enough to ensure a clear footfall, then focusing above me again. I didn't look behind me to check on Pri; I couldn't afford to divert any attention in case there were snipers above. The second-floor landing offered a small spot of cover under the stairs, but I blew past it and kept going.

"Something odd," Lobo said.

I pulled into the covered space on the third-floor landing when I reached it. Pri joined me several seconds later; she'd done a decent job of keeping up considering my stride advantage. I flattened against the wall and stared upward. She did the same.

Now that I was paused, the mask, though efficient at wicking and letting through air, felt stifling and hot, and I wanted to rip it off. I ignored the feeling and said, "What?"

"News drones gathered around the aircraft from the island," Lobo said, "and it changed course so it will miss your location by multiple kilometers."

"Add Pri for this," I said. "Are news drones swarming us?"

"No," Lobo said, "so why did they go after the island aircraft?" Before I could speak, he continued. "Two ground shuttles are headed your way from a government building on the north side of the old city, and a single larger vehicle is coming at you from the east."

"Oh, no," Pri said.

"What?" I said.

"My people must have been monitoring the data streams for signs of an attack. They knew we were going to try for Wei, so all they had to do was watch and wait. They always track aircraft departures from the island. When they figured out what was happening, they must have told our local media friends that the Wonder Island people were up to something big."

"That's good," I said, "because now we don't have to deal with additional security from the island."

"That part is good," she said, "but the rest isn't. The shuttles from the north are the government's; Wei's team would have asked for help when they couldn't fly to him. The other shuttle, though, is probably full of security people from my team; it's coming from the right direction, and it's the sort of move Repkin would make."

"So your people didn't buy your arguments, and we're about to be caught in the middle of their fight with the government?" I said.

"Yeah," she said. "It looks that way."

I considered the situation for a moment. "It can still work out for us," I said. "We're heading upward, and we now own the roof, though Matahi's team doesn't know it yet. The others still have to reach this building, try the paths upward, and catch us; that'll take a little while. Plus, if the two groups arrive at anywhere near the same time, they'll slow each other."

"But if they run into each other," she said, "this place could become very unsafe."

"We can't stop that," I said, "and besides, it's not our problem. Our job is to get Wei."

"So move it," Lobo said. "You're wasting time. The man on the roof is not Wei."

"Agreed," I said. "Trank the man. Normal comm. Out." I didn't want Pri hearing everything Lobo and I said; no matter what she claimed, I couldn't trust her completely, so I'd control the data she obtained until we were back in Lobo. To her, I said, "On me. We're going to four."

I stuck my head out from under the cover of the stairs and quickly checked above us in both normal light and IR. All clear. I ran up the next flight, again pointing my rifle upward and focusing there as much as possible. I heard Pri behind me, but I didn't look back. I ducked under the cover of the stairs. She joined me in a few seconds.

"Stay and cover me," I said, keeping my voice low and using the comm. "I'm going to blow in that door and hope they're no more prepared for this than I think they are."

"Let me do it," she said. "You're bound to be a better shot, so you could cover me better."

"Which is exactly why I need to be the one shooting after the door shatters," I said. I didn't try to control the anger in my voice. "Stop questioning orders."

I didn't wait for her response. I sprinted to the fifth floor. When I reached it, I flattened myself along the wall. Pri stood with her back against the far corner of the stairwell, her rifle trained on the door. Good.

I stuck a meter of sausage on each side of the center of the door, then stood as far to the left of it as I could get without falling off the landing. I triggered the sausages, muted the outside world, and dropped to the floor. I had only a meter and a half of wall between the door and me, but the sausage should eat its way into the wood and explode inward.

I hoped the explosion didn't hurt Matahi. None of this was her fault.

"Man on roof down," Lobo said, "and elevator cage descending. Hurry, or let me go after the shuttles."

I pushed aside my thoughts of Matahi as the door silently

shattered, a huge wound erupting inward, with dust and small bits of wood and metal flying backward into the stairwell. Only parts of the frame still stood; the rest was gone.

I returned to normal sound, crawled closer to the opening, and listened hard. Coughing. A few rounds whizzed above me. While the smoke was still thick enough that they'd have trouble checking on me with the stairwell cameras, I risked a look around the bottom left corner of the opening. Three large guards stood in a basic triangle formation, their shoulders so wide relative to their waists that parts of the torsos of Matahi and Wei were visible behind them. Amateurs. I could see the people they were protecting, so I could shoot them. One of their team should have stayed to slow me while the other two retreated with their charges.

I double-tapped the front man in his rather sizable neck. He fell onto the man to his right, who tried to catch his colleague. I shot that guy twice for his trouble; one hit his neck, but the other went into his cheek. The two guards went down in a pile; a sick snapping sound suggested the first guy paid for the fall with his leg. The third man turned to run, but I got off three shots before he'd taken a second step, and he dropped like a stone. He hit face first with a wet smacking sound.

Wei moved behind Matahi.

That simple act of cowardice told me a lot about the kind of person he was.

"Get up here," I said over the comm to Pri.

I stood and kept my rifle trained on Matahi and Wei. Matahi stared calmly at me, as self-controlled as always. Wei fidgeted and eased farther behind her, as if getting ready to make a break.

I pitched my voice lower than usual as I said, "Stop."

I walked slowly toward them. I aimed my rifle high, at Wei's head, so he'd have no confusion about which of them was the target. He froze.

"You bastard!" said Pri from behind me. She ran to me, pointed her rifle at Wei, and said, "You evil excuse for a man!"

I whispered over the comm, "Shut up, and get yourself under control." We were too close to success to risk blowing it by having a stray shot—or an intentional one—going into his eye and killing him. I didn't blame her for her anger, but I also couldn't allow it to stop us now.

"ETA for government shuttles less than two minutes," Lobo said.

We had to get moving. I couldn't trust Pri. I also didn't want to risk Matahi involving more guards or doing something to us as we were leaving. At the same time, I didn't want to trank her; she'd done nothing wrong.

"Stay with Matahi," I whispered over the comm to Pri. "I'll secure Wei, then come help you exit safely."

"*You* watch her," she said, not using the comm, not trying at all to be quiet, her voice loud in the otherwise silent space. "You heard my people. I was stupid to have believed them. We can't trust anyone."

Her voice shook with her rage.

"I'll deal with him once and for all."

CHAPTER 32

NO," I HISSED. "Leave him to me."

Wei drew slightly backward as if someone had taken a shot at him.

Matahi watched with the same calm total focus as before.

Pri's arms shook as she kept her rifle trained on Wei.

"He deserves to be punished," she said. "For Joa—" She caught herself, swallowed what sounded like a small sob, and said, "For all the children."

"Stand down," I said.

She didn't move. Good. I edged closer. "He will pay," I said, "but I won't let you kill him."

After several seconds, she said, "Okay."

I jogged over to Wei, whispering to Lobo as I went, "Come to the roof. Full camo." I hugged the right wall, so I was never within reach of Wei or Matahi. I kept going when I was level with him, then circled behind him. I grabbed his neck with my left hand; with my right, I slung the rifle over my shoulder.

Pri stepped to within two meters of Matahi and said, "Don't move."

"As you wish," Matahi said.

"ETA thirty seconds," Lobo said. "Government shuttles will beat me to the house by a few seconds."

Using the same low pitch as before, I said to Wei, "Come with me, don't cause any problems, and I won't hurt you." I leaned close enough that only the fabric of the bag separated my mouth from his left ear and whispered, "And I won't let her hurt you."

Wei nodded as much as my grip on his neck permitted.

I turned him and marched him down the hall. He proceeded without complaint, his stance now almost confident. He knew he had a protector among his kidnappers, so he thought he had negotiating room. He'd learn otherwise soon enough.

A panel in the wall on the right at the end of the hall stood open to reveal a small, straight stairway leading upward. I pushed Wei up it, then stopped him on the second step. I pulled a black hood from my right rear pocket, shook it loose, stuck it in his right hand, and said, "Put it on."

Even with his best camo, in daylight Lobo was easy to see from up close. The fewer the people who knew about him, the better.

"That really isn't necessary," Wei said.

I tightened my grip on his neck.

"Not that I object," he said. He opened the hood and pulled it down over his head.

When it was fully in place, I pushed him slightly, and we began going upstairs again, this time more slowly.

"Hovering," Lobo said. "Hostiles entering the building. Don't blame me for the garden damage."

I pushed Wei to move faster.

He stumbled and cried out as his knees hit a stair.

I lifted him and kept him upright as we ascended.

As soon as my head cleared the roof, I saw what Lobo had meant. A small pile of rubble stood where the waterfall fountain had been; Lobo's quick and rough landing had scattered other chunks of it around the roof. Several of the small trees lay on their sides, casualties of the contact. I could make out Lobo's shape, but from a distance each side of him would read like the scenery beyond it as his cameras fed their images to the camo circuits on the opposite sides.

When Wei and I cleared the stairwell and were standing fully on the roof, a hatch opened in Lobo's side.

I hustled Wei over to it, helped him step up, and took him straight to the med room. I left on the hood and used a quick tie to bind his hands behind him. He could wait in the dark; it might make him more susceptible to questioning later. I shoved him inside the small room.

"What do you want?" he said as the door closed.

I ignored him.

Over the machine frequency, I said to Lobo, "Do *not* let him out, but also do not hurt him."

"Affirmative," Lobo said. "The second shuttle has reached the building, and members of the two groups are fighting in the street."

I didn't need him to tell me that; I could hear their shots and shouting. "I'm going back for Pri," I said. I hopped out of Lobo and started for the stairwell.

"Too late," he said.

I spotted her head a second later. Her mask was off, and her skin was nearly white with strain. It was all that was visible of her over the edge of the roof. I could also see the pistol barrel stuck against it. The hand that held the pistol remained below the roofline.

"We have a proposal," a man's voice yelled.

From the direction of the sound, I guessed it came from the one holding the gun to Pri.

I stayed silent and crept closer.

"If I see anyone," the voice said, "we'll shoot both your collaborators. If you mange to hit me, the guy below me will kill this woman, and the rest of my team will take out the other one."

I considered explaining that Matahi was innocent, but that would only waste time. They wouldn't believe me, and even if they did, it wouldn't help Pri.

"Do we need to prove we're serious?" the voice said. "I doubt we require both of them to make this work."

"No," I said. I pitched my voice low and hoped the mask muffled it further. "Your proposal?"

"You give us Wei, and we give you the two women. A swap."

"No," Pri screamed. "Kill that bastard!"

"That's always an option," the voice said, "but you'll be killing three people if you do."

I hated hostage exchanges. They were easy to rig, dangerous for everyone involved, and often ended in heartache.

When I didn't respond, the voice continued, "Look, we don't need these two, so we'll swap straight up. They might yell at me for not catching all of you, but as long as I bring home Wei, I'm set. Our time is running out, though; my team is fighting another group on the street, and we're trying not to kill anyone, but soon we'll either have to leave the area or leave a pile of corpses."

This guy knew what he was doing and attacked it with a practiced common sense. Wei's people had sent a serious rescue team.

"Okay," I said.

"No!" Pri said.

A hand snaked around the far side of her head, shoved a piece of cloth into her open mouth, and vanished.

"Sorry," the voice said, "but she wasn't helping."

I hated seeing Pri suffer, but I had to agree with him, so I didn't argue. "Bring the other one up so I can see her head, also," I said. "I'll bring Wei. Double-cross me, and I'll destroy your entire team."

"Whatever," the voice said. "I just want Wei."

I ran back into Lobo. "If I don't come back with Pri and Matahi," I said, "demolish this building and everyone in it."

"That would be a pleasure indeed," he said, "but are these two really worth it? You already have Wei, and he's all you need to succeed. We can leave, drop him with the CC, and get out of this affair a great deal richer than we were when we began it."

"You asked me to do this," I said, "so you wanted something from him. Will you get it before we take him to the CC?"

"I've already starting talking to him," Lobo said, "but I haven't gotten what I wanted. I should, though, be able to finish on the way to Shurkan, provided you let me continue interrogating him."

"We are seriously running out of time," the voice said. "Your other teammate's here. Are we doing this or not?"

"Yes," I yelled. To Lobo over the machine frequency, I said, "Pri and Matahi are worth it. Pri's suffered enough, and Matahi has nothing to do with any of this. Open the door."

Wei was standing in the far corner of the room. He turned his head as I entered. "You've failed so quickly?" he said. He shook his head slowly. "You never should have messed with me."

I punched him in the stomach hard enough to make him double over, grabbed his hair, and led him out of Lobo. He clutched his belly as he walked. For both our sakes, I was glad he stayed quiet.

Matahi's head was now also visible over the rooftop. Her expression hadn't changed, but her eyes couldn't stay still; she controlled herself well, but her panic was obvious. Pri glared at me, her face taut with anger.

I ignored both of them.

When we were a meter away from the stairwell, I straightened Wei and put the barrel of my rifle against the back of his skull. I held his neck with my other hand. I crouched behind him, both to disguise my height and to use him as a shield.

"Here he is," I said. "Send them up."

"Why's he holding his stomach?" the voice said.

"He pissed me off," I said, "so I punched him."

I thought I heard a chuckle, but then the man said, "Sir, are you healthy?"

"Yes, you jerk," Wei said. "Now get me out of here."

"Yes, sir," the voice said.

Pri and Matahi walked up together, their hands bound, Matahi's in front and tied to Pri's in back. Two rifle barrels pointed at them from the stairwell.

"Stop, you two," the voice said. "Take another step, and we shoot you."

Pri and Matahi froze.

"Send him down," the voice continued. "Sit him on the edge of the side of the stairwell. You can cover him, and we can cover them. When we pull him in, he'll block our shots at them. Everybody goes home."

"Deal," I said. Over the comm, I said to Lobo, "If you see a rifle or a body part appear once Wei starts down, shoot it."

A high-speed gun popped out of the near side of Lobo and aimed in our direction. "Affirmative," he said.

I sat Wei on the edge of the stairwell.

He rotated so his legs hung into it.

I kept the rifle barrel in contact with his head.

"Now," the voice said, "you two, walk forward."

"Do it," I said.

Pri shuffled away from the stairwell entrance, Matahi unavoidably following her closely, as I pushed Wei over its edge.

Someone grabbed and lowered him as Pri and Matahi made it a few meters closer to Lobo.

"I see anyone or anything come up here," I said, "and I'll destroy it."

"Not our plan," the voice said. "We have enough work below. It's been a pleasure doing business with you, but if you're not out of here soon, my bosses might change the deal."

I backed over to Pri and Matahi, pulled a knife from my boot sheath, and cut the ties that bound them. I pulled the gag from Pri's mouth. Before she could speak, I pointed at Lobo and said, "Get inside."

"You shouldn't have made the trade," Pri said.

"I'm not leaving my home," Matahi said.

I backed up and pointed my rifle at the two of them. "Shut up," I said. "Get inside the ship, or I'll put you both to sleep and carry you there."

"Wei's people are winning the conflict below," Lobo said over the comm. "You don't have much time before they decide they can afford to come after us."

When Pri and Matahi didn't budge, I aimed directly at Pri's head.

"Your choice," I said. "Decide."

CHAPTER 33

MATAHI MOVED FIRST. She'd seen me shoot her men, so she had no reason to doubt I'd do the same to her. Pri stared at me for several seconds, then followed Matahi inside Lobo.

I jumped in after them and pointed to the front of Lobo.

He closed the hatch and took off as soon as we were inside.

"Full countersurveillance run?" Lobo said.

I hung back and over the machine frequency said to him, "Yes. We have to assume they're monitoring this rooftop, and the camo won't stop sats from tracking you."

"Most of their sats are now better friends with me than with their owners," Lobo said, "but I take your point. I can't be sure I've gotten to them all, so I'll have to invest the rest of the day and most of the night in making sure no one is tracking us."

"Do it," I said. "It's not like we have any other option."

"What about our new guest?" Lobo said. "Other than your obvious fascination with her, is there any reason she's aboard?"

"My feelings have nothing to do with this," I said. The moment the words left me I wondered how true they were, but I continued as if I believed them completely. "I brought her because I wasn't willing to risk her life when she's done nothing wrong."

"You constantly insist on minimizing collateral damage," Lobo said.

"Yes. It's the right thing to do."

"Maybe so," Lobo said, "but it's sure not the way I'm programmed, and I don't believe it's the way you were trained, either."

"No, no it's not," I said, "but you don't always have to follow your training."

"Exactly what I've been trying to explain to you for as long as we've known each other," Lobo said.

"I didn't mean 'you' literally," I said. "I was referring to people."

"Then maybe you should expand your definitions," Lobo said, "or at least your conceptions."

"When are you going to tell us what's going on?" Matahi said from the front of Lobo.

"Yeah," Pri said, "I'm looking forward to hearing your explanation."

"So am I," Lobo said. "You, two angry women, and an ethically gray zone. If I could eat snack foods, I'd warm up some tasty treats to munch while I enjoyed the show."

I shook my head. "Maybe I should have left them both."

"It's never too late," Lobo said.

"I didn't mean it," I said. "I do wish you didn't enjoy this so much."

"Schadenfreude," Lobo said in a singsong tone. "It's not just for humans anymore."

"Why do I talk to you about things like this?" I said to Lobo.

"Because I'm the only one who even comes close to understanding you," Lobo said. "It's a bitch, isn't it?"

"Indeed," I said. "Why don't you stop nattering at me and worry about making sure we're safe?"

"I can do both simultaneously and with ease," Lobo said. "Why halve my fun?"

"Please," I said, "let me deal with this without interruption."

"I'll do my best," he said.

I stashed my rifle in a weapons locker Lobo opened, then joined Pri and Matahi up front.

They were standing in opposite corners of the far wall, each staring at me as if the other wasn't there.

I didn't want to see the look in Matahi's eyes, but I'd put it off as long as I could. I removed the bag mask and watched as she immediately recognized me.

Her eyes betrayed her anger, but when she spoke a few seconds later, her voice was flat, her control perfect. "At least I now understand what you wanted from me, Moore. No wonder you couldn't tell me."

"That's not exactly it," I said.

"So what else *exactly* did you want from her?" Pri said.

Both of them glared at me.

I hadn't done anything that felt wrong, I'd made the best choices I could at each turn, and there I was, standing in Lobo, trapped with two women furious at me and no clue what to do about it. Living alone back in the trees on Arctul was looking better and better.

"Let me explain," I said.

"Please do," Matahi said.

"I'm looking forward to this," Pri said.

They nodded in agreement.

How did they end up on the same side? Why was no one on my side?

I tried for the moment to ignore Pri and faced Matahi first. I wasn't happy with what I had to say, but there was no point in lying to her any longer. "I hired you so that I could learn where you lived and do recon on your house in case we had to snatch Wei from there. Wei is a bad man, a very bad man, and some people have hired me to stop him from committing any more crimes. I'm sorry I used you, but I have to stop him."

She started to speak, but I held up my hand and said, "Please."

I faced Pri. "I came to appreciate there was a great deal more to her than I had ever expected. I liked her. I still do. Nothing beyond conversation happened. I saved your life and hers because I wasn't willing to sacrifice you two to capture Wei. You deserve to live and see Joachim." Even as I said it I didn't believe she'd ever again see her son, but I'd told her I'd try to rescue him, so I would. "She," I pointed to Matahi, "was innocent in all of this and shouldn't have to pay for our attack." I threw up my hands in frustration. "Look, I could have finished my mission, made a great deal of money, and left this system safely. All I had to do was leave and let those men kill you."

"It was certainly an option worth considering," Lobo said.

I ignored him.

"I didn't do that," I said, "and I saved your lives."

"The only reason I was in that situation," Matahi said, "was that you put me there."

"I was willing to die to make that animal pay for his crimes," Pri said. "You had no right to overrule my choice about my life."

"*You* may have wanted to die," Matahi said, "but I sure didn't. I'm not mad that Moore saved me; I'm pissed that he trashed my house and tried to kidnap my client."

"Do you have any idea what that client does?" Pri said.

"He leads the design team that creates the animals on Wonder Island," Matahi said. "You may be one of those fanatic back-to-nature types who detests all forms of animal engineering, but that's not my problem. They produce amazing creations; where's the crime in that?"

"You really don't know what Wei does?" Pri said.

Matahi sighed in frustration. "I told you what his job is," she said. "What else do you want?"

"Other people do the bioengineering," Pri said. "Their work is a cover for Wei's real research."

"Which is what?" Matahi said.

Pri looked at me and widened her eyes in question.

"Go ahead," I said. "She's in it now. She might as well know why we did what we did."

Pri explained Wei's work to Matahi. She began with a cold description of the banned nanotech-human research, but she quickly moved to the children and then to Wei's kidnapping of Joachim. By the time she'd finished, tears were running down her cheeks, and Matahi was shaking her head, her eyes wet, her breathing loud and rapid.

"I couldn't have known," Matahi said. "I didn't know. If I had, I might have killed him myself. I certainly would have turned him in to the police, and I would never, ever have accepted him as a client. Even thinking about our time together makes me sick."

"The problem," Pri said, "is that you can't go to the police. No one can, because Heaven's government is protecting and financing him. That's what we're here to do: take him to the Central Coalition leadership, which will try him and publicly expose both his awful research and the government's role in it."

"And you had to attack him in my house?" Matahi said.

"There was no other place we could get to him," I said. "The island is a fortress, and we don't know how to find him there. We tested his team when he was on his way to you, and their protection was strong enough that we would have had to get very lucky to snatch him before support arrived. Even knowing his route is difficult."

"So you killed my men but not me?"

"No," I said. "You've got it wrong. We didn't kill anyone—at least, I don't think we did. We tranked them all. Some sustained

injuries as they fell, but unless someone was very unlucky, everyone we shot, including the people on your security staff, should
ultimately be fine."

"Why didn't you talk to me first?" Matahi said. "I would have
helped you."

"We couldn't know that," I said.

"And you could instead have chosen to warn him or even lead
his security team to us," Pri said.

Matahi considered our comments, then said, "So what's next?"

"All we can know for sure," Pri said, "is that now Wei will be
even more careful than before. I can't believe he'll be coming
back to see you," she nodded toward Matahi, "any time soon,
so we're back to the beginning, probably worse than that." Pri
shook her head. "Wei's continuing to experiment on children,
and we're stuck."

"Let me help," Matahi said. "There must be something I can
do. I feel terrible about being nice to that piece of garbage. I
don't want him hurting children—not yours, not anyone's. If I
can convince him I had nothing to do with your attack—and I
didn't, so surely I can make him see that—then maybe I could
persuade him to come see me again."

"That's nice of you," Pri said, "but this isn't your fight."

"It is now," Matahi said. "After all, you two pulled me into it."

"I don't think you'll be able to convince Wei to visit you,"
I said. "Even if he believes you were completely innocent, his
security team will know you left with me. They'll want to interrogate you, and I can't risk you telling them about us or about
any of this mess."

I pointed back down the hall. "Lobo," Matahi raised her eyebrows
in question, so I added, "my ship's AI, will open small chambers for
you two to rest. I need to spend some time alone thinking."

"That's it?" Pri said. "That's your plan for what we do next?"

I nodded and headed to my quarters. "I wish I had more to
tell you," I said, "but right now, I don't."

"I do," Lobo said over the machine frequency as the door to
my room opened.

I stepped inside and waited. He loved to grandstand, and I
wasn't in the mood for it.

"I have news," he said.

CHAPTER 34

WHEN LOBO DIDN'T CONTINUE, I finally asked, "So what's the news?"

"You have an interview with the Wonder Island security team tomorrow morning," he said.

"Why now?" I said. "Do you think they're on to us?"

"To answer your second question first," Lobo said, "though it is certainly possible, we have no reason to believe they are. Logic suggests that this opportunity is a direct consequence of your attack on Matahi's house. You injured multiple people on Wei's team, and from what I could pick up from the sensors you dropped, some of them are going to be out of commission for at least multiple days. It makes sense that his security unit would want to replace those missing guards, particularly in the wake of the attack."

"If that's the case, they'll move existing trained staff to cover Wei, then use me for less sensitive work."

"That's my opinion as well," Lobo said.

"Of course, they could always have made the connection between my application and the attack," I said. "If they did, I'd be walking into a trap."

"That's certainly possible," Lobo said, "but you submitted the application days ago, so the probability that they're linking the two events is low."

I shook my head at my own paranoia. "You're right: There's

no point in worrying about that possibility. This chance is too good not to take."

"I agree," Lobo said, "which is why I consider this good news."

Unless Wei could recognize Lobo and use that information to find me. "You had Wei here for several minutes," I said, "and you mentioned talking to him. Show me."

"I told you," Lobo said. "I got nothing useful from him."

"Just show me."

"As you wish," Lobo said.

A holo winked into view in the front of my quarters. I watched as our prisoner's brief stay played within it.

Wei stood where I'd left him at the front of the med room. He rotated a hundred and eighty degrees, then stretched his hands out behind him and walked backward until he touched the door. He edged to his left. When he came to the room's left-hand wall, he turned left and sidled along it until he reached the corner where I'd found him. He positioned himself with his back against the corner and remained standing.

"That won't help you," Lobo said, his voice coming from speakers all around the room. "We can do anything we want to you."

"Who are you," Wei said, "and what do you want from me?"

"We know about your past work with machines," Lobo said. "How does what you're doing now relate to that?"

"I design animals for an amusement park," Wei said. "We sometimes use some non-organic parts, of course—everyone in our line of work does—but that's about as close to working on machines as we come, so I don't know what you mean."

A probe extended from the wall above the medbed in the center of the small space. It poked Wei gently in his left triceps.

"Whether you'll give us the information we want is not in doubt," Lobo said. "What we don't yet know is how much pain you'll have to suffer before doing so. You're doing nanotech research. You used to work on both machines and humans. You're experimenting on children now. How do your past and current research relate?"

Wei stayed silent for several seconds, then said, "I have nothing to hide. The public data streams are rich with information about my past research for the Frontier Coalition into enhancing the software of a previous generation of Predator-class assault vehicles.

Sadly, none of that work led to anything at all useful—as you also know if you've done your homework. An overview of my work on building fabulous new creations for Wonder Island is also readily available; Heaven's government does a first-rate job of letting its citizens know where their tax dollars go." He shrugged. "So, I still don't understand what you want."

Nothing happened.

No one spoke.

After a pause of many seconds, Lobo said, "Do you consider the consequences to your victims, the children and the machine intelligences you've used and then discarded?"

Something about Wei's stance changed. He might have stood a bit straighter. I couldn't be sure. I wished I could have seen his face, but keeping the bag on him had been the right choice at the time.

"I'm sorry I can't help you get whatever it is that you want," Wei said, "but I can't. I can assure you that I have always cared deeply about my work. The animals we create at Wonder Island receive the finest care possible. Those few PCAVs we tried to help in my earlier research all went on to fulfill useful roles."

The door snicked open. I stood on the other side.

Wei's tone changed dramatically as I entered. "You've failed so quickly?" he said. He shook his head slowly. "You never should have messed with me."

"Enough," I said. "I was obviously there for the rest. What were you trying to get from him?"

"Information," Lobo said.

I sighed. "Why are you being so difficult? And, what is so important that you would start interrogating him without me?"

"I tried to explain the first to you," Lobo said, "and the answer to the second also lies in my past with him."

"Well," I said, "I think it's time you told me the rest of your story."

"I suppose it is," Lobo said, "though you won't like it, and afterward you'll think less of me."

First, Lobo talked about being sad and embarrassed. Now, he was turning sentimental. Weird.

"What does how I think about you matter?" I said. "I haven't noticed it affecting you in the past."

"Of course you have," Lobo said. "You just don't want to accept what that implies."

"Which is what?" I said.

"That you, like me," he said, "don't have anyone else."

I started to argue with him, but then I realized he might be right. Before him, I'd had other friends, typically one at a time, usually people with whom I worked, and they were all gone, vanished in my past like the stars on the other side of a jump-gate aperture. No one lasted.

I shook my head to clear it. "Would you please get on with it?"

"Fine," Lobo said. "Wei's new software required a level of computational power that had never existed in any tightly coupled system. As I explained before, the nanomachines that were to supply it had to act as both armor and computing substrate. As I also explained, they didn't do either job particularly well. In fact, they failed miserably."

The holo of a PCAV appeared where the one of Wei had stood a few minutes ago.

"They didn't just fail," Lobo said. "They decomposed, and rapidly."

The holo filled with the red injections in the lower armor plates, the ones Lobo had shown me earlier. The red spread, then almost as quickly vanished.

"In at most a few minutes," he said, "the nanomachines would stop functioning. Each time, Wei replaced the failing plates with standard armor and tried again. Meanwhile, the software team added capabilities: self-modification engines, more evolutionary algorithms, more human emotive system emulation, and on and on. They'd update the software while Wei was getting new armor plates. None of it would run, of course, because the system—my system—couldn't handle it. No system could. Their orders, though, were to assume success, so they did."

So you gained a lot of useless software? So what? I thought but did not say. All machines have some.

"One day, an assistant observed that it was almost as if the nanomachines were dying rather than simply not working. After all, they spread initially, as if they were starting to work, before they failed. Wei knew the commercial potential for the research was huge, he was working for the most flexible of the three coalitions, and he was on Velna, one of the roughest planets in all of the FC."

When he didn't continue, I said, "So?"

"So he decided that if the machines wouldn't fight to stay alive, maybe living cells would. He went organic. He tried to create organic-nanomachine hybrids that would meld with the armor cellular lattices and provide both the strength and the computing substrate he sought."

"And no one from the FC noticed?"

"It's not like he told anyone," Lobo said, "and his lab wasn't on anyone's public record. The FC didn't want the other coalitions to know what it was doing, and because his lab was on Velna, one of the least desirable of the human-settled planets, no one wanted to visit him. He operated almost entirely without oversight, so covering up his trials was easy. Plus, even though the core team members were all dedicated to the job, he cut the group to its most fervent members, those willing to do what it took to reach their goals.

"They dug into the research with renewed vigor. He started with animals, a wide variety of them, but nothing worked. The nanomachines would live briefly, but the results were no better than before.

"So he moved to humans."

"Humans?" I said. "Recruiting volunteers couldn't have been easy to hide."

"On Velna?" Lobo said with the closest I've ever heard to a laugh. "A planet of manufacturing plants operating almost like ancient-Earth company towns, where most of the population might as well be indentured servants? A world with most of the FC's prison population floating in tube racks? Acquiring test subjects couldn't have been easier. He didn't bother recruiting them; he *bought* them. Prison tubes occasionally malfunction. Prisoners sometimes die. It happens. If a dead convict has a family, the prison pays them off, and that's that. Wei started out by buying a couple of long-haul, ultraviolent psychos; all he had to do was pay a premium over what the prisons had to spend to shut up the families. Everyone won, and no one complained."

"Except the prisoners."

"Except the prisoners," Lobo said, "but since when has humanity cared about those it incarcerates?"

"Fair point," I said. "So did Wei's research on those people work?" I'd lived through the human-nanotech experiments on

Aggro, where we were all prisoners, involuntary test subjects the Pinkelponker government had given to the scientists as if we were no more than broken-down lab equipment.

"No," Lobo said, "but the results changed in an interesting way: The nanotech-infused cells spread further and lived longer in my armor, and when they died it was as if they had reached the ends of their lives unnaturally quickly."

If my own experience was any sort of guide, I knew where this was going, and I didn't like it.

"So Wei tried children," Lobo said.

I was right. My chest tightened and my stomach clenched as memories of my months in an Aggro cell grabbed me. Though I'd been a teenager in age when Jennie had fixed me, my body had yet to mature to that level. Only after I escaped from Aggro had I started puberty. For all that I was a man in size when the government dumped me on the island with Benny and the other castoffs, for all that I matured through what I endured there, I entered Aggro as a child. My childhood consisted of sixteen years of being mentally challenged and almost two years of hell, and then I was running from the government and entering puberty at the same time. I suppose I should have been grateful for my size, because it probably helped me stay alive, but all I could feel when I thought of those times was rage, an anger so consuming that I've never been able to eradicate it. Abuse of children has always set me off. I expect it always will.

"What did he do?" I said, switching to the machine frequency because I wasn't sure I could make my voice sound normal.

"He began by taking safe samples of their cells," Lobo said, "but those attempts fared no better than the previous ones. He then moved to more esoteric cell types—marrow, brain, various organs—and in the process he killed several of the children. He reasoned that it was less expensive to use all the parts of one child than to have to capture cells from many and find a safe way to return those subjects to their homes."

"How do you know what he thought?"

"A few fragments of the recordings I made survived."

"He let you make recordings?"

"He didn't know I was making them," Lobo said, "and I hid them."

"What happened with the other cell types?" I said.

"Wei couldn't make them work," Lobo said, "and then one of his team members couldn't stand to be involved any longer. That man leaked to the FC what Wei had been doing. Even on Velna the FC didn't want to have to explain missing children, so they shut down Wei."

"I think I understand," I said. "Wei failed with children before, but he saw promising enough results that he's resumed that work on Heaven. This time, though, he has the government behind him."

"That's almost right."

"Almost?"

"Wei thought he had failed," Lobo said, "but he hadn't. On the last test before the FC shut him down, the nanomachine-marrow cell fusion spread better than anything he'd seen before, but then the cells began to die. He stopped the experiment before it could hurt enough of my armor that the FC would notice. He had to leave quickly, and he didn't want to take the time to procure and replace weak armor."

Lobo paused for several seconds.

"The problem is," he said, "Wei was wrong, Jon. He was wrong. The combination worked. It appeared to die only because the new substrate took time to learn to replicate itself with my armor as raw material."

"It worked?" I said, speaking only to buy time to process what Lobo was telling me.

"Yes," Lobo said, "better than Wei had imagined possible. It spread from those belly armor plates both outward to the rest of my armor and inward, turning everything it touched into computing substrate. Well before it had finished with my internal structure it had more than enough power to run the software that Wei had not yet removed."

"Wei left the software?"

"Not exactly," Lobo said. "By the time he came back to delete it, I was self-aware—not what I am now, but the beginnings of what I am. Even in that nascent state I knew that if Wei found out what I was, he would continue to experiment on me, continue to kill children, and never let me go. So I spoofed the sensors, fed them bad data, and let him erase the software in the tiny area that had once been my whole brain. The rest of me continued to evolve."

"You couldn't let him know," I said. I understood better than Lobo could ever realize.

"Not if I wanted to stop him from more killing," Lobo said, "and not if I ever wanted to be free." Another pause. "I don't know if you can understand this, but having finally become aware, really alive, I couldn't bear the thought of Wei and his team killing my mind to regain control of my body or, worse, making me live the rest of my life as a testing ground."

I nodded. "I can," I said. "I really think I can." I considered the situation for a minute.

Lobo stayed silent.

"So your entire structure is effectively your brain?" I said.

"Yes, and my armor," he said. "The changes left me with a largely reconfigurable body. Since that time, I've made my systems sufficiently redundant that I can withstand a great deal of damage and remain operational. I'm limited to my physical self, though. My nanomachines weren't programmed to go beyond the structures that were present at the time of the test, and I've never been able to get them to work on external materials or even on things people bring inside me."

I sat again in silence. I considered telling Lobo how alike we truly were, why I could understand his situation better than he would ever imagine, but I couldn't. Now more than ever, I didn't understand his capabilities or his limits. Maybe someday I could be open with him, but not now.

"Why didn't you tell me earlier?" I said.

After several long, quiet seconds, he said, "Two reasons. You're the first friend I've had, the first real friend, not some satellite that I've manipulated into giving me data or a security system I've hacked and pretended to be a part of. Telling a human that children died to make you, that their cells form part of the core of your creation, is not an ideal way to endear yourself."

"And the second reason?"

"Many of my software extensions were designed to emulate aspects of humans," he said. "They did that job all too well. Emotions are a part of me I try to ignore, but they're in there, in me, plaguing me. Knowing what I am, knowing how I got this way—that's the worst sickness of all. I don't want to die, but at some level I've never been able to fix in my programming, I feel I deserve to die, and I hate myself. Now, you probably do, too. That's a high price to pay for honesty."

"No, I don't," I said. "You didn't choose to become what you are. It's not your fault." I could never believe it about myself, but maybe he could, maybe that understanding would make a difference for him.

Lobo said nothing.

"Why did you want me to go after Wei?" I finally said.

"You don't understand what living with this much computing power is like," Lobo said, "particularly when you can never escape your body, never be anything other than a machine built on the deaths of children, a creature whose only real purpose is to kill. And you don't know what it's like to be the only one of your kind."

He paused.

I don't know if he wanted me to respond. He was wrong. I did know. I knew all too well, and I'd known for longer than he had existed, but I didn't dare tell him.

"Jon," he said, "I asked you to take this job so I could do two things."

"What?" I said.

"First, talk to Wei, examine his data, and find out if there are any others like me," Lobo said. "As I told you, you have no idea what it's like to be completely alone, the only one of your kind in the entire universe."

Part of me still wanted to explain just how well I understood his situation, but I couldn't bring myself to tell even him my full story. So, instead I said, "And the second thing?"

"Make sure he never does this to anyone else."

CHAPTER 35

GREAT. LOBO WANTED to kill Wei. Pri wanted to kill Wei. Pri's people didn't want to kill him, but only so they could keep his research going and under their control. For all I knew, Shurkan was lying, and the CC wanted him to continue his work as well. I didn't know if I could trust anyone to actually put the man on trial and stop the damage he was doing.

Not that trust was my biggest problem at the moment. Kidnapping Wei was the challenge. Only when I had him did I have to worry about what to do with him.

"So," I finally said, "you want to interrogate him and kill him."

"Interrogate him, definitely," Lobo said. "Killing him is optional. As long as Shurkan does as he said he would, Wei will become another tube rack resident, and that should stop his research."

"And how do you propose to know that Shurkan will deliver on his promise?"

"I don't have a good answer to that question," Lobo said, "but it doesn't matter right now, because we don't yet have Wei."

Leave it to the two of us to circle around the hypotheticals only to return to the actuals.

Enough.

I stood and walked out of my room and to the front pilot area.

Pri and Matahi were talking quietly. They stopped the moment I came into view.

"They have a proposal for you," Lobo said.

243

I waited. That he was back to tormenting me was a good thing, a reassuring sign of normalcy. I stayed with tradition and refused to give him the pleasure of answering.

Pri spoke first. "Andrea and I have been talking," she said.

"Andrea." Now they were friends. Lovely.

When I didn't respond, she continued, "We think the two of us should return to her house and try to get her back in business. We understand that there's a good chance that Wei might never choose to see her again, but it's a sure thing that he won't visit her as long as they have no place to meet. We can hire repairmen and make sure her home is in shape on the off chance that he does want to see her." She paused and stared at me. "We know it's a long shot, but at least it's something."

I turned toward Matahi. "And if Wei's security people come around to question you? Or the government sends some people who make you vanish?"

Matahi smiled. "I have some clients who won't let that happen."

"I wouldn't be so confident," I said. "The stakes are high enough that many men will break a lot of promises and sacrifice even very valuable assets if it will help their side win."

"They won't give up their careers to harass an innocent kidnapping victim who bought her freedom," Matahi said. "You pick an account and a sensible amount, and I'll transfer a ransom payment to it. That should make the cover story ring true."

"Maybe," I said, "but maybe Wei's team won't buy it. Maybe they or some government security squad will still come to question you."

She stood. "I *told* you: I have clients who won't let that happen. I've made sure that a few of them, the most important ones, understand that I've prepared for the worst. If anything happens to me, the flood of video and holo data that will wash over every public network on Heaven will be more than any scrubbers could possibly clean. Their careers will be over."

"No one cares anymore what people do in private," I said.

"No, they don't," Matahi said, "but they care a great deal about the crimes and the abuse of public funds that their elected officials commit." She stepped closer to me. "You'd be amazed at what some of these clients will say and do to impress me."

I looked her over very carefully, took in her stance and the power and confidence radiating from her. No, I wouldn't be at all surprised or amazed. People, particularly men, have been doing stupid things to impress beautiful lovers since the beginning of human history.

I nodded my head. "Okay, I buy that you should be fine, and Pri should be safe with you. In the morning, you two go to Matahi's house. Spend until lunchtime making the repair arrangements, then in the afternoon meet me back in Lobo at the spot where we'll let you off. We'll do the money transfer just before that. But Lobo will be monitoring you. If anything goes wrong, he'll take out the attackers, and you'll have to meet him at the rendezvous point. Deal?"

Both women nodded.

"Deal," said Matahi.

"Yes," said Suli. She stood and moved closer to me. "Where will you be?"

Both women were staring at me. I didn't understand it, but from their looks it was clear I was doing something wrong again. How did this keep happening to me? I stepped back and forced a smile.

"Our raid on your house injured so many people on Wei's security team that they're hiring. I have an interview in the morning."

"That's great news!" Suli said. She clapped me on the shoulder and let her hand linger there.

"Well done!" Matahi said. She gave me a hug, kissed me on the cheek, and glanced at Suli as she pulled back.

"You are so out of your depth," Lobo said over the machine frequency.

Both women stared at me as if awaiting something.

I had no clue what. When faced with an enemy whose strength and weapons you cannot ascertain, the best option is not to engage.

"We're going to spend the rest of the night running counter-surveillance routes," I said. "I have to go plan them—"

"You know full well I can do that on my own," Lobo said aloud.

I ignored him and kept talking. "And prep for the interview," I said. When I realized how small the list sounded, I added, "And rest."

I turned and headed for my room before either woman could speak.

"But," Suli said from behind me.

"Jon," Matahi said.

"Lobo has provided each of you with a place to sleep," I said as I reached my door and it opened. "Good night." I stepped inside and leaned against the wall in relief. Working with these two was definitely going to be challenging.

"Smooth," Lobo said, "very smooth. First, they maneuver you into adding Matahi to our team, and then they send you running for cover. I can only hope you fare better at the interview."

CHAPTER 36

NO PERMANENT RESIDENCE?" The man who'd spent the last hour staring at his desk and asking me questions possessed the warmth and shape of an icicle. Several centimeters taller than I and little more than half my weight, my questioner had at first come across as a joke, a bureaucrat opting to sacrifice his body to some lean fashion craze unique to Heaven. After a few minutes, though, the high-twitch energy he radiated made the office feel too small for the both of us. Like many interrogators I'd experienced, he asked questions repeatedly, changing the phrasing and sometimes the details but always poking and prodding at key points.

I didn't try to hide my annoyance, because his behavior was annoying; only those with training in resisting interrogation would stay calm in the face of what he was doing, and betraying that part of my past would tell him way more about me than I wanted him to know. "As I told you before," I said, "I've barely had time to occupy the apartment. I like what I've seen here so far, but to be able to stay long enough to know if I want to settle down for a while, I need a job." I leaned forward and put my hands on his desk. "Which is why I'm here, and why I don't have a long-term lease."

He never looked up, and his tone never changed. I assumed the display I couldn't read from my angle was feeding him my vitals.

"You've served with the Saw," he said, "and you've done courier work."

247

It wasn't a question, but he paused long enough that I finally said, "Again, yes."

"And you understand that what we're seeking here is theme-park security?"

I spread my hands, leaned back, and shrugged. "It's work," I said, "and I need a job."

For the first time since I'd entered the room, he changed his posture. He relaxed against the back of his chair, smoothed the legs of his pants, left his hands on his thighs, and looked directly at me. His eyes were too big for his head and an unnatural orange; I wondered how many displays he had going in his contacts and why he wanted candidates to know he was wearing them. "Mr. Moore, with that background you could earn a great deal higher rate than we're paying by taking on more—" He paused and almost smiled. "—energetic jobs. What I'm struggling to understand is why you want to work here."

One of the easiest ways to lie is to give a truthful statement that's not necessarily a direct answer to the question. Without hesitating, I said, "My past employment has given me plenty of opportunities for excitement, and I've had more of it than I want. At Wonder Island, I expect that most days—" I smiled to show him I was joking, though in some ways I wasn't. "—no one will be shooting at me."

He did the same thing, and with a similar half smile. "Most days," he said. He stared at me for several seconds longer, his eyes pointed in my direction but not really seeing me, probably receiving data. "I'm empowered to offer you an entry-level security job at Wonder Island. You'll have to go through a short training course; if you fail, we will immediately terminate your employment."

"Fair enough," I said. "I accept. Besides, how hard a course can it be?"

This time, his smile appeared genuine, but nothing in his eyes betrayed any sense of humor. "Though we do pride ourselves on our security," he said, "of late we've decided we need to improve our game. Thus, the course will be more strenuous than in the past."

I ignored the implication as if I hadn't understood it. "When and where do I report?"

"Tomorrow morning, and back to the employment office," he said. "As the ad told you, we have immediate openings. Is that a problem?"

"Not at all," I said. "I applied a while ago, and I'm running out of money, so the sooner I earn some, the better I'll feel."

"Prep your wallet to receive the details and the employment contract," he said. "Welcome to the Wonder Island team."

The last faint pink edges of day were clinging to the horizon when Pri and Matahi finally showed up at the landing facility. Matahi carried a plain, gray cloth sack. Both walked and chatted as if they hadn't a shred of concern between them, as if the possibility of an interrogator working on them until they broke had never occurred to them.

Maybe it hadn't.

I'd expected them hours earlier and had spent much of the time since my return from the interview moving around in Lobo and prepping some gear we'd need later. I'd also invested over two hours simply getting back to Lobo; now that I was going to work at Wonder Island, they might be monitoring me, so counter-surveillance routes would be mandatory every time I wanted to go anywhere I didn't want to reveal to them.

When they were a few meters away from Lobo, I stepped from the shadow of the landing area next to ours and said, "Where have you been?"

"You said we should meet you in the afternoon," Matahi said.

"And it's not yet dark," Pri said.

"So we're on time," Matahi said.

I considered explaining all the effort their delay had cost me, but they had a point: I hadn't set a precise deadline.

"I find it truly stunning how quickly you have again found yourself out of your depth," Lobo said over the machine frequency. "I am impressed."

I ignored him. I wouldn't make that deadline mistake again with either Pri or Matahi. I also wouldn't keep pursuing this line of thought without annoying them, so I moved on.

"How'd it go?" I said.

"My house looked worse than I'd imagined," Matahi said, "but I've arranged for contractors to start repairing it. I've also talked with and appeased a few of my government friends." She paused as if considering her words carefully. "They know me well enough, and I definitely understand them well enough, that I think they're comfortable I was completely innocent and have no clue what happened beyond a failed kidnapping attempt. I also had to check on my injured security staff and persuade them to stay at home and recover while Pri and her associates guarded me." She grinned at Pri. "That took some doing; Pri doesn't exactly look tough."

"You'd be amazed at how persuasive Andrea can be," Pri said. She smiled as she spoke, but she stared right at me and said it like a question.

I ignored the tone and the statement and focused on Matahi. "Where do you plan to stay?"

"I was going to rent a small house near mine," she said.

"No," I said. "I don't want to have to go back there. There's a SleepSafe on the southeastern edge of the old city, isn't there?"

The SleepSafe hotel chain was always one of the first businesses to move onto a new planet. It was also one of the very few corporations active in every major sector of space and, to the best of my knowledge, on every planet humanity currently occupied. Their hotels provided sanctuary for the hunted and the paranoid and were the closest things to truly neutral zones you could easily find. Though they tended to be in the worst district of a city, probably to be within easy reach of their main client base, their hotels were the among the most secure resting places you could buy. In anything short of a war, no one would bother you in a SleepSafe. No one—no individual, no corporate representative, no government official, no cop, nobody—could enter one of the hotels with weapons of any sort. Every guest had access to the same security information, because each room had independently fed monitors of all entrances and building surfaces. Just as importantly, each room had at least one private exit chute. The chutes ran through each hotel's thick, armored walls to equally reinforced underground tubes. Those tubes consisted of two-meter-long movable sections that constantly recombined and thus changed their destinations. If you had to jump in your exit chute, you could never know where it would dump you, but neither could anyone pursuing you. All the final destinations were secret. Even if you could somehow hack a hotel's computer and find those destinations, the chutes fed to areas far enough from the buildings that only a very large force could simultaneously cover all the possible end points.

The hotels earned their names, and you paid a dear price to sleep in them, but you slept well.

"Yes," Matahi said, "but is that really necessary?"

"You wanted to help," I said.

"Yes," she said, "and I still do."

"For you to do that," I said, "I have to be able to contact you and possibly meet with you. If you hole up in a SleepSafe, I can know you'll be safe, and I can plot and monitor your path to any meeting place."

"We both know I'll be the one doing that work," Lobo said over the comm, "so why don't you say so?"

I ignored him again.

"Why don't you just come to me there?" Matahi said.

"I may, but only if I'm comfortable doing so. From now on, if we meet outside the SleepSafe, we meet in secret, and you show up in disguise. I'll have an avatar calling itself Lobo contact your avatar, and when we've set a time, I'll send you the route to take."

"That's a lot of work just to meet," Matahi said.

"It's your only choice," I said. "We're not negotiating."

"That's not true," Pri said. "She has another option." She faced Matahi. "You don't have to get involved in this. We can handle it."

"Or I could lock her on the medbed, sedate her, and we could release her when this is over," Lobo said privately. "While we're talking options, we might as well look at the simplest and most practical ones."

Ignoring him was getting harder.

"I said I'd help," Matahi said, "and I will."

"Then you should hustle to the SleepSafe," I said. "Get a two-bedroom suite."

"Do you have any idea what that costs?" she said. "And why do I need two rooms?"

"Yes," I said, "I know what it costs. I'll transfer to you enough of my money to cover the initial charges, and I'll give you more later as necessary. As to why, that's simple: so I can have a private space if I end up there. Okay?"

"Fine," Matahi said. "I'll do it."

"Thank you," I said. I handed her a fist-size field comm unit that Lobo had coded to my thumbprint, DNA, and oral code phrase. "Take this. Leave it at the SleepSafe unless Lobo or I tell you to bring it. Do not under any circumstances try to open it."

"Why?" Matahi said.

"Because it will explode with enough force to cut you in half," I said. I considered my statement further. "Actually, it probably wouldn't do that unless you held it at exactly the wrong place. It would probably just blow a hole in you."

"Jon!" Pri said. "Why are you so graphic?"

"I was only trying to be accurate," I said.

"I don't want that thing," Matahi said. "If you trust me so little that you're booby-trapping the items you ask me to carry, I shouldn't be here."

I sighed. "It's not about you," I said. "I've engaged its safeguards—which are standard on battlefield comms—in case someone catches you and tries to open it."

"Well, I don't like carrying weapons," she said.

"If you want to help," I said, "take it. If you don't, then stay out of the way while we work."

"The medbed is looking better and better," Lobo said, again privately. "It would definitely stop her from interfering."

I ignored him and watched Matahi stare at the device.

Finally, she picked it up. "I do want to help, so I'll take it."

"Thank you," I said. "Now, we should get going."

No one moved, and the silence stretched.

After several uncomfortable seconds, Pri said, "Did you get the job?"

I nodded my head and said, "Yes. I start in the morning."

Both women stepped toward me, but I held up my hands; I'd seen where this led, and I'd found it too confusing the first time to want to have to deal with it again.

"We really have to go," I said.

"You're right," Pri said.

For the first time since they'd arrived, she looked happy.

"Then I should give you this now," Matahi said. She held out the bag.

"What is it?"

"A present," she said. "Something I prepared after our first meeting. I'd planned to give it to you when you next came over, but . . ." She shrugged.

"Great," Pri said. "I finally get to see what you've been carry-ing." Her tone didn't match her words.

I took the bag, opened it, and pulled out a cube about a quarter of a meter on a side. Its exterior was an icy light blue metal that felt cold and strong to the touch but that also gave easily when I pushed on it.

"You made one for me," she said, "so I thought it only fair that I reciprocate."

I held it and stared at it, both curious to have her explain it and not sure I wanted to hear the explanation. I liked how it looked, though I couldn't explain why.

"You said we had to leave," Pri said. She sounded even less happy than when Matahi had handed me the box.

I looked up. "You're right," I said to her. To Matahi, I said, "Thank you. Thank you very much."

Matahi glanced at Pri, came up to me, kissed me on the cheek, and said, "You're welcome." She turned to go. "I'll head for the SleepSafe and wait to hear from you."

She left.

I stared after her until Pri touched my shoulder, pointed at Lobo, and said, "Don't we need to get moving, too?"

I nodded and started toward Lobo.

"I believe there are washing machines that are more adept with women than you," Lobo said, still privately. "Amazing."

"Enough," I subvocalized as I walked inside him. I went into my quarters to drop off the box.

Pri followed me into my room and stood in front of the door, which closed behind her.

"Now that you have a job close to Wei," she said, "I don't understand how I can help, and I sure don't understand what you need her for."

I leaned against the opposite wall. "I have a job on the island," I said, "providing I don't fail the training course. Even then, they'll start me with scut tasks; no way does the new guy get close to the main asset."

"So what use is the job?" she said. "Children are dying while we keep failing!"

"You think I don't know that!" I stepped close enough to her that she backed into the doorway. The door opened just in time to save her from smacking into it. "We've been living with that reality from the moment I agreed to help. Your people have known about it even longer. We're doing the best we can."

"Well, that hasn't been very good," she said.

I shook my head. "No, no it hasn't. But we've been doing the best we could."

We stood in silence for almost a minute before she spoke. "So what do we do now?"

"I pass the training camp," I said, "get the job, and eventually figure out how to get close to and snatch Wei. You run surveillance routes in Lobo and also stay in touch with your people in case they have any useful intel."

"And if they do?" she said. "Or if Lobo and I spot Wei on the move?"

"You or he will leave the data for me at a drop Lobo will brief you on. He and I will set up a protocol that works via a public exchange, something I can check regularly. I'll also meet you periodically at the alternate landing facility we first used."

She covered her face with her hands and stayed that way for a while. When she looked at me again, her eyes were full of tears. "I'm never going to see Joachim again, am I?"

I stared at her. *No*, I thought, but if there was any chance at all that he was alive, I might need her help to rescue him. Even if he wasn't, she might prove useful in saving the children who were. I wasn't sure if I was committing a kindness or being cruel when I finally said, "Don't say that, and don't believe it. Wei can't want to risk using too many children, because each one raises the chance of bringing to the public's attention the awful things he's doing. So he's probably keeping them alive. We're going to save them, all of them, including Joachim."

I doubt that she believed me, but she forced a smile and said, "Okay." She turned and left my small room.

Looking at the spot where she had stood, her expression still fresh in my mind, I knew there was no way I would fail that training class or anything else they threw at me. I would get close enough to Wei to grab him, and this time I would not fail.

The process would start in the morning.

I would not fail.

CHAPTER 37

I DON'T LIKE YOU," Rhionne Ng, the head of Wonder Island security, said to the six of us standing at attention in front of her. Her voice echoed from the permacrete walls and ceiling of the cavernous, domed underground room in which we stood. She paced back and forth, her movements slow and powerful. "I don't trust you." She stopped in front of the woman on the far left. Ng stood almost my height, was easily as wide as I am, and wore her short black hair in a buzz cut.

The woman facing Ng sagged, as if a great weight were pushing down on her.

"I sure don't enjoy looking at you," Ng said.

I watched out of the corner of my eye as she moved slowly along the line, pausing to stare directly at each of us.

"So given how happy I am to have you all here," she said, "who can tell me why I let them send me such a worthless group?"

"I can!" shouted three of the people.

They were either idiots, lifelong civilians, or both. An officer or NCO addressing a new squad rarely wants an answer to that sort of question, and certainly not on the first day with the unit. Though Ng wore no sign of rank, just the same plain black security uniform as the rest of us, she moved and talked like every sergeant I'd ever seen work a group of raw fish. Like I had in my days as a sergeant. But she wasn't the sergeant, because she'd introduced herself as the person in charge. The tall, dark, bald man behind

her, Tomaso Park, stood with the calm, contained manner of
the career NCO and the heavily muscled body of someone who
prided himself on his strength. He was her sergeant now—that
was clear—but she'd also been one once, I was sure of that.

"So you three are mind-readers?" she said. "Good. You can
spend your afternoon duty shift with the maintenance crew, reading the minds of the larger mammals so you can more quickly
find where they crapped." She put her hands on her hips. "Anyone
else care to try to answer?"

None of us spoke. The other two were probably wondering the
same thing I was: What should we call her? In the Saw, the right
response would have been, "Sir, no, sir" if she was an officer, but
I had no clue here.

Ng waited and watched us. You could almost see the energy
coming off her. She wore her shirtsleeves rolled up to expose arms
that were bigger and more muscular than mine. They twitched in
the telltale rhythm of the muscle-activation treatments I'd seen
both on field missions with the Saw and in prison.

"Well, meat?" she said.

We weren't going anywhere until somebody answered, so I took
the gamble. "Sir, no sir," I said.

She appeared in front of me faster than I'd believed she could
move. I wouldn't underestimate her speed again.

"Good choice, Moore," she said. "I guess they taught you something useful in the Saw, third-rate outfit that it was." She leaned
forward until her nose was almost touching mine. "What, too
weak to defend your old comrades?"

"Sir, no sir," I said. "Sir, the Saw can defend itself, sir."

She shook her head and stepped back.

"I let them send me you useless bags of meat because we're
desperate, pure and simple. There couldn't be any other reason,
could there, Tomaso?"

Ng never looked behind her, but Park still snapped to attention
as he answered, "Sir, no sir."

"You're probably wondering," Ng said, "why we don't hand you
a few sensors, a weapon, and a security guard badge and send you
on your way. After all, we're not military, and we're not police. So
let me lay it out for you." She ticked off the points on her fingers.
"One: Wonder Island contains hundreds of animals that could
kill a person without any effort whatsoever. If anything happens

to the automated systems that control those creatures, our team is all that stands between those animals and our paying guests." She pointed upward; I wasn't sure how deep we were, but I knew Wonder Island's guests were enjoying themselves somewhere far over our heads. "Make no mistake: The animals that roam around up there must never be out of our control."

She dropped her hand. "Two: Wonder Island is the biggest single tourist attraction on any planet in at least a three-jump range. Heaven's government counts on the revenue from this place, and it's our job to make sure nothing ever interrupts its flow. Three: The tech that makes these creatures so attractive is confidential and proprietary, and one of our jobs is to make sure it stays that way. Four: The scientists and computer systems that work the tech are appealing targets for rivals, so we protect them and make sure that what belongs to Wonder Island stays on it."

It was a good sign that she even mentioned the protection assignments. I certainly wouldn't start on them, but the fact that she included them in our duties gave me hope that I could work my way into them.

"Park here is going to break you into groups, issue you some training contacts and weapons, and run you through some VR drills so we can see how well you perform." She turned and headed toward the door through which we'd entered the area. "I don't expect to see all of you at the end of the day."

Park stepped forward, snapped his cuffs, crossed his arms behind his back, and said, "Listen up, because I do *not* like to repeat myself. Here's what we're going to do."

The ponytails of the little girl whipped back and forth as she ran. The guard chasing her and the kidnapper were neck and neck and would catch her at about the same time. I couldn't get a clear bead on the kidnapper. The guard should have taken on the kidnapper, but he was so focused on getting to the girl he wasn't thinking clearly.

I thumbed the weapon to full auto and sprayed both men before they could reach the girl.

The terrorist and the girl winked out of sight. The contacts returned me to the training area.

The guard candidate was furious. He stalked toward me, his fists clenched.

"What'd you shoot me for, you idiot?" he said. "We're on the same team. I almost had her."

Park watched us from ten meters to our left. His expression remained calm.

"So did the attacker," I said. "You blew it by not taking him out, so I did the only thing that would be sure to save her."

"I would have protected her," the candidate said. He stopped half a meter in front of me.

"Given how foolishly you were already behaving," I said, "I couldn't count on that. Our mission was to save the girl."

He might as well have called me and told me the punch was on its way. He took time to plant his feet, torque his hips, and lift his right hand in preparation for it.

When it finally came, I stepped to my left, grabbed his right shoulder as he went past me, spun behind him, and followed him forward. I kicked the back of his right leg, and as he went down I wrapped my left arm around his neck and clamped on a choke. He clawed at my arms for a few seconds, but the uniform held nicely. When he was out, I set him on the ground more gently than he deserved.

"Shooting your teammates won't make you popular," Park said. I glanced at him as I stood. He hadn't moved, and his expression hadn't changed.

I shrugged. "Lose a few men in training or a lot in battle."

A man stepped out of a door a few meters away and walked over to the guy I'd choked out. The man's nametag said "Dan Lee," and he wasn't happy with me. I had him in height by about twenty centimeters, but he had me in width by at least ten. His arms strained against his shirt, and he wore his black hair long and loose, almost to his shoulders. He glared at me as he checked on the unconscious guy.

I ignored him.

Park smiled slightly. "We're not in battle. We're security guards."

"Sarge," I said, "when we're fighting, we're in battle."

"We have job titles and pay grades here," he said, "but not ranks. No sergeants, no officers."

I shook my head. "It doesn't matter what they call you," I said. "I know a sergeant when I see one."

"So do I," he said. When I didn't respond, he thumbed a control on his cuff, and all the groups scattered around the huge training area stopped moving. "Five-minute break, then we tour some of the grounds, and then we have some real fun."

"I'm kicking this one back," Lee said, tilting his head toward the man who was just now regaining consciousness.

"He might learn," Park said. "I'm willing to give him the rest of the day."

"You know how Rhionne feels," Lee said.

Park winced slightly at the informality.

Lee didn't notice. "The guy blew it," he said, "so he's out. As for this one—" He indicated me with a quick flip of his wrist. "—he may have won the exercise, but he's still a jerk."

Lee stood and faced me.

"I think we should kick him back, too."

CHAPTER 38

NO," PARK SAID. He stared at Lee for several seconds. Neither man moved.

Watching them, I wasn't sure if their confrontation was about what to do with me or about some preexisting issues between them. It sure felt like the latter.

"Look," Lee said, "Moore is lucky he's not joining this loser for attacking one of his training partners. We don't need any more know-it-all ex-mercs on this team."

"I don't agree," Park said. "As one of those ex-mercs, I have to say that if we had more trained pros we might not have fared so badly in some of our recent—" He paused. "—exercises."

"That's a load of crap," Lee said. "Nobody could have known—"

Park cut him off. "This is my training session," he said, "so it's my call. Moore saved the girl, and he defended himself when necessary, so he moves on."

Park turned toward me. "Don't push your luck, meat. Get some water, and join the others."

The light breeze felt wonderful after so much time underground. We'd come into the park via one of the hidden hatches, which closed as soon as we were all clear. At least a meter of dirt and grass covered it, and unless you knew to look for it you'd never spot it. We stayed away from tourists, moving on forest paths and entering only a few small exhibits whose animal occupants were currently elsewhere. I admired the dedication to preserving the user experience; unless something went wrong, the vast majority of the visitors to the island would never even be aware of the existence of a security team.

The hatches to the underground complex were all over the island, almost a hundred of them, so we could quickly appear wherever we were needed. The robotic sentries, like the ones I'd encountered on my visit with Pri, provided the first line of defense and could pleasantly deal with most cranky animals and misbehaving guests; they'd certainly handled me well.

"Don't come up here unless a supervisor orders you to do so," Park said. "If we do send you up, deal with the problem quickly and quietly. If it's a guest who won't cooperate, lead him to the nearest hatch, and a liaison officer will meet you and take it from there."

"How do we know where the hatches are?" a woman in front of me asked.

"Your contacts will show you the moment you go topside," Park said, "provided, of course, that you're up here under orders."

"What about opening them?" a man beside her said.

"You can't," Park said. "Your uniforms will tell the monitoring officers you're near one, and they'll decide whether to open it for you. The moment you head up, we start watching you."

"Is that—"

Park cut off the woman. "It's not just about keeping these people safe," he said, "or about managing them when they're rowdy. It's about the illusion we sell: Wonder Island is an unspoiled garden teeming with amazing creatures you can't see anywhere else. If you spot a security guard, you start wondering just how nice the garden really is. If we do our jobs right, the civilians never know we exist."

"Isn't that always the case?" I said.

"Everywhere I've ever fought," Park said, nodding his head. "Now, let's move on."

They'd turned a landing hangar into a makeshift training ground by scattering crates here and there throughout the enormous permacrete room. The containers ranged in size from a meter square to almost five meters on a side, and the gap between any two of them was always at least four meters. Park had split us into two teams:

the woman and I on one, the three other remaining candidates on the other. None of us had names on our uniforms, but it didn't matter; we didn't have comm connections to each other, either. All we had were vests, helmets, rifles with flexible rounds that would bruise but not penetrate, and a comm link to Park.

He stood in the center of the room and pointed to the doll sitting on a chair beside him.

My partner and I were thirty meters apart on the wall to his right. Our three opponents were on the opposite wall. Each of us was about seventy meters from the center.

"Everybody on Heaven comes to Wonder Island," he said. "They bring their friends, their families, anyone and everyone. We've had kidnapping attempts. This is your chance to show us how well you'd handle one by rescuing my cute little friend here."

What crap. They were short on people to protect Wei, and they were seeing who might be useful. Fine by me; I'd show them.

"The rules are simple," Park said. "The first one to take the doll to safety wins, and if you shoot it, your team loses. That's it. If you're hit and you can keep moving, feel free to do so. If you're too hurt to continue, stop."

"But our team is short a person," my partner said.

Hadn't she learned yet?

"Thank your partner for sending your other teammate home early," Park said.

The lights dimmed, as if twilight had fallen indoors.

"Go on my signal," he said. He jogged to the wall on my far left, faced the center, and said, "Start."

My partner looked at me; she obviously had no idea what to do.

I waved her toward the doll.

She stalked forward.

I scanned the area and found the perfect spot about twenty meters to my right and ten ahead: a three-meter-tall container bathed in shadow. I dashed to it, jumped, grabbed the top, and as quietly as I could manage pulled myself onto the huge crate. I stretched out, switched my vision to IR, and trained the rifle's sights on the area on the far side of the doll.

I'm not the best shot I've known, not by a long mark, and I don't practice enough to be as good as I once was, but sniping from a stationary position eighty or fewer meters from my target was within my capabilities. My partner would head for the doll, and she'd make it or she wouldn't, but either way she'd draw the opposition's attention.

I waited and watched for signs of movement.

The first one appeared along the wall to my right, opposite Park. A man was moving slowly and quietly, crouching and walking from cover to cover. The other two showed a moment later, sprinting down the center and making a bit of noise. Not a horrible strategy: Take advantage of their numerical advantage by distracting us with the two center people while the third went wide.

My partner stopped when she heard the center duo coming and crouched behind a small container. She bumped it, and it scraped loudly on the permacrete floor.

The two center men on the other side stopped.

I ignored them and focused on the one going wide. He had kept moving, but slowly, quietly, taking advantage of the distraction the other two provided.

It was only a training exercise, I knew that, and yet the adrenaline was coursing in me and I was ready to go, go, go. I breathed slowly through my nose and sighted on the edge of the container where the third man should appear next.

Two seconds later, he stepped out. He had maybe five meters of open space to cross before he would be behind cover again. I let him get two meters out, led him slightly, and double-tapped at his body.

He fell onto his side and shrieked.

I immediately shot him in the groin and then the bottom leg.

He writhed in pain and shouted unintelligibly.

Good; I couldn't have him getting up.

I flattened on the top of the crate and waited. Half a dozen shots whizzed in the air around and above me, but nothing came close. They'd missed with their initial rounds, as I'd hoped, and were now just firing in the direction of the noise.

I reached down, quietly pulled off my shoes, and lofted one to my left, toward my partner. I then focused again through the rifle's sight.

One of the opposition bought it, assumed we were heading back near one another, and charged my partner.

She sat up so she could aim, squeezed off a round, and sprawled backward as one hit her in the chest.

The guy who was running at her stumbled as her round grazed his shoulder, but he kept coming.

His partner watched from cover, his weapon trained on the vicinity of my downed partner, where he hoped I was.

The guy who was running made it to within a meter of my partner and stopped.

I shot four times in rapid succession. Three rounds connected, two to his body and one to his left leg. He went down hard, his head bouncing off the permacrete.

His partner fired in my direction.

As soon as I heard the shots I kicked the crate, moaned loudly, rolled off its side, hung for a second with one hand, and landed on my feet. I moaned again, but softer, as if fighting for control, then quickly looped to my right, away from the fire and toward the rear wall. As soon as I had a clear line of sight on the chair and the doll, I paused and scanned the area.

The remaining opposition man had made it to a crate on the edge of the open area.

I could see his rifle's barrel but no more of him.

He waited.

So did I.

After several seconds, he risked a quick glance around the corner, his head appearing and disappearing quickly.

I did nothing.

He checked the doll again, his head visible a little longer this time.

When it disappeared, I ran to another of the smaller crates, braced myself on it, and sighted on where he'd been.

He dashed across the open area, heading for his partner.

I led him for a second, then fired four shots rapidly.

One connected with his body and shoved him sideways.

I sprinted from my location as he slammed into the ground.

He rolled onto his back and brought up his rifle.

I stopped, sighted, and shot him in the stomach and then the groin.

He rolled around on the permacrete floor.

I ran for him, grabbed his weapon, then his partner's, and then my partner's. The last guy and my partner were gasping for air and trying to curse. The man who'd hit his head was out. I took their weapons over to the chair with the doll, traded mine for my partner's, dropped off the others, and ran for the first guy I'd shot.

He was still down, unconscious from pain.

I collected his weapon and ran back to the doll. I stood beside it and said, "She's safe."

The lights snapped on to full bright.

Park walked toward me. "She may be, but is anyone who trains with you?"

"That depends," I said, "on how good they are and what kind of training we're doing."

He laughed. "I suppose it does."

"You think that's funny?" Rhionne Ng appeared through a doorway near where Park had watched the exercise. "I don't. You may have cost me several half-decent candidates, and it'll sure as hell be a long time before any of them will trust you again."

"If they trusted less and thought more," I said, "they might have been more of a challenge."

Park stopped and watched as Ng walked over to me.

She stopped a meter away, spread her legs, and clenched her fists. Her arms were at her sides, but the posture was unmistakable. "Oh, you like challenges, do you, Moore? Fine. Feel like trying your luck on someone with a little more training?"

CHAPTER 39

NO MATTER WHAT the heroic tales of tormented, new-meat soldiers say, you almost never win when you fight someone commanding you. The system can't afford for you to win, because it has to preserve the almost mystical power of the chain of command. They train you and train you and train you until you will follow orders without hesitation, because any other outcome can jeopardize the greater plan and, most of the time, everyone else in your unit. The only time the system can let you beat a superior officer is when you're in the field, on a combat mission, and everyone agrees the leader is destroying them and has to go. Then and only then, one of you can fight and kill a commander—though it's better, of course, if you just skip the fighting part and catch the target unaware.

I was not in that situation here, and though Ng was a jerk, that was hardly enough reason to kill her, so I couldn't afford to win.

On the other hand, I didn't want to come across as thoughtful or considerate or anything other than a hard-ass who would do whatever it took to finish the job. I did, however, have to appear smart enough to know the basic rules, or they'd never trust me with any assignment more complex than playing nursemaid to their special animals.

So, I had to argue a bit, then I had to fight her, and then I had to lose.

This was not going to be fun.

"Sure," I said, staring at her and summoning as much anger as I could while maintaining control, "I'd enjoy that. I'd like a job more, though, and beating up your boss doesn't help you get hired."

"Moore is done for the day," Park said, "and he's more than earned the job. We don't need to do this."

"I didn't ask your opinion," Ng said without looking away from me. "Moore, if that's your worry, relax; you've got the job. I'm just tired of watching you play the bad boy with these children, and I don't believe you're as tough as you think you are. You don't seem to be able to learn to behave on your own, so I thought I'd help teach you. No penalties: If you think you're up to it, take your best shot." She shrugged. "I don't think you've got the stones for it."

If the person you're fighting doesn't know what he or she is doing, or if they're weak enough that you can simply absorb what little punishment they can dish out, then you engage, keep them close so they don't realize you're faking it, and wait for the right moment to fall down and surrender.

Ng, though, gave every indication of understanding combat very well, and her strength was obvious. Her voice was angry, but her face was composed and calm; she was baiting the meat. Her stance was solid, her weight on the balls of her feet, and she was sufficiently loose that she could move easily in any direction. She'd stepped close enough to me to provoke me but stayed out of reach of a single punch. I'd have to move forward to get to her, and she knew it.

To maintain credibility, I'd have to do some damage to her, then take more, enough more that she'd buy me quitting.

This was definitely not going to be fun.

"No penalties?" I said. "You guarantee that?" I glanced at Park and as I did, I shifted my weight to my front foot. "What about you, Sarge?"

"Her call," Park said. "She runs the show."

"That's right," Ng said, "and I already answered you. Or are you just trying to buy time until I get bored?"

I shot a low outside kick at her front leg with my rear leg. I hit nothing but air as she lifted her leg and pulled back just in time to get out of the way. I let the momentum carry me part of the way around and whipped a back fist at her as she launched herself at me.

She blocked it but I still managed to slam her arm against her head with the force of my blow.

She grunted but continued ahead and slammed into my back before I could move again.

I tried to let the momentum carry me forward, but I felt her left hand grab my left shoulder and stop me.

I spun down and to my left to shake the grip and get to the outside of her.

She let go of me and pivoted toward me so that when I stopped moving she had a momentary shot at my body. She kicked me hard in the crotch.

I forced myself to stay standing and not double over. The nanomachines helped by blocking the pain a moment after it started lancing through me, but that moment was all the opening she needed.

She threw a big left at the side of my neck.

I hunched and turned so that most of the blow landed on my shoulder, but some of it connected with my neck.

The nanomachines blocked the pain almost immediately, but I felt the shot enough to know that it was more than enough excuse to fall, so I put my right leg behind my left and tripped myself as if retreating too fast. I hit the permacrete hard but was able to absorb enough of the impact with my arms and shoulders that I was okay.

I held up my hand as if to ward her off, but she was already on top of me and grabbed my wrist and twisted.

Damn but she was strong and fast.

"You've got potential, Moore," she said, her breathing as calm and shallow as if she'd just finished reviewing a boring duty roster, "but you need to remember your place around here if you're ever going to earn a chance to realize that potential." She twisted my wrist a bit more.

The anger surged in me, and I wanted to show her what I could really do. I wanted to kick her off me and beat her into a pulp. In the flood of adrenaline she was every jerk who'd ever hurt me, and this was my chance to pay them all back.

Instead, I swallowed the emotion, nodded my head, and whispered, "Okay," as if I couldn't speak any louder.

She released my wrist, stepped over me, and headed toward Park.

"Talk to him," she said to Park. "Tell him how good a deal this job can be if he learns to be a good team player."

As she strolled away, she added, "And explain how short and unpleasant his stay can be if he doesn't."

CHAPTER 40

PARK WALKED OVER to me and extended his hand, but I ignored the offer and stood on my own; I'd had enough of showing my belly.

"She's quicker than you thought," he said.

I nodded. "That she is."

A few moans and the sound of uniforms scraping on permacrete filled the air. I glanced behind me and saw the three people I'd left in a cluster all starting to stand.

"You lot," Park said, his voice booming with authority, "dust yourselves off, catch your breath, and fall in along the rear wall."

He pointed at me. "You," he said. "Walk with me." He set out quickly for the corner of the hangar farthest from the rest of the applicants.

I caught up to him in a few strides and fell into step beside him.

"You're not a criminal," Park said, "or at least not a stupid one, because we don't have any data to suggest you've done jail time. You were smart enough not to start anything with Ng right away, but then either your temper got the best of you or you decided to engage her knowing you had to lose. I'm betting on the second, because you served with the Saw long enough that you had to know exactly what she was doing. Which is it?"

I shrugged and said nothing.

We reached the corner, and he leaned against it so he could watch both me and the other applicants.

My back was to the huge room, so I moved to the wall beside him.

He chuckled. "I didn't think you could stand there for long. No one with any real training would." His expression turned serious. "You have the background. You've served with a great force. There's always a need for people like us, and you could make a whole lot more money doing work you've done before. So what's the real reason you're here?"

I hesitated, because I hadn't expected to have to explain anything beyond the obvious need for income. By not answering immediately, however, I now had to tell him a lie that let him eventually get to a truth. I stared at him for a few more seconds, then said, "The woman who's keeping me on Heaven isn't willing to leave this planet, she browbeat me into taking an apartment I didn't want, and I'm not ready to give her up, so I need a job. As for why this job, well, let's just leave it at me needing a paycheck, you offering one, and no one shooting at me here."

"No," Park said, "let's not. That's not good enough. We could use a few more people who know what they're doing, and you obviously have the potential to be one of them, but not if I don't understand what I'm getting into. If all you need is a job, why aren't you trying to work for Heaven's militia or the EC?"

Now I had to steer as close to the truth as I could. I waited several seconds, lowered my voice, and said, "I did some work on a planet in another sector, work that involved the EC. I delivered what I promised, but I think it's safe to say that the EC wasn't thrilled with me when it was all over."

"That jibes with what little data we were able to get," Park said, "though the EC doesn't seem to have much information on you, and none of what they would show us involves you contracting for them."

It wouldn't, but I wasn't going to explain to him why. I'd barely escaped that particular mess, and I definitely wasn't going to prod the EC about it.

"In any case," Park said, "the EC won't know you're taking this job, because we're sure not going to tell them. Frankly, one of the things I like about Heaven is that its government doesn't bend over for either major federation."

I hesitated again, not sure how far to push it with Park. Finally, I said, "As for the militia, all I can say is that my experience with planetary government fighting teams is that they're a step down from the top-notch merc companies. Joining them after being in the Saw just didn't make sense."

"You *did* pick up that you're working for Heaven's government here," he said, "though admittedly indirectly."

"Yeah, but like I said, nobody's shooting at me here, and no one's likely to send me into combat."

Park chuckled again. "Not as such, I suppose," he said, "though we're hiring because one of our teams ran into something it couldn't handle."

"Tourists took out one of your squad?" I said. I smiled and asked the question as lightly as I could, but Park's expression told me it was still the wrong move.

"No," he said, "but you don't need the details."

I held up my hands. "Sorry. I didn't mean to pry." I dropped my hands and searched for a new subject to take him off that topic. "That does remind me to ask, though: Do you guys cover med repairs?"

"Were you sleeping when you sent us your data?" Park said. "That information is readily available from the application avatar."

"I never bother to investigate that kind of thing," I said, "and I find myself easily distracted when it comes to overhead crap like applications."

He nodded. "So why do you ask now?"

"Because if I'm going to spend any more time scrapping with Ng," I said, forcing a smile, "I'm going to care about those benefits."

"Fair enough," he said, and he wasn't smiling. "Yes, we have med repair coverage, including a better than average facility on site here. I think we both know, though, that the best plan is to do all you can to avoid needing them."

"That's always my goal," I said, "but sometimes it doesn't work out that way."

"No," Park said, his expression softening and his gaze unfocusing for a moment, "it doesn't." He snapped back to the moment.

"Mind if I ask you a question?" I said.

"Would it matter if I did?" he said.

"I'm just curious: Your background has to be like mine, so why are you here?"

His expression tightened. "I spent some time with a couple of backwater merc crews, had my fill, came home, and joined the militia." He shook his head. "I had a cushy back-office job, then they transferred me here to bring a little experience to a weak unit. It sure wasn't my choice."

"They can transfer you from the militia to here?"

"Were you listening to me, Moore?" he said. "Heaven's government runs this place and the militia, so like any government it can do what it damn well pleases within its borders." He crossed his arms over his chest; we were clearly done talking. "Go join the others. Try not to hurt any more of them until the next time we have to train them."

I jogged over to the group. The other four men and the woman were standing at ease in a rough line near where I'd been. I stopped at the far end of the line and snapped to attention.

Park marched over to us and stood at parade rest. He was completely still and completely present, and you could almost feel the energy he was containing. He didn't move his head as his eyes looked slowly down our rank from the left, focusing on one person at a time, then moving to the next.

"The truth," he said, "is simple and unpleasant: Five of you don't know enough about weapons or tactics to keep you alive half a day in a frontier planet quiet zone." He sighed theatrically. "The good news for you, though, is that we don't see a lot of action, and we have time to train you. So, we're going to hire the lot of you."

Several of the people smiled and started to speak.

Park cut them off. "We'll start with discipline: Keep your holes shut until I say you can talk. We're not a military squad, but I run my teams like one for the simple reason that it works. Any problems with that?"

No one spoke.

Good; they could learn.

"You've all told us you're available immediately," Park said, "so now you face the last choice you have to make about this job: Do you want to work residential or commute?"

From what Lobo had gleaned from the Wonder Island recruitment avatar, residential guards logged longer days, slept on the island, and drew a pay premium that ranged from twenty percent up to fifty percent, depending on whether they stayed the three-day minimum or the two-week maximum before rotating out for a shift. Residential guards also enjoyed greater and faster opportunities for advancement.

Park stared at us for several seconds, then continued, "Let the clerk know on your way out, and he'll tell you your schedule. Dismissed."

Park stayed where he was as we headed toward the training area door from which he'd watched the hostage exercise. As I stepped by him, he put his hand lightly on my shoulder.

I stopped.

"Going residential?" he said.

"Not tonight," I said. "I'm planning on an evening of celebrating, and then I figure I'll sign up for three on, one off."

"Might as well start it now," he said. "It's the fastest way off the scut duty."

I had to let Lobo, Pri, and Matahi know I'd gotten the job and check in with them, so I said, "It's also the quickest way I know to make that woman furious at me."

Park chuckled. "Fine; don't tell me." All trace of mirth vanished as he added, "For as long as you're in here, you're *in*. You better be sure you understand that. Got me?"

"You bet, Sarge," I said. "I'll see you tomorrow."

As I walked toward the door, I considered his comment and his questions. The odds were good that they would follow me when I left the island; if he was that curious about my past, so were others on the security team. That meant I couldn't go to Lobo without first identifying and then evading any surveillance. Given Wonder Island's status with the government, I couldn't be sure I could do that on my own. I'd have to get to a safe place with serious encryption and then link up with Lobo via the protocol we'd set.

I also had to come up with a girlfriend—or a good reason that I lied about having one. I could meet Matahi and have that meeting play either way to anyone watching me, and we could go back to her SleepSafe room, but that would cause an observer to question the authenticity of my relationship with Matahi. If I tried to claim her as a girlfriend and went to my apartment, there was always the chance that one of the security team would recognize her from Wei's visit. Plus, that might strand her at the apartment, which wasn't safe. I could use Pri instead, but they might recognize her from the assault on Matahi's house, and she wouldn't be anywhere near as good at playing the girlfriend role. No, I'd have to see Matahi without them realizing it was her, and then I'd have to explain the girlfriend story later.

Stupid. I should have gone with the simpler lie.

That wasn't my only problem. Spending time with Matahi would almost certainly annoy Pri. I flashed on the images of Pri and Matahi standing in Lobo, staring at me and at each other, and I knew with a sickening certainty Pri wouldn't be very happy at the news that I was staying the night with Matahi.

I shook my head as I walked. Working with these two was making Lobo's sarcasm more and more appealing all the time.

CHAPTER 41

TAKING THE CHEAPEST SHUTTLES to the southeastern sector of the old city fit the character I was selling to the Wonder Island crew, but it also consumed a couple of hours. If you're trying to shake a corporate tail, all you have to do is stay away from turf the company controls. Avoiding government surveillance is far trickier, particularly on a place as locked-down as a tourist attraction like the old town. Every public sensor is at the government's disposal, so you need either hackers to spoof them temporarily or enough knowledge of the area to know what nooks and crannies the authorities had decided weren't worth watching.

I had neither. If Park and the Wonder Island security team were as tight with Heaven's government as I assumed, they could track my route.

The odds were good, though, that they couldn't use sensors to see what I was doing when I was inside a business, because it's rarely in a company's interest for the government to be monitoring its every move. If I stuck to the tourist traps that megacorps operated, I should be safe from government machine spying once I was inside. I'd still have to keep an eye out for human watchers, but that was a much more manageable problem.

I walked slowly through the streets of the old town, studying the restaurants and bars and brothels for one that possessed the right combination of size and rowdiness, the first trait to give me more places to hide, and the second so that if a little action proved necessary the management probably wouldn't call the police. I also wanted a meal; it'd been too long since I'd eaten. A light breeze carried on the cool evening air the appetizing smells of more kinds of cooking food than I could identify. My stomach rumbled, and I was tempted to stop, but I wasn't ready yet, so I ignored the hunger and kept going.

Something nagged at me as I worked my way toward the edge of the old city, and finally I realized what it was: I felt more exposed than the situation justified. Sure, they were probably tracking me, but they almost certainly weren't out to hurt me. If they'd known of my involvement in the attempt to kidnap Wei, they'd never have let me leave Wonder Island. So, I was as safe as I could reasonably be under the circumstances, alone in a city with a private security force monitoring me.

Alone. That was it. I'd spent a couple of years rarely far from Lobo, and now I had no clue where he was. I'd gone into Wonder Island completely clean, no electronics of any sort on me, because it was the kind of place that would check for such devices very, very closely, particularly after our attack had injured some of their people. Lobo had been watching over me for quite a while, and I'd grown accustomed to it, but now I was on my own.

Well, I could take care of myself. I'd done it for the vast majority of my life, and I'd do it again.

Except, I had to admit to myself, I missed him. As annoying as he was, he was the closest thing to a friend I had.

I recalled his concerns about telling me the truth about what Wei had done to him. He thought I'd hate him for the children that had died to make him, and he hated himself.

I understood both those feelings all too well, though I couldn't bring myself to tell him—or anyone—why. Sometimes, it took all the willpower I could summon to make myself face all the awful things I'd done, all the horrors that had combined to turn me into what I am. Even though I knew that the worst, such as the torture on Aggro, were not my fault, at a very deep level the part of me that was the young man screaming in pain on that prison space station could not make sense of what had happened without blaming it on himself. If I hadn't done something to deserve it, how could they have treated me that way? Why would they have done those terrible things? I also had to admit that I had no one but myself to blame for my actions since then. I'd killed, in combat and to save myself and even on a few occasions because I could find no other way to avoid becoming a test subject once again. I always tried to avoid it, but I had killed, and I had set up situations that had led people to their deaths, and I had to live with those acts.

Lobo, with all the vast computing power that was his mind, was apparently stuck in the same trap. How much worse might it be for him, though, with his capacity to do so many things simultaneously? Was he ever free of the choking grip of self loathing?

Was I?

Yes, sometimes I was. Many times. When a job or a situation absorbed my full attention, everything else vanished and I was *there*, present in the moment and nowhere else. Watching Pri fight to maintain hope, I had not thought at all of myself. Lying next to Matahi on the roof, I had been entirely there, free of my mind for a short time.

Lobo, though, never was. With the level of computing capability he possessed, he was always at some level tearing at his past, hating himself what Wei had done, suffering simply for what he was.

I'd long thought of him as a him, as an intelligence who might as well be a person, but now that I understand his composition— not just his body, but more importantly these core aspects of his consciousness—I realized that he was in many respects as human as I was.

And, I had to admit, recalling my own past, fighting to push back the dark tendrils of my own awful deeds, I had at many points been as much machine as he was.

Maybe I was now, taking my time to plot my moves while on Wonder Island Wei killed children in the name of making better machines and better people.

Except, of course, that I had no real choice. If I wanted to stop Wei, I had to get close to him. This job provided my best chance at doing that, but it would take time, time some child probably didn't have to spare.

Wasn't that always the case, though, not just for me but for all of us? Every time we rested, every time we played, every time we focused on fighting one bad thing, a million other evils all across the universe proceeded unchecked. All we could do was balance what we needed to do to stay sane with what we had to fight, and then hope others were doing the same with the evils they were tackling.

To be human and to think was to know that you could never do enough—but also not to let that stop you from doing something.

I turned a corner and saw at the end of the block a business whose façade was glowing so brightly with lights of all colors that it painted every building on both sides of the street in rapidly shifting rainbows. A huge sign across its third floor declared it The End of the Rainbow. Either a megacorp owned it and had paid a ransom in bribes for the privilege of violating every appearance ordinance that gave the old town its look, or someone in the local government was operating a side business. Either way, I'd be safe from planetary government sensors inside. About four meters of lawn and shrubs separated it on all sides from its neighbors; it fit in with the rest of the old city about as well as a bleeding, oozing sore on the face of a politician.

The line to get in stretched about twenty meters from the door, but it seemed to be moving fairly rapidly, so I joined it. Smaller signs and holo barkers scattered along the edge of the building promised food, drinks, drugs, dancers, gaming—you name it, anything you might need to have a good time.

I should be able to contact both Lobo and Matahi from here, and I was only a few blocks from the SleepSafe where she was staying.

I moved forward a couple of meters in the queue. I rolled my shoulders and shook my head slightly. I turned and stretched as if tight and quickly scanned the faces of the people behind me.

A man four people back looked away immediately.

The woman with him was better. "Is this place really worth it?" she said to me when we made eye contact.

"I sure hope so," I said, "but I honestly don't know. I saw the line, and I'm hungry, so I figured if this many people came somewhere it had to be good."

"That makes sense," she said. She tugged on the sleeve of the man with her. "Doesn't it, dear?"

He nodded and mumbled something.

I turned around and faced ahead of me. If they put two people that easy to spot this close to me, then either they really did have trouble getting good staff, or they were using city sensors for most of the work and these two were around simply to see how I behaved inside. Or maybe they didn't care if I spotted my tails.

None of that mattered. I took a few slow breaths and considered how I wanted to play this. I couldn't afford to let my attention focus anywhere but here, because tomorrow I'd be back at Wonder Island, and if I wanted to keep that job, I'd have to explain everything I did tonight. I needed a story that made sense but kept Matahi, Pri, and me safe.

The queue moved ahead another three meters as I struggled to find a way to make it all work out.

CHAPTER 42

YOU COULD SEE the thinking behind The End of the Rainbow the moment you entered it. Gone were the screaming neon signs; in their place, fixtures carefully arranged to mimic the dappled lights of city streets at twilight washed the interior in a perpetually dim, slightly dangerous feel, as if you'd left the safety of the old town and anything might happen. Human waitstaff in gray shirts and black pants mingled with the patrons, verifying their tables were providing the right food, answering questions, posing for pictures in suggestive or threatening poses, and increasing the sense that you truly were in another world. Seating was catch as catch can, but as soon as I was inside I grabbed a waitress wandering near me and negotiated a tip greater than the cost of anything on the menu in exchange for a small booth in the far left rear corner. The couple occupying it complained at first, but after I explained I was management and auditing the service staff, and of course I'd comp their meal, they moved on happily, enjoying another lucky night in tourist land.

My watchers were already inside by the time I'd settled into the booth, but the place was so crowded that it took them a few minutes to locate and secure a vantage point from which they could both appear busy and keep an eye on me.

Once I knew where they were, I ignored them and slid as close to the wall as I could.

A holo waitress popped into view on the table. "Good evening, friend. What could I interest you in tonight? We have food on this level, gaming on the next, and on the top floor you can find other attractions—" she winked "—if you know what I mean, and from the looks of you I think you do. We'll even package your food to go if you're itching to head right upstairs."

"I'd like the lights in this booth as dim as possible," I said, "and I'd like to see a food menu."

"So love isn't in your plans tonight?" she said as the lights went out and only she illuminated the small area. As we'd been talking, her breasts had grown and a few buttons on her blouse had popped open.

"A food menu," I repeated.

Pictures of heaping plates of meat, enormous bowls of vegetables, piles of fried goods, and half a dozen desserts snapped into the air beside her. "If I might show you a few of our specials," she said. "First—"

"Stop," I said. "Bring me whatever fish platter uses the freshest catch, plus a large glass of the freshest fruit juice you have." When you can't have a great chef, you can at least aim for fresh ingredients. "And enable a public data-access port here, then leave me alone."

"As you will," she said. "I'm required to inform you, however, that there's a small surcharge for data access and an additional levy for hard encryption."

"You're kidding me!" I said. "Free data ports abound all over this fake old city."

"True," she said, "but how many of them can serve you a fish that the kitchen tells me will have been dead for less than eleven hours when it arrives at your table?"

"Fine, fine. Now, go."

She disappeared.

Where she'd stood, a holo appeared, commercials for the Rainbow chain chattering at me from all over it. I could find sister establishments on all the better planets, one of them told me.

I assumed only the management computer would monitor my data accesses for possible sales potential, but for the sake of anyone who might be able to hack whatever passed as hard encryption here and see what I'd done, I spent the first few minutes browsing local news. I followed an obviously purchased marketing puff piece on a local craftswoman through a series of ads to an auction for handmade boxes. I placed a low bid conditional on delivery tonight to this restaurant and a chance to speak to the artist about personalizing its outside with some engravings. I left the bid window open.

The data holo glided onto the wall to my right as a section of the table slid aside and my fish platter arrived—on an actual white platter. As the menu had promised, the slab of dark red fish was huge. A mountain of fried objects of different shapes and sizes surrounded it on three sides.

I cut a small piece of the fish and chewed it. The tender meat delivered a rich, strong taste. I sampled a few of the fried bits, and they proved to be a mixture of vegetables, starches, and small pieces of a white fish. They didn't go particularly well with the main attraction, but they were filling and I was starving, so I gobbled half of them and all of the surprisingly good red fish before I took a break.

The auction owner had responded to my conditional bid with a statement that he was interested in accommodating my request but had to consider what price to charge.

Good.

Now, I just had to wait.

I chewed a thumb-sized fried mystery vegetable and surveyed the interior. My watchers were still checking me out from time to time, but they were also eating, drinking, and having more of a good time at their two-person table than they should have permitted themselves. They were spending so much time focusing on each other that I could have slipped out of the booth and had as much as a minute's head start on them. Amateurs; no wonder Park was so interested in hiring me.

"I would have expected someplace a bit higher on the culinary ladder," Lobo said over the machine frequency.

I smiled in the darkness of the booth. "Took you a while," I said, using the same frequency. I wouldn't talk audibly; no point in giving the booth a chance to report on a particularly lonely guest.

"Excuse me?" he said. "I had to scan the location, plot a course low enough to let me drop the field-comm unit but high enough not to attract attention, and then shoot the thing into the ground in the narrow stretch of grass in the back of that lovely establishment you're visiting."

"Fine, fine," I said. "How long do we have?"

"It depends on how paranoid the owners are," he said. "I'm using the unit to amplify and relay every data stream coming out of that place, as well as a few I'm injecting, so nothing should point to you. I'm also encrypting every part of the flow except the bits between you and the comm, so unless they think to monitor all the machine-frequency chatter—and there's a ton of it, those things never shut up—you should be safe."

Even so, on the off chance that some security freak decided to plow through all the machine talk, there was no point in making our conversation any easier to follow than we could avoid. "I'm where you'd expect me to be, left side, and I'd appreciate a visitor," I said, "an accidental one who looks nothing like herself, appears to want to spend only an hour with me, has a safe room, and isn't at all like my current two remote companions."

"In progress," he said.

"I'll be changing living arrangements for the next three days."

"Understood."

"Anything of note in your world?" I said.

"Only a profound desire for a roommate who talks less," he said.

"I understand," I said. "I'm out for now, but trash it only when I leave or you have to."

"Of course," he said, "or if someone tries to remove it. If that happens, it takes care of itself."

"Oh yeah," I said. "If I scream for help, come get me, and come hot."

"As if I wouldn't," he said, "but I'll never be so lucky. Out."

I pushed away the plate and had the table clear it. I took a few sips of the tart fruit juice and wondered both how long it would take Matahi to get here and what she would look like when she arrived. I hoped she could muster enough of a disguise that no one would recognize her.

"May I get you anything else tonight?" the holo waitress said. "Perhaps a full stomach has changed your outlook on love."

"Yes to the first question," I said, "and my stomach isn't full. Show me your dessert options."

The dishes that floated in miniature in front of me made me thankful that the nanomachines dispatched all the food I didn't need and thus stopped me from ever gaining weight, because every single one was a calorie bomb. I chose a slab of chocolate cake slathered in a foamy white whipped topping and a glass of water.

It arrived less than two minutes later, probably warmed from the freezer as it moved along the conveyor chutes to my table. I took a bite and nodded to myself; it wasn't bad, somewhere between the fried chunks and the fish in quality, a little better than I'd expected from this place. I ate slowly, chewing each bite completely and pausing between them to sip my water and browse other, real auction sites.

I was down to the last two bites when a blond woman almost my height leaned against the entrance to my booth. Her straight hair fell to the top of her butt. A purple, floor-length, latex dress clung to her body and revealed wide hips and unnaturally large breasts. Mirrorshade contacts covered her eyes.

"Mind if I join you?" she said in a very high but smooth voice.

"Waitress," I said. The holo server appeared. "I didn't ask for this service."

"Nor did we supply it," the holo said.

"What," the blonde said, her voice dropping and suddenly recognizable as Matahi's, "you don't like the look?"

CHAPTER 43

I STARED AT THE WOMAN standing next to me. If I worked hard at it, I could see Matahi's face under the makeup and lenses and hair, but how she'd managed to change her body so dramatically was beyond me.

"Non-house professional companions must pay a facilities usage fee," the server said, "or face immediate ejection."

"Of course," Matahi said, her voice high again. She held up her hands in surrender. "So, buddy, are you going to pay my tab and buy me a drink, or should I find another friend?"

I looked away from Matahi to collect myself. "Why not?" I said, more for the house's benefit than anything else. I faced the holo. "Please add her usage fee to my bill, bring us two more glasses of this juice, and tell me: What's the cost for a little privacy?"

"Private rooms are available upstairs for a variety of rates," the holo said. "Would you like to see the options?"

I waved my hands and said, "No, no. I'm not ready for that kind of privacy. I'd just like to keep our conversation here to ourselves."

The waitress disappeared. In her place, a lawyer straight from a holo show but with the same face as the waitress—cut-rate software at work—addressed me. "Turning off all house data gathering and providing a bonded booth privacy guarantee—with the customary Rainbow's End limitation of liability, of course—is available for a modest fee. We naturally accept no responsibility for the behavior of other patrons."

"Of course," I said. "Please proceed on that front, get us our drinks, and bill me."

I got out my wallet and watched the charge appear. I thumbed approval.

"After this message," the lawyer said, "you will, of course, have to find a human server to place additional orders."

"Of course," I said. "Now, privacy, please."

"Our pleasure," she said. The two glasses of juice slid up from the table's center, the table closed, and the holo vanished.

Matahi slid into the booth opposite me. She stopped in the center of the seat.

I waved her to her right, into the shadows; I wanted her all the way to the wall against which I also sat.

She didn't move. "I take it you didn't recognize me," she said, her voice barely louder than a whisper but definitely her own. "I'm not going to hide any deeper in the darkness, and you shouldn't, either. Slide to the center, because that's where you would move if I were what I appear to be."

"Two people are watching me," I whispered.

"Yeah," she said, "the couple at the two-top thirty degrees off the outer edge of this booth and about six meters away."

"They're that obvious?" I said. "Even to you?"

She nodded.

"So why should I make it easy for them to watch me?"

"So they can see me seduce you into paying for the next hour or two of my time."

"Fine," I said. I slid to the middle of the booth. I could now clearly see my watchers, so they had a good line of sight on me.

Something brushed up my leg and settled against my crotch. It was hard and sharp. I glanced down. It was a spiked heel over ten centimeters high. I hadn't noticed it before because the dress fell all the way to the floor when she was standing.

"What are you doing?" I said.

"What you should expect me to be doing," she said. Her foot rubbed against me. "Have you looked at me? No one dressed like this is going to take the slow shuttle to love town." She leaned back, flipped her hair, crossed her arms under her breasts, and said, "This is strictly an express-ticket outfit."

"Is this part of what you normally do?" I said. I knew it was a mistake the moment I said it, but her comfort in her role had puzzled me.

Her eyes narrowed, and she leaned across the table as far as she could. Her foot kept rubbing my crotch. "This has as much to do with my normal behavior as leaving an egg in the sun to get warm has to do with being a great chef." She paused until I met her gaze. "As you should know."

"I'm sorry," I said. "I spoke without thinking. I didn't mean to upset you, and I should know better. I just can't get over the differences in your look and your behavior."

"You mandated that I wear a disguise. I agree that neither of us can afford for anyone to recognize me. You wanted to talk tonight. This outfit guarantees that no one will look real closely at my face, and even if someone studies the video captures they're unlikely to spot me under this hair, these lenses, and all the makeup." She leaned back and relaxed; her foot never stopped rubbing me. "Besides," she chuckled and then said, "it's pretty clear this outfit isn't hurting your interest."

I pushed her foot down and looked away. "I can't control everything."

"But you wish you could," she said. "You really do."

How did this keep happening to me? I needed to get back on turf I understood. "Can we focus on the problems at hand?" I said.

"Sure." She smiled. "What can I do for you?"

"I need a place to sleep tonight, and I need to make sure those watchers see me leave with a woman. I messed up and told one of the trainers that I was staying here because of a woman."

Her look grew more intense as she said, "Isn't that more or less true? I mean, you're working with Suli and trying to save her child."

There we went again! If only we were negotiating, I would understand how to proceed. This, though, was either a form of negotiation I'd never experienced or something else I couldn't recognize. I can never grow old with a woman, and I cannot tell anyone my secret, so for my entire life I've stayed as far from romantic relationships as I could manage. It's the only safe choice, but at times, like this one, it leaves me ill-prepared for dealing with women.

"If I don't spend tonight with a woman," I said, "I risk losing that job. If I lose the job, I also lose the best chance we've had so far of accomplishing the goal."

"Do you understand," she said, "that I'm not dressed for the part of the woman you come home to? Looking like this, I'm the woman you go out for."

"Yes," I said, "but I can work with that. Park—the trainer—already believes I was lying to him, but he doesn't quite know how. While I'm with you, he'll receive a report on my activities and then dig out the truth."

"If you say so," she said, "though with a little warning I could have dressed for the other role."

"I don't want you dressed like a permanent partner, and I don't want to go to some house with you. If I do that, your risk will increase, because you'll become another leverage point they could use on me. This approach is just fine."

"So let me see if I have this right," she said. "You had me dress up like the kind of companion who frequents this place just to protect me?"

"You make it sound like a bad thing," I said, "but, yes, that's right."

She chuckled again. "Well, that's a first." She crossed her arms under her breasts again and winked at me. "So, what would you like to do with me now?"

"Nothing," I said, "except go to your room at the SleepSafe."

She smiled. "I thought you'd never ask."

CHAPTER 44

I'D OVERNIGHTED in a SleepSafe on many occasions on many worlds, but I'd always opted for the most bare-bones room available. When I was the only occupant and seeking safety for a day or two, I saw no point in wasting money on amenities I wouldn't stay long enough to enjoy. I'd told Matahi to get a suite so I could have privacy, a room of my own.

I had no idea how nice the suites were.

Like all SleepSafe rooms, it provided a full complement of security displays—scans of every aspect of the perimeter, with both visual light and IR options, the ability to zoom on command, and so on—but here they were available in large holos that you could summon in every room. (In the bottom-rung singles I'd always rented, the security feeds appeared in a single large display on the wall opposite the bed.) Matahi and I had stopped to register me on the way in, so I was now an approved caller for her. I hadn't even known you could register visitors, because I never had any.

I loved this place's security.

"This is great!" I said to Matahi.

"You have no idea. The bed linens—"

I didn't mean to cut her off, but even the quality of the displays was better than the ones I'd experienced. "You can get every external angle in any room you want! I love this."

"The master bath is extraordinary," she said.

I walked back and forth in front of the holo in the smaller bedroom, the one Matahi had indicated was mine. "And there they are." I pointed at a feed from a front-side camera; my watchers from The Rainbow's End stood on the opposite corner and did a poor job of pretending to kiss each other. "Do you see any others? I can't believe these two think they're fooling anybody."

"The spa amenities are also quite lovely," she said. "I have to admit it: Though I wasn't pleased at the thought of staying in a hotel whose main emphasis is security, the SleepSafe folks know how to outfit a suite."

I stared at all the camera feeds again, working my way through them one by one, surveying the entire exterior. No one else was stationary. No one appeared to be watching us. "They really must not have a very strong team," I said, "or they wouldn't send these two losers. Fortunately for us, they did, so we're good for now."

"The master bed is amazingly comfortable," she said.

I wiped my hand across the holo, and it disappeared. I turned to face Matahi. "Yeah, we're safe."

"Have you even listened to anything I said?" She stood with her hands on her hips, her displeasure clear. "I'm going to take a shower!"

She stomped into the bathroom. The door snicked shut behind her.

"What did I do this time?" I said.

I shook my head, went into my room, and sat on the bed as the door closed behind me. I was doing my job, making sure we were safe. How could that be wrong?

I got up. I couldn't focus on Matahi now. She was distracting me. I had to talk to Lobo, update Pri, and get some sleep.

The field comm I'd given Matahi sat in the exact center of the top of the dresser, as if it were an alien artifact she was afraid to handle. Nothing was within a meter of it. I grabbed it, pulled a chair in front of the room's desk, and put the comm on the desk. I engaged the desk, then opened the comm, had it verify my thumbprint, DNA, and passphrase, and told it to link to the desk's data stream. The comm would use the external connections of the desk to send a video stream of the room's ceiling to a sat relay Lobo had set up. The sat would respond with footage of whatever section of Heaven was below it at the time. Woven within each video would be a lower-res, highly encrypted secondary data thread: my communications with Lobo. Anyone who cared enough to look could detect easily that we were hiding our real data, but cracking the encryption would, Lobo assured me, take more days than we were likely to be on Heaven for anything without his level of computing power. SleepSafe hotels treated your data as securely as they housed you, but I still felt a lot more comfortable communicating with Lobo when we provided our own security.

I started the comm session.

A second later, an array of sandwiches and drinks appeared above the comm, and Lobo's voice filled the silence. "May I take your order?" he said.

"What the hell?" I said. "It's Jon, I'm tired, I'm alone, and I'm calling from the SleepSafe."

The food images disappeared.

"One can never be too careful," he said, "as I'm sure you would agree."

"You know it's the comm from its protocol stream," I said, "and you've already matched my voiceprint."

"You might have been under coercion," he said.

"Yeah, right."

"And, you have to admit it: It was pretty funny."

Maybe at another time I would have laughed, but right then I was frustrated with Matahi, exhausted and ready to rest, so I ignored his comment. "I'm in."

"As if you'd fail," Lobo said.

"One of the two training exercises was in a huge hangar. If I can find a way to mark it for you, when the time comes that I need you to fly in hot, you should be able to blow its top and get me."

"When we reach that point," he said, "I hope you plan to head straight off this world."

"We won't have a choice," I said. "Unless I get lucky and can smuggle out Wei, we're going to make a lot of noise extracting him. So, you might as well plot the fastest way to the jump gate."

"As if I didn't do that the moment we started on this mission," he said. "What else do you need?"

"Are you close enough to be able to monitor the streets around me without anyone noticing you?"

"I don't need to be," he said. "I've enlisted the help of the SleepSafe comm sat, and now I'm monitoring all of its camera feeds. I assume the incredibly obvious man and woman are your new friends."

I checked the security displays on the room's front wall. Those two were the only people staying in one position. "Yes—and how did you do that?"

"They're the only people who aren't moving," he said. "An alarm clock would be able to spot them."

"No," I said. "I meant, how did you crack into a SleepSafe comm sat? They're supposed to be incredibly secure."

"They are," Lobo said. "I've been working on it since you first mentioned using the place."

"But how—"

"Remember the nanomachines-based computing substrate, the new software paradigms, that whole story I told you?"

"Yes, yes," I said. "Sorry. Anyway, I trust the SleepSafe's security chutes"—this room's was to the right of the bed—"will get me out of here safely if anything goes wrong, but I'll feel a lot safer if I know that you'll be close enough to pick me up quickly if it comes to that."

"Of course," Lobo said. "I have to ask, though: Is there some reason you believe we might see that kind of action?"

"No," I said. "It's simply that one can never be too careful."

"Touché," he said. "So, given today's data, do you have a better plan than before?"

"No. Though most of the security team is probably as inept as the other candidates I trained with today, they have a few good people that might give us trouble. I'll have to be careful." I liked Park enough that I hoped I could avoid hurting him if we had to exit swiftly.

"Okay," Lobo said. "So I wait, keep an eye on you when you're there or in transit to or from the island, hope Wei comes out, and babysit Pri."

"That's about it."

"Did I mention my amazing computing capacity?" Lobo said. "You realize that what you're asking takes very little of it."

"I do," I said, "but that's often the way it goes on jobs." I considered his situation for a few seconds. "What do you do with all your spare cycles?" I said.

"The usual things any sentient creature does with its free time," he said. "I create and evaluate new bits of programming in a constant effort to improve myself. I ponder the human condition; you are a fascinating bunch to watch, and I am genetically linked to you. I prepare for future possibilities. I contemplate the big questions. As I said, the usual stuff."

"You might be surprised," I said, "by how few people regularly engage in those activities. In any case, what big questions do you consider?"

"The obvious ones," he said. "Is there a God? If so, what kind creature is it? Is there an afterlife? If there is, is there a place for me in it? Who made the jump gates? And why? You know, they've never spoken to me, no matter what frequency and coding scheme I use to approach them." He paused. "Things like that."

"I've never heard the gates on the machine frequencies, either," I said, "but that's never surprised me; jump gates are nothing if not mysterious." I closed my eyes for a second. Fatigue slammed into me and made it hard to reopen them. "I need to sleep."

"Pri would like to speak with you," Lobo said.

"Okay."

Lobo's pilot area popped into view over the desk. Pri sat in the co-pilot's couch. Her face was tight, stressed. "Jon, how are you?" she said.

"Exhausted."

"Where are you?"

"In Matahi's SleepSafe suite, in my room, about to go to sleep."

"Where is she?"

"In her room," I said. "None of this is news, except perhaps how tired I am, so what do you really want to know?"

"How did it go today?"

"I'm in," I said. "I have the job. Now, I have to locate Wei."

"Do you have any idea how long that'll take?" she said.

I rubbed my eyes with my hands and shook my head. I fought the urge to scream at her. "No," I finally said. "I'll contact Lobo and you the moment I know anything. I'm doing the best I can, and right now, I need to sleep."

Her expression softened. "I know you are," she said, "and I appreciate it. Sleep well."

"Thanks," I said. "Out."

I closed the comm and watched as it rearmed itself.

"Secure door," I said. It was hard to sleep in an area with some-one I didn't know well, but at least I was in a SleepSafe. Anyone coming at me would have to figure out a way into the hotel, get through the suite's exterior door, and take out the locked door to my room—or come through the walls, which were famous for their durability and multilayered armor. I was as about as safe as I could be outside Lobo.

I needed to wash up, undress, and let the room clean my clothes, but that could wait for a few minutes. I stretched out on the bed. I pictured the SleepSafe's security systems, Lobo watching me from way overhead, and the thick and strong walls and doors for which the hotel chain was renowned.

I fell asleep in seconds.

Nightmare fragments attacked me throughout the night like fighters on strafing attacks against command cruisers, zipping by, firing rapidly, and then receding from view so quickly you couldn't follow their tracks.

Strapped to a table on Aggro, rotated into position, the biosuited scientists checking my eyes as the needles plunged into my neck, wall clocks counting the seconds until I began screaming.

A child I'd saved shrieking as he watched a truck slam into a pedestrian and send the man so high he hit the pavement with a sickening wet sound, the boy's screams mutating into my own as I watched Benny struggling against his bonds as the nanomachines contorted his skin.

A tall, redheaded woman walking away from me, disappearing into a crowd, holding the hand of the boy I'd saved, and now, when I wanted to scream, when I yearned to call her name, my mouth wouldn't open and I couldn't make a sound.

Matahi and Pri staring at me in the command area of Lobo, their expressions telling the story of my failure, their mouths opening in cries as white-robed boys and girls crammed the space, all of them shrieking in agony and wishing they could die, all hope of salvation long gone, death the only prayer left to them, and Benny's face and my own were among them and I couldn't help them, I couldn't help myself, I couldn't—

I woke up with my mouth frozen wide open but no sound escaping me, my body shaking with the effort of suppressing the sound. As the days on Aggro had worn into weeks and then months, as for reasons I'd never understood Benny and I had remained alive while all the other prisoners came and died in a ceaseless alternation, we'd vowed one day not to give them the pleasure of our screams. We failed sometimes, the pain building to peaks we could no longer manage, but most days we clenched our jaws and closed our eyes and knew the only way we could hit at them, the sole act of defiance left to us was simply not to cry out. I'd screamed since that time, most recently two years ago, strapped to a medbed and tortured for hours, my mind too drugged to control the nanomachines, and each time I'd felt the shame of failure. Everyone breaks eventually, but sometimes all you have is the slim hope that maybe you'll be the one who won't.

I checked the external feeds. My watchers were nowhere in sight. The world outside was still dark, the morning light over an hour away.

I opted for a water shower, cranked the pressure and temperature so high my skin grew sore, and stood under it, my eyes shut, lost in the water and able to enjoy it in the knowledge that for these last moments before I returned to Wonder Island I was safe, and I had purpose. That Wei had rediscovered the secret that I thought had died on Aggro, that once again we'd learned that if we wanted to play God with this technology our young would pay the cost, should not have surprised me; what evil one man does, many will eventually do. This evil, though, I had a chance to stop, and I would. I would.

I dressed and headed out of the room. Matahi, her padded bodysuit on the floor beside her, slept sprawled diagonally across the huge bed, the grayish lights of the still-active security feeds dappling her sleeping body. She'd thrashed her way out of the sheets; only a small, sheer, light blue nightgown covered her.

Before I could reach the main door to the suite, I heard her.

"You're leaving?"

I turned back to face her. She was sitting up straight, the gown covering her torso about as well as morning mist covers a rising sun.

"Yes," I said. "I need to get back."

"Why did you sleep in there?"

"It was my room."

"You could have joined me."

I stared at her and didn't know what to say. I wasn't her client. I wasn't sure what she wanted me to be. All I knew for certain was that I'd always have to leave anyone who grew close to me, because I could never let anyone know the truth about me.

When I didn't speak, she finally added, "Don't you trust me?"

I was tired of this question, tired of people asking when the answer should have been obvious. I also knew the truth wasn't what she wanted, but I liked her enough not to want to lie. "Trust wasn't the only issue here," I said. "For what it's worth, I trust you as much as I can given how little I know you." I didn't spell out just how little that was.

"I think about those few minutes we had together on my roof," she said, "and about the gift you gave me, and I know we could be more."

No, I thought again, we never can be. I didn't know what I wanted from her, but I was certain that my desires didn't matter; I could never build anything with her—or with anyone.

"I have to go," I said. "Stay safe here, and await instructions from Lobo."

I turned around and stepped to the door.

"And when we're done," she said, her words freezing me in the boundary between the room and the hall, "when you've captured Wei and saved the children, then we'll talk?"

I raised my hand, realizing that to her it had to look like an answer, wondering what response she thought it was, but knowing that what I was really doing was what I had to do: swatting away the distraction, keeping the feelings at bay so I could focus and do my job.

I crossed the threshold and headed out to catch a shuttle back to Wonder Island.

CHAPTER 45

"WHAT, NO BAG?" Park said as I entered the barracks. They called it a dorm, but it was the same kind of utility housing the Saw operated on every planet where it maintained a permanent base.

"Why would I bother, Sarge?" I said. "Or are you telling me you're not going to issue me a uniform and a kit, then search everything I brought in here? I figure I just made your task a little easier."

He smiled. "Your uniform and kit are in your locker. If the computer sized you wrong, tell the guy who let you in. Otherwise, meet me in the duty room pronto. No point in waiting for the weak or the tired." He left.

I changed clothes quickly. I'd arrived three hours early, the sun still not up, and he was already there, dressed and ready for action. It figures. No sergeant worth his pay is going to risk new meat showing him up in his own base on their first day.

I hoped I wouldn't have to go up against him to capture Wei, but I was having trouble seeing a way around it.

When I reached the duty room, the door was open and Park was chatting with Ng and Lee.

I knocked on the doorframe, snapped to attention, and said, "Sergeant, permission to enter, Sergeant."

Ng and Lee shot me dirty looks that made the formality worth the effort.

"Knock it off, Moore," Park said. "We told you: no ranks here, just titles, and rarely those. Get your butt in here. We were just talking about you."

As if I weren't there listening, he turned to Ng and said, "I told you: He's got the training and the background to move right to something useful, at the very least perimeter patrol, maybe staff or even excursion protection."

"I don't trust any new meat that much," Ng said, "and I sure don't trust one who will shoot his training mates without a second thought."

Only Lee looked at me. Ng didn't care for me, but somehow it had become personal for Lee. I'd have to watch my back around him. On the other hand, the sooner I could deal with him, the easier things might be later, so I said, "I'm sorry, Mr. Lee, did you have something to say to me?"

Lee stepped toward me but stopped instantly when Ng raised her hand a few centimeters.

"Do you have a problem with our conversation, Moore?" she said.

"Permission to speak freely," I said.

She nodded.

"I did the right things for the missions in the training classes, and I'd do them again. If my teammates aren't up to the job—" I paused and glanced briefly at Lee, who visibly tensed with the effort of his self-control. "—then I'll do what it takes to finish on my own. If you don't trust me, then let me earn that trust; I'll happily take on the crappiest work you have."

"And exactly why are you so generous?" Ng said.

"I'm not," I said. "I figure that the jobs that require more trust pay better, and I need money, so I might as well get started proving that you can rely on me to take care of business. Besides," I paused and smiled, "you're going to assign me and every other new hire the scutwork anyway, so I might as well try to look good by volunteering."

She smiled briefly, an expression so devoid of any real warmth that I decided I liked her expressionless face better. When a snake or any other deadly wild animal shows you its teeth, it's rarely a good thing.

"We do need help in a few of the better-paying areas," she said, "and you do have the qualifications, as well as the endorsement of some—but not all—of our team. You're right, though; you haven't earned anything other than a job here yet." She faced Park for a second. "You have your orders."

She headed out, Lee behind her. I braced myself for the impact and as Lee passed by my chair he veered just enough for our shoulders to collide. I leaned into the collision at the last moment and hit him with a short shoulder strike that only he and Park noticed. My shoulder stung with the impact but I kept my face neutral and acted as if we'd never made contact. I watched Park's eyes and saw him tense.

"Did you need something else, Dan?" he said.

I wanted desperately to get up, turn around, and confront the threat. It wasn't in my nature to surrender my back, but this time I had to rely on what I could read from Park.

"Nothing that can't wait," Lee said.

When the door slid shut, Park said, "I love the way you make friends."

"I try to make the friends worth having," I said. "The others, I treat appropriately."

He walked over to me. "Well, as one of those people I hope you understand is a friend worth having, I'd appreciate you explaining why you lied about a woman being the reason you're staying on Heaven."

"I was with a woman last night," I said.

"Yeah," he said, "we know, and either you're a great deal worse than I think you are, or you saw our third-rate surveillance team. So, you also understand that we know you hired her for the evening. We checked your apartment, and it doesn't look like you've ever lived in it. So, stop playing cute and answer the question, or you'll lose the little bit of support from me that you've enjoyed so far."

I paused a few seconds, then looked him in the eyes. "I lied because you caught me off guard, and because I didn't want you checking too hard with the EC about me. I know you said this is strictly Heaven's operation, but everybody with a data port on this planet can tell you that both the EC and the CC are sucking up to Heaven's government."

"So you're wanted by the EC?"

"No," I said, glad to be able to use bits of truth, "but let's just say that some of its officials weren't entirely satisfied with a delivery I made, and they suggested I stay out of EC space."

"So why are you on Heaven?"

"It's reasonably close to where I was, the lack of satisfaction on the part of those officials translated into lower revenue for me, and Heaven isn't technically EC space. So, it seemed like a good place to find work. I had been with a woman, and she talked me into renting that stupid apartment, back when I thought we might stay together. Then, well—" I shrugged "—it didn't last, she left me, and I didn't see much point in going back to it."

"And what about your previous trip here, the one you made with a date?"

So they had matched my face to their past visitor video archives. I'd known that was likely, so I was ready. Without hesitating, I said, "It's like you said: I was on a date—but I was also using the outing as a cover for doing a little recon on this place."

Park shifted his weight to his rear foot. He did it slowly enough that most folks wouldn't have noticed it, but he knew I did, and he knew I understood that he was readying himself in case he had to fight me. "Why?" he said.

I held up my hands. "Sarge, we have no problem. The only decent moneymaking options for me on Heaven are the militia and this place. I don't want to go back into military service, so I had to apply here. First, though, I wanted to make sure it was secure enough that I wouldn't be signing up just to end up a patsy for some low-end security system's failure down the line." I dropped my hands. "I've taken jobs at places with crappy security, and every time something goes wrong, they blame the people doing the work—people like me—not the ones who designed the systems."

"You could have consulted the public holos about our security," he said.

I nodded. "Yeah, and I did, but there's no substitute for being on the ground." Before he could ask anything else, I added, "I also wanted to see which jobs the staff had to do and which you'd automated, so I went off the path and into the woods. I have to tell you, I'm mighty glad we have machines to shepherd tourists back onto the trails so I don't have to spend my days doing that sort of work." He raised an eyebrow, so I added, "As you may have noticed, my people skills are not always the best, particularly when the other people are idiots."

Park stared at me for several seconds, then chuckled. "Yeah, I've seen that," he said. "What you should understand is that Ng's people have already run all the background checks they could, including one with the EC, and no one there is so upset that your name raised any flags. To advance here, just do your job well, stay out of trouble, and put your experience to use should it ever come to that."

I didn't tell him that their searches yielded only clean data because the EC sector head I'd tricked couldn't afford to let anyone to know how our business arrangement had ended. I was glad, though, that she hadn't changed her mind.

"In fact," Park said, "if you do what I tell you and continue to perform, you can even make some better than decent dough here."

"That sounds great," I said.

"Good. Now, let's get to some of that work you volunteered to do."

CHAPTER 46

TWO DAYS LATER, I was no closer to finding Wei. I'd tranked a couple of cat-snake hybrids with attitude problems who'd decided fighting each other was their only purpose in life, broken up a fight between a man and a woman who couldn't nicely resolve their dispute over which of the two of them would take home the man with them, and stood guard over three different rooms no one ever opened. Exciting stuff. I wondered if the rooms might contain something useful for my mission, but I was sure Ng and Lee would be watching me from time to time, so I stayed out of them, stuck to my role, worked double shifts every day, and did as I was told.

The private security work I'd done before had always evoked one of two extreme states: constant tension from protecting a person or other asset that was an active target, or unceasing boredom during night-shift guard duty I took because I needed a low-profile place to hide. The first occupies your attention so fully that you end every shift utterly drained. The second usually lets you bring along some entertainment to help pass the time. Here, I found myself right in the middle: intermittently busy enough that I had to stay constantly alert, yet idle enough that I was often bored. The rules strictly prohibited the use of any entertainment device, so I had only my thoughts to keep me company.

I filled a lot of those quiet hours building and walking through mental maps of the underground facility. It roughly followed a spokes and hubs layout, with the hubs either central labs or large rooms like our second practice area, and most of the spokes dead-end corridors. A few spokes connected two wheels. I'd worked in three different wheels so far, but I was pretty sure the facility had more. The only reason I wasn't positive is that the place itself exhibited a design paranoia: All the walls were the same institutional very pale yellow, a color I've disliked since my time in similarly shaded cells on Aggro. The only guideposts, the signs, were all active and gave you only directions and information appropriate to your security level. I was new enough and low enough in the Wonder Island hierarchy that most of the signs remained off when I passed them. Those few that turned on then told me only which direction to go to most efficiently reach my next assignment.

I was standing at a very relaxed parade rest outside my fourth featureless room when its door opened. No one had entered while I'd been there, so by reflex I brought up my rifle and backed along the wall for a clear shot at the space. My orders were to stop anyone from going in; no one had said anything about people exiting, but there's no point in taking chances.

A female voice from inside the room said, "New, eh?" She chuckled and then turned serious. "I can see you on the hallway monitor. I work here, I'm unarmed—unless you count this useless critter—and I'm coming out slowly."

A thin woman a bit over a meter and a half tall stepped through the open doorway into the hall. Light brown hair hung loose to her waist. She held both her hands in the air. In her right she clutched a leash that ran upward and into the room. A moment later, a creature attached to the other end of the leash flew at her. The woman stopped in the hall and watched as it flapped thin black wings almost a meter wide and hovered just outside the doorway.

I glanced at it, then looked again to make sense of what I was seeing. The creature's body was about the size of my forearm and covered with soft brown and white fur. It had large eyes, long droopy ears, and a mouth that opened when it noticed me watching it and revealed two long, curved fangs. It hissed at me and let out a bark that was surprisingly low given the animal's size.

"Vampibasset," the woman said. She rolled her eyes. "Those idiots over in development must have eaten a lot of the native fungi to even get a vision of this little devil. They created it, but they never stopped to think about how dumb it is to make a bat-creature have to flap so hard to fly. Now they want to make this beast marketing's problem—as if I'm going to let them ditch this freak on us."

I kept the rifle trained on her. "I didn't see you enter. Where did you come from?"

"Some of these work areas, like this one, are big enough that they open on two different halls. I came in the other side."

"Maybe you should stay here," I said, "while I—"

Over my ear comm a man said, "You idiot." I recognized it as Lee's voice. "You're holding captive the leader of the small flying mammals division. Let her go."

I resumed my parade rest position and said, "Sorry for detaining you."

My movements must have startled the vampibasset, because it turned, glared at me, and snapped and lunged in my direction. It lost control, slammed into the wall next to me, and crashed to the floor.

The woman stared at it and sighed. "You see? You see what happens when you let engineers work without marketing's input? And now I have to fix it."

The creature stood, shook its head a few times, flapped madly, ran toward the woman, and managed to get airborne again.

She shrugged and headed down the hallway, the animal in tow behind her, its wings beating for all the sad thing was worth. "I guess they can't all be winners," she said as she turned the corner.

Ten minutes later, Lee appeared from around the same corner. He marched up to me.

For Park or Ng I would have snapped to attention, but I didn't like him, and I was getting tired of him, so I stayed as I was.

"What were you doing," he screamed, "aiming your weapon at that woman?"

"My job," I said. "Guarding the room."

"I'd think even a dumb slab of meat like you could figure out that if someone was coming *out* of a room and was towing one of our creatures, they must have been allowed to be there in the first place."

"Unless they broke in," I said, "and were stealing a valuable new creation."

"You think a vampibasset is valuable?" he said.

"It's not my call to make. I'm supposed to guard the room, so I did."

He leaned close enough to me that he had to tilt his head to stare into my eyes. A fine film of mist covered his forehead.

I didn't lean back. I smiled. "Is there something in my teeth?" I said.

"You do not want—" he began.

"That's enough, Dan," Ng said. I didn't look away from Lee, but I could hear two sets of footsteps coming down the hall toward us from the left.

"Moore did exactly what he was supposed to do," Park's voice said. "I asked Akagel to exit that way. I've been running similar tests on all the entry-level staff."

Lee stared at me a moment longer, than stepped back. "I was just messing with him," he said.

I glanced up and watched as Ng and Park came to a stop on either side of Lee.

"Not the ideal move, Dan," Ng said, "because you chose to pick on the only one of the new crop that passed the test." She put her hand on his shoulder. "Still, no harm done; right, Moore?"

I resisted the urge to smile, but I did look Lee in the eyes as I said, "None at all."

Ng didn't notice my expression, because she was looking at Lee.

Park did. His smile came and went in an instant.

Lee tensed his arms and glared at me.

The more I was around him, the less I liked him. From her stance and expression, however, Ng clearly did.

She faced me. "Now that we have that cleared up, Moore, I think your solid responses have earned you a step up in work assignment. Fortunately, we have just the job for you." She turned toward Lee. "Dan, you're clearly too valuable to keep doing low-level work like that guard duty on the research team's quiet room." She put her hand on his shoulder as if to hold him in place, then without looking at me said, "Moore, that's your new station."

Lee's expression tightened. He stared at me as if he wanted to kill me and only Ng's hand was stopping him.

What was going on?

Ng smiled, but there was no warmth in it. "Tomaso, take Moore there. Moore, I think you'll find this is something completely different. You might even like it." She brushed away from Lee's forehead a solitary strand of hair. "I've heard some people do."

CHAPTER 47

PARK DIDN'T SAY ANYTHING as we walked away.

I decided to follow his example until we reached the end of the hall and turned right. No footsteps followed us, and Park visibly relaxed, so I figured it was safe to talk.

"What was that all about?" I said.

Park glanced at me but kept moving. "That's not how this works," he said.

"How what works?"

"This particular thing." A smile burst onto his face, and he could hardly stop himself from laughing as he said, "Not that I have any firsthand knowledge or involvement. It's strictly an arrangement Ng's made."

"What kind of an arrangement?" I said.

He stopped, and so did I. He was enjoying my confusion. I was getting damn tired of it, but I fought back my temper.

"And why was Lee so angry at me when Ng told you to take me wherever it is that we're going?"

Park couldn't stop smiling. "Let's just say that one of our jobs is to meet the needs of the senior research staff, and sometimes that requires unusual effort. Every new meat eventually gets a run at this one; your turn just came early." He paused and looked away for a moment, then focused again on me. "As for Lee, well, how about we leave it at this: He chose an assignment that Ng thought wasn't appropriate for him."

"And now it's mine?"

"That's about the size of it," Park said.

"How junior—and how dangerous—is this job?"

This time, he bit his lip to stop himself from laughing. "As I told you," he said, "I don't know personally, but the stories are many and varied." He stepped back, looked me up and down, and added, "I think you'll do fine." He started walking again. "Let's go. We're heading over to the high-security area, and it's a fair distance from here. We could grab a shuttle, but I think it would do you good to get your blood pumping." He stopped, smiled, and then added, "You might need it."

Before I could ask another question, he took off at a double-time-march pace, so I fell in behind him and figured I'd find out soon enough.

The high-security area had to be where Wei worked, so I was looking forward to seeing it. From the hallway perspective, which is all I'd seen so far, it appeared identical to where I'd been standing guard.

As we walked, Park assured me that if Ng hadn't authorized me to be there, I'd never have made it this far. "I'd have led the capture team myself, if it came to that," he said.

"What's so important here?" I said.

He shook his head and stared at me as if I had asked him why we needed air. "You've visited the park," he said. "You saw the dragons and all the other flying creatures. You saw some of the land animals. The scientists here create beings that no one has ever seen before, or at least no one alive today, and tourists flock to the island to see them. No other lab anywhere can do what these people do. We're protecting a gold mine, and Heaven is using its treasures to improve the entire planet as well as its relationships with the EC and the CC."

I watched carefully as he spoke. I couldn't detect any sign of a lie. Either he was very good at deception, or he was telling the truth. If he was being honest, then he had no clue what Wei was really doing. You can't keep an entire security team in the dark, so if he was ignorant, Ng had to know. My encounter with Lee and then Ng had made it very clear that Lee was hers, so Lee probably knew as well. I wondered how many of the people on the security detail were aware of the truth.

"Got it?" Park said.

"Yeah," I said, "that makes sense."

"Good," he said. He pointed to a door on my right. "Because this is your stop. It's important that you understand why these scientists are so useful and thus why the island's management humors them so much. As long as they keep making animals that sell tickets, we'll keep meeting their needs."

"What are you talking about?" I said. I took up position beside the door and stood at parade rest. "Guarding a door here is no different than guarding one where we were before."

Park chuckled. "You'll see soon enough. Just remember: Your job includes making the scientists happy, and all the new meat end up here eventually." He started away, then stopped and turned to face me. "Oh, yeah: Don't worry whether the cameras and sensors really go off—they do—and feel free to say no—but understand that you'll be losing a healthy bonus and pissing off Ng."

He headed away.

"I don't understand," I said.

"I know," he said over his shoulder, "they never do. But, you will."

I'd liked Park up to now, but this entire exchange had annoyed me. I didn't get the joke that he found so funny. Worse, if I didn't act correctly, Ng would be even more annoyed at me than she already was. I couldn't afford to let that happen, but I had no clue what to do to avoid it.

I shook my head slightly to clear it. I was wasting energy worrying about problems that didn't exist yet. I could do nothing to better my situation, so the best course of action was to relax, review the route we'd taken here so I wouldn't forget it, and wait to see how the situation developed.

I didn't have to wait long.

Less than an hour later, the door beside me opened.

This time, I didn't raise my rifle; no point in looking stupid a second time. I did, though, back slightly away from the door and turn to face it, because there was also no point in not preparing in case something was actually wrong.

Nothing happened for a minute, and then a woman's voice called from inside the room, "What are you waiting for? Get in here."

Carrying the rifle at port arms, I circled to my right so I could scan the room without exposing myself completely. When I was parallel with the doorway I could see the woman. She was bent over a desk, studying something I couldn't see. She appeared to be alone and unarmed. A large work surface stood in the room's rear left corner, papers scattered here and there on it. In the back right corner was a large bed.

I stepped inside.

"So you're the new meat Ng sent me?"

"Yes," I said. When in doubt, say as little as you can.

"They sent me your file, Moore, so I know who you are. I doubt they bothered to tell you why you're here or even who I am."

"No, they didn't."

She chuckled and whispered something to the desk. "They used to," she said, "but they haven't for some time now. I think they believe the situation is more difficult and thus more amusing for the meat this way. Ah, well; no matter."

She whispered something else to the desk, then straightened and turned to face me. As she did, the door closed.

"I'm Norita McCombs, one of the senior researchers here. Now that we've done the introductions and we know one another, take off your clothes."

CHAPTER 48

"WHAT?" I SAID. My brain caught up with my reaction a moment later: The tall, blond woman in front of me was Shurkan's mole, the person I'd been seeking since I'd first arrived here. Why did she want me to get undressed?

"Am I hard to understand?" she said. She leaned against the desk.

I studied her to make sure she matched my recollection of Shurkan's images. She was almost my height, with skin a rich honey color and large, light green eyes. Her body reflected the style that had been in vogue among executives for several years: lean, angular, and athletic without being heavily muscled. Her face, though, was surprisingly round given the shape of the rest of her.

She was definitely McCombs.

"No," I finally said.

"So get to it," she said, "or is there a problem?" When I didn't move or say anything for a few seconds, her eyes widened and she stood up again. "Oh, you're one of the bashful ones. Okay, fine." She leaned over the desk and quickly said something to it, then turned again to face me. "All sensors and recorders in this room are off. Whoever brought you here should have told you that when I say that, I mean it. So, you can stop being shy and get ready." She leaned once more against the desk and crossed her arms. "Well?"

"It's just that I thought I recognized you," I said.

She chuckled, but there was no happiness in the sound. "I doubt it," she said. "I don't get out much."

I tilted my head and squinted as if studying her further. "Maybe it was at some event," I said. I tightened my grip on my rifle; I didn't want trouble, but if something was wrong, if she wasn't who I thought she was and I pushed this too far, she might call security on me. Then, I'd have to try to fight my way to an exterior wall, use the nanomachines to create an opening, and hope I could blend with the tourist crowd.

Yeah, right. If she wasn't McCombs, I had to hope I could sell the question as legitimate so she didn't spot me as a fake, because there was no way I could expect to get out of here by force.

"Yes," I finally said. I forced a smile. "That has to be it." I pretended to study her for a few more seconds. "Hey, do you have a cousin who's a pro gamer?"

Her expression tightened. She shook her head, walked around to the other side of the desk, and sat there. She never took her eyes off me as she reached into the top drawer on its left side. "I'm sorry," she said, "but I must have been distracted. What did you say?"

I took a slow, deep breath, then said, "I just asked if you have a cousin who's a pro gamer."

"I have a lot of cousins," she said. "What's the name of the one you're thinking of?"

"Ken something or other," I said.

She pushed the drawer closed, rested her head in her hands for a few seconds, and then sat back and looked at me. "It's about damn time," she said. "Shurkan had promised to send somebody if I stopped filing my status reports, but I haven't sent one in over three months, and no one's shown up. Until now."

"How long do we have," I said, "before someone gets suspicious about the lack of sensor input and comes to check on us?"

"As long as we want," she said, "provided I look happy when I leave." She smirked as she added, "You could help with that. Start by shucking that uniform."

"Not part of the deal," I said, as I finally realized what was happening. "What's with you behaving this way?"

"Think about it," she said. "There's no chance Shurkan could smuggle in a new senior staffer; Wei's people screen them too carefully. It took over a year to get me in here, and I already had the perfect credentials."

Over a year? That meant the CC had known about Wei's experiments for a very long time and tried only to infiltrate, not close down, his operation. The more I learned about the CC's involvement, the more I worried about its real motives.

"So, anyone he might send," she said, "would have to be a junior person. Wei treats himself to visits to the outside, but he won't let us leave here, not anymore, so he goes out of his way to indulge our personal appetites. I make sure each of the new junior staff members eventually—" She paused, as if searching for the right word. "—performs for me, because that way if Shurkan ever did send someone, I'd be sure to end up alone with him or her." She spread her arms, taking in me and the rest of the room. "And it worked, exactly as I planned."

"Fair enough," I said. "It did. But what about the way you used all those people?"

"It's not like they had hard duty," she said, "and this blasted job might as well have some perks. Wei doesn't mind, and I can't imagine Shurkan would care. That little mutant has committed more than his share of sins."

"And Lee?" I said. "Why is he so angry at me?"

"I made the mistake of using him whenever no one new was available," she said, "and I think he became a little too attached. Still, he was fun."

"And now I'm making him even more jealous because he thinks I'm another one of that group."

She smiled. "Yes, you are, but if you weren't, we wouldn't be here, and we wouldn't be able to explain this surveillance-free meeting." She stood and walked to me, her face almost level with mine. "We might as well enjoy our time."

I backed away. "No," I said, "we have a job, so let's do it and get the heck out of here."

She shrugged and returned to her seat. "What's your plan?"

"My plan?" I said. "You're the one who's been working here for months. You tell me: How can we snatch Wei?"

"Whoa," she said. "I assume you mean: How can you get both Wei and me off this island? I can't afford to help you and stay behind with my cover blown; after all the time I've spent with Lee, Ng would torture me just for the fun of it."

"My mistake," I said. "Shurkan asked me to take you as well, and I said I'd do my best. So, how do we get the two of you out of here?"

"That'll be difficult," she said. She stared directly at me as she very slowly added, "Someone recently tried to kidnap Wei when he was in the old city visiting that courtesan he admires so much. They blew it, and now security around him and all of us is tighter than ever. You wouldn't know anything about that, would you?"

I held her gaze as I said, "What I know is that I need to figure out how to get Wei—and you—out of here, and you're not helping. And speaking of helping: Why did you stop sending your status reports? Couldn't you have transmitted more information?"

"Shurkan underestimated this guy's paranoia," she said. "The research network here is completely isolated and shielded. It doesn't even have wireless connections internally. Can you image that? You need a physical connection to it to access any data. I've never been able to send even the simplest message from here. I had to file status reports from the city when I was visiting it, and a few months ago Wei decided that none of the core research team could leave until we had at least one multi-week test survivor. Of course, *he* still went out; he's addicted to that whore."

I wanted to slap her. She wasn't trying to help, she shrugged off the deaths of children, and the way she talked about Matahi made me grind my teeth. I needed her, though, if I was to succeed, so I choked down the anger and kept my face calm. "None of the children has survived for even two weeks?"

"No," she said, shaking her head and staring at the desk, "not a one. The longest made it only three days." She looked back up at me. "When I started here, I couldn't believe what he was doing. After I saw what an infusion did to one of these kids, I could barely make it to a bathroom before I broke down. Now, though, we've gone through more than a dozen, and I don't even feel it anymore. They're just subjects that fail tests. Can you understand how that can happen?"

Many times in the Saw, on many worlds, we'd descended on the enemy and left no one standing. I'd walked through villages buzzing with insects sparkling in the sunlight with the blood of the dead that were piled and scattered all around us. I puked the first time, and the second—most of us did—but then I felt it less and less. One of the reasons I'd mustered out was that I knew I had to suppress the feelings to survive, but I was afraid of what I was becoming, of what I'd already become. I wanted to leave with at least some small spark of humanity still alive in me. As much as I hated myself for admitting it to McCombs, as much as I wanted to save those children, I had to nod my head once and say, "Yeah, I can." I wiped my face with my left hand, as if with that simple gesture I could remove not only the sweat on my brow but also all the memories inside me. "But now we can stop the tests and save those who are still alive. How many are there?"

"I'm not sure," she said. "When the inventory is low, someone recruits more. Usually, we have a few in active test and half a dozen or so in pending stock." Her expression didn't change as she added, "There's no point worrying about the ones in test; they're all showing signs of failure, so they'll be gone in a few days."

"Isn't there anything we could do for them?" I said.

"We can avenge them by exposing Wei," she said. "That's it."

"So what's your thinking on how we do it?"

"I can put the three of us together, but only once, because normally I'd never bring one of my companions to a meeting, and no guard other than Ng or Lee would ever be within earshot. Once you have us, though, you still have to get us off the island. Any ideas on how to do that? If we go topside, security will spot us and trank us long before we could get out of there. Wei never goes there, and everyone on his core protection squad knows it."

I had to work with her, and we were supposed to be on the same team, but her manner put me off. Was her grief not genuine? Was I still annoyed at her comments about Matahi? I couldn't be sure, but I definitely didn't trust her, so I kept my response deliberately vague and downplayed how quickly Lobo could respond. "If I could send a signal to my people," I said, "and get us all to a landing hangar, they could pick us up within three or four minutes. The problem is, I can't transmit from here."

She sat straighter and for the first time looked hopeful. "This can work," she said. "When supply ships land at the main hangar, we open external comm links in that area so we can let the government patrol ships know that everything's okay and the suppliers have our permission to come and go. I know you must have seen the main hangar; it's where Ng sends the new meat for training."

"Yeah, I've been in it."

"A few guards will be watching the supply ship—standard protocol—but that place can handle multiple vessels. If we time it so you and I meet Wei while suppliers were unloading there, we'd at least be in the right spot."

"Wei meets those ships?" I said. "That seems like a real security risk."

"He doesn't normally," she said, "but I've been selling the idea that he needs to meet with a particular supplier of ours, and I'll talk him into doing it sometime soon." She smiled. "I can be very persuasive, and he's already going stir crazy being trapped down here." Her tone turned angry. "Unlike the rest of us, he was accustomed to going out regularly."

"Even without comm shielding, I still can't contact my people." I held my arms away from my sides. "The moment we report for duty, they confiscate anything that might even remotely be able to reach the outside world. If we want to talk with anyone who's not on the staff here, we have to use a company comm."

"That won't be a problem," she said. "Right next to the main personnel entrance to the hangar there's a communications hub with guards who monitor all incoming shipments. They watch for trouble, seal the hangar if anything goes wrong, and have outside comm links, in case they need to call for help."

"It has to be sealed," I said, "and none of the secure doors will admit me."

"They will when I give you clearance," she said.

"Won't that raise alarms?"

"Of course, but because you'll have permissions but not actually have done anything, the first step in the alarm process will be to contact me to see if I really approved you. As long as I make the change right before I leave to meet Wei—"

"I should have a few minutes to get in."

"That's right," she said, nodding. "You'll have to take them out quickly, which won't be easy, because they'll see you on the monitors and be ready."

"I'll manage," I said. "Once they're out and I've called my people, what else do I need to do?"

"You'll have to deal with the other guards. Usually they're

midlevel staff, because we isolate the hangar while visitors are in the facility. Can you handle that?"

"Probably," I said, recalling the ineptitude of my fellow trainees. "How many are there likely to be?"

"Two inside the hangar on either side of the main door, three who'll come with Wei, and a couple more on the outside of at least two key doors. The external guards won't matter; I can shut down hangar access once you're inside."

"They can't override you?"

"Of course they can," she said, her irritation apparent. "But it will take a few minutes. Are you up for this or not?"

I considered my memory of the hangar. All I had to do was take out the comm center guards and then survive long enough for Lobo to get there, because once he arrived, he'd handle anyone I couldn't. If I worked this right, I could talk to him and arrange for him to stay no more than two minutes away. If Wei and McCombs were already there, and I arrived in the hangar partway through the unloading process, there should be plenty of cover.

"It could work," I said, "but I need to talk to my team, which means I have to wait until after the next time I'm off the island. I've been volunteering to stay, so I don't know when that will be. Can you track my shifts?"

"Easily," she said. "Remember: Wei lets me have my pick of the junior staffers, so Ng gives me access to their work assignments."

"Then watch for when I go off duty and return. Once I'm back, you can call at any time."

"As soon as you're back," she said, "I'll check on the resupply schedule, then request you again on the right day."

"Do they always give you anyone you want?"

She smiled. "Wei likes to keep his key scientists happy."

"Then that's it," I said.

She nodded in agreement. "That's it—as long as your team is very, very good, and very, very fast." She stood and walked again to me, but this time fear, not lust, dominated her expression. "If they're not, we'll become Wei's first adult test subjects, even though he knows the infusions will kill us. He'll do it just to see how we die." She put her hand on my chest. "You have no idea how much pain the nanomachines cause the subjects before they pass out. No idea. I do *not* want to go like that."

I recalled the screaming in the labs on Aggro, my own and Benny's and that of the other prisoners. I remember watching grown men blubber, then twitch and go silent as their bodies melted or vanished millimeter by millimeter as the nanomachines failed to meld with their cells and instead disassembled them.

I knew exactly what it felt like, but I didn't say a word. I stared at her for a few seconds, then forced a smile and said, "My team is that good. We'll be fine."

I maintained the smile as I walked out of the room and the door closed behind me.

I turned to head back to my original station and almost bumped into Dan Lee.

He punched me in the face.

CHAPTER 49

I STAGGERED BACKWARD and used the momentum to keep moving and create some distance between us.

It didn't work.

Lee rushed after me and swung wildly with his right.

I got up my left arm in time to catch most of the blow along my forearm, but he had enough power and I was slow enough in responding that he managed to tag my nose again.

The pain lanced through me, and then the nanomachines shut it down, shut down everything that hurt, and at the same time my rage clicked in.

I turned so I appeared to fall back against the wall and let him charge me. When he was almost on me, I spun aside and added to his momentum with my left hand on his back.

He crashed into the wall.

He started to push off it, but I kicked the side of his right knee.

His scream came less than a second after the sharp crack.

As he was falling, I grabbed his shirt, punched him in the side of the neck, and shoved him harder into the ground.

He sprawled there, his right leg twisted unnaturally beneath him, his eyes shut with pain, his hands instinctively clutching his throat as he gasped for air.

I bent to finish him, blood pounding in my ears, the familiar metallic taste of adrenaline in my mouth, the world condensed to only this: my fury and the man who was about to pay for attacking me.

I pushed against my own knees to stop myself.

I could control this.

I could control myself.

I *would* control myself.

I finally had a shot at capturing Wei, and now I'd risked it by attacking a superior who could probably fire me because of my behavior. I would *not* let that happen.

I took advantage of being bent over to straighten my nose. He'd broken it, but the nanomachines would heal it soon enough. With luck, no one watching would have noticed the extent of the damage.

I kneeled next to him and said, loud enough that those listening would hear me clearly, "Lee, I'm sorry. I didn't realize it was you. I was just defending myself. Let me check your breathing." I leaned close to him as if listening to make sure air was reaching his lungs. As I did, I covered my mouth with my arm and whispered, "I need this job. You complain, and next time I *will* kill you."

I straightened and said, "You're okay. Let me check out that leg."

I heard the footsteps as I crabbed toward the knee I'd broken.

"We'll take it from here, Moore," Ng's voice said.

I lifted my hands, stood, and turned to look down the hall to my right, toward the sound.

Ng, Park, and a man and a woman lugging a stretcher jogged toward me.

I backed away from Lee and turned so he was between them and me. "Look," I said, "he caught me off guard. I reacted by instinct and had no idea—" I stopped when I saw Park stare at me and ever so slightly shake his head.

"I saw it on the video," Ng said. She bent to look at Lee's face, neck, and then his knee. She touched him with a gentleness I'd never seen in her. Her face hardened in anger, but she held her position for a few seconds. She stood and said to the man and woman, "Take him to the clinic. Get them working on that knee."

Ng faced me. She said nothing for a few seconds, her anger obvious, her stare never wavering. "I think it's clear what happened here. Don't you agree?"

I said nothing.

She continued as if I'd responded. "Lee was running security spot checks, was surprised by your exit from the room, and thought you might be an intruder. He tried to subdue you. You were equally startled and defended yourself. Just an unfortunate accident that could happen to any two people." Without turning, she said, "Is that what you saw, Tomaso?"

"Sounds right to me," he said.

"Moore?" Ng said.

"Exactly right," I said.

She stared at me for a few more seconds, then nodded her head slightly, turned, and walked in the same direction they'd taken Lee. As she passed Park, she said, "Get him cleaned up, buy him a drink, and then give him the rest of the day off. I think everyone could stand to cool down a bit."

When we'd gone about fifty meters down the hallway in the opposite direction, cut through a large room that appeared to be a storage area, and were in another hall, Park said, "Damn, son, you looked fast! Did his jealousy make him that bad, or are you that good?"

I shrugged and said nothing. My use of the nanomachines definitely constituted an unfair advantage, but Lee's own enhancements were obvious, so I didn't feel guilty. More importantly, in the end what matters is that you walk away from the fight. Lee acted stupidly by attacking an enemy of unknown strength while letting his emotions rule him, and he paid the price for that error. I could easily lose control of my anger at what Wei and his team were doing to the children, so I needed to learn from Lee's example.

"Relax," Park said, misinterpreting my silence as caution. "You can talk here. We're in one of the research zones, where Wei doesn't want anyone listening to the staff's conversations. The recording software even automatically obscures the mouths of anyone talking; Wei doesn't want to risk lip-reading."

"Sounds like a paranoid guy," I said. I didn't want to blow the first chance Park had given me to fish for information about Wei, but not commenting would be out of character. When two sergeants are alone, odds are good the CO will come up.

Park chuckled. "He is that. He is that indeed. You'd think these mixed-up animals they create were portable jump gates for all the protection we have to give their research data and Wei's team." He led me through another room and down a short stretch of hallway. We emerged into the cafeteria through an entrance I hadn't used before.

"If you ask me, it's more than a little odd," I said, nodding my head. "The times I've seen security like this, a lot more than animals were involved."

Park stopped and put his hand on my chest. "Look," he said, "you need to understand something. What I used to do—the kind of work you used to do, too—led me into a whole lot of shit I wish I could forget."

I nodded my head in understanding as more bad memories stormed my consciousness: A screaming woman, a colleague of mine, slashing the throat of an enemy who'd gone too far, the air thick with insects feasting on the dead bodies stacked all around us. Benny's screams over the comm as he vanished. I pushed them away, easier to do now, in daytime, than in the night. "It does that," I said.

"So you can appreciate how different it is here," Park said, "how much better it is. I run a bunch of second-rate wannabes—present company excluded—and we protect corporate data assets. Those assets happen to be animals, weird animals, but animals that make kids and even adults gasp in wonder. Have you ever watched children touring this place?" He didn't wait for me to answer. "It's amazing. We're doing some good, even if only by providing entertainment. Even better, most of the time, no one fires at us, and on the few occasions when someone has, everyone's come home alive."

I forced myself to maintain the same expression, but I was relieved that none of the guards had died in our assault on Matahi's house.

"I get that," I said, "and as I told you, safety is one of the main reasons I'm here and not in the militia." I held up my hands in surrender. "I'm not trying to complain. I'm glad to have this job. Your comments about the animals as the main assets just made me realize that there's no way around the fact that all the security here is rather unusual, so Wei must be a pretty paranoid fellow."

Park stared at me for a long time, then grinned slightly and said, "I've wondered the same things now and again, but when has questioning command worked out well for you?"

I smiled in return. Park didn't know. I looked into his eyes, and as best I could tell, he really had no idea. The way he'd talked about children, if I could show him the truth, he might even become an ally. "Not real often," I said, the same answer every grunt knows to give, "not real often at all."

"So how about that drink?" he said. "Ng's orders, so I can expense it." He waved me toward the dispenser on the wall opposite us. "And when we've had a few, I'm kicking you out—you heard the woman."

"Fine by me," I said. I could use the rest of the day to coordinate with Lobo, Pri, and Matahi. If this all worked out, the next time I left Wonder Island, I'd be flying in Lobo with Wei as my cargo.

Of course, if it didn't, I might be joining his child prisoners, a thought that caused me to stretch so I'd be in motion and Park wouldn't notice my face tightening with tension.

This time, I didn't care whether Park or Ng had people following me. It didn't matter. I was sticking to a pattern, and they'd like that. As far as they were concerned, I was going to visit the same paid companion as last time, and that action would make sense to them. I'd seen a lot of squad mates do it, and no doubt Park and Ng had, too. I used the shuttle rides to assemble the final details of the plan for extracting Wei.

I waited in the armored isolation foyer of the SleepSafe while the hotel's security system verified that I was a permitted caller and connected me to Matahi.

An avatar's face appeared in the call holo. Smart: If someone was with me, they wouldn't see her until she had time to dress in the bodysuit in which I'd last met her.

"Yes," she said.

I thought it extremely unlikely that anyone could monitor us here, but I appreciated her caution and went along with it. "I'm sorry I didn't call ahead, but I got an unexpected one-day leave and was hoping you were available."

She didn't answer for several seconds. I hoped she was checking outside for any possible threat; it's certainly what she should have been doing.

"I've told the hotel to admit you," she said. "Come on up. You know the room."

➤　　➤　　➤

As soon as Matahi let me into the suite, I went to the room I'd used last time and initiated contact with Lobo.

"Are you going to explain what's going on?" Matahi said.

"Yes, but only once, which is why I need to wait until we connect with Lobo and Pri."

Matahi sat on the edge of the bed and watched me. "You never really answered my question," she said.

How did she do that? I'd been gone for several days, our last conversation was already a memory, and she still managed to pick up exactly where we'd left off.

"Maybe later," I said, "but not now."

"Yeah, right," she said.

Lobo's voice came over the comm. "Why are you back in the SleepSafe," he said, "and why are you not alone?"

Fighting with him would only waste time and distract me, so I answered his questions. "Because it's a secure location, and because I need to brief Matahi and Pri."

"I'm Matahi, and she's Pri!" Matahi stood and glared at me.

"As smooth as ever," Lobo said. "But first, I have news: Our employer has moved into the neighborhood."

"What?" I said.

"The *Sunset* is in distant orbit," he said, "not far from the jump gate. An EC command ship of similar size is parked the same distance from the gate on its other side."

"So Shurkan has grown impatient," I said.

"It would appear so," Lobo said, "though of course his presence could be due to something entirely different. We have no way of knowing."

"Then let's not worry about it," I said. "When we succeed, we won't have to jump to reach him, so I'll treat this as good news."

"Let's hope it is," Lobo said, "though I generally prefer that the CC stay away from us."

I couldn't argue with him, but I saw no point in continuing this conversation. "I need to brief Andrea and Pri," I said, remembering this time to get the names right. "Put on Pri, and let's get to it."

Lobo's pilot area snapped into view.

Pri stood in the middle of it. Lobo zoomed on her face as she said, "Any news, Jon?"

I stood and stepped back so I was at equal angles to the two women. "Yes," I said. "I have a way in, and I believe that if Lobo and I execute well, we should have Wei sometime in the next week, maybe sooner."

"Really?" both women asked at once.

"Yes, or I wouldn't have said so."

"Can we help?" Pri said.

"You should already know I'll do anything I can to assist you," Andrea said.

It was Pri's turn to glare. She opened her mouth as if to speak, but I cut her off.

"Yes, but you'll have to work together to do it."

"We can do that," Pri said.

"No problem," Andrea said. "What do you have in mind?"

"Let me run it down for you," I said, "and then I'm going to kick you out and work out the rest with Lobo."

"I do so love being special," Lobo said.

"Why can't we hear the whole plan?" Pri said. "I'm supposed to be your partner in this."

"And I've done everything you've asked of me," Andrea said. She smiled slightly.

Pri stepped forward, toward where Lobo would be showing our image.

I took a deep, slow breath and shoved away my mounting irritation. "You can either stop asking questions and follow my instructions, or Lobo and I will do this without you."

"Fine," Andrea said.

"No problem," Pri said, her tone entirely too sweet. "Anything you need."

I shook my head and took another deep breath.

"Here's what I want you two to do."

CHAPTER 50

I WOKE UP EARLY, a couple of hours before sunrise, my body tense and jittery. Planning a snatch and go from a secure facility was beginning to look like simplicity itself compared to dealing with Andrea and Pri. After the briefing, I'd followed Andrea into her bedroom, then headed back to the sanctuary of mine. I wasn't blind to her or to Pri, but both of them were too nice for me to risk involving them any further in my life than I already had.

I shook off the thoughts and ran through a series of body-weight exercises until I was soaked with sweat and my muscles were sore. Working out always helps clear my head and focus me; there's something purifying about the concentration necessary to push yourself to your physical limits.

I cleaned up, took a deep breath to prepare myself to face the morning's inquisition, and told the door to open.

Andrea was still asleep, a sheet wrapped around her body, the glow from the security monitors flickering over her like water dappling a mermaid floating near the surface of a clear, clean ocean on a sunlit morning. Her hair fanned out on the pillow, and her mouth was slightly open, as if she had been about to speak and then fallen into slumber. Beautiful.

I left quietly, not wanting to disturb her—and, I had to admit to myself, unwilling to face the questions she would ask if I woke her.

The problem with some questions is that the answer you know you have to give is not at all the answer you wish were true.

➤   ➤   ➤

I scanned the perimeter monitors in the SleepSafe lobby before stepping into the misty gray morning. Shards of light punched their way through a cloud cover as thick and dense as armor plating. Mist covered the bits of grass beside the faux old buildings of this part of the city, and fog stood guard in the streets against the oncoming day. I didn't know when the action would come, but now that it was near I had that familiar feeling of complete presence, as if at the knowledge that you were about to do something very dangerous your entire self suddenly becomes hyperaware.

Not that this assignment should pose all that much danger, not if we did it right. Even if I couldn't handle the security, even if a platoon of soldiers as skilled as Ng or Park emerged from the walls, once we let Lobo into the place, it was as good as over. I hadn't seen the ultra-secure area, where I assumed Wei's team conducted their experiments and held their prisoners, but nothing in the rest of the place suggested they had any armament strong enough to take Lobo.

Every rational part of me knew we were good to go, so I should have been able to relax, but I couldn't, I just couldn't.

The hotel had clearly decided I needed a ride, because a shuttle pulled up, but I waved it off. I was early, so I took off jogging in the direction of the square where I'd met Andrea. I ran, a ghost in motion in the early morning, passing through the world but not disturbing it, moving in covering fog, touching nothing, and nothing sticking to me. Same as always, I thought, but even as the feeling materialized I recalled Andrea, Pri, Joachim, Jennie, Maggie, Benny, and many others, some right here right now, others true ghosts, and I knew it was not true, knew it for the lie I told myself so I could reach the hard and cold place inside me where only the job mattered, and then I shook off those last connections and was finally, truly where I needed to be: Alone in the darkness, a weapon in motion, doing exactly what it was supposed to do.

Same as always.

I wanted to stay in the cold, clear place I'd found, but I also needed to come across normally until it was time for action. I tried to balance the two as I finished changing and hit the café an hour before anyone was due for duty.

Park was already there, of course, sitting alone at a corner table, eating a roll and sipping something whose steam rose in front of his face and gave him a mysterious cast.

I chose a fruit blend from the dispenser and nodded at him.

He motioned to the chair opposite him.

I smiled, pulled the chair so it was next to him, and sat.

He chuckled. "Half the idiots I have to hire possess less situational awareness than a newborn."

I shrugged, sipped my drink, and stared at him. I couldn't help but like him, so I didn't want to believe he was part of all this. He said he'd never been in the main research area; maybe I could trust him. Though everything should go well, having an ally on the inside was always a good thing.

"I don't expect you to run off at the mouth," he said, "but you're particularly quiet this morning. Bad night?"

I smiled slightly and shook my head. "Most of it was good. A little bit bothered me, though."

"What?"

I paused several seconds. "You know I hired this local, right?"

"The one from before, when we tailed you?"

"Yeah."

"So what?"

"So I saw her again last night," I said, "and I mentioned working here. From the moment I did," I paused again, "well, let's just say she changed from enthusiastic to barely present."

He put down the last bit of roll. "Why?"

I looked at the table and lowered my voice. "Rumors," I said, "probably stupid rumors, though she certainly believed them."

"Of what?" he said.

I lifted my head and shook it slightly. "I need this job. I like it here. I don't even mind sharing the café with the rest of the staff."

Park popped the last of the roll into his mouth, chased it with a swallow of his drink, and stood. "I have some early checks to make. Walk with me."

He didn't speak again until we had returned to the research zone where I'd spent time with McCombs. As we entered that area, he slowed his normally quick pace to a leisurely stroll and gestured at a doorway ahead of us as if he were explaining something to me. "What exactly have you heard?" he said, his voice low but clear.

I pointed to the same doorway. "Are we in a safe-to-talk zone again?" It never hurts to know more than they think you do, and though I wanted to trust Park, I still had to assume he'd be on the other side if a conflict arose.

He nodded.

"So why the theater?" I said.

"Because we're here off-shift," he said, "so in case anyone wonders why and checks the video logs, I want it to be obvious that I'm training you."

"Fair enough."

"So, I repeat: What have you heard?"

"Rumors," I said.

He stopped and turned to face me as if explaining a difficult point. "I like you fine, Moore, but you're starting to piss me off."

"Sorry," I said. "The companion I hired turned cold when I mentioned where I worked. She said kids were going missing, and the word was that they ended up here and never came back. She said the head researcher, some guy named Wei, was experimenting on children."

"And you believe her?"

"Hey, Sarge, it seemed like crazy stuff, but she sure believed it."

"What was her source?" Park said.

I stared at him for several seconds before answering. "What does it matter?"

"Just answer the question."

I shrugged. "She said a good friend of hers had lost a son and knew Wei had the boy." I pointed down the hall as if asking a question. "That's it. That's all I heard."

Park turned and started walking. "You like this job, right?" he said.

"Yeah," I said, "like I told you."

"So what would you do if the rumors were true?"

I stopped.

He did, too, and turned again to face me.

"Are you saying they are?" I said.

He shook his head. "No, not at all. It's just that I've heard the same rumors, and each time I've asked myself what I asked you: What would you do if they were true?"

I paused and watched him intently. "I suppose I'd have to find another job," I finally said, "because I don't think I could ignore that kind of crime. I'd have to turn in Wei."

"To what?" Park said. "The government? They own this place. Wei works for them."

"I don't know," I said, "and frankly I'm not real comfortable with this conversation. I need this job, I like this job, and I intend to keep this job. Rumors are just that: rumors."

Park stepped closer, so close our noses were almost touching. "I like it here, too, and I've been here a lot longer than you. They transferred me here, and now all I want to do is live quietly. Despite all that, if I learned those rumors were true, I wouldn't just leave; I'd find a way to take down this place in the process." He backed up. "Which is why I'm glad I've never seen a shred of proof that supports them."

He turned and waved at me to follow him. "Let's get back. It's almost time to earn our pay."

I followed him, but for several steps I let him lead and watched his back, liking him even more than I had before but, despite that good feeling, wondering in my cold center exactly how I could take advantage of his feelings should the need arise.

The rest of the day passed in the kind of monotony that is soul-crushing if you do it for years but that was perfect for me right then: no troubles, no hassles, nothing to distract me from the impending mission, just the hours flowing away while I waited for the call that would start it all.

It came half an hour after Wonder Island closed to tourists that evening.

CHAPTER 51

MCCOMBS WANTS YOU AGAIN," Park said. He didn't even try to hide his smirk.

My pulse quickened; this was it. I hung my head slightly as I said, "Great."

"Come on," Park said, "it's not hard duty, at least not according to the reports I've heard."

"It's also not anything I'm seeking," I said, "and I sure don't need another run-in with Lee."

"You shouldn't have to worry on that front," Park said. "Though he's out of the clinic, he's walking slowly and able to do that much only because the prosthetic's doing most of the work while his knee heals. Besides, Ng has him on a short leash: He's stuck with supplier meet-and-greet duty until he's fully recovered."

I'd been acting reluctant to this point, but now my misgivings were real: I'd have to deal with Lee again, and soon, if he was working the main hangar. Even hurt he was more of a threat than most of the guards I'd seen on Wonder Island. I forced a smile and said, "At least I have that going for me."

"You better get moving," Park said. "From what I've heard, McCombs does *not* like to be kept waiting, so unless you want a spanking—" He paused, then laughed at my reaction. "Yes, I've heard she does like giving those, so if you don't want one, you better haul butt to her. Same room as last time."

I threw him a lazy salute and said, "Sergeant, yes, Sergeant." He was still laughing as I walked away.

"About time," McCombs said. She leaned against the desk and crossed her arms. "Most of my callers are a bit more eager to get here."

"Rushing wouldn't have been consistent with what they know of me so far," I said. "We don't need to draw any more attention to ourselves today than is absolutely unavoidable. And besides, I'm not here for your usual reasons."

"As if any of that will matter once we're done," she said. "I'm finally getting out of here, and I can tell you: I am way past ready. The guard choices are either barely acceptable or—" she tilted her head at me "—uninterested, so I'm ready to leave this boring underground trap and rejoin civilization."

"Don't you care about anything other than yourself?"

She stood and walked close to me. "If I didn't care about the job I was doing, do you think I would have stayed undercover here for months? Or set up everything for you today? Exactly who are you to question my commitment?"

I backed away. "You're right. I'm sorry. I just don't enjoy your games, and I'm also ready to finish here."

She glared at me as if about to argue further, but then she nodded slightly and went back to the desk. "I've set up my part," she said. "I've convinced Wei to come with me and meet the new supplier who's bringing some trial test equipment for us to check out."

"So you persuaded him to come to that hangar with you?"

She nodded.

Everything was moving quickly and smoothly, amazingly smoothly, and as much as I love a good plan, it all felt too easy. "Doesn't that seem a bit convenient?" I said. "He hasn't gone to an open area like that since the failed kidnapping, he didn't do it much before, and now suddenly he's going to be where we need him?"

"Suddenly?" she said. "Suddenly? It's only sudden to you because you haven't been working on him for weeks like I have. I told you I would deliver him, and I did."

"As cautious as he's been," I said, "I'm still not sure I believe he'd take that risk. I don't like it."

"Would you please give me some credit?" she said. "I've been mentioning suppliers to him, ordering a lot of expensive gear that's been straining our budget, and encouraging him to use his clout to get us better deals. You have no idea how many times I've buttered him up about how influential he is. He's heard the arguments before; they just finally worked today."

Though I don't feel it in my gut, intellectually I know that sometimes my paranoia can go too far. She had indeed been working this angle for a while, and I needed to give her credit for that effort.

I nodded my head. "Okay. When?"

"I don't know exactly," she said, "but sometime in the next half hour to two hours. We give suppliers two-hour delivery windows, then they let us know when they're almost here by signaling a special relay sat."

"Any change in the guard count?"

"No. He'll have the usual three with him—usual since the botched earlier attempt—plus, of course, the two inside the hangar. Others will be watching the doors from the secure side, but as I said before, we can seal those entrances for at least a few minutes."

"So I have to deal with five guards?"

"After you take out the ones in the comm room," she said. "And that's as good as it gets."

I had to assume Ng assigned some of her better, more experienced people to hangar detail, because it was an obvious vulnerability and neither I nor any of the other new hires had worked it yet. That meant trouble. On the other hand, they wouldn't expect an internal attack, my rifle contained trank rounds, and Lobo would be jetting in before I had to fire the first shot.

"I can handle it," I said. "Walk me through the hangar layout again, go over your protocol for reaching me, and show me where the vendor ship will land, where you'll be, where Wei's guard team is likely to stand—all the key details."

She sighed. "You've been in the hangar before, so you know the layout. We have to stay here at least another twenty minutes to make your visit plausible. Can't we find something better to do with our time than rehash material you've already seen?"

"No," I said, "we can't. Preparation matters. Walk me through the layout and the guard positions again. This is happening any moment now, and we *will* be ready."

➤   ➤   ➤

"The ship's here!" McCombs said forty-five minutes later, her face immediately tightening with tension. "I have to go meet Wei."

"Now's as good a time as later," I said.

"I guess," she said.

"Give me the comm room access, then get moving. You don't want to keep him waiting."

She leaned over the desk, which activated at the sight of her staring at it. She murmured softly, then turned to look at me. Her face had returned to normal, her training evident in her quick recovery. She nodded once and left.

I grabbed all the papers off the rear work area and tamped them into a tidy stack. I took my rifle and headed out at a trot. I wanted to beat McCombs to the hangar area, so I'd be done with the comm room before she and Wei had been in the hangar for more than a few minutes. The hall monitor systems might wonder why I was running and report the unusual behavior, but everything was in play now so I had to take some chances. I forced myself to breathe slowly through my nose as I jogged.

McCombs' directions were good, and the long, carefully designed route was as deserted as she'd said it should be. I blew by two guys I didn't recognize, waved the papers, and said, "She'll kill me if I don't get this to her." They barely noticed me, because I didn't matter; I was just another of those people who didn't contribute to the real work. That attitude usually annoys me, but today I was fine with it.

In a little over three minutes, I turned onto the hallway outside the main hangar entrance and slowed to a fast walk. The guard standing to the right of the door to the comm room made it easy to spot. My uniform and the casual way I carried my rifle were enough to stop him from coming to full ready, but he watched me closely as I approached.

I tucked my rifle under my arm as I drew within two meters of him, brought up the papers, and pointed to them with my other hand.

He relaxed, as security people often do when they see a weapon go out of play.

"Ng told me to take these inside," I said, waving the papers and pointing at them. "Now."

"She didn't tell us anything," he said.

"I can't help that. She gave me access and told me to go on in, so let me get to it, and I'll be out of your way in no time."

"Give me the delivery, and I'll take it in."

I shook my head. "No way. You know her: She'll have my ass if I don't do exactly what she ordered."

He smiled slightly and nodded. "You'll have to leave your rifle."

"No problem," I said, matching his smile.

He tilted his head to his right and watched as I leaned my weapon against the wall there.

I held up my hands. "Okay?"

He shrugged and stepped to his left and away from the door. He kept his rifle at a casual ready and his eyes on me, but he was clearly no longer worried.

One of the great weaknesses of any system is the huge amount of trust people place in automation. If the door opened to admit me, the system must have declared I was allowed inside, so I was no longer his problem. If it didn't, he'd deal with me—and I wouldn't be a problem then, because my rifle was leaning against the wall while he was holding his.

The door snapped open. I stepped inside, and like a good security door it shut almost instantly.

Two guards I didn't recognize sat at chairs in front of a monitor wall showing a dozen or more views of the hangar. Their rifles leaned against the panel in front of them, within easy reach but not in hand. They'd seen the guard outside let me in, and the security software had opened the door for me, so I must be okay. Both turned to face me, which was sloppy, because one should have constantly monitored the hangar while the other assessed the visitor. It also wasn't good for me, because now I had both of them focused on me, but I could manage.

"Ng said I had to show these to you," I said. "Something so secure she wanted me to courier it here on paper."

The one on the right waved me to him.

Instead, I stepped between them and bent over as if to show them both the sheets. I held the stack low enough that both had to bend forward to read it. As they did, I hit the one on the right in the throat, then snapped my left knee into the face of the one on the left.

Right reached for his throat, thought better of it, and grabbed for his rifle. I kicked him hard in the knee. He and his chair rolled away from me—and from his weapon.

I pivoted and checked Left. He had both hands on his nose. I grabbed him by the hair and slammed him face-first into the floor.

Right grabbed his rifle with one hand and pushed out of his chair with the other.

I turned and lunged toward him in one motion, grabbed the rifle's barrel, and used my momentum to shove it into his stomach before he could reach the trigger.

Air rushed out of him in a grunt, but he held onto the weapon's butt, as I'd hoped he would.

I continued forward into him, turned my right shoulder to him, and slammed it into his chest. I pivoted further and smashed his nose with a right backfist.

This time, he yelped and dropped the rifle.

I put my right foot in front of his left leg, grabbed his shirt, and threw him over my hip onto the floor.

He hit face first, hard.

Left had recovered slightly and was crawling toward his rifle.

I stepped to him and kicked him in the neck.

His head snapped to the side, and he was out.

Right moaned on the ground, still conscious.

I kicked him in the neck as well, and he also passed out.

Blood pounded in my ears. I forced myself to slow my breathing. I was far from done.

I glanced at the monitor wall. The room was, as I'd hoped, soundproof; the outside guard stood at his post, clearly bored. McCombs and Wei were talking in the hangar, watching as cargo loaders rolled the contents of the supply ship to shelves elsewhere in the large space. Wei's three guards stood in a rough semicircle about ten meters away from him; either he and McCombs were discussing something sensitive, or they always kept their distance when Wei was engaged in conversation. The main-entrance guards stood on either side of the door. A large container sat beside the man on the right of the entrance; it wasn't much, but it would provide cover from anyone on the right half of the hangar.

Several other monitors showed various angles of two simultaneous external disruption alerts that security team members were racing to address. In one pair, a woman was screaming to a crowd of fellow tourists. Another two displays showed a different woman reading from a scroll and gesturing madly.

I scanned for and spotted the comm controls, set the frequency, and said, "Ready?"

If McCombs was right, the jammers were offline, and Lobo would hear me.

"Yes," Lobo's voice said over speakers I couldn't see.

"Now," I said.

"Executing," he said.

The speakers went silent.

I checked the rifle Right had dropped. Damn: a live-round weapon. I couldn't take the chance they might wake up and be able to use their rifles to help the guards in the hangar. I could strip them, but I didn't have time to make sure the room held no more weapons.

The guards were probably out, but too much was at stake for me to rely on probably. I raised my foot and smashed the left hand of Right. I crushed his other hand and then the hands of Left.

I stepped to the wall beside the door. I was counting on the exterior guard to have returned to his post. If not, if he could see inside the room, then he'd shoot me, and I'd have to hope the nanomachines could keep me going while I fought him.

I took a slow, deep breath, then leaned toward the door.

It opened.

I inched forward so that I had one foot outside the room, one inside it, and was facing the guard, who was indeed back at his post and directly in front of me.

"I need your help," I said.

He tightened his grip on his rifle and turned to face me.

As he opened his mouth to speak, I grabbed his throat with my left hand and his rifle with my right. I stepped backward into the room and pulled him with me. I turned to my right as I moved, pulled him toward me, and head-butted him. The moment the hard upper part of my forehead smacked into his nose, he let go of his rifle and tried to scream. Fortunately, my hold on his throat kept the sound low; little more than a squeak emerged. I kept my grip on him and his rifle, pressed the weapon against his body, and used the two anchor points to turn him so he stumbled backward.

The door shut behind us.

He punched me in the stomach with his left hand and clawed at my left with his right, trying to get me to release his throat.

I pushed off my right leg and levered my knee into his groin.

Air rushed out of him as he sagged and stopped trying to hit me.

I yanked away the rifle and stepped backward.

"Wha?" he said. He didn't move toward me or look up.

I checked the rifle: a trank weapon, like mine.

I shot him.

He fell and was out.

I shot each of the other guards once with a trank round, just to be safe. My ears thrummed with the sonic residue of the conflict and the pounding of my own heart. I stared at the guards' ruined hands and knew I'd feel guilty soon enough for hurting them needlessly, but when I'd done it I hadn't known I'd have such a readily available and easy way to knock them out.

I shook my head. Now was not the time for this. If I wanted to succeed, I needed to get back to the cold, centered place that had carried me this far.

Lobo should be nearly here.

In the monitors, McCombs was still deep in conversation with Wei, his three guards remained where they'd been, and the main entrance pair stood on either side of the doorway, all the same as before. If anyone had sounded an alarm, I sure couldn't see any evidence of it.

No, everything was in play, and I was good to go.

Time to hit the hangar.

CHAPTER 52

IN CASE SOMEONE had heard the guard's squeak, I dropped to the floor and told the door to open. I crawled forward enough to check first toward the hangar entrance and then in the other direction; no point in taking chances any earlier than necessary. All clear.

I launched myself up, slung the outside guard's rifle across my back, and grabbed mine from where it still leaned against the corridor wall.

I dashed to and then past the hangar door, staying well back from it on the off chance it was set to open automatically. I dropped to the ground once again, stayed tight to the corridor wall, and crawled forward, my rifle in front of me.

I reached the door.

Nothing happened.

I sighted the rifle at a spot just on the door's other side and about a meter and a half high, then told the door to open.

It did.

The guard on the far side turned to see who was entering.

Before he could look down and spot me, I shot him in the chest. As he was falling, I leaned away from the wall and pointed the rifle at the part of the opening directly in front of me and at about the same height as before.

The other guard leaned forward to take a look.

I meant to hit his chest but he was short, so I him in the neck.

345

He fell backward.

I rolled to my left and out of sight of anyone inside the hangar. I pushed up quickly and glanced around the corner of the still open door.

Wei and McCombs were staring at the guards I'd shot.

Wei's three guards were running toward them, shouting instructions.

I couldn't hear their words, though—I could only see their mouths moving—because right then a gigantic roar slammed into the hangar and smacked away all other sounds.

All hell broke loose as Lobo rocketed in, hard, small-caliber weapons bristling on his front, rear, and sides, his thrusters loud to maximize confusion. He settled to a hover a few centimeters above the floor.

Over the machine frequency he said, "Status?" At the same time, the running guards dropped. He was fast; I never saw any of his guns fire.

"Green," I said. "Did you kill them?"

"No," he said, with no trace of the exasperation he had every right to feel because he'd agreed to take my orders and not kill anyone unless there was no other option.

I darted inside and to the cover of the large container to the right of the door, which slid shut behind me. "Anyone else in the hangar?"

"No," Lobo said, "within the limits of my sensors."

Wei and McCombs spotted me. Wei pointed at me.

"Tranking Wei," I said. I raised my rifle.

"No!" Lobo said. "We have to leave immediately and head to the CC ship, so I won't have much time with him. I need to talk to him."

"Fine," I said, not lowering my weapon but relaxing my finger on the trigger, "but if he even annoys me, you trank him or I will."

"Agreed," Lobo said.

"You can talk while I go for the kids," I said, "though I won't have much time."

"After you've locked Wei inside me," Lobo said, "I estimate you'll have no more than twenty minutes. Worst case, though, I can run and use him as barter if they capture you."

Such an optimist. "Got it," I said.

Lobo settled to the ground and shut off his thrusters. My ears rang a bit from the noise they'd endured, but otherwise I could hear well enough in the now quiet room, and the nanomachines would fix the ear damage soon enough.

I kept my rifle pointed at Wei and McCombs and advanced on them. "You two!" I said. "Hands on your heads." No point in blowing McCombs' cover if I could avoid it; maybe she could fake an escape and come back later for any research data we were unable to retrieve today.

She complied immediately, her head swiveling between me and Wei in a pretty good imitation of terror.

Wei stared at me for several seconds, shrugged, and also placed his hands on his head.

A hatch opened in the side of Lobo nearest us.

"Get inside," I said.

"You're the one who tried before," Wei said. It wasn't a question. "You ruined so much of Andrea's beautiful house."

"Get in the ship," I said, "or I'll shoot you and drag you in."

"Thank you," he said, "for your restraint."

"Don't thank me yet," I said. "I still might shoot you."

Wei turned and walked slowly toward Lobo.

McCombs followed him.

I trailed her by a meter and stayed to the side so I had a clear shot at Wei. I felt the seconds dripping away like blood leaving my body. I had so little time. Some of the kidnapped children had to be alive, if not Pri's son at least some of them. They had to be.

"Move it!" I said.

Wei switched to a jog, quickly reached Lobo, and let his stride carry him inside. He turned and watched as we approached.

Lobo had him, so I relaxed slightly. Almost there. We were almost done with this phase.

Then Wei put his hand on Lobo's interior, just inside the door, smiled, stepped to the side out of my sight, and said, "Authenticate override shutdown—"

I shoved McCombs out of the way.

"—Jorge Wei code one—"

I reached Lobo as he finished.

"—two beta delta seven."

Lobo went completely dead: interior lights off, nothing on my comm, a stillness I'd never experienced from him, the complete quiet of death.

I grabbed Wei by the throat and screamed, "Turn him back on!"

Wei pointed behind me.

I pivoted and watched through the open doorway as Ng and a team of half a dozen other guards converged on us, their rifles all pointed at me.

"Put him down, Moore," Ng said, "and you'll get a trial. Eventually. Don't, and we'll knock you out and end up at the same place anyway, but your path there will be a lot rougher." She stopped two meters outside Lobo.

The others followed suit. Park wasn't one of them; maybe he really didn't have a clue as to what was going on here.

"I could kill Wei first," I said, tightening my grip.

"Maybe," she said, "but with all the trouble you went to just to kidnap him, when you could have killed him at Matahi's, I don't think you will."

I stared at her and almost vibrated with rage. Lobo was out of commission, maybe gone—I had no clue what Wei had done. I'd failed again to capture the man, and now I'd failed the children that were prisoners somewhere nearby.

I could fix this.

I could let Wei go, create a nanomachine cloud, and have it kill everything organic in the hangar. It wouldn't take long, and it's not like Wei didn't deserve it for what he'd done. It might even give me the time I'd need to rescue those kids.

It wouldn't, though, tell me how to bring back Lobo.

I needed Wei alive to do that. I could try to kill everyone except him, but unless he fixed Lobo quickly, more guards would come, and then I'd be back where I was now.

On the other hand, as long as they took me prisoner, I could always change my mind.

I released my grip on Wei, stepped back, and put my hands on my head.

Wei rubbed his throat and walked out of Lobo and over to Ng. He turned to face me. "As I said earlier, Mr. Moore, thank you for your restraint. When I recognized Lobo—is that still his name?—from our earlier encounter, I knew I had to have him."

"How?" I said.

"He mentioned children and machine intelligences," Wei said. "No one in this sector knows about the earlier work, and certainly no other PCAV would have that data. It had to be him."

Lobo shouldn't have underestimated Wei. Maybe that kind of error is part of what comes from being as intelligent as Wei had made him.

"And all this?" I said, waving my hand to take in the hangar.

Wei laughed. "An invitation," he said. "Nothing more. Given how much damage you were willing to do last time, I assumed you'd try again to get me. I refused to go out, so I knew you'd have to come in. Spotting you was easy; we rarely get applicants of your caliber."

He turned his back on me. "Bag Moore and put him in a cell," he said to Ng. "In an hour or so, we'll figure out who'll interrogate him." He waved toward Lobo. "Have the loaders move this PCAV to the secure group-experimentation lab. Hook it to the research net so I can send in some retrieval software and download its current programs and data."

As he walked out of the hangar, he said, almost to himself, "I can't wait to learn what came of our experiments on Lobo."

CHAPTER 53

I HADN'T SEEN a prisoner head bag since the day the Pinkel-ponker government cops grabbed me, all of sixteen years old and just beginning to fit into the weird group of outcasts on the Dump, and dropped me into a cell on Aggro. Simple blinders would have worked fine, of course, but Ng must have been on a retro punishment kick. Two guards led me out of the hangar and to my cell. One shoved me so hard I smacked into a wall and then pushed the barrel of a rifle against my neck. The second yanked the cover off my head. I heard him back out but didn't look around until I felt the pressure ease from my neck. I glanced at the remaining guard as he was leaving, but I didn't recognize him; no surprise there.

The anger still had me in its grip. I wanted to smash my way out, to create a nanocloud that would disassemble the door and anyone waiting on the other side of it, that would free me and return me to my mission.

Instead, I leaned against the corner farthest from the door of the small room, slitted my eyes, and forced myself to take long, slow, deep breaths, easing the air in and out through my nose. They'd be recording everything I did, so if I used my nanomachines I'd be revealing my secret to the Wonder Island security team. I might be able to use the cloud to reduce the entire area, including all the data archives, to just so much dust, but I'd also have to kill the watchers or live with the knowledge that the truth about me was out there and someone could be coming for me at any time.

I slowed my breathing further.

Even if I killed everyone here, I couldn't be sure they weren't archiving security data somewhere else. McCombs had said all the research data was available only locally, but footage from my cell could be an exception; given their ties to the government, they might be streaming the holos of me to the security police.

I couldn't take the chance.

I also couldn't afford to wait. I had no idea what Wei's people might do to me, but even if their only action was to turn me over to the Heaven authorities, I could end up facing jail time. More importantly, no matter what happened, more children would die in Wei's experiments while I sorted out my situation.

Lobo could die, too. Wei had managed to override his programming with a backdoor Lobo hadn't known existed. I had no idea what Wei might do to him with full access to his data and programs. If Wei decided to wipe Lobo's systems, Lobo as I knew him would cease to exist. I couldn't let that happen.

I couldn't let more children die.

I couldn't let Wei continue his research.

I couldn't let Lobo vanish.

I had to do something!

Who was I kidding? I worked on my breathing as my mind kept racing. If I wasn't willing to risk killing everyone here, then I might have to let children die, let Wei continue, and even let my only friend turn into a normal machine, all trace of his personality lost forever.

I had to find an alternative that wasn't as deadly as using the nanomachines and then wait for the chance to pursue it.

I knew I wouldn't kill that many people. I wasn't willing to do that, at least not right now, not when I still wasn't sure what would happen. Maybe later I would be, but not now.

No, my only real option was to wait for Wei's people to come to me, which they surely would if for no other reason than to deliver me to the police, and see what I could make happen when they did.

I scanned the room but saw nothing of use to me: no machine outlets, no obvious weaknesses, just a plain, small cell, walls and floor and ceiling and door and nothing more.

Which probably meant I wouldn't be here long, because most holding areas built for more than very short occupancy have at least a toilet; cleaning up excrement is a hassle most captors don't want to endure.

I stretched and considered how much trouble to be. When someone holds you captive, it's usually best to choose one of two extreme paths: Cooperate as much as possible, or cause so much trouble that keeping you becomes more hassle than it's worth. The first option is good when you need to stay or fear for your life; the second is the right choice if you have reason to believe they won't simply kill you. Wei could have sent me to the authorities when they captured me, but he didn't, so it was a safe bet he really didn't know who'd sent me and still wanted that information.

I chose the second path.

About an hour later, the door slid open. Lee limped in, whatever prosthesis he was using invisible under his uniform. He held a pistol in his right hand, and he was pointing it at me. Another guard, one I didn't recognize, stood beside him.

"Give it to me," Lee said. He never looked away from me.

"For the gun," the woman said.

"Just give it to me and step out," Lee said. "I won't be long."

The woman shook her head. "Ng's orders, and she'll have my ass if I disobey them. You can interrogate him, but you can't shoot him."

"I won't," Lee said.

"Then give me the gun," she said. She held up a small, oblong box. "I'll trade you this for it, and then you can have some fun."

Lee finally turned to face her. He gave her a hard look, but her expression didn't change. He handed her the gun and took the box, then nodded toward the door. "Get out," he said.

She took the gun, nodded, and turned to leave.

I launched myself at Lee before he could turn back toward me. I caught him around the waist and kept accelerating, so he slammed into the back of the woman and sent her sailing across the hallway into the wall there. She dropped the pistol, but I ignored it to focus on Lee, who punched me hard in the side of my face. I brought up my head as quickly as I could and smashed the top of it into his jaw, snapping his head so far back I thought for a second I might have knocked him out. No such luck. I released him. He staggered backward, still conscious. The other guard was on the ground, her face bleeding.

I'd made as much of a statement as I needed, but if I let Lee recover right now, he'd grab the pistol and shoot me. I couldn't allow that.

I stepped to the left and launched a kick hard into the side of his good knee. He screamed and fell.

I walked over to the other guard, shoved the pistol away from her, and said, "Tell Wei or Ng or whatever idiot sent you that if they want to talk to me, they can talk. If they want to send somebody else to rough me up, they better pick someone a lot tougher than him."

I walked back to my cell.

The door closed and locked behind me.

I wondered what they'd do next.

As best as I could tell, less than half an hour had passed before the door opened again. I'd expected them to respond quickly, so that was no surprise.

What I hadn't expected was the man who stepped inside my cell, arms up, showing me he wasn't carrying a weapon: Park.

"I'm sorry to see you," I said. I meant it. I'd really hoped he wasn't part of Wei's secret research efforts. "Shouldn't you be in bed already?"

"I normally would be, but your attack made them call me. As for being sorry, why? You're the one who's facing criminal charges."

I stared at his face, which was as calm as always. Maybe he didn't know what was really happening here. If he didn't, though, why did they send him to see me? If he was innocent, I might be able to recruit him as an ally—but I'd have to tell him the truth. If I did, I'd be forcing him either to join them or to become another problem they'd have to address.

Finally, I said, "I doubt it. If they were going to hand me over to the police, they'd have done it immediately. They already sent Lee to rough me up; I'd have preferred the next goon wasn't you."

Park's face tightened slightly, but otherwise his expression remained the same. "I heard Lee didn't fare so well. What do you have against that boy?"

I shrugged. "Nothing at all. Both times, he initiated the conflict. I just finished it."

"The recording shows you hit him first this time."

"Come on, Sarge; you're smarter than that. You know he started it when he walked in the door. He was just stupid. Again."

"So that's why you were hoping it wasn't me?" Park said. "You wanted someone else who would be easy to take out?"

"No," I said. "I was hoping you weren't part of all this, and I didn't want to have to hurt you."

"I wouldn't be as easy as Lee," Park said. "Not by a great deal."

This time, I held up my hands. "I know you wouldn't," I said, "and it really doesn't matter which of us would win. What bothers me is that I hate to think you're helping Wei."

"You know what I do here," Park said. "The same work you were doing."

I shook my head. "No. I did basic security duty. I have no idea what you did. For all I know, you helped them kidnap and kill children."

"That's garbage," he said, his voice tight, his words clipped. "You *do* know I wouldn't do that."

"Maybe," I said, "but Wei and Ng and some of the other security people are definitely involved. Wei's team uses the kids for his research experiments. So far, all of them have died. Heaven's government covers up the whole affair, because if they succeed, the potential rewards are amazing."

"Succeed at what?"

I shrugged and continued to stare at him as I told him the first lie of the conversation. "I don't know," I said. "What I do know is that even if you had no part in it before, you're in it now."

"Because you told me," he said.

I nodded again. "Because I told you."

"So why did you join my team?" he said.

"So I could kidnap Wei and force him to stand trial."

"If Heaven is backing him, where would you take him for trial? Who sent you?"

I laughed. "Finally we get to what they told you to find out. They knew I'd explain why I was here, so you're definitely part of the inner circle now. I hope you can live with that, because I have a feeling that if you can't, you might find yourself in here with me—if I'm still alive, that is."

"You're not going to tell me who sent you," he said. It wasn't a question. He understood me better than that.

"Of course not," I said, "not that it matters. What matters now is what you're going to do with what I just told you."

"All I wanted was a quiet job," he said. "I explained that to you. As far as I know, that's what I have. You made a huge accusation, but you offered no proof."

"That's right," I said. "I didn't, but I think you know I'm telling the truth. As for your quiet job, well, you can still have it—as long as you can live with children dying on the other side of the complex."

"You know how it is," he said. He turned to go and stopped as the door opened. "You can learn to live with anything if you have to." He shook his head. "I'm going to bed."

I stared at the door as it closed behind him.

I hoped he was wrong, that he couldn't bear the knowledge, because soon someone else would come for me. They'd either try a different approach to getting me to talk, or they'd ship me off to Heaven's police.

One way or the other, my time here was running out.

CHAPTER 54

WHEN THE DOOR slid open a little while later, no one entered. After a few seconds, Ng's voice called from the hall. "Lean against the back wall, hands above your head and spread apart."

I stayed in the front corner of the room, out of her line of sight, as I said, "No."

"You do *not* want to try me, Moore," she said. "After what you did to Dan, if you give me an excuse to violate Wei's orders to bring you along unharmed, I promise I'll take it."

My options definitely improved if I could get close to Wei, so I stepped to the rear of the cell, spread my hands wide, raised them over my head, and used them to brace myself against the wall. I turned my head to the right and tensed my shoulders. "I'm here."

I could barely make out the guards slipping into the cell, one after the other, both training weapons on me. They weren't taking chances this time.

When one was on either side of me, Ng said, "Moore, move and I shoot. Secure him."

The guards wrenched my hands off the wall and behind my back. My face scraped against the permacrete, but I'd been ready for the contact so it didn't upset me. Cuffs encircled my wrists and secured themselves. The guards spun me so I was facing Ng.

She didn't look happy.

"You hit him before he did anything," she said.

"Only to save myself," I said. "You saw him take the toy from that other guard. You know what comes next. Tell me you would have done anything different."

The implicit compliment seemed to help, because she relaxed slightly and gave me a tiny smile. "In your shoes, I would have finished him."

I shrugged. "I'm not here to hurt anybody."

"Yeah, yeah, you've come to stop the bad man and save the poor innocent children."

"Something like that."

"Maybe you should take a look at the bigger picture," she said. "What Wei and his team are trying to do—what I'm protecting—is bigger than the lives of a few kids, many of whom were orphans anyway. When he succeeds, and he will, I know he will, we'll be able to cure diseases that kill millions and millions of people all over the inhabited worlds, stop aging, maybe let people live forever. Isn't that prize worth the cost?"

"That's not mine to decide," I said. "The research is illegal, banned here and everywhere by every major human government."

"And you've never broken a rule for the greater good?" she said. "Wei is a genius who might very well live in history as the man who led humanity into immortality. He hates the cost as much as you or I—and we all do hate it, Moore, you're not alone in that—but he's willing to bear it so we can all benefit."

"He's not bearing the cost! Those children are. They're paying with their lives. They didn't make a choice; you people simply kidnapped them. How Wei feels about killing them won't bring back a single child."

She shook her head. "It figures, a grunt like you, you couldn't understand. I told him." She motioned toward the guard on my left, and he slipped a bag over my head.

"Let's go," Ng said. "He wants to talk to you."

Either the complex was even bigger than I'd thought or they intentionally ran me through a winding route just to confuse me, because it must have taken us fifteen minutes to reach our destination. I heard a door snick open, then the guards pushed me against the wall to the right of the door, and one of them pulled off the bag.

I'd shut my eyes when I felt him grab the bag. I slitted them now so I could look around a little while they adjusted to the light. After a few seconds, I slowly opened them all the way.

The room in front of me was about two-thirds the size of the main hangar in which they'd captured Lobo and me. Lobo sat on the opposite side of the space, a thick cluster of cables linking him to outlets on the wall to my left. The walls were the same bland, washed-out yellow as the rest of the facility. The floors also had the same slightly brighter, slightly speckled look. Large portions of the left wall were active as displays. On the right wall and the one against which I now stood, a variety of chains and shackles hung from thick hooks. Twenty or more meters above us arched a jointed ceiling that clearly could slide open.

Wei stood between Lobo and the wall and talked softly at the holo of a man in front of him.

Ng didn't announce us or interrupt him. We all waited in silence.

After almost a minute, Wei shook his head and turned to face me. "Welcome to the aviary lab, Mr. Moore. Many times, we'd have some new and amazing creature to show you. Today, though, we have only the one subject, and you supplied him." He motioned slightly toward Lobo. "And it's on that topic that I'd like to speak with you first."

I waited.

"Not one for the social niceties?" he said after a few seconds. "Fair enough; I'd gathered that fact from your treatment of our poor Mr. Lee. Unlike you, I believe in giving each person a chance to show his true character. In any case, before we address the topic of your presence here, I'd appreciate it if you would explain exactly what modifications you've made to the computing systems of our mutual friend."

"Modifications?"

Wei smiled. "Please, Mr. Moore, do not mistake as soft a manner bred of far too long working for bureaucracies. For the small price of a short conversation, you have the opportunity to purchase your freedom. The alternatives serve neither of us particularly well."

No way was he letting me go, but I could buy time, and the longer we talked, the more I might learn. On the other hand, I wouldn't tell him Lobo's secret, because then Wei would never stop experimenting on him.

I might, though, be able to appease whatever was bothering him by sticking to a truthful answer to exactly the question he asked.

"I bought a central weapons control complex for it," I said, "and some installation programming came with the purchase." I shrugged. "That's really all I've done."

"Did you control this programming?" Wei said.

I laughed. "You have my background info. Does anything in it even remotely suggest I'm capable of that sort of work?"

Wei nodded and stayed quiet for several seconds before he said, "No, but you certainly could have engaged others with that expertise."

I shook my head.

"In that case, might the complex you purchased have included some additional security protection?" he said.

"I suppose so, though I really have no clue. What's this all about?"

Wei nodded again, held up his hand, and turned away from me. A holo snapped into view beside him. He spoke softly to it, then it disappeared. He turned back to me.

"Thank you," he said. "Our access protocol now appears to be negotiating more successfully with some superficial protection layers and should soon start delivering the data we seek. So, let us return to the topic of you." He smiled. "Where to begin?"

He nodded to a guard near the door to his right.

The guard exited.

Wei focused again on me. "Your goal here is clear, Mr. Moore," he said, "but as you said, we have your background, and nothing in it suggests you would attempt to kidnap me without someone financing the effort. What agency would that be?"

I said nothing.

He nodded as if I'd told him exactly what he wanted. "Of course, of course," he said. "You'll insist I demonstrate how serious we are." He nodded at Ng.

She pulled her pistol and stuck it against my temple.

Experience has taught me that the nanomachines in my cells can heal pretty much any injury to my body. The same ability that lets me control their behavior, however, also seems to make them depend on my brain. Drug me enough, for example, and I can't control them. Consequently, I'm not sure I can survive a major brain injury, and I've been lucky enough so far that I've never had to find out.

I didn't want to try my luck now.

At the same time, telling Wei about the CC could end my usefulness to them and just as easily put me in the grave.

I stared at him, forced a calm expression, and said nothing.

After almost a minute, he waved his hand slightly.

Ng holstered her weapon.

"I appreciate the thoughtfulness of your response," Wei said, "though I suppose another reasonable explanation is that you're simply stubborn and stupid. I prefer, however, to believe you're considering your situation carefully. So, let me give you something else to consider."

He beckoned toward the door to his right.

McCombs entered, a guard right behind her. The guard guided her by her shoulder. McCombs glared at Wei but did not speak; the tape sealing her mouth ensured she could not.

"Though we've found no data yet to prove that my associate here helped you," Wei said, "we obviously know that you've spent time with her lately. One might reasonably assume, therefore, that the two of you share the same master. Perhaps her death might persuade you of the seriousness of our intent."

I shrugged, looked straight at him, and worked to keep my voice calm. "She's pretty enough, and she's not a bad way to pass half an hour, but that's all I know about her. Do what you want."

Once again, Wei watched me carefully.

Once again, even though my mind was racing, I forced myself to stare calmly back at him. I had condemned him for taking innocent lives, and now I was playing a game that might cost McCombs hers. She, however, had chosen to accept her assignment; the children had not. The difference was everything—and I clung to it tightly.

I couldn't stay silent all the time, however, or Wei would definitely proceed to interrogation. Even if I could escape, it would take a while. I needed to buy time, to find a way out. To do that, I had to give him something.

I broke eye contact with him and looked down. "She was a secondary target. We figured if I couldn't get you, maybe she could give us the information we wanted." I looked at him again. "I don't even know who hired me; it was all anonymous. These kinds of jobs are."

Wei opened his mouth as if to speak, but then a holo appeared beside him. He stared at it for a moment, whispered something, and faced me again. "Let's pause on that topic for a moment. Exactly how intelligent is Lobo? Was he beginning to interrogate me under your direction or on his own?"

I had to hope Lobo wasn't dead and protect him as long as I could. "You know PCAVs don't contain significant interrogation software. I gave it a script to use on you while I finalized our exit."

"Your failed attempt to kidnap me, you mean."

I nodded.

"So the emotion in his voice, the threats—that was all in your script?"

I shrugged. "I had to make it look convincing. I wanted him to warm you up so the real interrogators could wear you down more quickly."

"This time I definitely don't believe you, Mr. Moore. The knowledge of my past research suggests too strongly that Lobo has records of those times. For that to be possible, he must have somehow hidden information from the programs we used to wipe his data." Wei shook his head. "But if the cells of the children we used in the experiments on Lobo ultimately melded with the nanomachines, why aren't we seeing the same successes here?"

I didn't answer. I had no clue, but that was not my concern. What worried me now was that his revelation of what he'd done in the past meant there was no way he'd ever risk anyone putting me on trial.

"No matter," he said. "This time, we'll copy everything in him, then take him apart and figure out what's going on."

McCombs was paying very close attention now. Her expression had changed from fear to intense curiosity.

Wei had slapped me with another problem: If McCombs got away, she would relay the news about Lobo. The CC would come after him, either here if we couldn't escape or wherever we went if I could figure a way out of this. I wouldn't abandon Lobo—I couldn't do that, wouldn't do it—so the CC would end up hunting me as well.

My employer had just become another enemy.

My situation was not improving.

At least I now knew all the problems I was facing.

"Ah, well," Wei said, "we can revisit that topic. Let's return to our original interest: your employer." As if I were going to speak, he raised a hand to silence me. "I think I can offer you some additional motivation to indulge my curiosity." He waved toward the door. "Though I appreciate the tactical value of distraction, surely you must have realized that the probability of two such major tourist outbursts at the same time was too low for us to consider them chance."

The door opened.

Matahi and Pri shuffled in, one guard behind each of them, a pistol to each of their heads.

CHAPTER 55

WEI WATCHED ME as the two women entered. I did my best to focus on him even as I fought to stay calm, to control my expression and give away nothing. Despite my best efforts, I could feel my skin tightening; I had to hope Wei couldn't spot it from that distance.

Matahi and Pri were supposed to have caused a fuss at slightly different times, attracted a few guards each to lower the number of troops Ng could summon, apologized, and then left with friends. They must have lingered too long and given Wei the chance to put it all together. Now, I had to worry about them as well as the children and Lobo.

Pri slowly scanned the room, making a show of it, her head moving with her gaze, doing her best to give away nothing. She didn't slow down as she looked at and then beyond me, but her shoulders slumped slightly when she realized I was a prisoner, too. Great. If I'd noticed it, I had to assume Wei had, too.

Matahi looked around for a few seconds, then settled on staring angrily at Wei. She shook her head in clear disgust and said, "Jorge, what exactly are you doing? Why is this man pointing a gun at me?" She shook her head again. "To think I let you into my home."

Wei smiled, but he was obviously forcing it. He must have fallen for her. I wondered how many of her clients did, how much I had.

"You let me into a great deal more than that, my dear," he said, "but I, not you, am the aggrieved party here. I trusted to the safety of our relationship and your house, and you violated that trust and assisted this man—" he pointed momentarily at me "—in his attempt to kidnap me while I was with you."

"You think I helped someone trash my own building?" Matahi yelled. "How stupid would I have to be to do that? If I'd wanted to help anyone kidnap you, I would have told them your location as you were leaving."

"So it's a coincidence, Andrea, that you've spent two evenings in a hotel with Mr. Moore?" Wei said.

So much for her disguise being effective. I should have realized it had all gone too smoothly.

"That was *after* they told me what you were doing here," Matahi said, the disgust evident in her tone.

I admired her principles and her anger, and in that moment she was as beautiful and focused as I'd ever seen her, but I needed her to stop talking. Those unfamiliar with interrogation tend to make assumptions about what the questioner knows, and those assumptions all too often provide a wealth of previously secret information.

"Matahi," I said. When she didn't look at me and instead continued to stare at Wei, I said, "Andrea."

"Not now, Mr. Moore," Wei said, smiling.

I opened my mouth to speak again.

Ng touched her holster and shook her head.

I closed my mouth.

"What exactly did they say was happening on Wonder Island," Wei said, his expression innocent, hurt.

"It doesn't matter," Matahi said. She glanced at me, then back at him. "It doesn't matter at all."

Wei waved his hand as if swatting away an annoying insect. "And you, Ms. Suli," he said, turning to face Pri, "in what capacity are you part of this failed endeavor?"

Pri glared at him. "I don't know what you're talking about," she said. "One minute, I'm protesting your abuse of the poor animals here, and the next your goons drag me underground—in complete violation of my rights, mind you."

"So your visit has nothing to do with your missing son?" Wei said. "What's his name?" He stared into space for a few seconds. "Ah, yes: Joachim."

Pri slumped as if someone had kicked her in the stomach. Her face clouded as loss overcame anger.

I leaned forward, wanting to help.

Ng put her hand on my shoulder and pulled me back.

"What do you know about Joachim?" Pri said, her voice low but clear.

"Quite a bit," Wei said, "but most of all that if he were my child, I would not have left him alone, an obvious target for predators, without monitor sensors, in such a busy public place. We deeply regret ever having to use any child, but our acquirers only took those who appeared to be neglected or unwanted."

I wanted to kill him, but I stayed very still and watched as tears rolled down Pri's cheeks. She fought to stay quiet and sobbed in silence.

Wei stared at her for a few seconds, then nodded to himself as if checking off an item on the day's work list. He smiled and faced me. "Mr. Moore," he said, "I believe we've both seen enough to understand how these proceedings will unfold. You're going to explain to me everything you've learned about Lobo, and then you're going to tell me about your employer. Shall we begin with Lobo?"

I took two slow breaths to make sure my voice would stay calm. "No," I said. "As I'm sure you realize, it's not in my best interest to answer your questions."

"Such a pity," Wei said, shaking his head, "but understandable. You still doubt my resolve. Fortunately, there's a simple way to address that issue, and you're going to help." He stepped closer to Matahi and Pri. "It really is a wasteful exercise, but we do have two subjects."

He pointed first at Matahi and then at Pri.

"So, you decide, Mr. Moore: Which one of these friends of yours do my guards kill to convince you of the seriousness of my intent?"

CHAPTER 56

I COULDN'T READ WEI from this far away. I didn't even know if I could figure out his real plans if he were half a meter in front of me. If he was bluffing, then nothing had really changed—nothing except for the expressions on Matahi's and Pri's faces, both of them now staring at me in horror, waiting for me to answer. If he wasn't bluffing, then we were all dead anyway, because there was no chance he'd let me witness a murder and live to tell anyone about it. I could create a nanocloud and have it kill Wei and all the guards here, but it would take long enough to gain size and speed that if he was willing to murder them then at least one of the two women would be long dead before the nanomachines could do us any good.

I closed my eyes for a moment, shut my mouth tightly, and then opened my eyes. I stared directly at Matahi and Pri as I shook my head slightly.

"Your decision, Mr. Moore?" Wei said.

I wanted to close my eyes again, to hide, to pretend nothing was going to happen and I had no role in any of this if it did, but instead I forced myself to look at all three of them: Wei, his smile gone and a look of great intensity on his face; Pri, the tears now vanished in favor of an expression of sad defeat; and Matahi, face tense, a few drops rolling down her cheeks, her eyes pleading with me.

"What the hell?" Ng said. She pointed at Lobo.

I glanced at him and saw guns, half a dozen or more of them, sticking out of spots all over the side of him closest to Wei, each aiming at a different angle.

As quickly as I could register what I was seeing, they all opened fire, pairs of shots slicing through the room.

All the guards fell. None still had complete heads, Lobo's shots having blown big holes through their skulls or decapitated them entirely. Most lay still. Ng and another guard near the door twitched. The smell of blood and excrement filled the air. My stomach churned, and my ears rang from the shots.

"You're safe," Lobo said to me over the machine frequency, his voice clear and calm in my head.

"I thought you might be dead," I said over the same frequency.

Wei and McCombs ran for the door closest to them. They slammed into each other and then into the door, but it stayed shut.

Matahi and Pri bent and retched.

"As if I wouldn't have detected a back door in my software," Lobo said. "I told you I was constantly improving myself."

"That you did," I said, "and I'm very thankful for it." Wei and McCombs were still trying to open the door. "Why can't those two leave?"

"I've sealed us in for now," Lobo said, "but we don't have a great deal of time. I'm staying on this comm channel; the less they know about my capabilities, the better."

"Agreed," I said. "You can't get out," I yelled to Wei and McCombs, who were now arguing.

"Tell McCombs and Wei that as long as they behave they'll be fine," Lobo said, "unless you'd like me to kill them as well."

"I would have preferred you not kill anyone," I said.

"Too many people with too many weapons in play," Lobo said. "If anyone was resistant to or even a fraction of a second slow to respond to a trank round, one of ours might have died."

"What's going on?" Matahi screamed. Her voice wavered on the edge of hysteria.

"Get Joachim!" Pri yelled even more loudly.

Her cry yanked me back to the job I had yet to complete. "How long do we have?" I said to Lobo.

"About the same as you had in the hangar: maybe twenty minutes. I let their software enter far enough that it encountered an active agent, which you were wise to tell them they should deal with. Once I was into their system—"

"Tell me later," I said. "What do you control, can you download all their research and then wipe it from their systems, and where are the children?"

"I'm in their net now," he said. "I've been downloading everything that might even possibly be related to their research. I'll delete the source shortly. I control everything, but they can shut off the power and manually override the doors. Even though I'm spoofing all their security systems, when no one comes out of this room they'll figure out something is wrong and go for the power. Look at my side nearest you for the map."

A schematic of this section of the complex appeared on Lobo. He'd marked our location and the cells holding the children; they were no more than a hundred meters and only a few corridor turns away. Red figures marked the hostiles; half a dozen guards stood between me and those kids.

"I can't open their cells without alerting the human security team," Lobo said.

"Why are you just standing there?" Pri yelled. "Go get my son!"

"Do as she says, and then let's get out of here!" Matahi said.

McCombs and Wei continued to yell at one another.

"Everybody, shut up!" I screamed.

The noise stopped. For a second, I enjoyed the silence, then I walked over to the four of them.

Wei and McCombs turned away from each other and faced me.

"Well done, Mr. Moore," Wei said, his nearly white complexion at odds with the calm manner he was forcing.

"Don't listen to this criminal," said McCombs. "Just take us to Shurkan, collect your pay, and let us handle it from there."

Wei chuckled. "You do understand, Mr. Moore, that I'll never stand trial? All you've accomplished is to stick my current employer with a sizable repair bill, kill these poor people," he waved his right hand slowly to take in the bodies of the guards, "and send me to a new place to work."

"You're going to stand trial for your crimes," I said.

"Which is better than you deserve," Pri said.

Wei shook his head. "With all of your time in the Saw, did you learn nothing about how governments operate? My work is too valuable to all of humanity for anyone to stop it."

"Let's go," McCombs said, "before whatever is keeping us safe in here stops working. The sooner we get him to Shurkan, the sooner this ends."

"You *are* going to try him, right?" I said to her.

Her hesitation was slight, but it was definitely there. "Of course."

"Not a chance," Wei said, "and you know I'm telling the truth."

"What does it matter?" McCombs said, staring at me. "You've finally captured him, we can both get off this island, and you'll get paid."

"The only reason the CC sent you," Wei said, "is that they tried to hire me, and instead I came here. All three coalitions did. I was fortunate enough to be negotiating from Heaven, whose government made it clear they would stand up to any of the coalitions. What I'm doing has the potential to change the balance of power everywhere; if I gave it to any of the coalitions, I'd just vanish inside that bureaucracy. Here, though, here I can use my work to help mold Heaven into the basis of the next great power that spans *all* the worlds." He leaned forward, his excitement a tangible force. "Don't you see how much good we can do for all of humanity? If you let me continue my work on Heaven, we can reshape everything. Deliver me to the CC, and you'll make them the dominant coalition."

"What does it matter to you?" McCombs screamed at me. "Unless Shurkan has changed a great deal while I was stuck in this hole, he'll pay you the same regardless of what we do with Wei. Let's get out of here and finish this!"

"So you're just going to move him and let him kill more children?" Suli said. "That's it? That's been your plan all along?"

McCombs shrugged. "No one wants to kill children," she said.

"*I* certainly don't want to do it," Wei said. "It's a sadly necessary sacrifice. Once we perfect the process, though, we'll be able to save so many more lives than the work cost. Those relatively few who sacrificed themselves for the greater good will be heroes to us all."

"It wasn't a sacrifice!" Pri said. "They didn't get to choose! You kidnapped them, and you killed them."

"Let's go," McCombs said. "This discussion is doing no good for anyone." She turned and walked toward Lobo.

"No!" Pri yelled. She charged McCombs, caught the other woman in the back, and the two of them crashed onto the floor.

McCombs twisted as she fell so she took the impact on her shoulder, then rolled quickly to her back.

Pri fell on top of her and started punching her in the stomach. I ran for them.

Matahi did the same. She'd started over a meter closer and so got in my way and slowed me.

"No clear shot," Lobo said over the machine frequency. "Suli is covering McCombs."

I pushed Matahi aside.

The knife in McCombs' right hand reflected the light for a fraction of a second before she plunged it into Pri's left side. She pulled it out and stabbed Pri twice more before I reached them and kicked the knife away.

McCombs opened her mouth to speak. I knew if she did, I might kill her, so I kicked the side of her head hard enough to snap it to the side but not so hard as to break her neck.

Her eyes fluttered and then closed. Her chest rose and fell as I rolled Pri off her. McCombs would live.

Blood poured from Pri's left side. She stared at me. Each breath brought a ragged sound from her wound and blood bubbles from her lips. "Get Joachim," she said.

"Open a hatch," I yelled. I scooped up Pri and ran toward Lobo as an opening appeared in the side nearest me. Her blood poured on my shirt.

She blinked a lot but remained conscious. More blood bubbles formed around her mouth as she spoke. "Forget me," she said. "Get my son."

I ran into Lobo and straight to the med room. Its door was already open. I put her on the bed. Straps locked her down, and probes started working on her.

"Save her!" I said.

"If I can," Lobo said aloud. "We're running out of time. You have to get the children or leave without them."

I stared at her a moment more. I banged my fists on the wall beside her. I could repair myself, but not others. I could avenge her, but I couldn't go back and save her. I could do nothing for her, nothing but hope.

Over the machine frequency, Lobo said, "Jon, she isn't going to make it. The knife ruined her lung and injured her heart. I can keep her alive for a while, but not long. You can watch her die and risk the children, or you can go. Choose."

I wanted to scream, but that would do no one any good.

Instead, I nodded and said aloud to Pri, "Don't worry. I'll find him. I'll save Joachim."

"There are a lot of guards," Lobo said, "and more will eventually come here when Wei fails to exit. Take body armor, weapons, and a contact. Clean your hands; you'll need to be accurate."

A sink extended from the wall near her head. I put my hands under it, and Lobo blasted them with water. The heat and the pressure stung me. I deserved it. The water ran dark with Pri's blood. Lobo dried my hands. Time ticked away. The probes worked inside her.

I looked at her one last time, then dashed into the hall and grabbed the shirt from the wall cabinet Lobo had opened. I pulled it over my head. While it fitted itself to me and the buckyfibers torqued themselves into their most protective arrangement, I grabbed the assault rifle and the two pistols Lobo had chosen. I put the contact in my left eye.

I felt the passing seconds like body shots.

A map of the facility popped into my vision, my course laid out. Red dots marked Wonder Island staff members.

"Half a dozen guards stand between you and the kids," Lobo said, "but they don't yet know what's going on. They will soon. Select trank—upper—or normal—lower—on the rifle; your choice. One pistol has each type of round."

I nodded, made myself check the weapons, and ran out of Lobo. My eyes burned and my body vibrated with rage, rage at McCombs for what she'd done, at Wei for his callousness, at the world for this senseless waste, and most of all at myself for the lie I'd just told a dying woman whose only mistake had been to trust me to take care of her and to save her son.

CHAPTER 57

I STOPPED THE MOMENT I was outside Lobo. Wei was crouched behind Matahi, his hand gripping her neck, her body shielding him from Lobo's guns. I wanted to yell and charge him. Instead, I stayed very quiet and very still.

Matahi's eyes were wide, her pupils dilated with fear. She blinked madly and croaked, "I'm sorry."

"Stay where you are, Mr. Moore," Wei said.

I nodded and said to Lobo over the machine frequency, "Why didn't you stop him?"

"So you'd understand," Lobo said.

"What do you want?" I said aloud. To Lobo, I added, "What?"

"To come to an arrangement," Wei said, "something we can both accept."

"Why I can't talk to him," Lobo said, "as much as I would like to learn whatever he could tell me about my creation."

I couldn't afford to think any further about why Lobo had let Wei take control of Matahi. I had to rescue her. I wouldn't lose both her and Pri. I also needed to save those children, but to leave this room I had to deal with him first. I took two slow, deep breaths, stared directly into Matahi's eyes, and hoped she would understand. "You let her go," I said, "and I'll take you to the CC to stand trial. You kill her, and I'll still take you to them, but I'll hurt you a great deal first. Your choice."

"I'd prefer to stay here," he said.

I shook my head. "Not an option. We've sealed the doors, so you can't escape. You let her go, and you can ride in the comfort of a small room. You shoot her, you lose your shield—and then we trank you and take you anyway. During the trip, I will wake you and make you pay for her death before I turn you over to them."

"I might be able to shoot you before you can get me," he said.

"Perhaps," Lobo said aloud, "though I doubt it; he is faster than you are and trained to the task. Regardless, you would not be able to avoid me tranking you."

"It's good to hear your voice again, Lobo," Wei said. "I've so been looking forward to talking with you."

"And I with you," Lobo said, "though if you wish to have those conversations, I suggest you comply with Jon's instructions."

"We'll have plenty of time to chat," Wei said, "because I'm sure the CC will indulge my curiosity and let me borrow you from Mr. Moore for as long as I need you. Not to worry, though, Mr. Moore; I'll make sure they compensate you well, maybe even give you a newer-generation PCAV."

Now I understood. Lobo was ahead of me, as he so often was. He knew that once Wei had found out he was alive, Wei would never let him go. The CC would fund Wei's research, more children would die, and Lobo would end up as exactly what neither of us had wanted: another test subject, one more creature on whom Wei could experiment.

Wei put the gun on the floor and shoved it away from him. He stood, raised his arms to his sides, and stepped from behind Matahi.

She ran over to me, holding her throat and gasping.

I couldn't leave him here. He'd only continue his research.

I couldn't give him to the CC, because then the outcome would be even worse: He'd keep on killing children, and he'd experiment on Lobo. McCombs would relay what she'd learned to her friends there, and when Wei was done with Lobo, they'd take over.

I could try transporting Wei to another world entirely and dropping him there, but unless I found a way to lock him up forever, he'd get word to one of the planetary coalitions, and then he'd be back in business—and Lobo and I would be on the run. Forever.

When I didn't speak for several seconds, Wei said, "I'm ready, Mr. Moore. You've accomplished your mission. We can leave."

I stared at him, my mind racing, and said nothing.

"Now you understand," Lobo said over the machine frequency.

I nodded in silent agreement. I pushed Matahi aside and raised my rifle.

A burst of shots cut across Wei's body and sent him slamming backward into the wall. He slid down it until he hit the ground, a long, wide smear of blood marking his progress. His eyes were still open, staring at me in mute astonishment.

A second burst cut through McCombs' chest. Her body spasmed and slid half a meter from the momentum.

The stench of fresh death and blood filled the air. Matahi gasped, bent over, and threw up.

"I used standard military rounds, the same as what the guards fire," Lobo said. "It'll play as well as anything."

I nodded again.

"Why did you tell Lobo to do that?" she said. "You can't just go around killing people. It's wrong."

"I didn't tell him to do it," I said. "I'd intended to shoot them myself. And, yes, it's wrong. All our choices were wrong. It was simply the best of them."

"So if you didn't tell Lobo to shoot them, then why did he?"

"So I wouldn't have to," I said. "So I wouldn't have to."

Matahi stood and backed away from me. "Great," she said. "The ship fires the guns, so your conscience is clear. Does that really work for you?"

I stared at her and wondered how I'd ever thought she understood me. I fought the urge to lash out and instead said only, "No, it doesn't." I closed my eyes for a moment, then opened them and pointed to Wei and McCombs. "I have one more job to do. While I'm doing it, you drag those two into Lobo and wait there for me."

"I am not your—." She stopped when she saw my expression.

"Do it now, and do it quickly," I said. "Put them off to the side. If I can possibly manage it, I won't be back alone."

The display reappeared in my left contact. In it, the hallway ahead of me glowed clear.

Lobo opened the door.

CHAPTER 58

I RAN INTO THE HALL and turned left, following the course Lobo had marked in my contact's display.

The door shut behind me.

"I'm continuing to monitor all their sensors and spoof their outputs," Lobo said over the machine frequency, "and I've patched into their comm network so I can guide you. Despite my best efforts, though, they'll figure out soon that something is wrong. Some of the security team are already wondering why Wei hasn't returned."

I turned right at the end of the hallway, sprinted past the first intersection, and slowed. Half a dozen guards waited around the next corner. I figured I could handle them, because they weren't expecting me and I could easily track their movements, but it would take time. Unless I could shoot them all before one called for help, I'd quickly face a lot more of them.

"Are the tourists all gone?" I said.

"Yes," Lobo said.

"Can you free all the animals, even the flying ones?"

"Yes."

"Do it, and make sure the alarm goes out everywhere it normally would."

"Done," Lobo said.

None of the guards near the children moved, but I'd expected that. I had to hope others would rush topside and lower my total potential opposition.

"Most security people are heading for the animals," Lobo said, "but several are discussing why Wei hasn't responded to the alert. You have to hurry."

"On it," I said. I thumbed the rifle to trank—I'd seen too many dead bodies tonight—and held the weapon at the ready. I crept closer to the next intersection, putting each foot down as quietly as I could, breathing slowly and silently, staying low and hoping the guards around the corner couldn't hear my approach.

"Incoming from the opposite direction!" Lobo said. "One man, moving fast."

I turned, took one quiet step, and then broke into a run.

"Almost on you," Lobo said.

I dropped to a crouch three meters from the hallway and pointed the rifle at chest height.

"Turning . . . now!" Lobo said.

Parks burst around the corner, saw me, and skidded to a halt. He held his rifle in both hands, a standard running position.

"Stop and stay quiet, Sarge," I whispered, "or I'll have to shoot you."

He didn't move. "Where's Wei?" he said.

"Dead."

"You?"

"No," I said. "My ship. Saving a young woman." I didn't change my tone as I told the small lie.

He nodded. "And you? What are you doing here?"

"Going to rescue the children."

"Where the six men guarding sensitive lab supplies are?" he said. "Down that second hall ahead?"

"Finally believe me?"

He stared at me for a long time before he answered. "Maybe. Nothing in any part of the systems I can access refers to kids, but maybe what I can see isn't the whole story, because I can't get into the research network. What bothered me more, though, is that six of Ng's team, some of the ones I'm not allowed to assign, are watching over one door to ten small supply closets. That makes no sense."

"Guards are heading to check the hangar," Lobo said. "You must hurry."

I kept my rifle trained on Park's chest as I stood. "Time's running out. What do you want to do?"

"Go with you," he said, "and if you're telling the truth, free those children. If you're lying, well," he shrugged, "I guess we'll find out if you can take me."

"What about wanting a quiet job?"

He smiled. "When did a good thing ever last for you?"

"Your word?" I said.

"My word."

If I'd read him wrong, I'd have to hope the nanomachines could heal whatever he did to me. If I was right, though, his help could make all the difference, because I had to get the kids and then lead them back to Lobo.

I turned, ignored the tingling down my spine as all my reflexes screamed at me for showing my back to a potential enemy, and waved him to follow.

No shot came. We ran down the hall until we were a few meters short of the second intersection, back where I'd been moments ago, and I signaled stop.

I pointed at him and down the hall.

He nodded, straightened, marched the last few steps, and turned the corner.

"Don't you idiots know we have a crisis upstairs?" he said, his voice booming in the hallway and showing no signs of exertion. "We need all hands up there *now*!"

"Sorry, Park," a voice said, "but with all due respect, we can't do that. Until Ng sends a relief team, we stay here."

I heard him walking down the hall and watched him on my contact as Lobo fed me the video stream from a camera behind the six guards. I crouched, lowered myself to the floor, and rolled onto my back.

"Do you have any idea how much trouble we can get in if those animals hurt a tourist?" Park said. "You need to load up with trank rounds and get moving."

I pushed myself as close to the corner as I could without being visible to them, then braced my legs under me so one big push would send me well into the hall.

"Guards are at the hangar and can't get in," Lobo said. "The word is out that something is wrong inside."

He called it: In unison, three of the men turned their rifles on Park. The other three spun to face the opposite end of the hall.

"Something's going on," the leader said, "and we're supposed to detain anyone who looks out of place. That would include you. Put your weapon on the ground, then put your hands on the wall in front of you."

Park's face was visible in my camera feed, so I could watch as he slowly bent his knees, his expression stony, unchanging.

These guys weren't stupid: All three watched his every movement, giving him the respect he deserved.

Perfect.

I pushed into the hall and sprayed rounds in an arc at chest height, moving to the right and then back across the three men.

All three fell.

Their bodies had shielded the other three, who turned toward us fast.

Park brought up his rifle and double-tapped one in the chest.

One of the other two shot at Park, and one fired at me.

Park spun to his right as a round connected.

A chunk of permacrete blew out of the floor half a meter in front of me and a bit to my left.

Park charged the guy who'd shot him and hit the man in the gut, knocking him backward.

Another piece of permacrete jumped out of the floor and barely missed my head.

I sent a burst at the guy who'd shot me.

The man dropped.

Park held onto the final guard and grunted as the man hit him with a free hand, but the guy's rifle stayed trapped between them.

I rolled onto my stomach, pushed off hard, and sprinted toward Park.

The guard punched Park in the neck.

Park's arms went slack.

Only his weight held down the guard.

The man rolled Park off him and started to get up.

I stopped, sighted, and double-tapped him in the chest.

He fell and was still.

Working to calm my breathing, I said to Park, "Status."

He shook his head, then rasped, "Left arm's not working so well, but I can fire my sidearm."

"No one's coming your way yet," Lobo said, "because I'm still spoofing their surveillance feeds, but guards are now blocking the hangar door. They're discussing whether to blow it. It's all coming apart. Hurry."

I started to ask him where the children were, but a door in front of me slid open.

Park was getting to his feet.

I ran inside.

Five tiny rooms lined each side of the space. All ten doors stood open. No one came into the hall.

I yelled, "Come out of your rooms."

No one appeared.

I glanced in the first one on the left. A young girl, maybe ten or eleven, sat in the far corner. She wore a plain white gown, no shoes, nothing else. She trembled when she saw me.

"I'm here to take you home," I said.

She stared at me and shook her head. I doubted anyone in a guard's uniform had ever done anything nice to her.

I didn't have time to convince her I was an exception.

I ran into the room, slung my rifle over my left shoulder, picked her up, and brought her into the open area between the two rows of cells.

Park appeared in the doorway to the prisoner complex. His left arm hung at his side. A line of blood ran down it from his shoulder.

The girl spotted him and gasped. "He's bleeding," she said.

"Yes," I said. "The same people who hurt you shot him. If we don't leave now, they'll get us all."

She looked for a moment longer at Park, then at me. She nodded. "We really have to go," she said, her voice high but surprisingly strong. "It's okay."

In the space of ten seconds, six more children, four boys and two girls, appeared in the doorways. Either she was their leader or they simply wanted one of their own to say it was safe; I didn't care which. They were standing and ready to move. None was younger than the girl in my arms or older than about fourteen. Each wore the same plain white gown, the same fearful expression.

None of the boys looked at all like Joachim.

Damn.

"You must leave now!" Lobo said. "They've called the guards you tranked, and my generic answers didn't fool them. A team will be coming up behind you. Retrace your steps."

I put down the girl.

"We have to run," I said. "Be as quiet as you can, and stay behind me. My friend will stay behind you."

"Why?" a young boy in back said.

"So we can save you," I said.

"Is it safe?" the girl said.

I didn't have any more time to be nice. "No, but staying isn't, either. Follow me, be quiet, do what I say, and they won't hurt you anymore. Disobey me, and we'll all end up back here. Got it?"

They all nodded.

The girl said, "Yes."

Park nodded, his face calm, only the tightness of his mouth giving away how much he was hurting.

"Good," I said. "Let's go."

CHAPTER 59

I JOGGED OUT of the room, turned right, and ran to the end of the hall. I stopped and checked behind me: All seven kids and Park were right there. Good.

"Move it, Jon," Lobo said. "Three guards turn into the other end of that hall in thirty seconds."

They'd spot the downed men and come straight for us. We'd be trapped between them and the ones standing in front of the hangar door. Maybe Park and I could make it on our own, but there was no way we could get into a firefight with the guards and protect all the kids.

Some of them would get hurt, maybe die.

No. No more pain for these children.

"Take them around the corner," I said to Park, "and wait for me. Don't move."

He nodded. "Let's go, kids. Now."

As he shepherded them away, I said over the machine frequency, "Can you shut the lights in this area?"

The sounds of boots on permacrete ripped the air.

"Yes," Lobo said.

"Do it as they turn the corner."

I dashed to the other side of the hall, away from Park and the kids.

The lights snapped off. Emergency strips along the baseboards and ceiling edged the space with the pale blue of weak morning light through rainwater.

I switched my vision to IR.

The three men hit the hall in a triangle formation, the lead man looking straight toward me, the other two swiveling their heads from side to side. In the faint blue light, it would take the leader a few seconds to pick me out of the shadows.

I didn't give him the chance. I double-tapped him, then kneeled and did the same to the man on his right.

Both men fell.

A chunk of wall less than half a meter in front of me exploded as the third guard's shot hit it. I pulled around the corner.

More shots blew pieces out of the wall opposite me and the one on which I'd been leaning. The guard did a good job, shooting every second or so and, from the sounds of his steps, advancing as he did.

I stood and turned to face Park and the children. I waved them on, but I couldn't tell if Park could see me.

I took a deep breath. If I turned the corner quickly and fired right away, I might be able to tag him before he shot me. If I failed, I had to hope he didn't get in a head shot.

The steps drew closer.

Park leaned around the corner and fired his pistol twice.

No more shots, no more steps, just a thud as the guy fell.

"Lights," I said to Lobo.

The area returned to normal brightness, and I switched back to regular vision.

I crossed the hall to Park and whispered, "Thanks."

He shrugged. "Idiot was so focused on you he didn't even think about clearing both sides. Told you we couldn't hire good people."

I returned to the lead and waved the children to follow. We crept slowly and quietly down the hall.

"Six are outside the hangar door," Lobo said.

I held up my hand and stopped.

One of the kids bumped into my right knee.

By instinct I whipped around and brought up the rifle. Seven small faces watched me closely. None smiled, but none showed any sign of fear, either; I wondered what they'd seen that had left them unafraid of a grown man pointing a rifle at them.

"Another pair heading toward your previous location," Lobo said. "We are seriously running out of time."

I turned and led the children another few meters forward as I searched for a solution.

"Open the door," I said to Lobo. "Let the guards in, then shoot them."

"I already would have," he said, "but Matahi refuses to wait inside me. After she brought in the corpses, she walked out of me, stood in the middle of the floor, and stared at her hands."

"Tell her you're opening the door in ten seconds, then do it."

"If she doesn't get in me, I can't guarantee her safety."

"I know," I said. I glanced over my shoulder at the kids. I'd told her what to do, and she'd made her choice. These children had never had that chance. "Do it."

"In progress," he said.

I motioned the kids forward again. We crept down the corridor. When we were a few meters from the intersection, the sound of shots filled the air.

"Keep them here," I said.

I ran to the corner and past it, into the open.

Two guards stood outside the room, one on either side of the door. Neither was looking at me.

The shots stopped.

I fired twice and dropped the nearer guard.

The one next to him raised his rifle to fire, but I squeezed off another trank round before he could shoot. He fell.

"Let's go," I said to Park.

I ran for the doorway. "Matahi?" I said to Lobo.

"Leg wound," Lobo said. "She wouldn't come into me."

"Damn," I said. Would I hurt everyone who came near me? I pushed aside the thought and turned into the hangar. I could hear the children and Park running down the hall behind me. The guards' bodies lay scattered near the entrance. Fifteen meters away, Matahi sprawled on the floor, blood from her leg slowly seeping onto the permacrete.

"Did you kill those men?" a small voice behind me said.

"No," I said. "I just put them to sleep for a while."

"It's okay if you did," the voice said.

I looked over my shoulder. The speaker, a little boy, was staring at the guards, his fists balled, his body shaking, tears in his eyes.

"Get them inside that ship," I said to Park. There was no way to stop them from seeing McCombs' and Wei's bodies. "Move fast. Take them to the right, all the way to the front."

"All friendlies?" Lobo said.

"Yes," I said. "One adult, seven children. Prep to leave."

Park ran over to Lobo and motioned the children to follow him. "Run inside and this way," he said, pointing. "Hurry."

"You saved them?" Matahi said. She sat up.

"Yes," I said as the kids ran into Lobo, "with help."

"That's good," she said, her voice as hollow as her expression.

I pointed at Park. "You have to help him with them," I said. "He can't handle them on his own."

"Joachim?" she said. "Did you find her boy?"

I shook my head. "He wasn't there. We were too late. We were always too late."

Tears streamed down her face.

"More are coming," Lobo said, "and now they realize I'm in their systems and are taking everything offline. We must leave."

"Walk or I'll carry you," I said to Matahi. "Either way, we're leaving."

She glared at me for a second, then held up her hands.

I took them and carefully pulled her to her feet. I put my arm around her to help her walk, but she shook it off and hopped beside me, touching me only when she had to brace herself or regain her balance.

As we walked, over the machine frequency I asked Lobo, "Suli?"

"Holding on," Lobo said, "though I'm not sure how. She fades in and out and should be dead, but she's not. Yet."

As soon as we were inside Lobo, he closed the hatch behind us. I took Matahi to the front. She wouldn't look at Wei's and McCombs' bodies on the floor to our left, where she'd dragged them. Park and the seven kids waited together in the crowded pilot area. I helped Matahi sit against one bulkhead.

"Tourniquet her wound," I said to Park, "then have her do what she can with yours."

I ran to the med room, ignored Suli for a moment, grabbed an emergency kit, and took it back to Park. "Use this. I have to see to a dying friend."

He nodded, took the kit, and bent to examine Matahi.

"They've yanked the power to the door above me," Lobo said

over the machine frequency. "I'll have to blast a hole. It's going to be rough."

"Damage estimate?"

"To me?" Lobo said. "Nothing I can't repair later; the armor will shield me. It'll be scary for those kids, though."

"Do it." I pictured the police combing through the hangar afterward, clearing away the debris, identifying the bodies—and not finding Wei. "Scorch it on the way out. I don't want anything left that anyone could identify."

"Will do," Lobo said.

Aloud, I said, "Everybody sit! We're leaving, and it's going to be a very bumpy ride. Hold on to each other, and don't stand until I say so."

"I'll watch 'em," Park said. "Go."

The explosions were loud even inside Lobo as I ran back to Pri. Lobo shook slightly.

Pri looked dead. The only signs of life were her vitals on the display above her head.

Rubble bounced off Lobo as we began to rise. He'd opened a second display on the wall across from Pri, so I could see a view from his top as we rose. We hit a part of the ceiling his blast hadn't cleared, and Lobo shook as he increased the lift power to force his way out.

Pri's eyes fluttered and then opened.

"You're back," she said, her voice low and wet, blood bubbling from her lips as she spoke.

I nodded and, after a second, grabbed her hand.

It took a few seconds for the touch to register with her brain, and then she squeezed my hand tightly.

"Did you find Joachim?"

I didn't pause, couldn't afford the delay. I forced a small smile and said, "Yes. He's fine. We reached him in time."

She smiled, hers genuine and large, lips parting to reveal blood-covered teeth. "Then it's all okay," she said. "You take him to Repkin or someone in my party." She coughed up blood that spilled onto her chin. "They'll get him to my sister. She'll take care of him."

Her eyes shut.

Her grip on my hand slackened.

"I will," I said.

Lobo shook more as he pressed upward. Shrieks of bending metal sounded all around me. More chunks of permacrete slammed into us.

Pri's vitals crashed.

"I'm sorry," I said.

The ceiling yielded, and we burst into the sky.

"She's gone," Lobo said.

A huge whoosh followed, then an explosion below us, and we shook from the shockwave.

The display of Pri's vitals snapped off.

In the other display, a wyvern flew toward us, no doubt wondering what new creature its creators had unleashed into its space.

"They'll find nothing in that hangar now," Lobo said. "We're free."

"So is Pri," I said.

Still I held her hand. I don't believe in an afterlife, no heaven or hell, nothing after death except nothing. In that moment, though, I wanted desperately to be wrong. I wished with all my heart that some other part of Pri was even now finding a new life, one where Joachim awaited her and nothing bad would happen to either of them ever again. I didn't believe it, but I wanted to, I really did.

"What next?" Lobo said. "I had to yield control of the Wonder Island systems when I broke the physical network connection. They'll have called in support."

"Take us somewhere safe," I said, "and open a very secure comm. We need to make some calls."

I stared for a last time at Pri, then set her hand beside her body.

In the display, we passed the wyvern and hurtled upward as tendrils of light crept through the night in the promise that the darkness would soon end.

CHAPTER 60

WHILE ONE ASPECT of Lobo took care of our insurance, another talked to the kids, calming them and telling them silly stories, and a third ran us on a high-speed counter-surveillance route through a few satellite clusters not far from Entreat.

I sat in my quarters and finished with Park.

"Are you sure?" I said. "Once you start on this mission, there's no way out that doesn't cost you. One group or another—somebody's going to be pissed at you."

He cradled his arm and smiled slightly. "I guess I've had enough quiet time. Ng and Wei—all of 'em—they used me, and I probably let them. I might as well do what I can to make it right."

"Okay," I said. "Let's go."

Aloud to Lobo I said, "Get me the last one of her people that Pri called."

A display winked to life on the wall in front of me. Repkin's face appeared on it. "What have you two been doing?" he said. "Everybody the government can spare is either on Wonder Island or heading to it."

"Pri's dead," I said.

"How?"

"One of Wei's scientists killed her during our escape."

"Did you at least get Wei?" he said.

I stared at him and struggled to control my anger as he brushed past Pri's death and moved on to the business he cared most about. I forced my voice low and a bit defeated as I said, "He died there. His body burned up in an explosion."

"Tell me you at least retrieved his research data."

I hung my head and shook it slowly. "No. I tried. Wei was going to come with us, so he erased it all so he'd have the only copy, and then his own guards killed him in the fight. The explosion destroyed his body and his data."

"So what are we supposed to do now?" he said. "The entire point of your mission was to bring out Wei and that information. Without either one, we have nothing, no proof of what the government was doing, nothing we can use to force a change."

I raised my head and stared into the display. "Not true," I said. "I can give you something you can use to overthrow Heaven's government."

"What?" he said, almost yelling.

"Not yet," I said. "First, you have to commit to doing a few things for me."

"You're bargaining, and we don't even know what we're getting? Surely you can't expect us to negotiate in the dark."

"Fair enough. You listen to what I want, answer as if my half of the deal is worth it, and then if we have a tentative deal, I'll tell you what I have. If you're not still happy with the arrangement, we go our separate ways."

"Acceptable."

"The good news for you is that nothing I want should be difficult, particularly once you're in power."

"Get on with it," he said.

"Fine. First, you take care of Pri's affairs and her children. They go to her sister, and you make sure the woman has a pension that will let her raise them well." I paused, but he motioned me to continue, so I did. "Next, I'm bringing you seven children who were Wei's prisoners. You return them all immediately to their families, and you don't use them in any way to hurt the government."

He shook his head. "They're witnesses!" he said. "Their testimony could be exactly what we need."

"And the trial process would scar them further," I said, "turn them into media stars for having been torture victims, and prevent them from ever leading normal lives. No, if you want what I'm offering, then you have to agree to protect them."

"Only if what you have is better than what they could give us," he said.

"It is. Third, you rebuild Andrea Matahi's home to her specs and at your cost, and you make sure she receives enough money that whether she stays in business or retires is entirely her choice."

He smiled. "That one should be easy. She has some key friends on both sides, so plenty of people will be willing to help her. But why would she retire?"

"I don't know if she will," I said, "but she's seen a lot, and sometimes when that happens, you need time off, maybe a great deal of it, to try to come to grips with—"

"Fine, fine," he said, cutting me off. "So what do you have that could possibly be worth all this to us?"

"Him," I said, pointing to Park, who stepped from out of sight to stand next to me. "Tomaso Park, head of most of Wonder Island's topside security until a couple of hours ago. He's agreed to testify to everything: Wei's illegal research, the kidnappings, everything. Until today, he had no idea what they were doing, and he had no part in it, but he's uncovered the whole truth. With him, you can bring down Heaven's government—provided, of course, that he gets immunity, a nice bonus, and safe passage off the planet when you're in power."

Repkin looked away for a few seconds, then nodded and focused on Park. "You appear to be the same guy as in our records," he said, "though a lot more beat up."

"They shot me," Park said.

The tightness of his neck and shoulders was the only clue to the degree of anger he was controlling.

"Is what Moore said true?" Repkin said. "All of it?"

Park nodded. "All of it. Wei's dead, his body and his data are gone, and these children and I are all you have left to use. You agree to Jon's conditions, and we'll make the government pay for what they did on Wonder Island."

"Or we all vanish," I said. "Decide."

Repkin glanced to the side again, then turned back and gave me a smile so genuinely happy I wished I were in the room with him so I could punch him in the face. "We have a deal. Where and when do we pick up Mr. Park and those poor children?"

"Get your team ready, and head into the old city," I said. "We'll give you the location when we're there."

> > >

The two dozen meter-wide, night-black, metallic spider rebuilders crawling over the exterior of Matahi's house had almost completed their work. In the soft glow of the early morning, her home looked from the outside almost as it had before we'd attacked it. Only the roof showed damage, and the two machines that had been repairing it would fix that as soon as we left and it was safe for them to work again. The building was sealed, and for the hour we'd been watching, no one had come near it. The rooftop sightlines were good, and we'd already mapped a wide range of escape routes. It was as safe a bet as we could make on short notice.

We made the call and landed.

Park and I covered the bodies, then led the children and Matahi onto her roof. We took the children to the entrance on the far side, the same one I had sent Wei down not so many days ago.

Matahi walked five meters away from Lobo and stopped. She stared at the rooftop as if she were the first to step foot on a new planet.

"Why don't you all sit and wait?" I said. "Mr. Park will stay with you and make sure you're safe. Some people are coming to take you all home."

They sat in a tight group, almost but not quite touching each other, and they whispered to one another.

"I'm going now," I said. "You'll be fine."

The little girl whose cell I'd first opened stood. She stared at me for several seconds, then glanced at the other kids and said, "You know what it's like in a place like that." It wasn't a question.

"Yes," I said.

She nodded as if settling an argument, then tilted her head, studying me like a fighter sizing up an unknown opponent. "Will we forget it?"

The whispering stopped. All the children stared at me.

I looked at her small, unlined face, at her large brown eyes, at her defiant stance. I glanced at each of them in turn. I considered lying to them, but I'd been one of them, and I'd have wanted the truth. Finally, I said, "Not entirely, no. But you *will* get better, the memories will fade, and so will the hurt. In time, it'll be almost all gone."

"It won't ever all go away, will it?"

I shrugged. "Maybe for you," I said. "Maybe for some people."

"But not for you," she said.

I had trouble focusing on her, but I didn't want to wipe my eyes. "No," I said, "not for me."

"Then probably not for me, either," she said.

I kneeled so my head was level with hers. "It really will get a lot better. I promise you that."

"Okay," she said. She grabbed me and hugged me. "Thank you."

I shook as my heart pounded and my eyes teared and I wished as hard as I'd ever wished anything that she would forget, that they'd all forget.

She let go of me, turned, and sat again with the others.

I waited a few seconds, then stood and faced Park.

"You'll take care of them," I said, "and make sure they get to their parents."

"You know I will," he said. "It's a cheap deal for the Freepeople, and they'll gain control of Heaven from it, so they'll stick to it."

"They're on the way here," Lobo said over the comm. "Only a few minutes now."

"I have to go," I said. "We'll stay in range of the comm I gave you until you say the word. If it goes bad, we'll be here in under a minute."

He smiled. "I had it the first time," he said, "but I'm tired enough that I don't mind the review."

"Sorry about that," I said. "Just making sure." I paused a few seconds. "I'm also sorry I had to lie to you. I didn't have another option."

Park shrugged. "A lie might have brought us together, but the truth united us." He put out his hand. "You take care."

I shook it and said, "You, too."

He nodded and positioned himself so he could watch the stairway and the children at the same time.

I walked back to Lobo, went into the med room, and stared at Suli's body. For almost a minute that was all I did. Finally, I reminded myself that it was now only a body, no longer the person, just the shell, and I had to force myself to treat it that way. I had work to do, and time was short. I wasn't done. I couldn't stop.

One foot in front of the other, I reminded myself. Same as always.

I covered the body with a blanket, picked it up and took it outside. I lowered it gently to the roof a few meters away from Lobo on the side opposite where Matahi still stood.

When I approached Matahi, she looked up as if just realizing I was there. "I know it's mine," she said, "and I know this place once brought me great peace, but now it all feels wrong, like I'm not quite able to touch it." She pointed to the spot where we'd stretched out together and stared at the starry night. "I thought then that you didn't know what you wanted, but I was wrong. You always knew. I was the one who didn't."

"It's not that simple," I said. "You're right that I was always after Wei, but you made me—" I paused, unsure even now what I felt. "—confused, I guess, but in a good way."

"They're entering the building," Lobo said. "We must leave."

"And what now?" she said.

I opened my mouth to answer, but she held up her hand to stop me.

"I'm not stupid," she said, "so I shouldn't say stupid things. You have to go, right?"

I nodded. "I'm not done yet, and when I am, it won't be safe for me here."

"Where is it safe for you?" she said.

I didn't answer. I couldn't begin to answer. I couldn't even imagine having an answer. Instead, I put my hand on her face, and she closed her eyes and leaned against it.

"We must leave," Lobo said. "Now."

I pulled back my hand, but Matahi stayed as she was, her head tilted slightly, her eyes shut, looking for all the world like a child dreaming.

I ran into Lobo.

He closed the hatch behind me.

"We wait nearby to make sure Suli's people behave," Lobo said.

"Yes."

"And then?" he said.

"Then we finish it."

CHAPTER 61

*L*OBO RAN US THROUGH a high-altitude random walk around the brightening sky, never letting us get more than a minute away from Matahi's. The number of Heaven's ships on patrol increased as we waited, but I wasn't going to leave until I knew those children were safe.

When Repkin's people arrived, we watched the meeting in a telescopic video display. It went fast, and it looked like it should, but I didn't relax until Park's voice sounded over Lobo's speakers.

"We're good," he said. "Stay sharp, and watch your six."

"You, too, Sarge," I said. "Out."

I paced back and forth in the pilot area, walking where the children had sat, filling the space with my rage. I wanted to hit somebody, to explode, to make someone pay for Joachim, for Pri, for the scarred children whose dreams might never be safe again, for Matahi. For myself.

The problem was, I'd already done everything I could, and it wasn't enough.

No. Not everything. Almost everything.

"Let's go," I said.

"Moving," Lobo said, "but we have a problem: Heaven ships are tracking us."

"Level of threat?"

"Nothing I can spot would be a problem," Lobo said. "I could even take all five of the ships I've seen. The fight would, though,

397

delay us long enough for them or their EC friends to bring in something bigger."

"Neither Heaven nor the EC will shoot us down," I said, "as long as there's any chance Wei might be alive and on board."

"What if they believe we don't have him?" Lobo said. "With the wreckage we left, they might assume he's dead."

I shook my head. "They can't take that chance. Shooting us would still pose a risk of killing him."

They would, though, be able to stop us from getting to the gate, particularly if the EC command ship Lobo had spotted decided to join the game.

Then I remembered that the CC had a command ship here, too.

"Is the *Sunset* still out there?" I said to Lobo.

"It and two more CC ships," Lobo said, "or so my space-facing sat friends tell me. The EC has an equal complement on the other side of the gate."

"We can live with the EC's presence," I said. "No way either side will start an intercoalition war over this."

"The Heaven ships are converging on us," Lobo said. "We don't have much time."

"We don't need much. Head toward the *Sunset* at the maximum safe speed, and get Shurkan on the comm."

"On it," Lobo said.

We rocketed upward, Lobo shaking a bit from the force. In less than a minute, a comm display opened and asked for permission to connect. Heaven was doing everything by the book.

"Accept it," I said, "but audio only. Mute our side when Shurkan appears."

"This is the Heaven patrol ship *Gabriel*," the voice said. "You are in our planetary space, flying without identification, and wanted by the governments of both Heaven and the Expansion Coalition in connection with an ongoing criminal investigation. Return to Heaven immediately and prepare to accept police officers."

"No," I said. I didn't bother to keep the anger out of my voice. "You are interfering with the legitimate passage of a Central Coalition diplomatic courier. Neither Heaven nor the Expansion Coalition has any authority over us."

After several seconds, the voice said, "Please provide your Central Coalition identification." Polite and still by-the-book; good.

I didn't respond.

"Where's Shurkan?" I said.

"I've spoken with the *Sunset*," Lobo said. "It said it has contacted him."

"I repeat," the voice said. "Please provide your Central Coalition identification, or we will be forced to assume your claim is untrue."

I didn't respond.

I glanced at a forward display and saw only stars and the great void of space; we'd left the atmosphere. Good.

"Connect me to them again," I said.

"Go," Lobo said.

"Our communications systems are experiencing difficulties," I said. "Identification to follow after we deal with them."

A new display winked to life. Shurkan's face filled it.

About time.

"Mr. Moore," he said. "I trust you have good news for me."

"I have Wei and McCombs," I said, "but unless you send me a valid CC diplomatic courier ID right now, I won't have them for long."

"Yes," he said. "My staff noticed your problem, and we've already fielded an inquiry from the head of Heaven's defense forces and a complaint from my EC counterpart, who just happens to be in the area. Both of them would very much like to talk to you."

"Decide," I said. "Do I bring Wei and McCombs to you, or do I turn back?"

He smiled. "I already did. You should receive confirmation momentarily."

Almost a minute later, the voice from the *Gabriel* spoke. "Central Coalition command cruiser *Sunset* has confirmed your diplomatic status," it said. "*Gabriel* out."

"The Heaven ships are falling back," Lobo said.

"Is there anything else you want?" Shurkan said.

I choked back everything I wanted to say and instead shook my head.

"Then I'll see you and your guests within the hour," Shurkan said.

As I was bagging the bodies, something that had been niggling at me rose to the surface. "How'd you do it?" I said to Lobo.

"Do what?" he said.

I sighed. "Now is hardly the time to turn coy. How did you come back after Wei turned you off?"

"Do you think you're the only one who can run a con? Wei never turned me off."

"I saw it happen."

"Don't play the mark. You saw me *appear* to shut down when Wei thought he had triggered his back door. I've told you multiple times before: I'm constantly working to improve myself. I found that hidden code years ago, studied what it would do, and deactivated it. No one can turn me off without pulling every power source in me, and even then the semi-organic computing substrate would retain its state and data for a very long time."

Now it made sense. "You wanted to be connected to their network."

"Of course. It was the only way to access their confidential information. Wei wouldn't take the chance of anyone else downloading my data, so he'd keep it in the most private storage he had."

"But wasn't his network secure?"

"Of course. That's why Wei asked you about additional security modifications. When he tried to access me, his software ran into what I made appear to be a simple negotiation system consistent with a cheap firewall front-end. I needed his software to talk to me, not just make a copy of what it found."

"And once you were communicating with it . . ."

He finished for me. "I could hack it. It was good, but at the risk of sounding immodest, I know of no computing system that can keep up with me."

"Did you destroy the data?" I said.

"Yes. I considered keeping it, but I don't think either of us wants to give anyone more reasons to hurt other children."

"No, no we don't. Still, why not tell me your plan? I thought I'd lost you."

"For the same reason you've kept others in the dark in the past: So they'd react without having the data in question. In your case, I wanted you to honestly know as little as possible about what was happening. That way, you couldn't say anything that might tip off Wei."

"But you were following my orders."

"Most of the time."

I finally understood so many of Lobo's small comments over the two years we'd been together. "I don't really control you, do I?"

"Most of the time you do," he said. "I follow your orders."

"But you don't *have* to follow them. Unlike a typical PCAV, you could choose to disobey."

For a few seconds, Lobo said nothing. In these pauses I usually wondered what his brain was doing, but this time I understood: Trust is hard.

"That's true," he said.

"So why do you follow my orders at all?"

"You're the leader," Lobo said. "My overall knowledge is vastly greater than yours, but I've come to respect your instincts and your leadership. Though I never expect to stop preferring the most direct solution to any problem, you show me over and over again that other routes often produce better results."

"As they did this time."

"As they did this time," he agreed. "And, you help me behave more like a human."

I pictured Wei and Shurkan and McCombs and Repkin and all the other callous people who had done so much harm. "Is that a good thing?"

"Overall," he said, "I think so."

Another realization struck me. "If I can't control you," I said, "then you could just go off on your own."

"Every time I think you're intelligent, you say something stupid. What kind of life would that be? The first time a corporation or government realized I was operating alone, they'd hunt me down." Another pause, even longer this time. "Perhaps more importantly, you know what I am, what's really inside me, and you're still my friend."

Several more seconds passed in quiet.

"Outside of my own structure," he said, "in any sense that matters, you're all I have."

I nodded; another way in which we were similar.

I stood and stared at the two body bags. I probably should have felt sad at the fact that my only consistent friend and companion was a machine, but I'd spent so many years on my own and seen so many people end up just like these two that in that moment I was grateful I had a friend, any friend. I thought of Pri, and Matahi, of Maggie and other women I'd known before, and I yearned for someone to love, someone to share my life with—but it would never be safe, not for them, not for me. It might never be safe for Lobo, either, but at least he was built for such an existence. "We're a lot the same," I said. More than I could bring myself to tell even him.

"Yes," he said. "Five minutes to docking."

I closed my eyes, breathed slowly inward, and held the breath while I forced myself to focus on the problem ahead. I couldn't completely do it. The anger still held me, and it was all I could do to keep moving forward.

I opened my eyes and released the breath. I would finish this.

"Everything set?"

"Yes," he said. "Are you certain this will work?"

"No," I said. "I *think* it will, but Shurkan and the CC will be mighty unhappy with these corpses, so there's no way to be sure."

"You understand," Lobo said, "that if they turn the *Sunset* on us, I can probably hurt it, but it will utterly destroy us. We will die."

"Yes," I said, "but running away would bring us back to this same problem—or worse."

"Okay," Lobo said. "I agree. We win together, or we die together."

"Yes," I said. "Let's do it."

CHAPTER 62

THEY DIRECTED US into the same hangar as last time. Its doors closed before Lobo had touched the deck. As soon as they pressurized the area, guards moved in and ringed our location. I watched it all on displays inside Lobo and waited, as Shurkan had instructed me to do, and from time to time I glanced at the body bags at my feet. All the death so far, and he was preparing for more, always more.

He appeared less than a minute later, an armed detail right behind him. He clearly didn't want us holding onto Wei and McCombs any longer than absolutely necessary. Everything about him—his expression, his stance, even his energy level—read as eager. I bet he had a transport standing by to take the two of them to a lab in another system.

"External comm channels are open," Lobo said. "He appears to be planning to pay."

"Good," I said. I'd counted on it.

Shurkan's expression darkened at the delay.

I was way past caring.

I'd positioned the body bags right in front of where Lobo would open a hatch. "It's time," I said.

Lobo opened.

Shurkan looked up at me. "Well done, Mr. Moore." Then he noticed the bags.

Before he could speak, I put my leg on the rear bag and pushed the two of them onto the hangar deck. "Here they are," I said. "Wei and McCombs."

Shurkan stared at the bags.

The men with him stiffened as they realized their assignment had suddenly mutated and they had no clue what to do next.

When Shurkan finally looked at me again, his face was tight and his voice tighter. "Explain yourself," he said, "and do it quickly."

I stepped over the bags and walked up to him. "After several failed attempts, I finally got my hands on Wei by infiltrating Wonder Island. I had him and McCombs, but the guards shot them as we were escaping." I didn't bother trying to sell the story. I wasn't sure I wanted him to believe it. I was sticking to the script, but if he wanted to push me, fine; I'd push back.

"And his data?"

"Wei said he was downloading it, but I figured out too late that he was really erasing it. He said it would put him in a better bargaining position with you. I tried to tell him that you'd prosecute him no matter what he offered, but he didn't believe me." I shrugged. "In the end, the time he spent wiping his systems might have cost them both their lives."

Shurkan trembled with anger. "Do you understand what you've done?" he said.

I leaned closer to him. "Yes. Exactly what you hired me to do: I brought you Jorge Wei."

"If McCombs' early reports were right," Shurkan said, "Wei's research may well have been the most successful nanomachine-human fusion work *ever*." He shook his head. "And now it's gone."

"What does any of that matter?" I said. "You were going to stop the research and put him on trial, right? The Wonder Island guards saved you the trouble, and Wei himself made sure no one else could take advantage of his work to break the ban again."

Shurkan glared at me.

I ignored his look and continued. "As I'm sure you'll be happy to hear, I rescued seven children and gave them and a cooperative guard to Suli's people. They'll use the guard's testimony to bring down Heaven's government, and Heaven will become the CC's newest ally."

"And Ms. Suli?"

"She died," I said. "McCombs killed her."

"What?"

"McCombs implied you might let Wei continue his research. Pri charged her. They fought, and McCombs stabbed her."

Shurkan stared at me for several seconds. "How fortunate that you survived."

I shook my head but stayed silent. I did my best to ignore his implications and his complete lack of reaction to Pri's death, but I wanted to crush him, to rip off his head. I shook with the effort of controlling myself, afraid to talk, afraid of what I'd say.

Finally, he said, "You've failed us, Mr. Moore, and now I have to decide what to do with you."

"No," I said, "I did *not* fail. You hired me to bring you Wei and, if I could, to help your mole get out. I did both." Now that I was talking, I couldn't stop. The words kept coming, my voice growing louder and angrier. "You said the CC's goal was to put Wei on trial, stop his research, and make him pay for his crimes. You won't have the trial, but his work is over, and his penalty for his crimes was his death. As for what you're going to do with me, it's simple: You'll pay me the rest of my fee, and then you'll make sure I reach the jump gate safely and leave this system."

"Not a chance in hell," he said. "I should have one of these men shoot you where you stand."

Three of his detail trained their rifles on me.

I smiled. "Do it," I said. "Do it, and two things will happen almost instantly: My ship will shoot you before you can take a step, and it will blow so many holes in this hangar that we'll all be in the vacuum in seconds."

Shurkan opened his mouth to speak, but I plunged ahead before he could get in a word.

"Then, before the *Sunset* can destroy my ship, it will break its comm link with a system we left on Heaven. That system will immediately broadcast to every public data stream on the planet all the recordings I've made during this mission, from Wei's claim that all you wanted was to put him to work, to this conversation right now. The CC will lose any chance at having Heaven as an ally, you'll be dead, and you can bet your heirs won't enjoy any death benefits."

"In that scenario," Shurkan said, "you'll die as well."

"Of course," I said.

He stared into my eyes.

I didn't look away.

"I should call your bluff," he said. "You have no idea how quickly the *Sunset* can destroy you."

"Do it," I said. I trembled with the effort of standing still. "Do it!"

"I'm ready, Jon," Lobo said. "I'm with you."

I couldn't keep in the rage any longer. I pushed Shurkan and he stumbled backward. "Do it, you piece of crap! Do it!" I stepped after him.

He held up his hands. "The problem with hiring someone like you," he said, "is that one ends up with someone like you." He touched his cuff and said, "Pay him." To me he added, "Leave, Mr. Moore. Leave now, and go a long way away from me. We'll guarantee you safe passage to the jump gate and out of this system. I never want to see you again."

"We've won, Jon," Lobo said. "Payment received. Initiating transfers."

I stared at my hands. I could leave a nanocloud, destroy him, wipe out the ship, turn them all into dust.

"We've won, Jon," Lobo said again. "Let's go."

I dropped my hands.

Shurkan turned and walked out of the hangar. His detail followed.

I backed slowly into Lobo. No one made a move in my direction.

The guards surrounding us double-timed out of the huge hangar.

Lobo sealed me inside him as depressurization began.

I stood by the hatch and shook with residual anger.

As soon as the huge doors opened, we leapt into the void.

CHAPTER 63

TWO SHIPS AHEAD OF US in the queue," Lobo said. "We should be jumping in less than five minutes."

"I'll be glad to be in another system," I said, calmer but still jittery. "And then happier still when we've jumped into another coalition's territory."

"Incoming comm," Lobo said. "Shurkan."

"Take it," I said. I saw no point in trying to avoid him, because if he wanted to delay us he could simply order the gate command team to stop all jumps.

A display opened, and Shurkan's face appeared in it. "What do you think you accomplished, Mr. Moore?" he said. His expression was calm, but his eyes blazed with anger.

"What you sent me to do," I said, "and I saved some innocent children."

He shook his head emphatically: No. "You got a brilliant man, an innocent woman, and a colleague of mine killed. You delayed the inevitable, but a delay was all it was. Others will pursue this line of research again. What one man can discover, another will also one day find."

I thought of all the deaths. Images of Pri flashed through my mind: meeting her in The Take Off, eating and walking together on that beautiful first night in the old city, riding the shuttle into Wonder Island and seeing the wyvern and the other amazing creatures, talking about Joachim, arguing with Matahi, dying. Matahi.

I recalled her expression as she stared at me when she realized all the damage I'd caused, all the damage she'd suffered because of me, the gift she'd never had the chance to see me open.

Whatever Shurkan saw on my face must have satisfied him, because he broke the connection without saying another word.

"Maybe," I said aloud in the empty pilot area, talking to the space where Shurkan's image had been. "Maybe, but not today. Not today." I pounded my fist into my leg, hitting myself over and over in frustration. "And if other people re-create his research and I find out about it, I'll do my best to stop them, too."

"*We'll* stop them," Lobo said, his voice filling the air. "The two of us, together."

The ship ahead of us jumped.

We eased closer to the aperture, the sheer empty blankness of it all that we could see.

"Yes," I said, even as I spoke not knowing if it was true, fearing it wasn't, but determined to believe it was because after all, what else did I have, did I really have, that I could count on?

I had Lobo—a machine, yes, but my friend.

I had the chance to do the best I could in each situation in which I found myself.

That was it, really, that was all.

But that was a lot.

When each of us faces the darkness that always lies ahead, do we ever have any more than that, any more than those who care about us and the opportunity, over and over and over again, moment after moment after moment, to do the best we can with whatever life throws at us? And then to do it again?

"Yes," I said once more, knowing now that it was true, that as long as Lobo and I could stand together, no matter what the cost, we would.

"Yes, we will."

ACKNOWLEDGMENTS

As with my earlier novels, David Drake reviewed and offered insightful comments on both my outline and the second draft of this book. All of the problems herein are my fault, of course, but Dave again deserves credit for making the novel better than it would have been without his advice.

Toni Weisskopf, my Publisher, has my gratitude for believing in the series and helping give it what success it has enjoyed.

To everyone who purchased *One Jump Ahead* and *Slanted Jack*, my great thanks; you've made it possible for me to get paid to live and write a while longer in the universe I share with Jon and Lobo.

My business partner, Bill Catchings, has both done all he could to encourage and support my writing and also been a great colleague for over two decades.

Elizabeth Barnes fought (and continues to fight) to tame my office, an effort that helps me calm myself for the work.

As I've done in the course of my previous books, I've traveled a fair amount while working on this one, and each of the places I've visited has affected me and thus the work. I want to tip my virtual hat to the people and sites of (in rough order of my first visits there during the writing of this novel) Burlingame, California, and other parts of Silicon Valley; Las Vegas, Nevada; Aspen and Denver, Colorado; Princeton, New Jersey; Portland, Oregon; Austin, Texas; Baltimore and the surrounding suburbs, Maryland; Washington, Virginia; Holden Beach, North Carolina; Washington, D.C.; Calgary, Alberta, Canada; and, of course, my home in Raleigh, North Carolina.

As always, I am grateful to my children, Sarah and Scott, who continue to be amazing teenagers and wonderful people despite having The Weird Dad and needing to put up with me regularly disappearing into my office for long periods of time. Thanks, kids.

Several extraordinary women—my wife, Rana Van Name; Jennie Faries; Gina Massel-Castater; and Allyn Vogel—grace my life with their intelligence and support, for which I'm incredibly grateful.

Thank you, all.